"THIS IS A BAD IDEA . . ."

Shane murmured into her skin as he broke from her mouth to trail kisses down her neck. God, she smelled unbelievably good. He unzipped the front of her coat to dive lower into the neckline of her sweater, letting his tongue dance across the planes of her collarbone.

How could she taste even better than she smelled?

"Mmm-hmm, I know," Bellamy groaned, yanking off her gloves to rake her hot, bare hands through his hair. He was on the bullet train right to hell, but Shane didn't care. He could feel her pulse hammering through the vein in her delicate neck as he swept his mouth from the angle of her shoulder back to her lips, and it only spurred him on harder.

"Just for the record," she bit out on a gasp when he slid his hands to her hips and pulled her in tight to his body, leaving no space between them, "I *really* like bad ideas."

Shane's smile grew wicked against her parted mouth as he tightened his grasp on her. "Then you're gonna love this."

Read more Kimberly Kincaid in

The Sugar Cookie Sweetheart Swap

Published by Kensington Publishing Corporation

Turn Up The Heat

KIMBERLY KINCAID

ZEBRA BOOKS
KENSINGTON PUBLISHING CORP.
http://www.kensingtonbooks.com

ZEBRA BOOKS are published by

Kensington Publishing Corp.
119 West 40th Street
New York, NY 10018

All Kensington titles, imprints and distributed lines are available at special quantity discounts for bulk purchases for sales promotion, premiums, fund-raising, educational or institutional use.

Special book excerpts or customized printings can also be created to fit specific needs. For details, write or phone the office of the Kensington Special Sales Manager. Attn.: Special Sales Department. Kensington Publishing Corp., 119 West 40th Street, New York, NY 10018. Phone: 1-800-221-2647.

Zebra and the Z logo Reg. U.S. Pat. & TM Off.

First Printing: March 2014
ISBN-13: 978-1-4201-3283-0
ISBN-10: 1-4201-3283-0

First Electronic Edition: March 2014
eISBN-13: 978-1-4201-3284-7
eISBN-10: 1-4201-3284-9

10 9 8 7 6 5 4 3 2 1

Printed in the United States of America

To Darrin,
because without you,
none of this exists

Acknowledgments

It is an absolute myth that writing is a solitary endeavor. The following people are my own living proof.

To my amazing agent, Maureen Walters, whose savvy is the size of an ocean. I am so grateful. To my incredible editor, Alicia Condon, who not only lets me take the ball and run, but encourages me along the entire length of the sideline, thank you. You both make my dreams come true on a daily basis.

Deepest and heartfelt gratitude to my parents, Anthony and Marthe, for never once saying no when I begged for "just one more book." I owe my passion for words all to you.

Bottomless thanks to Alyssa Alexander, Tracy Brogan and Jennifer McQuiston for your never-ending reads, advice, and friendship. You are shining examples of a whole being greater than the sum of its parts, and I could not write without you. Also, you put up with my corny food jokes (hardy har har). I love you more for it.

Robin Covington and Avery Flynn, without whom Friday would be just another block on the calendar. Thank you for Man Wars, for your dedication to the perfect road trip, and for having an advanced degree in talking me off the ledge. Martini lunch is on me.

Thank you to the Washington Romance Writers for being an amazing home-base, to Amanda Usen for your never-ending patience with my rookie questions and for setting the bar so deliciously high, to John Carnes-Stine for being the living embodiment of selfless friendship, and also for your extreme patience with me on the Internet. Much love to the Ambrose family for teaching me how to persevere, to Stephanie Khan for taking me shoe shopping when the going gets tough, and to Wendy Corsi Staub who wrote the e-mail that started it all. I am thankful beyond measure.

Big thanks to Sonja Brow, for giving The Double Shot its name, and also to the staff at Clarke's Grill and Sports Emporium for letting me behind the scenes.

A sha-la-la thank-you to singer/songwriter/man of awesome facial hair Matt Nathanson for writing "Come on Get Higher," which kicked off the inspiration for this book. It was playing when I wrote both "Chapter One" and "The End," and a lot of times in between.

To my daughters, who are the light of my life. Thank you for happily eating Cheerios for every meal when mommy is on deadline. Now we can have the ice-cream sundaes we talked about.

And lastly, thank you to my incredible husband, for your knowledge of muscle cars, transmissions, and snowplows, as well as answering to all those calls of "Mom!" while I was locked in the writing cave. The reason my characters can fall so deeply in love is because art imitates life, and the first love story I ever knew was you.

Chapter One

The contract on Bellamy Blake's desk was a doorstop waiting to happen. She flipped through the pages absently, rolling her eyes at the legalese. Hell, it could be *Portuguese* as far as she was concerned. Being a real estate analyst for the second largest bank in Philadelphia had sounded so much better when she'd started, fresh out of graduate school. After three years, an endless supply of doorstops and a boss who made Attila the Hun look like a lapdog, the whole thing had lost most of its luster.

Bellamy sank back in her sleek leather desk chair and stared at the waste of foliage that was her current contract, trying to ignore the headache forming behind her eyes. Still, the doorstop-slash-contract wasn't going to negotiate itself. It was time to buck up and take one for Team Paycheck, headache be damned.

Bellamy had no sooner waded to her knees in fine print when the phone on her desk rang. She was so grateful for the distraction that she didn't even check the caller ID before she scooped the phone to her ear. Maybe it would be a cheesy office supply salesman with a well-rehearsed spiel on the virtues of buying toner cartridges in bulk. That would be good for at least twenty minutes of distraction.

This had to be an all-time low.

"Bellamy Blake," she murmured, pushing her blond curls over her shoulder to tuck the phone to her ear.

"I cannot *believe* you didn't tell us you're moving to San Diego, you hideous bitch!"

Bellamy sat back, unfazed at her best friend Holly's theatrics, and grinned. This was even better than the toner guy. "Slow down there, Encyclopedia Dramatica. What are you talking about?" she laughed. "And by the way, hello is usually customary for the whole phone-greeting thing. Just so you know."

"Screw hello! You're *moving*?! If you told Jenna and the two of you kept it from me because you knew I'd freak out, I'm killing you both!" Holly wailed. Man, her flair for the old melodrama was on fire today.

"Are you out of your mind? I just re-upped the lease on my condo. Why would I . . . oh! Hold on, my cell phone is ringing." Bellamy paused to dig through her purse. "You know how my boss is. If I let her go to voice mail even once, she'll light that thing up like Times Square on New Year's Eve until I answer."

"Boss, schmoss! For once, the Wicked Witch can wait!"

The caller ID made Bellamy sag with relief. "Oh, it's Jenna! Hang on." She slid her cell phone under her other ear and tipped her head toward it.

"Hey, Jenna, let me call you back. I've got Holly on the other line, and she's ranting about—"

"California? God, Bellamy! Did Derek propose or something to get you to go? Why didn't you say anything?"

Did anyone stick with a good old-fashioned *hello*

anymore? And what was with the idea of her moving across the country?

"Okay, remind me not to sample whatever Kool-Aid you and Holly have obviously been sharing. I'm not moving to California, and I'm *definitely* not getting married. What the hell is going on?" If her friends wanted to pull one over on her in the practical joke department, they needed to work on their skills, big-time.

"You're getting *married*?" Holly's screech from the forgotten office phone rivaled that of a tornado warning going full bore, grabbing Bellamy's attention.

She fumbled as she scooped the other receiver back to her ear. "No! Jeez, Holly. I just said I'm *not* getting married!" Bellamy huffed, starting to get exasperated.

"I'm Jenna, not Holly," her other best friend replied from the cell phone, confused.

Bellamy released a heavy sigh. "Holly's on my office phone, and I've got one of you on each ear, even though you're both insane. Look, if this is some kind of sick candid camera thing that you guys are planning to throw on YouTube, so help me . . ."

"Bellamy, are you watching Derek's newscast?"

Whoa. What was with Jenna's talking-down-a-suicide-jumper voice? She only reserved that for Holly when she was going full-tilt, so something must really be up. Bellamy paused.

"Just because he's my boyfriend doesn't mean I watch all of his newscasts, Jenna. I'm at work, and my boss just dropped a couple hundred pages' worth of contract on my desk." Bellamy's stomach shifted uncomfortably. "Why?"

"Oh my freaking God. You don't know," Holly breathed.

Bellamy pressed her office phone to her ear, feeling like

a human Ping-Pong ball. "Don't know what, Holly? Come on, you guys. What's going on?"

"Derek's moving to San Diego," they replied, in stereo.

Bellamy's brows knit together in confusion, and her first impulse was to laugh, although it came out more like a nervous croak. "That's impossible. I think he'd have told me if he was moving across the country." It wasn't as if San Diego was a hop, skip, and jump from Derek's upscale Philadelphia brownstone. It was on another coast, for God's sake.

"Uh, sweetie, maybe you should call him," Holly offered.

The croak made a repeat performance. "Okay, first of all, that's going to be kind of hard seeing as how both of my phones are tied up at the moment. Secondly, he's clearly on the air right now, saying something that's making the two of you lose your marbles." Ugh, what was that tightness in her chest? Who'd have thought turkey and Swiss could give a girl heartburn like this.

"Google him, or grab the live stream from the Internet or something," Holly tried again. "Because I'm telling you, I'm not making this up."

Far be it for Bellamy to be a spoilsport, especially if it would put an end to this weird little charade. "You want me to Google my boyfriend to prove that you're playing a practical joke on me? Okay, fine. Whatever blows your skirt up," she laughed.

Bellamy no sooner had her hands over her keyboard than Jenna's panicked voice cut through the phone line attached to Bellamy's other ear. "Wait, did Holly tell you to . . . wait! Bellamy, don't . . ."

Too late.

Bellamy's heart did the pitter-patter-holy-shit in her

chest as her eyes focused on Channel Eight's home page. The headline *Anchorman Derek Patterson Bids Philadelphia A Fond Farewell* was splashed over a handsome headshot that was all too familiar.

Her boyfriend was moving to California, and he hadn't told her a damned thing.

There weren't a whole lot of places Shane Griffin would rather be than up to his elbows in an engine block. He swiped a flannel-clad forearm past his eyes in an effort to relocate the swath of black hair that had fallen into them.

No luck. He needed a haircut like nobody's business.

The side door to the garage swung open, bringing with it a nasty wind and a soft, steady footfall that Shane could recognize from a coma. He straightened up from the frame of the 1969 Mustang Mach 1 in front of him, wincing.

"Damn, Grady! You're bringing some nasty weather with you," Shane called out, tipping his head in the old man's direction.

Grady gave up a gravelly chuckle. "We're in the Blue Ridge, son. That weather's part of the territory now that it's winter. And I ain't bringin' it with me. Somethin's comin' down the pike all on its own. Feels like a doozy, too."

Shane shook his head and laughed, flexing his stiff fingers. "Whatever you say. I don't go for that superstitious crap." Man, Grady bought into all of that stuff, right down to using the twinge in his knee to predict the snowfall. Like the whole warm-front-meets-cold-front thing had nothing to do with it.

Come to think of it, Grady's accuracy *was* kinda freaky, though.

"You're young. You'll figure it out eventually," Grady quipped in his gruff voice. "You still messin' with that Mustang?"

"Yup. I finished Mrs. Teasdale's Lincoln, so I figured you wouldn't mind. You know that thing's older than I am," Shane grumbled.

"So's the car you're workin' on," Grady said.

Hell if he didn't have a point.

"Yeah, but the Mach 1 is a classic. Mrs. Teasdale's Continental is more of an antique." Shane eyed the Lincoln through the filmy windows of the garage. The thing was built like a Sherman tank and was about as pretty.

"Gets her from point A to point B just fine." Grady leaned against the rickety wooden workbench that ran the length of the far wall, blowing into the cup of coffee he'd just poured.

"It does now," Shane corrected with a smirk. It had taken him the better part of yesterday to get that carburetor straight, but right about now, the car could do everything short of sing show tunes. Thing ran like the day it rolled off the lot.

In 1979.

Grady eyed him, his demeanor changing slightly. "Listen, kid. You got another call from that loan office. Something about your payment going up. I left the message on the machine in the back room. Thought you'd wanna know."

Great. As if the promise of bad weather wasn't bad enough to wreck Shane's day.

"Thanks, Grady. I'll figure something out." Okay, now Shane was just plain talking out of his ass. A hundred and fifty grand wasn't exactly something you just *figured out*.

He scrubbed a hand down his face, tempted to tell his five o'clock shadow that it was only ten in the morning.

Guess that was yesterday's fiver. Oh well. It wasn't like Shane had anybody to impress.

"I'd pay you more if I could, Shane. You're worth every damn penny."

Shane's head snapped up just in time to catch the conflicted look on Grady's weathered face.

"You pay me just fine, Grady. You know this is something I've got to work out on my own." He let his eyes rest on the Mustang, his gut flickering with unease. "If it comes down to it, I can sell the car." The words tasted like a battery acid lollipop as they came from his lips.

"Shane," the old man started, but Shane waved him off.

"I'm going to return Mrs. Teasdale's car, then go for a run on my way back. Unless you need me for something here?" The look he gave Grady said the conversation was over.

Grady nodded slowly. "You know you're gonna freeze your ass off, don't you?"

Shane tipped his dark head at Grady and went to grab the spare set of running gear he always kept in the office. "I'll be fine."

Sure. As long as money grew on trees, he'd be freaking stellar.

"Let me get this straight. You took a job in San Diego and you're starting next *week*?"

Well. Didn't Bellamy just put the sucker in sucker punched?

Derek cleared his throat and looked largely uncomfortable. "That's putting a rather fine point on it, but, yes."

He smoothed a hand over his perfectly arranged hair and looked down at her with an equal mixture of sympathy and guilt.

She should've known better than to trust a man who was prettier than she was.

Bellamy watched the waiter place their lunches in front of them and let him depart before she replied in disbelief. "Were you going to, I don't know, *tell me* at any point?" She wanted nothing more than to be angry, to deliver the words with the sassy-girl malice she knew she should be feeling right now at his lack of candor.

Somehow, though, she just couldn't work it up.

"It's, ah, a little more complicated than that." Derek leafed through his spinach salad with quick, nervous stabs, refusing to meet her eyes.

Bellamy's brows popped. "It didn't seem complicated when you told your entire viewership about it a couple hours ago." Okay. Maybe she could drum up a *little* attitude. He'd practically dumped her in front of a bazillion people, after all! A girl had her pride.

"Look, Bellamy." He shifted his crystal blue eyes around the room. "It's not you, okay? I got this great job opportunity, and I couldn't pass it up. My career is very important. People depend on me, you know."

A hot prickle of irritation filled her chest. He was an anchorman, for God's sake. It wasn't like he was going to give Mother Teresa a run for her money or anything.

Derek smiled and patted her hand. "And, let's face it, the long-distance thing just never works out. You understand, don't you?"

Bellamy couldn't handle another nanosecond of delaying the inevitable, and the whole thing sent her stomach into a quick churn. "Frankly, I don't. You couldn't have told me this when it was all coming about? Jeez, Derek. Did you think I'd flip out or something?"

He cleared his throat ever so softly. "Well, I *am* a public figure. I didn't think a scene would be in either of our best interests. Like I said, it's really nothing personal."

Wow. She could admit to maybe being a little bit star-struck in the beginning, but how had she missed the fact that this guy was sporting an ego the size of Mount McKinley? Her intuitive skills needed one hell of an overhaul. She opened her mouth to give him a piece of her mind when the last six months flashed over her with startling clarity.

There really wasn't anything *personal* about it at all. Kind of like their entire relationship.

"You know what, Derek? You're absolutely right." Bellamy's pride overrode the sting of Derek's words, and she gathered her purse in a swift grab while offering up a saccharine smile. "Although I've got to say, for someone with such a *prominent* position in the field of communications, your one-on-one skills suck. Good luck in San Diego."

Before she could even register that her legs had shifted to accommodate the weight of her body, Bellamy had turned on her heel to stride out of the restaurant.

"I'm sorry, Mr. Griffin. There's really nothing I can do."

Shane had known the words were coming, but his gut sank anyway. "Look, my payments have always been on time up until now. Isn't there some way we can put off the increase just a little longer?"

Way to work that last-ditch effort, my man.

"We've already deferred the increase longer than we should have," the woman apologized.

Right. He'd been trying to block out the phone call he'd made to them three months earlier. Shit.

"Okay, well, thanks for your time." Shane hung up the phone and leaned back in the ancient desk chair that served as the only place to sit in the entire garage. For the first time since arriving at Pine Mountain a little over a year ago, he was flooded with unease. Short of an unexpected windfall or an angel to illuminate some unknown path out of this mess, there was no alternative but the obvious. A debt was a debt, and as much as he hated it, his had to be paid.

The thought of his Mustang going to that smarmy dealer in Bealetown, or worse yet some chop shop for parts, made his stomach do the up-and-at-'em against his ribs. That car had been the only thing of value that Shane had brought with him to the mountains, the only thing he'd ever worked for and earned himself, no strings attached.

But selling it was the only way out.

Shane shuffled through the papers on the desk until he came up with his checkbook, not pausing to glance at the "balance" column. He knew damn well there were far too few numbers left of the decimal, and to see it written out in front of him conjured up images of how well the words *insult* and *injury* could go together given the right frame of mind.

Shane stuffed a check into a pre-printed envelope and sealed the sucker up tight, knowing that by sending it he'd all but bleed his bank account dry. His careworn running shoes crunched over the loose gravel of the drive as he walked his last thirty days of freedom over to the mailbox, letting the wind cut through him on his way back inside. Letting out a long sigh, he returned to the office and punched a couple of digits into the phone before he lost his nerve.

"Information? Yeah, I need the number for Louie's Auto Traders in Bealetown. Yeah. I can hold."

Chapter Two

After the tenth time her phone rang like the Liberty
Bell, Bellamy buried it deep in the bottom of her purse.
Everyone from her sister to her dental hygienist (okay, so
they'd been friends since college, but still) had called to
find out if she was moving to the Golden State, and she
was sick to death of rattling off the same answer.

A big, fat, resounding *hell no*.

Although she wasn't proud of it, Bellamy had taken the
cheater's way out and called her boss's desk phone ten
minutes after the weekly management meeting for their
department began. One fake gynecologist's appointment
later, Bellamy was out of the office, more than ready to
block out the contract on her desk and the freshly minted
ex who had left her for greener pastures.

She did a mental tally of the ingredients in her pantry.
It had been at least a month since she'd gone on a baking
binge—something that always made her feel worlds better
when she was having a craptastic day. Spending the afternoon in her kitchen, hand-mixing pastry dough from
scratch sounded like pure, uncut heaven right about now.
Bellamy guided her feet toward the postage stamp–sized

parking lot at the end of the block where her car lay in wait, but stopped short at the glitzy department store between her and her destination.

Half-off designer shoes *and* the afternoon spent in her kitchen? Bellamy grinned and pushed her way into the cool, air-conditioned shopping Mecca known as Macy's. This day might be looking up.

"Can I, like, help you with anything, ma'am?"

Maybe not.

Bellamy winced, turning to look at the young, blond salesgirl in front of her. Holy Paris Hilton, Batman! The girl teetered on her hot pink stilettos, and Bellamy wondered how anyone could possibly wear them and remain vertical.

"I'm just looking for now, thanks," Bellamy murmured, watching the girl click-clack away.

Bellamy browsed through the racks for exactly three minutes before her phone made a bid for her undivided attention. At the very end of her patience, she fished it out from the bottom of her purse.

"Hello?"

Ten minutes later, after she had quietly and repeatedly assured her mother that no, she wasn't packing her bags, and yes, she and Derek had broken up but she was fine, Bellamy reached critical mass. She switched her phone to vibrate and pitched it back in her purse, vowing to ignore any callers who might utter the D-word.

Right about now, Bellamy would give her left arm for something, *anything*, that wouldn't make her think of Derek and the miserable day she just couldn't seem to get away from. Her gaze caught and snagged on the display in front of her and she gave up a wicked grin.

Yup. Racy bras would do the trick.

Forty minutes and six bras later, Bellamy cruised past the window display in search of matching panties that didn't look like dental floss. Her general rule of thumb was that if she herself had to have an ass, then by God, her drawers would provide a place to park it. The sound of the salesgirl snapping her gum brought Bellamy's head up to full attention.

"Can I help you find, you know . . . a size?"

Bellamy chewed her bottom lip. "I was wondering if these come in a different, ah, style?" She held up the microscopic scrap of fabric. Good Lord, it was see-through on top of everything? Honestly, what was the point?

"Nope. Fourteen different colors, though." The salesgirl started flipping through the racks to prove it when Bellamy felt her purse do the tango on her shoulder.

"Oh! Hang on, I'm vibrating," she muttered, and the salesgirl laughed.

"A good thong will do that to you every time."

Bellamy shook her head and held up her cell.

The girl nodded, a little slow on the uptake. "Oh, right. I'll just be over here if you need me."

Bellamy expelled a breath of relief at the caller ID and tucked the phone to her ear. "Hey, Holly. What's up?" She slid into the plush waiting-for-my-wife chair on the other side of the display.

"I just wanted to make sure you're okay."

Bellamy sighed. "I'm fine. I'm out bra shopping."

"Don't take this the wrong way, sweetie, but don't you think you're dealing with just a touch of denial here?" Holly ventured.

It was all Bellamy needed to go completely code red. "You know what? I *wish* I could be in denial, because at least that would mean I wasn't dealing with it. Every time

I turn around, someone's asking me what happened and if I'm okay. I think I'm *over*-dealing with it. I wish, just for today, I could go somewhere where nobody's even heard of Derek Patterson!"

The salesgirl's bottle-blond head popped up from the next aisle over. "Derek Patterson, like the news guy? He's hot."

Bellamy couldn't have fled the store any faster if it had been engulfed in flames.

"Okay, Bellamy. Stop and take a deep breath, honey."

"I'm in the middle of the street, Holly," Bellamy snapped, instantly feeling like a jerk. "Sorry. I'm just fried, you know?"

Holly didn't skip a beat. "Look, why don't you meet me at your place? I'll call Jenna and we can grab some pizza and ice cream. You can do that weird cooking thing you do, and then we can watch *Shakespeare in Love* 'til we pass out. What do you say? Joseph Fiennes, yum yum yum," Holly cajoled gently.

Bellamy knew she should give in. Her friends meant well, and she could spend the night immersed in the classic breakup routine of chick flicks and Häagen-Dazs for dinner. Better yet, if she called in sick tomorrow, she could even put off worrying about her drill sergeant of a boss until Monday morning. By then, she'd be more than ready to get on with her normal, albeit kind of boring, life. Bellamy opened her mouth with every intention of saying she'd meet Holly at her place in fifteen minutes.

And then she saw the billboard over the bus stop.

Pine Mountain Ski and Spa Resort, only 100 miles from Philadelphia. Come for the weekend. You'll want to stay for a lifetime!

Bellamy's mouth curved into the first genuine smile

she'd managed all day. A thousand bucks said no one at the Pine Mountain Ski and Spa Resort had ever heard of Derek Patterson.

"On second thought, Holly, call Jenna and tell her to pack her bags. We're headed on a little road trip."

Shane practically gritted his teeth into dust while Louie Sinclair took yet another slow turn around the Mach 1. Louie didn't so much walk as he slithered, stalking the car as if it was a side of beef and he hadn't eaten in weeks.

Everything about this was wrong.

"It's a nice car," Louie proclaimed, as if it was a gift. "Paint's going to be a problem, though."

Shane cranked his hands into fists, but willed himself to chill out. "The body work's done. You won't find a scratch anywhere on her. About the only thing she needs is prep and paint." He'd spent hours, hell, *months* making sure that every line on the car was spot-on.

"Where did you say you came across it, again?" Louie eyeballed the primer-gray of the car one more time, not missing a thing.

"I didn't. But I bought the car six years ago outside of Philly. Everything's been rebuilt, including the engine." Normally, Shane would have popped the hood with pride and showed the 428 Cobra Jet off like it was his kid, but he didn't want Louie to lay his beady eyes on it.

Of course, Louie asked, so Shane had to oblige. After Louie had done everything but take the car out for a nice steak dinner, he rocked back on his heels and gave Shane a look.

"Mind if I ask why you're parting with it?"

Shane didn't even flinch. "Yeah, I do."

Louie's thin brows lifted in surprise. "Well, I'll tell you. Demand for Mach 1's is iffy right now, economy being what it is. This one's in pretty good shape, though."

Screw that. Shane knew it was pristine because he'd made it that way. He opened his mouth to tell Louie to forget the whole thing.

But with Mrs. Teasdale's car done and no other jobs in sight at the garage, Shane needed the money. As much as he wanted to, Grady couldn't pay him if there was no work coming in.

He closed his eyes and braced for impact.

"I could give you eighteen for it, if you're willing to part with the car today."

Shane made a mental note to do a way better job of cleaning his ears. "Eighteen thousand? That's it?" So much for subtle negotiating.

Louie frowned, his cheesy smile disappearing like fog in the sun. "It needs a ten-thousand-dollar paint job, Mr. Griffin."

"And when it gets one, it'll be worth forty-five grand," Shane snapped.

"*If* I can sell it. And that's a big if. These Mustangs are popular, sure. But there are lots to choose from." He swept a glance over the car that was more of a leer than anything else. "Twenty would be my final offer, and that's a stretch."

Shane knew that even though the offer was total bull-shit, he had to take it. He had twenty-nine days and counting to figure out where that next loan payment was coming from.

Nope. He just couldn't do it.

"Sorry for wasting your time." Shane stood firm, eyes flashing over Louie's in a way that suggested he wasn't just playing hard ball.

The guy smoothed a hand over his greasy hair as if he was waiting for Shane to recant, then he gave up a humorless smile when he saw that it wasn't going to happen. "Give me a call if you change your mind."

As Louie's Corvette left a cloud of gravel-turned dust in its wake, Shane leaned over the hood of the Mustang, palms against the quarter panel, head hung low.

Shit.

"I take it that didn't go the way you wanted." Grady shuffled out from the office, his timeworn face etched with fresh lines of concern.

Shane's head snapped up. The last thing he wanted was for the old man to worry about his problems. "Guess not."

"Look, Shane. I don't meddle in your business. It's not what I do. But maybe it's time you—"

"No." He'd rather sell his car a hundred times than go down the road Grady was steering toward.

Grady nodded once, resigned. "All right. If you change your mind, let me know."

"It's not going to happen, Grady. But thanks." Shane stood up and hooked his thumbs through the belt loops on his jeans. "It's Friday. Why don't you start your weekend a little early? Nothing's doing here, and I'm just going to stick around to mess with the car. I can always call you if something comes up."

"It ain't even much past lunch, Shane. You tryin' to get rid of me?" Grady's chuckle lifted a smile out from underneath Shane's crappy mood.

"Yup. You got me."

"Just look out, would you? Meant what I said yesterday. This wind is bringin' somethin' with it. Might knock you on your ass if you ain't careful." Grady's steel-gray eyes glinted in the overhead lights of the garage as he served Shane with a boyish grin that defied his years.

"It's going to take a lot more than some wind to knock me down. But if it'll make you feel better, I promise to stay on my toes." Shane skimmed a hand over his hair before turning back to the car, chuckling. "See you Monday," he called out.

"Not if I see you first." Grady flipped back his standard response from where he stood in the door. "And don't stay too late, you hear me? Too much work'll kill ya."

"I'll survive."

As soon as the side door to the garage slammed shut on a gust of wind, Shane high-tailed it over to the radio. He didn't have to flip through the stations to find what he was looking for; he just fired the thing up and it was good to go.

Nothing like Mozart to get a gearhead's brain good and straight.

After forty-five minutes under the Mustang, Shane had all but forgotten about his shitty morning and the dilemma that accompanied it hand in hand. The parts of the car were like a puzzle in front of him, and he finessed each one right down to the smallest detail. They made sense to him in a way that nothing else did, lining up with gorgeous precision, flawlessly finding their way home under his hands . . .

A sudden blast of wind under the car rattled him down to his bones.

"Hello? God, please tell me there's someone here. Hellllloooooo?" The feminine voice shot through Shane like a chaser on the heels of the wind that brought it. He pushed with both feet, rolling the Creeper out from under the car so fast that he was momentarily dazed.

The woman's face was pinched from the cold, and her blond hair flew around her in a wild riot of curls. For a moment, gazing at her from his upside-down position on the floor, Shane felt as if he'd been scattered to the four corners of the garage.

She looked angelic, except for the fact that she seemed pissed.

"Thank God at least *one* thing in my day is working out! This is a garage, right?" Her green eyes flooded with relief as she scanned the drafty space, taking in the oil-stained floors and the scattered tools.

He straightened up and gave her a quick once-over. His gut tightened as he registered her expensive clothes, right down to the understated yet elegant classic Tiffany pendant around her neck. Her boots alone probably cost more than he made in a solid week's worth of work, even though the three-inch heels were caked with mud. Shane knew her snobby type like he knew his own reflection, and the pang he'd felt when she crossed the threshold was gone just like that.

"Wow, you're perceptive," Shane quipped, eyes hardening over her. Okay, so it came out more rudely than he intended, but girls like her didn't usually care what people like Shane thought, anyway.

"Look, I just walked two miles in the freezing cold to get here, so I'm not really in the mood. If you can't help me figure out what's wrong with my car, that's fine. Just point me in the direction of the nearest phone and I'll be on my way."

You've got to be kidding. No way was Shane letting some stranger call him out like that. He didn't care *how* freaking sexy she was when she put a hand on her curvy little hip and arched her brow.

"Oh, I can figure out what's wrong with your car, I guarantee it. But if it'll make you feel better to call someone else, be my guest. Phone's in the back." He jutted his chin toward the office, watching her mutter to herself.

"I can't believe I'm stuck in the middle of God's country with a stupid cell phone that might as well be a paperweight. Hasn't anyone ever heard of service towers out here?"

She drew in a deep breath as if she was reaching for her patience, and the swell of her chest underneath her thin, red sweater made Shane suddenly forget the chill of the wind she'd brought with her. "Okay. My car died by the side of the road, and I don't have a clue what's wrong with it. Is there somebody here who can maybe take a look and help me make arrangements to have it fixed?" Her jaw was set in fiery determination that contradicted the graceful lines of her face.

Shane shrugged. "Unless you want me, you're out of luck, Princess. Grady's is the only game in town, and as far as mechanics go, I'm it for the rest of the day," he offered with a grin.

She opened her bow-shaped mouth to answer him, and for a second he thought she was going to turn on her heel and huff her way back out into the cold. But then she set her lips back into a stubborn line and settled for giving him a humorless smile.

"Great. Are you available to come look at it?"

Something about her dared Shane to do a little boundary-testing, even though he knew it was probably a bad idea. He worked up the most bored voice he could manage. "Let me check my schedule," he said, without moving.

She waited about twenty seconds before crossing her arms over her chest. "If you'd prefer, I can just call someone from the city to have it towed back there. I wouldn't want to put you out."

Shane froze. "Wait." No matter how minor her car trouble turned out to be, they needed the business. Plus, although he'd messed with her a little bit just to get on her nerves, he didn't feel right turning her away just because she was a sassy little rich girl. Stranded was stranded, no matter how you cut it, and he knew those dealers in the city all too well. They'd rip her off six ways to Sunday, and just because she had the money to spare didn't make it right.

"Sorry, I was just giving you a hard time, that's all. I can come take a look at it. Those jack-wagons in the city will charge you by the mile for the tow alone, and you don't wanna know how much, either."

She shifted her weight, and if Shane didn't know any better, he'd think that was relief on her pretty face. "It's a couple of miles up the road," she said.

"Got a truck around back that'll make quick work of that." Shane wiped his hands on the front of his jeans, noticing that it didn't really do anything to improve their appearance. "Shane Griffin." God, her hand was so slender and delicate compared to the meat hook he'd just thrust out.

"Bellamy Blake."

He couldn't help it. He laughed. "Your name is Bellamy?"

She stiffened. "It's French."

Translation: highbrow and verrrrry expensive.

"Right. Well, the truck's this way." Shane gestured to the side lot where his beat-up F150 sat, ready to go. Another gust of wind rattled the windows in their frames, and man, it was really getting nasty out.

"Okay," Bellamy murmured without enthusiasm as she sauntered to the door and went to push it open.

He barely had his jacket all the way on when another burst of wind slammed into the building, even stronger than the last. The clean-linen smell of Bellamy's shampoo filled his nose from her sudden closeness, and before he could register what the hell was happening, she had pitched into his arms.

Chapter Three

Bellamy was caught completely off guard by the blast of wind shoving its way into the garage with a rude hi-how-are-ya. The steel door swung on its hinges so hard that she was forced to either move out of its path or let it body check her for her trouble.

Well *that* was a no-brainer. She stumbled backward, only to be met by an immovable object that turned out to be Shane's chest.

"Look out!" He shoved his arms beneath hers in a rough yank, and she fell into him just as the door slammed against the doorstop hard enough to leave a dent.

"Oh!" Bellamy's breath exited on a hard gasp. Sharp pain streaked through her ankle, which she knew without looking must be turned at a rather unnatural angle, because it hurt like crazy.

"Jesus! Are you okay?" Shane murmured into her hair as it blew around both of their faces in the biting wind.

Bellamy's ankle sent up a chorus of *hell no*, but there was no way she was going to admit it out loud, especially not to a total stranger, and definitely especially not *this* particular stranger. "I'm fine."

Sure. If *fine* meant clumsily tumbling into the arms of a brooding, borderline obnoxious car mechanic with the hottest smile this side of the Mason-Dixon line, then she was just peachy.

Didn't Guinness have records for weeks this bad?

"You sure?" Shane didn't loosen his grip, as if he thought she were bluffing. Which she was, but *he* didn't need to know that.

"Yeah, absolutely. You can let go. Thanks."

"Suit yourself, city girl." He shrugged and let her go without preamble.

Bellamy's cheeks flamed as she tested her weight on her throbbing ankle. After a few ginger steps got her through the door and into the parking lot, it looked like her pride had taken a bigger hit than anything else. What the hell else was new? She flipped the handle of the battered pickup truck and climbed inside.

"So, what kind of car do you drive?" Shane asked, getting in and starting the truck.

"A Mazda Miata."

He shifted his weight and looked out the driver's side window so she couldn't see his expression as they pulled away from the lot, and her heart sank. Maybe the sporty convertible was out of his area of expertise.

"Is that going to be a problem?" Bellamy asked, rubbing her hands together.

Shane scoffed, flipping the heater on high. "No. They're just a pain in the ass to fix, that's all. Pardon my language." He muttered the last part, like he was actually embarrassed he'd let the curse slip. "Can you tell me what's wrong with it?"

Bellamy looked at him blankly. "Um, it doesn't run."

Shane's smirk-and-eyeroll maneuver translated to

a glaring *Hello, Captain Obvious.* "Yeah, I got that part. I was thinking more along the lines of what happened to make it that way. Weird noises, dashboard lights, stuff like that." He gave her a sidelong glance.

Her cheeks flooded with heat. "Oh. Well, come to think of it, it *has* been acting a little funny lately. Every once in a while it makes this grinding noise. I figured it just needed a tune-up or something."

Again with the well-duh look. So she'd skipped a freaking tune-up. Was it really that big a deal?

"Anyway," she continued, after biting her tongue. "Just now, a whole bunch of white smoke started coming out from under the car. It kind of jerked a little, made the noise again." She broke off, wracking her brain. There had to be technical terms for her botched explanation, but hell if she could come up with a single one. "Then it just kept lurching forward instead of really going anywhere, even when I hit the gas, so I pulled over. That's pretty much it."

Shane's frown was less than encouraging. "You just passing through?"

"Sort of." God, what a mess this bright idea of hers was turning out to be. "I'm supposed to be meeting friends of mine at the Pine Mountain Resort for a long weekend."

Wait, did he just roll his eyes again before he looked out the window? Really?

"That's only a couple of miles from here. You'll need to call someone to get a ride."

Bellamy pulled back, frowning. "Do you think it's that bad?"

Shane's black-coffee eyes met hers for an instant. "I don't think it's good. At the very least, I'll probably have to come back with the tow truck to get it to the garage for a better look."

She must have done something cosmically terrible to have karma bite her in the ass. First Attila the Boss, then Derek, and now this. "That's me, right there." Bellamy pointed through the window to where she'd left her car on the narrow, muddy shoulder by the scenic overlook.

"Yeah, I figured. Not too many two-seater sports cars on the side of the road up here. Especially in January." Shane pulled over, but not before she caught the cocky smile he tried to hide as he looked over his shoulder to check his blind spot.

Wow, his shoulders were broad.

"You coming, or do you want to wait here? I can leave the truck running if you want," he offered without much enthusiasm.

Shit, when had he gotten out too?

"No thanks. I'd like to see what you're looking at, if that's okay with you." Clumsiness notwithstanding, she didn't want him to think she couldn't handle herself. Her pride had suffered enough in the last twenty-four hours, thank you very much, and he already seemed to think she was some spoiled city girl. It couldn't be rocket science to keep up with a quick look-see under the hood, right?

Shane lifted a dark brow. "Suit yourself." He stood in front of the car and hooked his thumbs through the belt loops on his jeans, waiting.

Bellamy's heart did a repeat swan dive toward her belly. What was he looking at *her* for? Didn't he know where to start?

"I'm, ah, going to need you to pop the hood so I can look at the car."

She swallowed her full dose of *hi-I'm-an-idiot* in one hard gulp. "Oh, right!"

As soon as the car was unlocked and her butt sank into

the driver's seat, Bellamy's first order of business was to clutch. Come on, she had an advanced degree in business, for God's sake! How hard could it be to pop the stupid hood? The knob, or button, or whatever, had to be here somewhere. It had to be . . .

"Aha!" Bellamy crowed under her breath, her hand shooting out for the lever marked with the little stick figure lifting the hood. She gave it a triumphant yank, smiling from ear to ear.

"Bellamy?" Shane's grin wiped the confidence from her face. He put a hand on the door frame, leaning in. "I might be just spit-balling here, but I don't think the problem's in your trunk."

If his laugh hadn't been so deep and downright sexy, in that moment she'd have hated his guts. He and the stick figure could kiss her ass.

"Sorry, must have pulled the wrong one," she glowered, spying the correct lever right next to the trunk release. She gave it a decisive snatch, and the hood lifted up by about an inch.

"Mmm," Shane answered, closing the trunk before going around to look under the hood. Bellamy got out and stood next to him, watching with awe as he moved his hands over the inner workings of the car with both care and purpose. How the *hell* all of that stuff came together to create a whole bunch of get-up-and-go was totally beyond her.

Finally, she couldn't stand it anymore, though barely five minutes had passed. "How bad is it?" she asked, chewing her bottom lip.

"Go ahead and try to start it for me."

"I don't think anything's going to happen," she offered politely, trying to save him from wasting his time. The car had seemed in pretty bad shape when she'd pulled it over. If the damned thing was going to start up now, after all she'd just been through, she was going to be *pissed*.

"Yeah, I've done this once or twice before. Why don't you humor me and give it a whirl just for grins, city girl."

Bellamy bit her tongue to trap the rather unladylike voice in her head threatening to tell him exactly where he could shove his *princesses* and his *city girls*. The reality was that the garage had been the only thing she'd seen for miles, and as much as she wanted to tell Shane to pound sand, it looked like the only option that wouldn't get her left by the side of the road was to humor him as he'd asked.

His expression sure suggested he could use it.

"I was only trying to help," Bellamy muttered under her breath as she put the key in the ignition. Of course the damn thing purred right to life just to spite her.

"Okay, you can cut the engine," Shane said, crouching down to look under the car.

"So is it fine?" Bellamy asked, confused. "I really wasn't imagining things," she insisted, sliding out of the car.

Shane's grim expression suggested that he believed her. Bracing one hand against the fender, he reached down and swiped his fingers through a dark puddle of something seeping out from under her car in a thick, ominous stain.

"No, you really weren't." His frown intensified as he stood, looking again at the inner workings of the car. "How long have you had this thing?"

"Um, four years. Five in June." She leaned in to look over his shoulder.

Yup. Still broad.

"Should've known better than to hope it was still under warranty. It looks like your transmission's blown."

Her mouth fell open. "Are you sure?"

Shane broadcast a look that all but screamed are-you-kidding-me. "Unless you have transmission fluid coming from somewhere else, yeah."

Bellamy quickly calculated her options, realizing that she had only the one. She had to get home in a couple of days, after all. "Can you fix it?"

Shane didn't flinch. "Absolutely."

Finally, some good news! "How much is it going to cost?"

The slight wince he gave wasn't lost on her, and he shifted where he stood. "I'd have to look up the cost for the parts, but assuming you need the whole thing replaced, trannies for these things aren't cheap. We can work something out for labor since it's going to be a longer job, but it's still going to be expensive."

Bellamy exhaled. "Okay, can you elaborate on that a little more?" There was a difference between nice-dinner-expensive and diamond-earrings-expensive, after all. Maybe she could get away with nice-dinner car trouble, just this once.

"Parts and labor? You're probably looking at close to three grand."

"Are you *serious*?" she yelped.

"'Fraid so. I told you they were expensive."

"Wait." Bellamy felt like she was on a thirty-second delay, with Shane's words taking their sugar-sweet time to sink in. "Define *longer job*. How long is this going to take, exactly?" She had the sinking feeling that the extended weekend she'd allotted for her relaxing mountain getaway wasn't what Shane had in mind.

He scrubbed a hand over the stubble on his chin. "Orders on parts have probably shipped for today since it's already after noon, which puts the next ship date as

Monday. My guess is that it'll take everything three days to get here."

She squeezed her eyes shut, but stayed silent as Shane continued.

"It's going to be another day and a half for me and Grady to put the new tranny in once we get it. Good news is I can start yanking the old one this afternoon if you want, but because of the lag time, it'll be at least next Friday before we can finish."

"Do I have any other options here?" Bellamy managed in an unsteady voice, pinching the bridge of her nose with freezing fingers.

"Sure."

Her head sprang up, surprise popping through her veins. "I do?"

Shane nodded, sending his black hair down over his eyes. "You can have it towed to the city, where they'll quote you a price of about four grand instead of three. You're welcome to call them to double check me, if you want. And before you ask, it'll take them just as long to get the parts. Barely anybody stocks those, so I'd bet you're still looking at about a week that way."

Bellamy felt like a day-old party balloon. "Any other suggestions?"

"You could get a new car."

Even better.

"I need to make a few phone calls." Out of habit, she tapped her cell phone to life. The *no service available* message still flashed across the display, and Bellamy resisted the urge to hurl it over the guardrail. "You said I could use the phone back at the garage, right?" Frustration bubbled within her chest, filling her veins with its thick heat.

Shane nodded, and his piercing stare did nothing to make Bellamy feel less vulnerable.

"Yeah, sure."

"I guess we can head back, then."

As he dropped the hood back to the frame of the car with a firm bang, it was all Bellamy could do not to cry.

As soon as they got back to the garage, Shane knew right then and there he was screwed. His pickup had no sooner rolled to a stop on the gravel than Bellamy made a beeline for the office, and she hadn't been subtle about closing the door, either. Fifty bucks said she was on the phone with the Mazda dealership in the city, making plans to have her car towed even though he knew he was right about the mark-up those frickin' apes would certainly throw at her. Figured a girl like that would want the pros to work on her precious car no matter what the cost.

It would've been a royal pain in the ass to drop a new tranny in that Miata anyway, even though the money would have meant at least one more worry-free month on his loan. The business wouldn't have hurt Grady, either. Well, at least there was the upside of not having to deal with a pretentious rich girl who was too smart for her own good.

Even if she was kind of cute when she got flustered.

"Excuse me? Shane?"

Speak of the devil. Shane straightened up from where he'd been tinkering with the Mustang and met Bellamy's bright green stare.

"My friend is on her way to come get me, so I should be out of your way in a couple of minutes." She bit her lip but didn't lower her gaze.

Aw, hell. He *had* kind of dropped a bomb in her lap

about her car. Even if she could probably afford to have it fixed in the blink of an eye. "No problem. Listen, good luck getting it fixed."

The confusion on her face was obvious. "Uh, shouldn't I be saying that to you?"

Looked like confusion was contagious. "What?"

"You said you can tow it back here and start today, right?" Her eyes were on him, unwavering and all business.

"You want me to fix your car?" Shane breathed, relief spreading over him.

The edges of Bellamy's lips kicked up into a smirk. "You're perceptive."

Fuckin' touché.

He laughed under his breath. "That's your freebie, sweetheart, but only because I deserved it. Yeah, I can tow it back here this afternoon."

Her hand went back to her hip in a move he'd bet was unintentional, and Shane had to admit it. He was totally turned on.

She gave up a catlike smile. "Tell you what. You can keep your freebie just as long as you get me back on the road no later than one week from today, *sweetheart*. Do we have a deal?"

An odd ripple went up Shane's spine as he tipped his chin at her and grinned.

"One week. It's a deal."

Chapter Four

"Oh, Bellamy! Honey, are you okay?" Holly's arms were around Bellamy in a tight embrace before she and Jenna could even cross the threshold of their suite.

"Holly, it's my car that's toast, not me," she managed to breathe out through the tumble of bright red curls falling over her friend's shoulder. "I'm fine. I can think of about fifty things off the top of my head I'd rather do with that money, but what choice do I have?"

Bellamy looked around the gorgeously appointed common room of their suite, which was both cozy and utterly lavish. The breathtaking view of the Blue Ridge Mountains surrounded by the whispering hints of sunset should have been a complete tension buster, and she sighed as she gazed at the panoramic sight beyond the glass.

It was going to take something stronger than the stunning landscape outside her window and the promise of imminent spa treatments to kill the stress that had set up camp in her shoulders. Something along the lines of 80 proof, bearing the moniker Jose Cuervo would do the trick just fine.

Holly flopped into a luxurious overstuffed chair,

curling her petite legs beneath her. "Well, I hope you're not getting ripped off. Are you sure this mechanic guy knows what he's talking about?"

Bellamy thought of the intense way Shane's hands had moved over her car as he assessed the damage. He might be a cocky SOB, but he was the only mechanic who'd ever given it to her straight.

"Not for a fact, no. But I double checked with the Mazda dealership in the city when I was sitting in his office, and he wasn't wrong about the wait *or* the prices. Do you know that those guys charge over a hundred dollars an hour for freaking labor? I'm in the wrong damned business," she mumbled, slumping into the couch.

Jenna popped her honey-colored head in from the tiny kitchenette, holding a block of cheese and some garlic and herb crackers. "You got another estimate?"

Bellamy crinkled her nose at her friend. "You're not really going to put those crackers with that kind of cheese, are you? They totally don't go together."

"Oh, I forgot. The food Nazi's here. You want to do this, then?" Jenna laughed, bringing the hospitality basket over.

"Mmm, fig preserves. Nice." Bellamy rooted through the basket of goodies, lifting an approving eyebrow at the contents. "And hell yes I got another estimate. Getting swindled isn't my idea of fun." She paused, sweeping a few items onto the coffee table and going to work. "But Shane seems to know what he's doing, plus he said he'd start today. As it is, I have no idea how I'm going to manage not having a car for a whole week."

God, she really wanted to forget every single second of the last couple of days. Missing a week's worth of work because she was stranded in the mountains was probably going to send her boss into the stratosphere. She'd have to come up with a way to go home and come back for her car next week, or risk having Bosszilla so far in her shit that she'd never be rid of the woman.

"Yeah, that's kind of a no-brainer. Have it hauled back to the city for more money or leave it here and let some totally hot mechanic have his way with it," Jenna laughed, nudging Bellamy with one long leg as she sat down next to her on the floor.

"I didn't leave it with him because it was cheaper! I left it because it was *faster*," Bellamy asserted, her hands stopping over the assembly line of snacks she'd laid out.

"Whoa, whoa, whoa, nobody said anything about the mechanic being hot!" Holly interjected nosily, giggling from her perch in the nearby chair.

Bellamy flushed. "He's not *that* hot," she protested, knowing it was a bald-faced lie.

Shane was hot as hell.

Jenna gave a no-nonsense snort. "You're full of shit, sister! I could see how smokin' hot he was the minute I walked in the door to come pick you up! If you didn't have dibs on him, I'd be half tempted to go yank something important-looking out from underneath the hood of my car and show up on his doorstep needing a little repair job of my own," she snickered, popping one of Bellamy's hors d'oeuvres into her mouth.

Bellamy hopped up and made a beeline for the kitchenette to look for wineglasses. "Okay, first of all, I don't have *dibs* on him. What are we, in the seventh grade?" Her frown sent a knowing look between her two friends that Bellamy knew she had to nip in the bud right away. "And secondly, if you'd like my three thousand-dollar car trouble or the screeching reaction my boss is sure to have over the whole thing, you're welcome to it. I've been handed enough crap over the past couple of days without having to worry about some backwoods mechanic who has some grudge against all things city on top of it all," she sighed.

"He likes you." Jenna's brown eyes sparkled as she waggled her light brown brows at Bellamy.

"That's crazy." She stopped in the middle of the carpet, three glasses in hand. "How do you know?" Was she seriously holding her breath?

"Because when I came in to pick you up, he was pretending not to look at you, even though he was *totally* looking at you. And these are amazing, by the way." Jenna held up another cracker before polishing it off in one bite.

A nervous laugh spilled from Bellamy's lips. "Thank you. And he was *not* looking at me," she countered. Shane had been way more interested in the lone car sitting in the garage than anything else. The only second thought he'd given her had come in the form of eye rolls and cocky smirks, she was sure of it.

Now *those*, she had caught.

"How do I always miss the good stuff?" Holly pouted dramatically. "Hot mechanic guy checking out my bestie on the sly? Seriously, next time, *you* can stay here," she said to Jenna, tossing her auburn hair. "Damn, these *are* good, Bellamy."

"They're even better with the spicy mustard on them. Here." Bellamy passed the jar to her friend with a shake of her head. "And nobody checked me out," she insisted.

"If that's what you think, then you *definitely* didn't catch him looking at your ass when we left."

The jaw-dropping look on Bellamy's face sealed her fate. Both Jenna and Holly were overcome with a fit of giggles that no amount of arguing was going to erase.

"Shut up," Bellamy groused, but a tiny smile played on her lips.

"Oh, come on, B. You've had the week from hell. Let's go downstairs and get mani-pedis, indulge in a dinner where calories totally don't count, and then you can let me and Holly take you out to drown your troubles. We're in the mountains. You can get embarrassingly snockered if you want, and there won't be any witnesses." She paused to grin. "Well, none that you'll ever see again, anyway. What do you say?"

Now *that* sounded like a plan. "I say I need a drink like nobody's business."

After all, it wasn't as if anything else could possibly go wrong.

"Not a whole lot of people in the Blue Ridge who actually *want* to yank a tranny on their Friday night. Guess you're just special."

Shane didn't have to turn around to know that Jackson Carter was wearing a smartass grin that matched his personality with absolute perfection.

"You say the nicest things." Shane didn't even break stride with the wrench in his hand, even though he was far from ignoring his closest friend.

Jackson laughed, sauntering into the garage with a cold wind at his back. "Asshole."

"Stop. I'm blushing." Shane cracked a grin, finally swinging his gaze from the underside of the Miata. He'd had it on the lift for a couple hours now, and it was every bit the pain in the ass he'd predicted it would be. But considering the paycheck that would come out of the deal, he really couldn't bitch.

"So, did you come all the way out here just to blow sunshine up my skirt?" Shane dragged the rolled-up sleeve of his flannel shirt over his brow and eyed Jackson with a smirk.

"Nope. I'm a man on a mission." Jackson ducked his six-foot-four, I-ate-a-linebacker-for-breakfast-and-went-back-for-seconds frame under the tiny red sports car and lifted his eyes with a frown. "Do I even want to know where you came up with this?"

Shane thought of Bellamy's fiery green eyes and the way her hips looked in those expensive designer jeans for a long second before answering. "Probably not."

"Right. So what say we go grab some beers at the Double Shot? Come on, buddy. I'm buying."

Shane's brows popped. "That's your mission? Are you honestly that hard up for someone to drink with?"

"Matter of fact, I am. Word is Samantha Kane just broke up with Jimmy Bowman."

"Jesus, is that the girl you've had the crush on since sixth grade?" Shane laughed. How anyone could have a jones like that for someone else was beyond him. Dating, he got. Hell, even casual sex made sense as long as both parties were on the same page. But unrequited love? Not happening to Shane in a million years.

"If you want to get technical, since December of the fifth grade. But anyway. She's bound to be out tonight, and I'm not going to impress her if I show up alone. I need a wingman, and you, my friend, have special charm. Even if you never use it. Whaddaya say?" Jackson arched a brow toward his blond crew cut and grinned, but something flickered in his stare.

Shane tilted his head at Jackson. "Did Grady put you up to this?"

Shane had called Grady right after Bellamy left the garage to let him know the job had come in, although he'd deliberately fudged the truth about when he planned to pull the tranny so the old man wouldn't come back in to work. The lines on Grady's face lately suggested that being in the garage was wearing on him, and Shane didn't mind picking up the slack.

Just so long as Grady didn't *know* he was picking up the slack.

Jackson stared at his scuffed work boots. "Not really."

"You suck at bending the truth," Shane offered, pressing his lips into a tight line. He raked a hand through his hair, exhaling slowly.

"Well, the Samantha Kane thing is true," Jackson started, and Shane saw the honesty in his expression. "But yeah. I saw Grady in town a little while ago and he said something about you bein' here an awful lot. So I thought I'd see if you wanted to go grab a few. It's not like it'll hurt anything. This time tomorrow, you'll have that tranny out, and for what? A three-day wait on parts? Come on." Jackson tipped his crew cut toward the door. "This fancy bucket of bolts will be here tomorrow, no worse for the wear."

As much as Shane hated to admit it, Jackson had a point. Plus, the last thing Shane needed was Grady thinking he spent too much time in the garage. He worked his ass off because he loved it, period. It had been that way ever since the minute Grady hired him.

Hell if that wasn't a thread Shane didn't feel like pulling.

He grumbled, mostly to cover up his smile. "I'll only go on one condition."

Jackson lifted his brows at Shane in question. "And that is?"

"Your ass is coming back in here tomorrow to help me muscle this tranny out."

Jackson shook his head like he should've known better. "Let me guess. Damn thing seized? You know those things are a pain no pill can reach, right?"

Thinking of how the car had come to be here in the first place, Shane had to laugh. "You think that's bad, you should see its owner. Come to think of it, a couple of beers might not be the worst way to end this day after all."

Bellamy eyed the faded sign over the side of the worn wooden building and giggled.

"Okay, you guys. You're seriously taking me to a bar called the Double Shot in an effort to make me feel better?" She was feeling the effects of the two gin and tonics she'd had with dinner, especially since they'd been strong enough to take the paint off her car.

The very car that was currently sitting in some back roads garage, waiting for parts that cost more than a Mexican beach getaway.

She wasn't drunk enough.

"Yes. We plugged 'hot men, local bar' into the GPS and this is what popped up. Go figure," Jenna said.

"Bellamy's here to forget men," Holly reminded her, slamming the car door.

Huh. In the wake of all the crappy events raining down on her today, Bellamy hadn't even thought twice about Derek. He seemed like small potatoes compared to her French-fried transmission and its sky-high price tag, not to mention the fact that she still had to deal with calling the boss from hell to try and weasel a whole week's worth of days away from the grind.

"I'm here to forget *one* man," she corrected. "And to be honest, I don't really think it's worth my energy to be pissed at Derek."

Jenna tipped her head as they hustled through the busy parking lot. "You're not mad at Mr. Fantastic anymore?"

"He wasn't that fantastic, obviously," Bellamy griped.

"How great can a guy who colors his hair be?" Holly said, giggling. "I swear, he was more of a product whore than me, and that is totally saying something."

Bellamy laughed, letting the bone-chilling cold take her buzz down a notch. "I'm not talking about that." Oh, thank God. They had finally reached the door. "What I mean is, now that I think about it, the whole thing was kind of just . . . meh."

If her relationship with Derek was as exciting as dry wheat toast, then she'd found its polar opposite in the bar she'd just entered. The place was packed with people, all in various states of drunk and disorderly, and between the low lighting and the loud, freely flowing music, Bellamy knew they'd discovered the perfect place for her to drown her sorrows.

"Yeah, no offense, honey, but Derek wasn't exactly riveting. Although *he* thought he was," Holly half shouted over the din as they made their way toward the crowded bar.

"Please. I can say this now that he's a thing of the past. The guy was an asshat," Jenna said, frowning.

Bellamy stopped short a few steps from the glossy wood of the bar top that ran the entire length of the room. "Did you always think so?"

Jenna chewed her lip for a second. "Yeah, kind of."

"Why didn't you say anything?" Bellamy gasped.

"Because I wasn't the one dating him. You seemed to like him, and that was good enough for me. His pretentiousness wasn't that offensive in the grander scheme of things. It's not like he kicked puppies or stole money from little old ladies or anything."

"Still! You're supposed to be my friends. If anything, you should've told me for my own good," Bellamy said.

Holly looked at her as she leaned against the bar. "Derek's a complete weasel, honey."

"It's not retroactive," she sighed.

Of course, neither one of them was wrong. Derek wasn't necessarily horrible. But he sure wasn't as great as he thought he was. In more ways than one.

"Oh. Okay, well have a drink, then," Holly said brightly, passing her a fresh beer.

The unexpected pang at the memory of her lackluster sex life with Derek made Bellamy's cheeks flush, and she took a long draw from the bottle. It wasn't like a through-the-roof sex life would've saved the relationship in the end.

But it wouldn't have *hurt* anything, either.

"I've got bigger fish to fry than Derek. How am I going to get home on Monday without a car? Bosszilla is probably already losing her mind at the fact that my cell service is spotty at best up here." The discovery of cell service within the boundary of the resort had been the only bright spot in Bellamy's otherwise trying afternoon. Right up until the three voice mails and nine texts from her boss popped through, anyway.

"Oh, no you don't. We're not worrying about any of that crap until tomorrow. Tonight is supposed to be about you *forgetting* your sorrows," Jenna reminded her. "Now knock it off before I find out whether or not that karaoke

machine is functional. I'd love to see you belt out some
Lady Gaga."

Bellamy had a retort on the tip of her tongue when she
heard the sound of a very deep, very male throat being
cleared.

"Excuse me, ladies. My friends and I were wondering
if you'd like to join us for a drink."

No pick-up line, no nonsense, no veiled suggestions of
any kind. Now *this* was something she could get on board
with. Bellamy turned to look at the source of the voice.

The man's eyes were right on hers as she peered up into
his classically handsome face. His blond hair was slicked
back with a suspicious amount of product, but then again,
she could do worse than a guy who cared about his appearance. She exchanged a look with Holly, who had already
gotten the subtle nod from Jenna.

What the hell. If they were going to get their drink on,
they might as well make it a party. The guy seemed nice
enough; plus, how bad could it be with Holly and Jenna at
her side?

"Why not," Bellamy said, giving up a smile.

"Marcus Lawrenson." He extended his hand. His handshake was softer than she expected, but the smile that went
with it had potential.

Marcus was *not* prettier than her.

Which made him absolutely perfect in her book.

Chapter Five

Shane leaned a forearm onto the bar and took a lazy draw from his beer. The Double Shot already teemed with its typical Friday night crowd, and even though going out wasn't necessarily Shane's thing, it was hard to find anything wrong with a cold beer after a long day.

"So, can I ask you a question?" Jackson gave him a look that suggested he was going to no matter what Shane's response turned out to be.

"Shoot."

"How come you work so much? I mean, I like cars as much as the next person, but really? Every guy needs a break. Hook up with a girl on the side, maybe get a little drunk here and there, go fishing with his buddies. You? For the year I've known you, all you've ever done is put your nose to the grindstone. What gives?"

Shit. Shane knew this question was overdue, yet he'd still been dreading it. "Nothing gives. I'm just a get-it-done kind of guy, that's all." Shane shrugged, hoping Jackson would drop it.

Not a chance. "Look, I know you saved Grady's business from going down the tubes after he had that heart attack last year. If you hadn't drifted into town when you did, he'd have probably ended up having to sell the place. But still, you gotta loosen up, Shane! Life's too short, you know?"

Shane had all but drained his beer during the course of their two-minute conversation, and he was gonna need another one, stat. "I'm loose enough, man. Really, you're worried over nothing."

Jackson's laugh turned a couple of nearby heads, even with the music blasting from the speakers. "Really? When was the last time you got laid?"

"That's a little personal, don't you think?" Shane placed his empty beer on the bar and signaled the bartender for a replacement, dodging the question like a pro.

"Sounds like it's *nothing* personal to me. Come on, Shane. There are tons of pretty girls in this bar. I'm not saying you should marry one of them, but it wouldn't kill you to get somebody's number, would it?"

"I just haven't met anybody I'm interested in, that's all," he replied, wanting nothing more than for the conversation to end. Jackson's eyes scanned the bar with careful precision, and Shane narrowed his gaze on his friend.

"What are you doing?"

"I'm trying to find a girl who looks interesting. What about her?" Jackson flicked his gaze down the bar and let it settle on someone in the crowd by the door.

"Marcus Lawrenson? I don't think he's my type," Shane chuckled.

Jackson let out a breath, exasperated. "Not Captain America, you dick. The girl he's talking up."

Shane smirked, finally enjoying himself a little bit as he turned around. "Oh, all right. Let's see who Marcus has his sights set on tonight."

As soon as Marcus shifted his stance, giving Shane a clear line of vision to the girl leaning against the bar, his stomach did a lurch-back flip move that shocked the hell out of him.

Across the room, Bellamy Blake smiled up at Marcus like he was God's gift to women. And was she holding his hand? Shane's beer suddenly tasted bitter, and he rolled the bottle around to check the expiration date.

Jackson lifted a brow. "What?" Unfortunately for Shane, Jackson hadn't missed a thing, and the big oaf was smarter than his *who me?* charm let on. Shane hadn't given any girl a second look since he'd moved to Pine Mountain; he wasn't about to start now.

"Nothing. That's, ah, the girl who belongs to the toy car sitting up on the lift at Grady's."

Jackson's eyes glimmered with interest. "Lemme guess. Not your type either?"

This one was a total gimme. "Definitely not." Yet his eyes disobeyed his brain and arrowed in on Bellamy again. Okay, so she wasn't holding Marcus's hand. It must have been the guy's poor excuse for a handshake that Shane had witnessed. Right.

Why did he give a shit?

"She's cute. You sure she's not interesting enough for you?"

Shane didn't need to feed Jackson's imagination any further, especially not when it came to his being interested in a snobby little blonde from the city. Which he wasn't. At all.

"She's plenty interesting if you want to date a prissy pain in the ass. Me? I'll pass. Hey, isn't that Samantha Kane over there, looking at the jukebox? You should go talk to her, my man, before someone else swoops in and steals her away." Shane jutted his chin at the willowy redhead standing by the jukebox with a gaggle of her friends.

Forgoing subtlety, Jackson swung his head around and studied the situation. "If I'm going to talk to her, I ain't goin' alone. Why do girls travel in packs like that, huh?"

Shane exhaled in relief at the shift in focus. "Relax, Lover Boy. I'd be a poor excuse for a wingman if I didn't go with you." He barely registered his subconscious glance in Bellamy's direction before his eyes were back on his friend. "Who knows. Maybe one of her friends will be interesting."

Jackson finished his beer and looked at Shane with a grin. "Atta boy. You might get lucky tonight after all."

Bellamy spent more time listening to the conversation around her than participating in it, which proved to be increasingly amusing as the night—and the drinks—wore on. About two beers into her bender, she'd spotted Shane leaning against a wall, looking like James Dean spit him out. By beer number three, he was getting cozy with a sexy brunette wearing a top cut so low that it earned wardrobe malfunction status in Bellamy's book.

By beer number four, she realized that she really needed to stop giving a flying fig what the man did.

"So, Bellamy, tell us what you do," Marcus purred, his voice sounding like it was covered in chocolate.

Since both Holly and Jenna were suddenly engrossed in conversation with Marcus's friends, Bellamy wasn't exactly sure who the *us* was, but what the hell. She'd play along just for grins.

"I'm a real estate analyst for the second largest bank in Philadelphia."

Whoa. Note to self. Don't use the big words around Marcus. He looked so bewildered that even deer stuck in headlights would be embarrassed for him.

"Beauty *and* brains, huh? Nice combination," he finally managed.

"Uh, thanks, I think." The pause that followed reeked of awkward, so she figured she'd bail the poor guy out. "What about you?"

Marcus's chest puffed and he flashed his pearly too-whites. "I'm a ski instructor at the resort. I heard Jenna say you're staying until Monday. If you want to hit the slopes tomorrow, I could show you a thing or two."

Oh my God. Did he just give her the double-barrel-wink? Honestly? Who did that anymore?

"Oh, ah, wow, that's really nice of you. I didn't bring skis with me this trip," she apologized.

Much to Bellamy's chagrin, Marcus was completely undaunted. "Oh, that's fine. We've got tons of that stuff you could borrow. Really." He leaned in so close that the cloying scent of his cologne hit her nostrils full force, and between that and the alcohol coursing through her veins, dizzy was her new middle name. "There are all kinds of trails on the mountain with romantic views. They're perfect for a private lesson," he said on a deep croon.

The thing about anything covered in chocolate was, if you had too much of it, you tended to throw up.

Bellamy straightened up and gave Holly the signal for *help me out or I'll kill you.* Bless her best friend's heart, her response time was less than ten seconds.

"Bellamy, I need a drink! Do you want one?" The flush on Holly's face suggested that she needed a drink like she needed a tax audit, but Bellamy was in the mood to pick up her friend's slack if necessary.

"Oh, ladies, allow me," Marcus murmured, moving to join them.

Bellamy brushed his sleeve with her hand. "That's really not necessary, Marcus. I'd like to have a quick conversation with Holly about our itinerary for the weekend. We won't be long."

Marcus got caught up in her use of multiple syllables like they were a smart-girl force field, and he gaped like a grouper on deck. "Oh, uh . . . right. I'll just wait here, then."

She pressed her lips together to hold in a smile, but as soon as Bellamy turned toward the bar, her smile died on the spot.

Shane was standing not ten feet away, leaning against the wall and staring at her with eyes so dark, they all but glittered black in the low light spilling down from overhead. Bellamy froze where she stood in the middle of the hardwood, unable to do anything but stare back at him, until Holly's voice finally snagged her attention.

"Hello? Earth to Bellamy?" Holly followed Bellamy's line of sight across the bar, eyes landing directly on Shane. He'd shifted his weight and casually turned his attention toward the absolute mountain of a guy next to him, but Holly caught him well enough in profile to put two and two together. Her mouth curled into a quick, wicked grin. "What's the matter? Hot guy got your tongue?"

Bellamy's cheeks went from zero to five-alarm-fire in two seconds flat, and she stalked the rest of the way to the bar. "I don't know what you're talking about," she said casually, flipping her hair for emphasis.

Holly snickered. "I'm drunk, not stupid. But whatever you say."

Come to think of it, Bellamy wasn't exactly sober, herself. "Well, thanks for the save over there. I owe you one."

Holly leaned an elbow onto the bar, and within a minute, two fresh beers graced the counter in front of them. "So, Marcus is a no-go, huh? Not that I'm shocked, really. He's, um, how should I put it . . ."

"Cheesier than Velveeta?" Bellamy supplied, and Holly choked out a laugh.

"I was going to say too enthusiastic. Is he that bad?"

Bellamy sighed, linking her fingers around the frosty neck of her beer. "Yes. No." He definitely wasn't her type, but just because he was your basic cornball didn't mean he was that bad of a guy. "I think I might need a break from men after all. Just for a little while." Of course, her eyes zeroed in on the spot where Shane had been standing. And of course, he was still standing there, unmoved, looking almost bored.

And wildly sexy.

"I think I need something stronger than this," she mumbled into her beer.

"Well, why didn't you say so?" Before Bellamy could protest, Holly had lined up two shots of Patrón Silver, along with one look of approval from the bartender.

"Jeez, Holly. Guess we're not going halfway," Bellamy laughed.

"Nope, not a chance. Now be a good girl and drink up."

Wait, what was the adage? Liquor then beer . . . no wait. Did those gin and tonics count anymore? Beer then liquor . . . uh . . .

Fuck it.

Bellamy tossed back the shot, and it rode like a lightning

strike to her belly. She shifted her weight and leaned against the glossy bar, suddenly very aware of her body. Standing upright after being seated for a while over in camp check-out-my-ski-slope brought on a sensation Bellamy couldn't ignore.

"Hey, Holly, I've gotta find the loo." How had she managed to keep four beers in her thimble-sized bladder, anyway?

"Ha, the loo. You're so freakin' proper. They didn't teach you the word *pee* at that Ivy League grad school?"

"Come on, you know my mother hates that word. I've never said it in my life."

"You're the only twenty-seven-year-old I know who worries about what her mom thinks." Holly paused to frown. "Ah, shit. Jenna just sent me the get-your-ass-back-here look. What do you want me to do?"

"Please. I might be skirting the edges of blotto, but if I can't take myself to the bathroom, then there's something wrong with me. I'll be right back."

Bellamy turned, her eyes tracking the bar for any sign of the ladies' room. She was loath to admit that her brain's response time involved some serious slack, especially on the heels of that shot of tequila.

"Okay. If you're not back in ten minutes, I'm coming after you," her friend warned.

"I'm sure I'll be fine." What could go wrong on a trip to the loo?

Assuming she could find the damned thing.

Anticipation prickled through Bellamy as she casually surveyed the bar. Like her eyes needed another excuse, they landed on the spot where Shane had stood, staring at her.

He was gone.

Just as well, she grumbled to herself. Now maybe she

could get back to normal instead of making goo-goo eyes at someone she didn't even like.

Finally, Bellamy located the bathroom at the very back of the bar. Navigating the narrow hallway with its handful of identical doors was a challenge to her beer buzz, but she managed to locate the correct one without too much fanfare. After going to the bathroom, she ran a hand through her hair in the dingy mirror, realizing she had a flush on her face that matched the one on Holly's. Well, at least she'd managed to achieve one goal today, anyway. She'd temporarily forgotten about her ex, her hideous boss, and her car. The same car she'd left with the mechanic who had both made fun of her and sent her a stare that doubled as a dark, sexy, hot-man laser.

Oh, holy shit, it was time to go to bed.

Bellamy decided to forgo reapplying her lipstick, lest it encourage Marcus. What she really wanted more than anything was her nice, warm, king-sized bed back at the resort, and the prospect of recovering from her hangover courtesy of a gourmet breakfast and a massage. She made her way back into the narrow hallway to go find Jenna and Holly. Forgetting her troubles had been nice, but it was time to go sleep off the liquor before fate found her and messed with her evening like it had messed with her day.

As if destiny heard her thoughts like a homing beacon, the only thing standing between Bellamy and the sweet dreams she craved was Shane Griffin.

Literally.

Chapter Six

The minute Bellamy's eyes locked in on his as she sauntered from the back hallway where he'd been heading, Shane's first impulse was to look away.

So it was really weird when he found he couldn't.

Instead, he stopped to lean against the wall in the alcove leading back to the bar, sinking his thumbs through the belt loops on his jeans. She paused by way of a tiny stutter step, then straightened her shoulders and promptly ignored him even though they were the only two people in the alcove.

Typical. Man, girls who did shots from fifty-dollar bottles of tequila were so not in his best interest, no matter how sweet the curve of their hips looked.

Goddamn designer jeans.

Of course, he knew about the tequila because he'd been watching her carefully, even though it was a bad idea. Chalk it up to the fact he was pretty bored, and that, contrary to his hopes, none of Samantha Kane's friends was the least bit interesting. Kind of tough to work up a whole lot of appeal if you had the IQ of a doorknocker, even if you had the other kind of knockers to make up for it. As far as Shane was concerned, the trade-off wasn't worth it, not even for a night.

And the pinnacle of his so-so evening was going to be the cold shoulder routine from a girl he didn't even like? Thanks, but no thanks. Bellamy's emerald-green eyes were focused squarely on the path back to the bar, and she looked as if she was going to breeze right past him even though he knew she'd seen him. Shane scoffed and pushed off of the wall with disgust, ready to beat her to the punch and let her watch his back for a change.

But before he could turn all the way around, she stumbled off course and walked smack into the support pole in the dimly lit alcove.

Shane swung back toward her, his legs giving up an impressive response time to cover the space between them. "Whoa! Bellamy, are you okay?"

Both of her hands flew up to her right cheek, and without thinking, he covered them with his own. "I'm fine. It's fine," she insisted, but her voice betrayed her hurt.

"It's not fine. Christ, let me look at you." Shane guided her beneath the one decent overhead light in the back of the alcove, and she didn't fight him. "Here, lean against the wall."

"Don't be stupid, I told you I'm—ow!" She winced and yanked her head away from his gentle touch, smacking it into the wall behind her.

Shane raked a hand through his hair and sighed. "Could you knock that off please, before you give yourself a concussion?" Maybe if he made light of it, Bellamy would ease up and at least let him take a look. God, she was tough.

"Oh, that's nice. Go ahead. Make fun." She scowled, but her voice was tenuous.

"I'm not trying to make fun of you. I'm trying to look at your face." She couldn't lose the bravado for the ten seconds it would take for him to make sure she was okay? Jeez!

Shane took two fingers and very gently lifted her stubborn-as-hell chin so he could get a better look at the angry welt on her cheekbone. "You need to get some ice on this," he murmured, frowning. He'd had a few shiners in his day, and he wouldn't be surprised if the mark on her face bloomed into a nasty bruise before morning.

Bellamy closed her eyes and slumped against the wall. "I don't want any ice," she whispered, chin trembling beneath his fingers.

Something inside his gut went completely soft, and his lips parted in surprise. "You're going to have a bruise, Bellamy. Plus, you hit your head kind of hard. Maybe you should go to the emergency room or something." He turned to see if one of the bouncers was milling around near the back hallway.

"Shane." The tone of her voice made him turn back around, mid-movement. "Please don't get anyone, okay? I promise I'm fine. I just . . ." She broke off, her green eyes flashing with tears that she seemed to be fighting with every ounce of her willpower. "I've had a really, really bad week. The whole walking into a pole thing? Let's just say a trip to the ER would be the miserable icing on the cake of my issues right now, okay?"

He opened his mouth to argue with her, but the sliver of nice-guy that lurked in his subconscious recognized her embarrassment and wouldn't let him. "All right. Let me at least get a good look at it, though." She didn't resist, *finally*, so he leaned in for a closer inspection. "You don't feel dizzy? Nauseous, anything like that?"

She let him turn her head under the light for a better look. "Of course I feel dizzy and nauseous. I was just doing shots of tequila."

Welcome back to square one. Even hurt, she was a pain in the ass.

Shane stiffened at the mark on her face as he ran his fingers along her jaw. He was no expert, but the bruise that was forming looked small and fairly straightforward. "I think you're fine. Let's see your eyes." Not like he'd really be able to see her pupils in this light, but at least he knew that if they were round, it meant she was okay. Her attitude sure was intact.

"I told you, I'm really fine." Bellamy turned her head back toward his, making a show of opening her eyes as wide as they would go.

It was right in that moment that time slowed way the hell down, and Shane realized that her face was less than a couple of inches from his. Her green eyes glinted as he looked into them, and he was struck again by the very odd sensation of not wanting to look away. Insane as it was, he wanted to be closer.

He wanted to kiss her.

Shane cleared his throat, not moving. "How many fingers am I holding up?" The lag time between his brain and the rest of him made him wonder if he sounded like an idiot.

Her eyes crinkled around the edges, and she smiled a little even though it looked like it hurt. "None."

Affirmative on the idiot thing.

"Looks like you're fine," Shane said, his voice low. His fingers were still on the side of Bellamy's face, and somewhere in his brain, a voice screamed that he should move them.

But she looked like she didn't want him to.

"Mmm-hmm," she agreed.

It was a really terrible idea, but Shane didn't care. Something high-powered, almost magnetic, was in charge of his actions, charring his free will like toast right there in the alcove.

He placed his lips on hers in the barest hint of a whisper, and for a second, she didn't move. Tracing her uninjured cheekbone with the pads of his fingers, he curved them beneath her chin and tipped it carefully upward, increasing the contact between their bodies. Bellamy sighed into him then, parting her lips to accommodate his, her soft skin opening to reveal enticing heat.

God, she tasted like pure electricity.

Not wanting to hurt her, but not willing to let go, Shane swept his tongue across her bottom lip, letting his teeth follow in the gentlest of grazes. Bellamy arched up to him, her tongue darting into his mouth tentatively at first, then filling him so boldly that he wanted to do a lot more than kiss her. He slid his hand around the back of her neck, cupping her hot skin, getting tangled and lost in her soft golden curls, until . . .

"Bellamy? Are you back . . . oh, *shit*!"

Bellamy's entire body seized beneath Shane's hands, and he pulled away from her in a flash.

A pair of giggles lifted over the muffled background noise of the bar beyond where they stood, while Bellamy wrapped her arms around herself and blushed, clearly embarrassed. "Yeah, I, uh . . ." She trailed off, unable to finish.

"God, we're sorry." The friend who had picked Bellamy up from the garage earlier eyed both of them with a half smile as she stopped short in the dim hallway.

Bellamy's expression went from embarrassed to mortified in less than a breath. Well, shit. Who could blame her? Her highbrow friends had just caught her kissing the lowly car mechanic. What was he *thinking*?

The tall honey-blonde stammered. "We just wanted to make sure she was okay, but it seems . . . well, that she is. So we can just . . ."

Desperate, Shane cut her off. "No, no. It's a good thing you came along. She hit her head, over there by the pole and I was just taking a look."

Bellamy's expression morphed into a glower before she averted her gaze from him completely.

"Oh, God, Bellamy! Are you okay?" The girl Shane hadn't met, a petite redhead, came rushing over to Bellamy, and the awkward circumstances seemed to be quickly forgotten by her friends.

"I'm fine. It was a total idiot move, really," she muttered, a swath of blond curls falling across her injured cheek as she tried to hide her face. "I guess I wasn't paying attention to where I was going."

In the low light of the alcove, Shane could see the look of despair that crossed her pretty features, and he remembered the admission of her bad week. Bellamy opened her mouth, presumably to elaborate on what had happened, but he cut her off.

"It was totally my fault. I wasn't looking where I was going, and I plowed right into her. Knocked her right into the damned thing. She really needs some ice."

Bellamy's head jerked up in surprise, causing her to yelp in pain, and her eyes narrowed on his in confusion for a split second before he looked away.

This was his out, and he was taking it. "So, if you girls can wait with her, I'll go get some ice from the bar."

Translation: I'll send someone back here with some, and then I'll hightail it out of here as soon as she's taken care of. Had his brain gone on a complete walkabout? As Bellamy's friends fussed over her, gasping at the mark on her face, he knew she was in capable hands.

He never should have kissed her. And judging from the way she'd glared at him and was now refusing to look in his direction, Shane wouldn't be making that mistake again even if he wanted to.

He'd be surprised if Bellamy Blake would touch him with a ten-foot pole.

"Room service!"

Bellamy squinted at the clock on her bedside table and groaned. Now she knew what Wile E. Coyote felt like when the Road Runner managed to dump that anvil on his head.

Oh, to be a cartoon so someone could erase it all.

"Jenna, it's nine in the morning." Bellamy nestled deeper into her pillow, unable to ignore the marching band in her head.

"I know, but you slept for eight hours, so I wanted to check on you." Jenna balanced a room service tray between both hands as she entered, silhouetted by the sunlight trying to breach the drapes in Bellamy's bedroom.

Bellamy made a face, which she instantly regretted. God, that hurt. "I *told* you two not to Google 'head injuries.' This so doesn't count." She made a mental note to kill Shane for outing her like that to her friends. It figured he'd feel the need to draw attention to her getting hurt. It had been the perfect getaway for him, after all. The whole walking-into-a-pole part had really just been the pièce de résistance of her night.

Unless you counted the whole kiss-and-run thing. How could she have fallen for something so stupid?

Jenna cleared her throat gently, bringing Bellamy back down to earth. "Are you sure it doesn't count? Maybe you should bite the bullet and take a look at your shiner," she offered, placing the tray on the dresser.

"You've been taking drama lessons from Holly. I don't have a black eye." The smell of fresh coffee perked Bellamy's senses to life, and she left the rumpled confines of her bed to inspect the tray.

Jenna snickered. "If you say so. You looked like an extra from *Fight Club* before you even went to bed."

Bellamy sighed. "Okay. Fine." She glanced at the mirror over the dresser, wincing as Jenna swung the drapes open. Since when was the sun so malicious? "See, I don't have . . ."

An inch-long bruise the size of a nickel glared at her from her reflection, as if it was made of spite.

"Oh, you've got to be *kidding* me!" She leaned toward the glass until she was so close that her breath fogged her reflection. The bruise wasn't big or terribly swollen, but it was definitely noticeable.

She would never, ever try to look cool in front of a guy again. Who gave a shit what Shane Griffin thought, anyway?

Well, apparently she did, because she'd been so torqued up over breezing past him that she'd smashed into a stupid pole.

"It's really not as bad as I thought it would be, considering how nasty it looked. I bet it hurts like a bitch, though." Jenna sat down on the edge of the bed while Bellamy examined the bruise from every possible angle.

"Oh! You're up," Holly said, bouncing into the room. "I brought you a couple of things from the store. You know, for your head injury." She held up a plastic bag that was full to the point of straining.

"Okay, you guys, really? It's just a bump," Bellamy griped, padding back to the bed with a mug of coffee between her palms.

Holly ignored her and opened the bag with glee. "Motrin, one every four to six hours for pain. The pharmacist said for a really bad headache, you could even take two. Portable cold packs—you really should ice it again, you know. Look how cool these are, all you do is just . . ."

"I'm pretty sure I know how to take Motrin." Bellamy scowled, then blew out a breath. "Sorry. I know you're just worried. But really, it's fine."

Holly peered at her, unfazed. "S'ok. I thought kissing the hot mechanic guy last night might improve your mood, but I guess not. Was he a bad kisser?"

"No!" The need to deny that the whole thing even happened propelled the answer out of Bellamy before she heard its implications. Neither of her friends skipped a beat.

"So he was a good kisser? He *looked* like a good kisser," Holly mused.

Jenna broke in, snagging a scone from the tray before sitting back on the bed. "Told you he's hot."

"I hate you both," Bellamy muttered without malice. She should have known they'd do this. Hell, if the shoe was on the other foot, she wouldn't hesitate to dole out a little friendly ribbing.

"We're okay with that. You're the only one of the three of us who scored last night. Come on! Dish a little," Jenna said, scrunching up her nose.

"I didn't *score*. To be honest, I think the whole thing

was a mistake. And why do you look like you just bit into a lemon?" Bellamy took a long swallow of coffee, and the warming sensation helped lift the edges of her hangover.

"These scones are like hockey pucks. Go with the bagels if you value your life." Jenna tossed the half-eaten scone back on the tray with a thunk.

"That's what happens when you overwork your dough." Bellamy shrugged, taking a cinnamon raisin bagel from the platter and tearing off a hunk. "Hey, toss that Motrin over here, would you?" It was as close as she would get to admitting that her head really did hurt.

"So you're not going to give up any details about your rendezvous with Mr. Goodwrench? Really?" Holly poured some orange juice for Bellamy to swallow the pills, looking disappointed.

"I would, but there aren't any. I told you, it was a mistake," Bellamy mumbled around the Motrin.

Jenna laughed. "What, like forgetting to pay your cable bill? Come on!"

Bellamy blushed, heat creeping all the way up to her ears. "No. I meant the kind of mistake that involves beer goggles," she said, ripping her bagel into tiny pieces.

"Um, you've got some rose-colored beer goggles, sweetheart. Jenna's right. That man is fine." Holly cracked open a cold pack and passed it over wordlessly.

"Not me, him." Bellamy's words were so quiet, they almost qualified as a whisper. She leaned into the cold pack, feeling the ache of it seep into her cheekbone. It was embarrassing enough that she'd walked into a pole trying to look cool in front of the cocky jerk, but then to go and kiss him like a groupie on top of it all? Insult and injury were supposed to be metaphorical, for God's sake!

Jenna lifted her gaze from the bagel she was buttering, confused. "But he seemed sober."

Bellamy cut off her thoughts with a wave. Nope. Her ego was a sinking ship as it was. She simply couldn't dwell on it. "Either way, it was nothing. As a matter of fact, it was less than nothing." Shifting the cold pack, Bellamy traced a line down her half-numb cheek. "Hey, does this look bad enough to get me out of work for a couple of days? I'm thinking I should milk it for all it's worth, and fifty bucks says Bosszilla asks for photographic proof of bodily harm before she gives me another couple of days off."

"Oh, come on! Your car is about to be in a bazillion pieces. She won't let you off the hook?" Holly rolled her eyes.

Bellamy smirked. "Clearly, you're forgetting the time I took two days off for my great-aunt's funeral in New Jersey. She made me give her the obituary so she could call the funeral home to verify everything."

"Well, the bruise isn't terrible, but we could Photoshop you to make it look really awful," Holly suggested, falling for the change in subject hook, line, and sinker.

Bellamy played right along. "Knock yourself out. I have twenty-four hours to come up with a viable excuse, or else my boss is going to go full frontal bitch. And trust me when I say, it's not a pretty sight."

She sank back against the headboard as Jenna and Holly argued over whether being mauled by a bear in the mountains was a viable excuse. The subject of Bellamy's clandestine barroom kiss had been all but forgotten, swept under the rug as if it had never happened. Which was just the way she wanted it, because the whole thing had been a mistake of epic proportions.

Now if only she could get the feel of Shane's mouth, hot and oh so male, out of her head, she'd be just fine.

Chapter Seven

By the time lunch rolled around, Shane had been under Bellamy's Miata for three hours, and that was after running the five mile loop behind the old log cabin he rented. The unease he'd felt all morning sloshed around in his belly by the gallon. If a five mile run and yanking a transmission that was as stubborn as its owner didn't work to lighten his restlessness, Shane was out of ideas for what would.

"Lemme guess. You've been here a while. And by a while, I don't mean twenty minutes," Jackson drawled from the side door of the garage as he came in, huddled deep in his jacket against the January cold.

"A while, yeah." It wasn't Shane's fault he couldn't sleep, for God's sake. He had work to do.

"Tell me you at least stayed in bed until after the sun was up, you freaking workaholic."

"Whatever makes you feel better, man." Getting paid meant getting it done, and Shane had waited long enough to start pulling the tranny on this thing. Plus, if he kept his hands busy on Bellamy's car, then maybe he wouldn't be so tempted to be doing other things with them. Christ, it was a good thing this tranny would take all afternoon.

Maybe he'd offer to tune up Jackson's truck, just for good measure.

Jackson shook his head, joking as he ducked to stand under the car. "Don't you ever rest?"

"Got plenty of time to rest when I'm dead," Shane quipped over his shoulder with forced humor.

"Aren't you just a ray of frickin' sunshine?"

"Sorry. This thing's a pain in the ass." It took Shane all of three seconds to notice his buddy's ear-to-ear smile. Damn, those things were contagious. He couldn't help but return the favor, and was relieved to feel his bad mood get knocked down a few pegs. "What's with you?"

"I am taking Samantha Kane to the Pine Mountain Resort bonfire tonight, that's what's with me." Jackson's grin turned downright goofy as he looked up at the work Shane had done so far.

Shane laughed. "That explains the shit-eating grin, I guess."

Jackson's hands went up, signaling *guilty as charged*. "Well, if you hadn't taken off so early last night, you'd be in the know. Where'd you get to, anyway? One minute, we're standing there throwing back a cold one and the next thing I know, you're a ghost."

Good thing Shane had the bored look down pat, because he was giving it a workout right now. "Yeah, I was just beat from working all day. I'd have said good-bye to you, but you looked kind of occupied."

Jackson went for round two with his grin, and Shane just shook his head as he continued. "So it all worked out, huh? You were pretty cozy with her when I left."

"Yup. She even let me kiss her good night. Man, that woman can kiss. Hot enough to singe my toes, dude,"

Jackson said, lost for a second in what was probably a vivid recollection.

"I don't think that's your toes," Shane volleyed, but then suddenly, he was caught up in a recollection of his own. One that didn't involve *his* toes, either.

Well, shit.

"Yeah, yeah. She's not that kind of girl. Not yet, anyway," he laughed. "She stuck pretty close to the safety net of her friend just to make sure I wasn't a consummate creep. And speaking of her friend—" Jackson narrowed his eyes as Shane busied himself again with the car overhead. "You gotta come to the bonfire with me tonight. Melody was really into you. If you'd stuck around, maybe I wouldn't have been the only one who got kissed senseless, you know?"

Shane skipped around the irony of those words and the mention of Samantha's friend, dodging both like the land mines they were. "Yeah, I'm going to pass on the bonfire. I've got a couple of things I have to take care of." Never mind that those things would probably take all of an hour. As far as Shane was concerned, even a flimsy excuse was a good excuse to stay away from that fat-cat resort.

Jackson shot Shane a look of disbelief. "What could you possibly have to take care of on a Saturday night?"

Crossing the room to put his wrench down with a clank, Shane shrugged. "If I don't hit the grocery store, I'm going to be stuck eating ketchup for dinner. Plus, I gotta swing by Grady's." The way the old man had looked the other day still played at the back of Shane's mind. He'd looked tired, and not for lack of sleep.

"Well, you should come to the bonfire after. I know you avoid the resort like the plague, but I'm telling you, you won't be disappointed."

Shane looked up from where he'd been carefully straightening the tools on the workbench. His trip to the Double Shot last night had been enough social interaction to last him a month. The faster he could get back to working in the garage, paying off his loan and forgetting everything that had happened in the back room of that bar, the better.

"If you say so, Jax. Now are you gonna help me yank this tranny, or are you just gonna stand there looking pretty?"

Just like that, Shane's life went back to normal.

Bellamy examined the fridge in the suite's kitchenette with disdain. "We made pretty fast work of that hospitality basket, huh?" The only signs that it had even existed were some lonely slices of cheddar cheese and a jar of spicy mustard with nothing but dregs at the bottom.

"Yeah, sorry. I got the munchies last night after we came back," Holly said, looking sheepish from where she lay sprawled on the couch.

"That's an understatement. No lie, I thought she was going to lick the jar." Jenna laughed, moving just in time to dodge Holly's elbow.

Bellamy cracked a grin. The hourlong massage and matching facial treatment she'd indulged in had gone a long way toward improving her mood, especially since the aesthetician had put special effort into reducing the bruise on her face. With some strategically placed concealer, she'd be good as new.

"Well, we can't have you licking the jar. It's just embarrassing," Bellamy said. She pondered room service, but breakfast had been lackluster at best. Which was to say that it basically sucked.

"You're one to talk, Bruiser." Holly giggled, throwing a pillow across the common room toward the kitchenette.

The pillow missed by a mile, but the reminder of Bellamy's faux pas and the kiss that went with it stung. "Just for that, I might consider not going to the grocery store in town for more snacks." Bellamy arched a brow at her friend, noticing that it hurt a lot less than during previous attempts throughout the day.

Jenna tossed her the keys to her BMW without pause. "You will not, you big, fat foodie! The crappy room service has to be driving you bazoo. I don't suppose you'll get me a good old-fashioned bag of chips, huh?"

Bellamy wrinkled her nose as she slipped into her black wool peacoat and threw a knit hat over her tangle of curls to properly hide their disarray. "Since it's your car, I guess I can hook you up," she grumbled. Damn, she missed her car.

Nope. Not thinking about it. Not even a little bit.

"Okay, you brats. I'd say call me if you think of anything else, but, well, you know." She rolled her eyes at the idea of her worthless cell phone as she hustled out the door. To be honest, as much as she knew she'd probably pay for it in the end, it *had* been kind of liberating not to worry about the stupid thing all day.

Bellamy made her way down the curvy mountain road at a snail's pace. Part of her care came from the gut-clenching drop-off on the other side of the guardrail, but most of it was so she could take in the breathtaking view. Afternoon sun peeked through the high, thin clouds, bathing the tall, thick evergreens in sparkling light and smokelike shadows. The sky, a mix of watercolor blue and iron gray, was a perfect canvas overhead, and by the time Bellamy reached the grocery store, her mood had crossed the threshold of decent for the second time that day.

She parked Jenna's BMW in front of Joe's Grocery, squaring her shoulders before going inside. Bellamy didn't have high hopes for what lay beyond the doors, but with a little luck, she'd be able to work some magic and do better than the surprisingly mediocre room service food at the resort.

"Okay, Joe. Let's see what you're made of, baby," Bellamy murmured under her breath.

As soon as she stepped inside the grocery store, a warm pang erased every ounce of trepidation she'd carried in with her. This wasn't your typical, institutional mega-mart, with fluorescent lighting and symmetrical stacks of ho-hum produce. No, Joe's was set up like a cross between a country store and a cozy gourmet market, with buffed hardwood floors the color of warm honey, and large bushel baskets overflowing with gorgeous red apples and bottom-heavy, green pears at the height of ripeness. There were assorted cheeses in a refrigerated dairy case against one wall, and a counter boasting prepared salads, half a dozen kinds of fresh bread, and pastries arranged on mouth-watering platters, all right before her eyes at the front of the store.

No two ways about it. Bellamy had found her own personal version of the Promised Land.

"Afternoon, miss. Can I help you find anything?"

It took Bellamy a full minute to realize that the pleasant man behind the counter had been speaking to her. "Oh! Ah, I'm not sure. I think I'm a little overwhelmed. To be honest, I wasn't really expecting . . ." Oh my God. Were those wheels of Brie in the cheese case? And figs in the basket next to it? Seriously?

The man laughed. "Not a whole lot of people do. In fairness, if you head back that way, you'll find the normal stuff, too, so if you're hankerin' for Froot Loops, don't fret."

Bellamy blinked, unsure where to begin. "Oh, no. This will do just fine. Thank you." When she saw the basket holding fresh avocados, it was all she could do to suppress a squeal. She could make guacamole like nobody's business. How much more perfect for nighttime munchies could you get?

By the time she'd made her way from the brisk scent of the grapefruits and navel oranges to the impressive selection of cheeses and deli meats in the case along the wall, the basket draped over Bellamy's arm was heavier than a stack of phone books. She had much more than she needed, but caring was the furthest thing from her mind. Her mood was lighter than it had been in days; hell, *months*. Enjoying it was her number one priority before she had to face reality in the form of a boss who could screech like a howler monkey and an insubordinate car that had stranded her at the foot of a mountain with nothing but an arrogant mechanic to show for her troubles.

Make that an arrogant mechanic who could make a girl forget she had knees with the heat of a single kiss, then saunter off like it was no big deal after he was done.

Bellamy turned toward the bushels of deep red Fuji apples, flushing to match their color as she forced herself to shove the thought aside. She'd forgotten about her wonder-ex, Derek, for God's sake, and they'd kissed a hell of a lot more times than the whopping once she'd shared with Shane. Mentally ditching the image of one measly kiss should be a piece of cake. Except Derek's kisses had never felt anything like that.

Come to think of it, nobody's had.

She squeezed her eyes shut for a brief second to block out the memory once and for all before swiping a couple of apples to top off her basket. Exhaling a slow breath, Bellamy turned toward the checkout line, leaving all thoughts of Shane Griffin in the dust.

Shane was taking the shortcut to the frozen dinner section in Joe's Grocery when he caught sight of a fall of blond curls that could only belong to one woman. Great. He had to run into Bellamy at the grocery store, of all places. She couldn't eat room service like everyone else up at the resort? And was that a wheel of Brie in her hand?

Christ. Kiss or no kiss, he sure had her pegged. He turned, intending to slink behind the tall stand of fresh cut flowers in order to avoid her. But the way she looked in profile made him stop, halfway hidden from where she stood, and stare.

Bellamy's face was shrouded by a light blue hat that softened her features, and her fair hair spilled down her back in its trademark ringlets. Shane could see the bruise on her cheek, right by her eye, and he was shocked to see it was already starting to fade. Her green eyes glittered in the light pouring through the giant store windows, and she wore a smile that was as honest as a day's worth of work.

What rooted him to the spot wasn't any of those things, although each of them captured his attention. The thing that made him pause, watching surreptitiously from behind buckets of lilies and greenery, was the look on Bellamy's face. She studied everything she touched with tender reverence, cradling the avocados carefully as she chose the ones she wanted, letting her fingers sweep over the pears like they were made of glass. The sight fascinated the hell out of Shane.

Right up until she turned around and caught him blatantly staring at her.

"Oh!" Bellamy gasped across the row of apple bushels, her eyes flying wide. "What are you doing here?"

The way Shane saw it, he only had two options. He could either stand there like the dumbass he currently was, or he could joke his way out of this mess.

And he'd never been too partial to looking like a dumbass.

"Well, it's a little known secret, but we mechanics do eat." He stopped to let out a half smile. "I'm grocery shopping. What are you doing?" Shane stepped away from the flowers and met her gaze head-on over the bins of produce. It wasn't lost on him that Bellamy got kind of cute when she was unnerved, and he both hated and was turned on by how endearing it suddenly made her.

"Grocery shopping," she said, as if she wished she had something more clever to say.

"Imagine that," he bantered back. The edges of her lips curved upward into the barest hint of a smile.

Okay, that was hot.

Not quite sure how else to fill the silence, Shane figured he'd give polite conversation a go. "I, ah, managed to get your transmission out today. The parts should be shipped first thing Monday, so it looks like you're on track. Should be done by Friday afternoon as long as everything arrives on time."

Bellamy's smile made a full appearance then, and it

prompted him to forget all of the fire and brimstone he'd seen from her yesterday.

She looked happy.

"Thanks. Although I have to say I hope you're better at fixing cars than you are at grocery shopping," she replied, nodding toward his empty basket.

Shane's grin covered his face before he could rein it in. "I eat as well as the next guy," he argued, and she crinkled her nose at him from across the produce display.

"That's what I was afraid of."

Damn, that little half smile thing was disarming! He wanted to make a courteous excuse, grab some Hungry Man dinners and get the hell over to Grady's. He really did.

But then she laughed, and his legs made it clear that carrying him away from the spot where he stood wasn't on the current menu of options.

"Okay, smarty-pants. What've you got in there that's so good, then?" He made a show of peering over the low aisle and into her basket.

Bellamy tipped her head, and her curls tumbled across her shoulder as she looked down. "Oh, nothing really. I mean, we barely have a kitchen in our suite, so, you know. Just some stuff to tide us over. The room service at the resort is, um. Just okay."

"That's not exactly a ringing endorsement," Shane said, lifting a brow.

She bit her lip, which jacked Shane's cute-o-meter up a little higher.

"Well, you said it, not me." The look on her face suggested the room service was pretty bad.

Shane catalogued the contents of her basket in his head. "How many avocadoes does one girl need?" he queried, keeping his face as serious as possible. What a weird thing to have four of. You didn't exactly eat them out of hand like apples.

Bellamy gave a nonchalant shrug. "When the girl in question is making guacamole for her two friends who will certainly hork it down after consuming way too much alcohol at a bonfire? You err on the side of caution."

Shane's mouth popped open in surprise. "You're *making* guacamole? Doesn't that stuff come in jars just like everything else?"

Bellamy's wry laugh caught him right in the chest. "Shane, you took my freaking *car* apart. Do you really think making a little guac is rocket science in the face of all that?"

He stammered. "Well, I don't know. At least I'm sure I won't screw the tranny up. The guacamole, not so much."

"Oh, it's not hard," she said, eyes sparkling. "Now homemade pasta, that's a pain in the ass."

"Okay, wait. You can *make* pasta? As in, the dried stuff in aisle three?" Shane tried to rope in his complete shock, but failed. She might as well have told him she was going to whip up a quick batch of butter.

Bellamy served up a look that suggested homemade pasta was the garage equivalent of a simple oil change. "Sure. It's more time-consuming than difficult, which is what makes it a pain. Kind of a fun way to kill a Sunday afternoon, though. The results are definitely worth it."

Boy, if that didn't make watching a football game from the old recliner look downright lazy. Shane's brows drew inward. "So are you a chef or something, then?"

She barked out a laugh. "Oh God, no. I just cook for fun."

"What a coincidence. I eat for fun." If Shane had known how freaking provocative her giggle was, he might've tried harder not to piss her off yesterday.

Don't look now, but you're flirting with the rich girl.

The thought jammed into Shane, freezing his blood in his veins. "You know, I should let you go." Hell if this part of the conversation wasn't ten minutes too late. "Your friends are probably waiting for you to go to that bonfire, and all. I don't want to keep you."

Bellamy's laughter shorted out like a faulty fuse. "Oh. Well, it doesn't start for another couple of hours, I guess, but yeah. Yeah, you should get on with your shopping, too." She paused, chewing her lip. "Thanks for the update on the car. Have a good night."

"Bellamy, wait," Shane blurted, thinking only of the smile that had now faded from her lips. "Maybe I'll see you. Later. I'm going to the bonfire with a buddy of mine."

Her mouth lifted at the corners, the faint suggestion of her smile playing there for only an instant. "You are." The words were the verbal equivalent of Switzerland, so neutral that Shane couldn't read her tone at all. Still, something about that sexy laugh she'd given before spurred him on before he could think.

"Yup."

I am now, anyway.

Chapter Eight

"Let me get this straight. You made a date with hot mechanic guy in the middle of the produce aisle and you didn't even *tell* us?" Holly's expression was an equal mixture of shock and wicked grin as she halted a steaming mug of Irish coffee halfway to her lips.

"A little louder, Holly. The people in the way back didn't hear you," Bellamy hissed through clenched teeth, her breath puffing into the frigid night air.

The bonfire had been roped off for safety, separated from the milling crowd by an eight-foot circumference of rope and resort staff. It still gave off a decent amount of heat and a hell of a lot of atmosphere, although the plunging nighttime temperatures could knock the breath right out of a girl.

Or maybe it was her recollection of the mechanic with a smirk so sexy it should be illegal that was doing the job all by itself.

Bellamy sighed. "And I didn't make a date with anybody. I ran into Shane at the grocery store, and when I mentioned going to the bonfire, he said he *might* see me.

I hardly think it's a date if he was planning on being here anyway."

Jenna rolled her empty coffee mug between her gloved palms. "I don't know. Was it a casual 'maybe I'll see you'?" she deadpanned, giving an off-the-cuff wave. "Or was it more hopeful, like 'maybe I'll *see* you'?" She added a waggle of her dark blond brows for emphasis.

"He said maybe he'd see me, like a normal person," Bellamy insisted. "It's not a date. He doesn't even like me, for Pete's sake."

Holly scoffed at the protest. "I still think 'maybe I'll see you' qualifies as a date. It implies intent," she pressed, taking a long draw from her mug.

Bellamy arched a brow. "What are we, in court? A date involves phrases like 'pick you up at seven' and 'are you up for sushi?' 'Maybe I'll see you' doesn't count."

Holly rolled her eyes. "Sell stupid somewhere else, sweetie. You tried on three different sweaters and you've got that sexy-tousled thing going on with your hair. This is such a date! And by the way, your hair looks fabulous," she added.

Jenna nodded her approval, huddling closer for warmth. "You *do* look rather kittenish, darling," she said, and both women dissolved in a fit of giggles.

"Screw you," Bellamy muttered, although she couldn't help but laugh, too. "How's that for kittenish?"

"I don't know what the big deal is. After the kiss he laid on you last night, a date seems like the next logical step," Holly said, recovering from her laughter.

"That's a little backward, don't you think? People are supposed to kiss *after* a date, not before it. And this isn't a date, anyway."

Because if it was, Bellamy was on the precipice of getting stood up.

Jenna reached out to squeeze Bellamy's arm. "Well, whatever it is, it looks kind of cute on you."

"Thanks for the ego boost. The reason my hair looks decent is because I used those pricey samples from the spa, by the way. And Shane probably only said something about seeing me here because I mentioned that we were going. It was pretty causal, sorry to disappoint you."

Except that when he'd looked at her with those dark eyes and that gut-stirring smile, she'd have sworn that he *was* hoping to see her.

And now she was the one who was disappointed.

Jenna rubbed her gloved hands together, deciding for the moment to let Bellamy out from beneath the date-or-no-date microscope. "God, it's cold out here. Another coffee would hit the spot. Or at least maybe help me feel my toes again."

"Oooh, I'm game. Irish coffee is goooooood!" Holly said.

"That's because you've had three, and we've only been here for an hour, you lush." Jenna linked arms with Holly and nodded toward the lodge, with its inviting fireplaces and cozy armchairs. "Bellamy? Aren't you coming?"

Bellamy shook her head. "Nah. After last night, I'll pass. One night of alcohol-induced embarrassment is all this girl can take. I'll wait for you guys here."

"You sure?" Jenna hesitated.

"Yeah. But if you wimp out and stay inside to cozy up in one of those chairs by the fireplace, I'm coming in after you."

As soon as they had turned toward the resort, Bellamy wrapped her arms around her ice blue down parka and rocked back on her heels to try and generate a little body heat. She let her eyes scan the crowd, flitting from face-to-face for a full minute before commanding herself to knock it off. Shane had definitely said maybe, and there were hundreds of people out here, huddled around. He'd probably just come up with something more interesting to do, that's all.

Like that brunette from the bar last night.

"Oh, don't be stupid," she muttered, her breath escaping in puffy wisps.

"Ouch. I haven't even said hello yet."

Bellamy's eyes flashed wide as she whirled toward the sound of a very male voice coming from right behind her.

As Shane walked through the east gate and onto the near-frozen grounds of the resort, his unease made an encore performance by way of tap dancing through his gut. It was cold as all get-out, there was a playoff game on that would've looked great from his nice, warm Barca-lounger, and being at the resort made him want to break out in hives.

What was it, exactly, that had possessed him to shoot his mouth off like a two-dollar pistol and say he would do this?

Right. The thought of Bellamy's lips, turned up into that sweet little half smile, that's what. Ten minutes, Shane rationalized. If he hadn't found a reason to stay in ten minutes, he'd hit the road.

Probably.

After nine and a half minutes of milling through the growing crush of the bundled and huddled, a familiar voice called out from behind him.

"Shane? Hey! I didn't think you'd show."

Jackson's voice caught Shane by surprise, but he turned and played it cool, as if standing outside with a couple hundred strangers 'til his legs went numb was his idea of unparalleled fun.

"Yeah, well, I was at loose ends after swinging by Grady's. Figured I'd come check it out after all."

Jackson nodded toward the resort. "You've got good timing. I'm running to grab a round of coffee for me and Samantha. I could do without the frilly whipped cream, but I gotta say that the Irish whiskey in those things knocks the chill right outta ya. Why don't you come hang out with us?"

"I don't want to go all third-wheel on you, dude." Shane shifted his weight and skimmed the crowd again with a careful glance.

"Are you kidding? There are tons of people here. It's not like you're interrupting a private party. Yet," Jackson added on a smirk.

A flash of ice blue and blond curls caught the corner of Shane's eye and held tight, but as soon as he focused, his gut sank.

Bellamy was standing, sweet as could be, maybe ten feet from them. At about ten feet, four inches and much too close in Shane's opinion, stood none other than Marcus Lawrenson. From the look of things, the old cheese bag was laying it on as thick as molasses in the winter, too, leaning in toward Bellamy as she spoke.

Damn it, Shane knew coming here had been a bad idea. A classy girl like her belonged with the ski instructor set, anyway. He turned to give Jackson a sorry excuse and cut a path directly to his recliner. If he was lucky, he'd be able to catch the second half of the game before falling asleep in the thing.

But then the look on Bellamy's face registered in his brain. Her tight, awkward smile seemed forced, and so at odds with the one she'd given at the grocery store. Shane's legs did that independent-thinking thing again, refusing to move while he stared at her. He watched as her eyes skirted the crowd, darting toward the resort whenever Marcus wasn't paying attention.

She was looking for a lifeline.

"You okay, man?" Jackson waved his hand in front of Shane with a nonverbal *hello, in there*.

Shane nodded, crafting an idea in his head. "Yeah, sorry. Listen, I left my gloves in the truck. I'm just going to run and grab them." He made a show of rubbing his bare hands together and blowing into them, even though they weren't really that cold. This was either going to work like a charm or it was going to get him slugged. Shane took one last look in Bellamy's direction.

If she slugged him, it might be worth it.

"Couple of Irish coffees and you won't feel a thing," Jackson said with a laugh. "We're on the other side, over by the west gate. Just come over on your way back."

"Right."

His feet were moving toward Bellamy before the word was all the way out.

"Bell-a-meeee," Marcus sing-songed, and for the first time ever, Bellamy hated the sound of her own name. "I can't believe you didn't come down for a lesson today. The powder was as good as the view," he continued, his tone sickly sweet as he leaned in close enough for her to smell the breath mint that was failing to cover up whatever he'd eaten for dinner.

"The day must have gotten away from me, I guess." Where the hell were Holly and Jenna? This was going to turn into a code red, Bellamy could feel it. Somebody should really invent a best friend panic button for these kinds of situations. She threw one last glance through the crowd while Marcus slicked back his hair with a hand.

Nothing.

"Well, we can't let that happen again." Marcus arched a brow at her in a way that made her want to bathe in Clorox, but then she felt a tiny pang of remorse. He wasn't hurting anything, although she was a little worried about getting caught in the creep shrapnel if things went downhill. Still. For now, maybe there was a way out of this that didn't involve her running and screaming.

"Listen, Marcus, I, ah, should probably tell you. I'm waiting for . . . somebody." Bellamy edged backward to regain her personal space and waited, hoping he'd jump to the wrong conclusion and get the not-interested vibe she was broadcasting on all channels. Never mind that 'somebody' was either Jenna or Holly, or better yet, both.

"The more, the merrier, sweetheart," he cooed, her implication going unnoticed.

Bellamy groaned an inward curse. She should've known better than to expect a logic leap from a guy who used his head primarily as a hat rack.

Marcus leaned in again, not seeming to notice that she took a step backward as he did. His voice reached Barry White status as he shuttered his lids to look at her. "Your girlfriends are always welcome to join us, if you want."

Okay, *ew*. Bellamy had reached her limit. "You know what, I—" Before she could even finish her sentence,

Shane sauntered up and wrapped his arm around her, planting a kiss right on her lips just as easy as you please.

"Hey, babe. Sorry I'm late. Parking was a bear." His dark eyes flew to Marcus for a split second before returning to hers with an almost imperceptible nod.

Holy shit. The fake-boyfriend routine was the oldest trick in the book.

Shane was bailing her out.

"Oh, I'm so glad you made it," Bellamy gushed, playing it up by snuggling under the arm he'd left around her. "Shane, this is Marcus. He was just keeping me company while I waited for you."

Marcus was too busy picking his jaw up from the ground to do anything other than stammer. "Oh, uh, yeah. We know each other. Hey, Shane."

"Marcus. Thanks for looking after my girl while I parked my truck." His dark eyes flashed over Marcus's, glinting in the orange glow of the firelight.

Wow, Bellamy thought. Shane was good. He really had the whole protective boyfriend act down cold.

"Bellamy, you, ah, didn't mention that you . . . knew Shane," Marcus tsked weakly.

"We only just met recently, but it's been quite the whirlwind." She smiled. Okay, at least that was the truth.

"Well." Marcus cleared his throat. "Maybe I'll catch you another time."

"Maybe." Shane's tone flattened over the word.

She waited until Marcus had taken about twenty paces through the crowd before pulling back to look at Shane. "Your *girl*?" she asked, trying to keep a straight face.

He cracked a boyish you-got-me grin, and it snapped through her like a current. "Sorry. Too much?"

Oh, God. Not enough.

Bellamy blinked, her rib cage feeling like the new home for a fleet of hummingbirds. "Uh, no. No, I think it did the trick. Thanks. Did I look that desperate?"

"Truth?"

She gave him a look that said she expected nothing but. "Of course."

"You looked like you'd rather have a root canal," Shane admitted.

Bellamy's laugh bubbled out of her, mostly because he wasn't far from the mark. "Wow. You really know how to flatter a girl."

His baritone chuckle mixed in with her laughter. "Look, you're the one who asked for the truth."

"I guess I did. I'd rather people just lay it on the line, you know? Then I know what I'm dealing with." She shrugged, watching the warm breath of her words defer to the cold air that carried them.

Shane fastened his gaze on hers with an unwavering smirk. "Okay. Let's try this, then. I'd really like to buy you a cup of coffee. What do you say?"

Bellamy grinned from ear to ear. Now *this* was a date.

"I say that sounds great."

Chapter Nine

"Can I get those in to-go cups, please?" Shane looked through the crowded lodge to the spot where Bellamy stood with her friends as the guy behind the coffee counter snapped plastic lids on both cups. When she'd agreed to have coffee with him, her smile had traveled down his spine in a straight shot, overriding the circuitry in the rational part of his brain. Maybe it hadn't been fair to judge Bellamy based on her car, or the fact that she sported diamond earrings that probably cost more than his truck was worth. She had a killer laugh, and while she could've easily flipped the bitch-switch to get Marcus Lawrenson to beat it, she hadn't.

Plus, as soon as he fixed her car, she would head back to the city, no harm, no foul. What could a cup of Joe and a couple hours outside hurt? He took a long swallow from one of the cups, letting it warm him before walking across the room, coffee in hand.

"Ah, to-go cups. I take it you're planning a field trip." Bellamy tipped her head at the Styrofoam cup he passed her way as she took two packets of sugar from the bowl on the side table. Shane had no idea what she did to her hair to get it all shiny like that, but man, he was tempted to reach out and touch it.

He took a long look at his cup and wondered what the hell was in his regular old black coffee to make a stupid thought like *that* take over his gray matter.

"As long as you're okay with a little off-roading, I figured we could head up to Carrington Ridge," Shane said, looking at the two other women. "You're both welcome to come. It's not far, but the Ridge is pretty cool." One of the added benefits of the Ridge was that not a lot of non-locals knew where it was, which made it virtually unpopulated by the hot toddy–sipping jet-setters who frequented the resort. As it was, standing inside the massive lobby, with its blazing fireplaces and yuppie crowds, was giving Shane the sweats.

"That's really nice of you to offer." Bellamy's friend Jenna gave a genuine smile. "But honestly, I don't think Holly's going to budge from the couch now that she's figured out how much better Irish coffee tastes *indoors*."

"Sing that," Holly acknowledged with a nod. "But thanks for the invite," she added, toasting Shane with her mug.

"I'll be back in a bit," Bellamy murmured. Jenna flashed her a knowing glance that looked like it might mean something in girl-speak, but then it was gone, replaced by Jenna's dimpled smile. What did he know about complex women-codes, anyway? Guys were so much simpler. If you didn't mess with another man's livelihood or his woman, you were pretty much set.

Bellamy fell in step beside him as he headed toward the exit leading out the back of the resort. "Okay, so what's Carrington Ridge?"

He held the door for her, waiting until their feet were back in rhythm together before continuing. "It's on the other side of the mountain from the resort, facing Big Gap in the east. The resort has the market cornered on skiing and snowboarding, but all of its trails are over here, on the west side." Shane paused, gesturing over his shoulder. The night trails were lit up like a beacon, dotted with skiers gliding over the largely manufactured snow.

"So it's not part of the resort?"

He chuckled. "If it was part of the resort, it wouldn't be the best kept secret on the mountain, that's for sure." They walked in perfect rhythm together for a minute before Shane continued. "It's one of my favorite places up here. Most people who know about it go for the great sunrises. They're really something else." Shane wasn't much of a landscape guy, but if there were words to do justice to the sunrise over the valley at Big Gap, he sure couldn't string them together.

"Looks like it," Bellamy said as they reached his truck and he unlocked her door.

Shane paused. Maybe she'd gone off the tourist trail and seen it already or something. "Oh, sorry. Have you been there?"

She gave a slight shake of her head, just enough to jostle the waves of her blond hair before she got into the truck. "No, I just assumed it must be something pretty special, judging from the look on your face."

Shane blanked his expression out of instinct. "Yeah, the view is even better at night." He went around to the driver's side and got in. As he started the truck, a ripple of something odd made its way up his spine. Shane couldn't remember the last time anyone had pegged his emotions just from the look on his face. It sure as hell hadn't been since he'd moved to Pine Mountain.

'Course, he just had to slip up in front of the prettiest and most intuitive girl he could find, didn't he?

Bellamy cleared her throat delicately. "Okay, I'll bite. How is the view so good if it's dark outside?"

Shane scrambled to catch up to the moment, realizing she'd been waiting for him to continue telling her about Carrington Ridge. "Oh. Uh, well, it's what you can't see that makes it so cool, actually."

Her puzzled expression warmed him up faster than any heater, but he flipped the thing on high anyhow, watching her crease her brow in thought.

"I don't get it," she admitted, lacing her fingers around her coffee cup and taking a sip.

"You will when we get there," he said, enjoying the frustrated frown he got in response.

"So you're just going to leave me hanging, then." The playful edge to her voice teased around Shane's ear, and he reached out to crank the heat down a notch. Man, the truck got hot quick.

Or maybe that was just him.

"You're a smart girl. Figure it out."

In the dim glow of the dashboard lights, he could see her face, bent in concentration. "How do you know I'm smart?"

"Law school or MBA?" Shane's pulse quickened.

"MBA. But you didn't answer the question."

He looked at her for as long as the road would allow before returning his stare to the windshield. "Just a guess. Boy, you really weren't kidding. You kinda like it right out on the table, don't you?"

"Yes. You're seriously not going to tell me how we're going to take in this spectacular view in the dark?" Bellamy persisted, not giving him an inch.

She should've been a lawyer.

"Nope," Shane replied, grinning at her frustration.

"Are you *trying* to get under my skin?"

He smirked and let the question hang. "How'm I doing?"

She arched a pale brow back at him. "You're a natural."

They rode in silence for a few minutes before he found the turnoff from the main road. Shane angled the truck through the space that would've been nonexistent to anyone who didn't know just where it was, guiding them onto a narrow dirt road.

"Hold on, it gets a little bumpy." He maneuvered over the back road as far as his aging F150 would let him before pulling onto a grassy stretch of land overlooking the twinkling lights of the valley below.

Bellamy's face was set in confusion as she squinted through the windshield. "Okay. There's nothing here."

"Or everything. Just depends how you look at it." Shane reached around to the tiny storage space behind her seat and grabbed the old army blanket he always kept there in case he got stranded in the snow. He'd kept her in the dark, so to speak, long enough, and although he had to admit that the irritation on her face was turning him on like a light switch, he didn't want to piss her off completely. "Come on."

He walked around to her side of the truck, eyes adjusting to the darkness that came not just from the sun having long since set, but from the fact that there weren't any city lights to speak of for miles around. The tiny town that lay at the mouth of the valley showed itself in a sprinkling of warm porch lights and barely visible streams of shadowy chimney smoke rising to greet the cold night air.

"Are we going far? Because I'll be honest. I can't see a

thing," Bellamy admitted with an unsure waver in her voice.

"Yeah, this is a totally different brand of dark than you get in the city. Here." He captured her gloved hand in his bare one, just meaning to help her get her bearings.

But the way she squeezed him made him forget his own.

"Sorry." She laughed nervously. "You probably think I'm an idiot. I'm not normally scared of the dark."

He commanded his legs to move, leading her away from the truck. "Don't worry. I felt the same way the first time I came up here."

"Well, sure. You were probably like eight or something when that happened, though."

Shane's thoughts darted to the first time he'd stumbled upon Carrington Ridge, but quickly stuffed the memory away. By the feel of the hard, flattened grass under his boots, where they stood right now should do the trick. Most of the snow that had fallen the week before had melted, exposing big gaps of frozen earth. Shane stopped about halfway through the field, eyeballing it in the dark shadows. Yeah, this was good. He made quick work of unfurling the blanket, kneeling down to make sure no sharp twigs would poke through and hurt Bellamy when she sat down.

Nope, not even a stray rock or anything below the dirt. This was perfect.

"Okay. This'll do it." He sat down on the blanket, making sure there was plenty of room for her to sit next to him, but she hesitated.

"You coming, or what?" he asked, jerking his head toward the space on the ground next to him.

"Where?" she asked back, sounding thoroughly confused.

Shane's laughter felt warm and good as it left him. "To

see the view, of course. It's been right in front of you the whole time."

Bellamy's eyes had finally adjusted to the dark, which now looked less like a pitch black abyss and more like layers of shadow on shadow. At least now she could make out Shane's silhouette against the background of the night around them, with his legs kicked out casually over the blanket he'd put down. He seemed to be measuring her with his look, head tilted to one side, but she couldn't quite tell in the dark.

"So, you think you can trust me for a second? It's better with your eyes closed."

Bellamy was tempted to retort that of course she trusted him, she'd ridden right into the heart of no-one-can-hear-you-screamville with him, for God's sake, but instead she just gulped. The closest breathing person had to be miles from here. She and Shane were very, very alone together, and he'd just asked her to sit down next to him, close her eyes and trust him.

Oh, God, she wanted him to kiss her again.

"Um, okay." Since when did her voice sound all breathy and soft? She sat down next to him and extended her legs toward the edge of the blanket. Bellamy closed her eyes, wishing she'd had the wherewithal to pop a breath mint after downing that cup of coffee. "There."

Shane was so close to her that she could smell his skin, a combination of woodsy cedar-scented soap and lean, strong man that made her want to breathe him right into her body. "Okay," he murmured, his clothes rustling as he shifted his weight next to her. "All you have to do is lean back and open your eyes."

She clutched. "Lean back, like lie down?" Bellamy squeaked. Ohhhhh, as much as she was attracted to him, this might be more than she'd bargained for.

"If you want."

And then she got it.

Bellamy braced herself with her palms and eased back onto the blanket, keeping her eyes shut but unable to suppress her Cheshire-cat grin.

"Shane?" She tipped her head toward him as she spoke, inadvertently landing her ear on his shoulder.

"Mmm?" he asked, breathing into her hair in reply.

If she hadn't been so preoccupied with one-upping him, she'd be turned on right down to her toes. "Why didn't you cut through all the crap and just say we were coming up here to look at the stars?"

His sexy, no-boundaries laugh spilled out of him again, and it froze her breath in her lungs.

"Open your eyes, spoilsport."

Bellamy's lids fluttered open. Stars littered the sky like an ocean of diamonds over a velvet canvas, some burning so brightly that they were unmistakable; others, so dim they barely smudged the space with light.

She gasped, eyes flying wide. "Oh!"

It was easily the most stunning thing Bellamy had ever seen in her life, the simplicity of the stars themselves so at odds with the complexity and depth of the way they were strung together in the sky. Tears formed, hot in the corners of her eyes, and mirrored the glitter above them in flashes of starlight.

"*That's* why," Shane whispered.

Chapter Ten

As soon as Bellamy's soft sigh registered in his brain and then followed through with a whisper to his anatomy due south, Shane knew he was going to need a cold shower to get out of this hot mess. Still, rendering her speechless was worth it.

He gave her a few minutes before bringing her down out of the sky. "How's your astronomy?"

She didn't move, save for the rise and fall of her chest that sent the breath from her body in small, billowy clouds. "Truth?"

"Of course."

"Pretty bad."

Well, at least she was honest.

"Oh! Wait!" Bellamy sat upright, rummaging through her coat pockets. "I've always wanted to use this!"

Shane laughed as she brandished her iPhone with a triumphant flourish. "What are you doing?"

"I'm using the constellation app!" she crowed, swinging the phone upward with glee. "All we have to do is point it up at the sky and it'll tell us . . ." Bellamy's voice faded out on a curse.

"That you still don't get cell service up here," he finished, shaking his head. "You don't need it anyway."

Her pout was obvious, even in the dark. "How am I supposed to know what I'm looking at, then?"

Shane crossed his feet at the ankles and folded his arms beneath his head, getting comfortable. "Well, if you'd lie back down and listen up, I'd be happy to tell you."

She swung her head toward him, probably to glare, and the smell of her shampoo filled his senses like clean laundry on the line. If she lay back down, he was in for a long night.

"Fine," she grumbled, getting situated next to him, bringing the heat of her body with her.

Long night, for the win.

"Okay." Shane cleared his throat, willing himself to concentrate on the sky. "See those three stars, right up there, that are kind of in a line this way?" He pointed up at Orion's Belt.

Bellamy snickered. "Shane, there are like six billion to choose from. Can you be a little more specific?"

Looked like they were going to do the Smartasses Guide to Astronomy tonight. He gave her a playfully dirty look, hoping she could make it out in the shadows. "As a matter of fact, I can." Shane used his right hand to scoop up her left, lining his fingers up under her palm. Extending his index finger lifted hers along with it, and he aimed them right at Orion's Belt.

"Lean your head in and follow the line of my finger straight up. See them now?"

Wordlessly, Bellamy curled her hand around his and did the lean-and-look. "Oh! Those three, in the middle of that hourglass shape?"

Bingo. "Yup. That's Orion's Belt. And you've already

got the basic idea of the rest of the constellation from the hourglass. That bright one down there"—Shane dipped their hands lower and to the right—"is Rigel. And the reddish one up on Orion's shoulder is Betelgeuse."

She peeked at him over her shoulder, then shifted her hand over his. Crap, after having Marcus put the sleazy moves on her earlier, she probably thought this looked just as bad. After all, they were out in the middle of nowhere and he was lying in the dark holding her hand. Not that he hadn't planted a kiss on her himself, but that had been more in the interest of public service. Even though her lips were just as soft as he remembered.

"Sorry." Shane replaced her hand down by her side. "It's just the best way I know to show someone the sky." Maybe this had been a mistake.

"No, it's actually helpful. If you don't mind, I mean." She paused, inching her hand back toward his. "What else is up there?"

She didn't have to ask twice. Shane pointed out a handful of the bigger constellations, using their entwined fingers to trace the night sky. The fuzzy patches of stars forming the few nebulae visible to the naked eye were easy to make out against the clear canvas overhead, and Shane gave her the *Reader's Digest* version of some of the stories that went with the bigger constellations. They were lucky—there wasn't even a hint of a cloud in the sky. Still, despite the clear weather, the crisp, earthy smell of impending precipitation hung in the air. If he didn't know better from the weather report he'd caught over at Grady's, Shane would swear a decent snowfall was on its way.

"So how do you know so much about this stuff? I mean, the iPhone app isn't exactly going to spit out the mythology you just told me, and you know right where everything is." Bellamy dropped her arm back down to her side, but didn't let go of Shane's hand.

He shrugged. "My grandfather taught me when I was a kid."

It was the first thing Shane had said about himself out loud for over a year, and it tumbled out of his mouth before he even realized what he was saying. His muscles pulled taut, freezing the words in place, and the ensuing silence was palpable as it wrapped around them in the frigid air.

"Ah." Bellamy shivered, sinking down into her coat a little further, but didn't press him for details. Which was good, because he'd already opened his yap more than he should've.

Shane stiffened. It had been a little too easy to bring her up here on the spur of the moment, and it occurred to him that he'd never been up to the Ridge at nighttime with anyone else. Sure, flirting with her had been fun, and yes, she was definitely sexy when she got irritated, but there was no way around the bigger picture. Being up here with her topped the list of very bad ideas, and they really shouldn't stay.

Shane had an exit strategy on the tip of his tongue when she turned to her side to look at him, her face so close to his that he couldn't possibly ignore her.

"Can I ask you something?"

His gut buckled down, and he didn't return her stare. *Just play it cool so you can wrap this up.* "Sure."

"Why did you kiss me last night?"

He whipped his head toward her, wide-eyed and stunned. "What?"

Bellamy's eyes shone on his, unwavering in the starlight. The girls Shane knew wouldn't have dreamed of being ballsy enough to bring up something potentially embarrassing like that—after all, he and Bellamy had kissed under some strange circumstances, and they'd both been skirting around the issue. But she just stared at him, no-nonsense, waiting for an answer, and all he could think of was how badly he wanted to do it again.

"Truth?" he whispered, and he felt her breath hitch as she nodded.

"Of course."

"I have no idea."

Unable to resist the heat of her, he closed the space between them, his mouth on hers as if it had never left. She tasted even sweeter than the night before, warmth drawing him in and keeping him like a secret. Shane parted her lips with his, searching with intensity, and she responded with a deep, drawing sigh.

"This is a bad idea," he murmured into her skin as he broke from her mouth to trail kisses down her neck. God, she smelled unbelievably good. Shane unzipped the front of her coat to dive lower into the neckline of her sweater, letting his tongue dance across the planes of her collarbone.

How could she taste even better than she smelled?

"Mmm-hmm, I know," Bellamy groaned, yanking off her gloves to rake her hot, bare hands through his hair. Oh, *shit*, he was on the bullet train right to hell, but Shane didn't care. He could feel her pulse hammering through the vein in her delicate neck as he swept his mouth from the angle of her shoulder back to her lips, and it only spurred him on harder.

"Just for the record," she bit out on a gasp when he slid his hands to her hips and pulled her in tight to his body, leaving no space between them, "I *really* like bad ideas."

Shane's smile grew wicked against her parted mouth

as he tightened his grasp on her. "Then you're gonna love this."

In one swift motion, he pulled her on top of him, keeping as much contact with her as possible while he guided her over his body. Even through the layers of clothing, she fit over his body perfectly, and the heat shared between the lock of their hips made him bite back a groan. Unable to keep his hands off her, he sat up to cradle her in his lap. Shane slid his hands into her open coat and wrapped his arms around the soft curve of her back, taking in every nuance of her movement with care that was fueled by raw desire.

"Shane." His name escaped from her lips on a velvet sigh, and she kissed him hungrily, fingers tight on the back of his neck, keeping their bodies entwined. Thick need shot through him, screaming to be acknowledged, and the way she arched into him in all the right places did nothing to make him want to deny it.

Bellamy curled her legs around his waist from where she sat, balanced in his lap, and sent a path of hot kisses from his ear to his neck. Her tongue flickered and teased over his skin, heightening the raw want building within him. A slide of her hips over his cock brought a sigh from her lips, and the thrust Shane gave in response turned it into a moan.

"*Oh* my God." The rhythmic rise and fall between them grew faster, more urgent as she dug her fingers into his shoulders, grinding against him in a graceful frenzy. She caught his mouth with hers in a greedy, searching kiss, the ache between his legs reaching epic proportions as she tightened her thighs around him and let out another lusty sigh. The kiss intensified, and Shane wanted nothing more than to linger in her and take her all at the same time.

But if Bellamy didn't stop kissing him like that, not only was he going to keep kissing her back, but he wasn't going to be able to resist the magnetic grab of her until they were pared down, raw and vulnerable and very naked in the back of his truck.

She had to stop.

"Bellamy." Shane cupped her face between his palms, pulling away. The skin on her cheeks was flushed with dewy warmth, and he resisted the urge to return to kiss her slightly puffy lips. Pushing her away like this was wrong, he knew. But not more wrong than what was bound to happen if they didn't stop, because he didn't have any intention of seeing her again after the last bolt on her transmission was tight and ready to roll, no matter what kinds of ideas his body had to the contrary.

"What's the matter?" She froze against him, and even though every fiber of his body roiled against his brain's command to do it, he slid her carefully from his lap back onto the blanket.

"We can't . . ." He broke off, raking a hand through his hair. "I'm really sorry, but I never should have brought you up here." God *damn* it. There had to be a way to say this without hurting her feelings. "It's not—"

"If you so much as *imply* the words 'it's not you,' so help me God, I will scream," she said, cutting him off with the steady, controlled whisper of a hiss.

Ah, shit. Of course she was going to be pissed. She didn't seem like the kind of girl to go the weepy route, after all. "Well, it's . . ." Shane stopped midsentence at the flash of unadulterated anger in her eyes, the only thing he could make out in the glow cast down by the sea of stars over their heads. He tightened up and cleared his expression to a blank slate before finishing.

Better for her to think he was a jerk, anyway. Hell, right now, she wasn't far from the mark.

"I should get you back."

Bellamy had snatched her gloves off the blanket and whipped them over her hands before he could even register her movements, springing up from the blanket in one nimble motion to find her feet beneath her.

"That would be great," she said, her tone hollow, and she started walking without pretense toward the truck. The fine line between sweet and sexy that she'd been straddling all night was gone from her voice, with nothing there but the memory of it to make Shane feel like a complete jackass.

It was better this way, he reasoned. For both of them. He wasn't interested in opening up to anybody, least of all a top-shelf city girl, no matter how good the sex might be. And like it or not, something about the sinuous curve of Bellamy's body and the dulcet inflections when she said his name told him she was more than he'd bargained for.

And he'd learned the hard way that being a betting man was a bad idea all around.

Ruined pride still ran deep, and Bellamy got all the way through the terrible, silent ride back to the resort before hers crumbled. She mumbled a good night to Shane before turning on her heel to march away from his truck, and he refused to answer her or even meet her eyes, the coward. At least Derek had been able to deliver the stupid "it's not you" line with a little bit of feeling.

Shane had delivered it like a lie.

Bellamy inserted her key in the door to the suite and tiptoed into the darkened main room. Jenna and Holly were passed out cold on the couch, with the remnants of the guacamole she'd made in a big bowl next to a near-empty bag of tortilla chips and a Lifetime original movie on the TV, volume down low. Normally, this would crack a smile over Bellamy's face, even after a crappy date, but tonight she just couldn't muster it.

She bit down on the tears that threatened to fall, refusing to give them the time of day—or night, as it were—as she went into her bathroom and started running hot water into the luxurious, claw-footed tub. Peeling off her clothes, she pinned her hair into a loose knot on top of her head and sank into the blanket of bubbles that rose up to meet her.

Yes, it had been impulsive to run off with Shane in the first place, and no, she didn't know if she'd have had the nerve to actually sleep with him right under the stars after knowing him for all of two days. But still. Getting the "it's not you" speech before she even had to make that decision had caught her completely off guard. And it stung. Hard.

Bellamy sank into the water up to her chin and cried.

Chapter Eleven

"If you don't dish, and I mean *right now*, I'm going to explode!"

Holly held out a steaming mug of coffee, which Bellamy took with a grateful grunt as she padded from the common area to the kitchenette, wearing her bathrobe and a face full of determination to forget all about her night with Shane.

"Good morning to you, too."

"Screw good morning! I need details!" Holly followed, hot on her heels, as Bellamy rooted through the fridge to unearth a tiny carton of half-and-half.

"There aren't any." She shrugged, much to Holly's exasperation. No *way* was Bellamy going to admit being within nanoseconds of reaching the summit of Mount Oh-My-God while getting her fully clothed grind on. Especially since the guy in question had put the brakes on the whole shebang by uttering the three worst words in the English language.

Nope. Bellamy was in no mood to relive the craptastic events of her night. How many times could a girl hear "it's not you" before she got the message loud and clear that it was, in fact, very much her?

Jenna trudged in from her room, bleary-eyed, just in time to watch Bellamy's dodge-and-deflect. "Oh, hey B." Jenna yawned and stretched. "Could you please tell her about your wilderness hike with Mr. Fix-It before she erupts? Spontaneous human combustion is so messy."

Was it too late to go back to bed? "I hate him. How about that?" Bellamy asked sweetly, downing half her cup of coffee in one swallow. "Ugh, this stuff is *awful*." She grimaced at the horrible mix of bitter and burnt invading her taste buds. Damn. Room service couldn't even get coffee right.

"Wait, you can't hate him. How can you hate him? I thought he was a good kisser." Holly pouted.

"I can, and I do." *And yes. He's a fan-freaking-tastic kisser. Not that I'll be making that mistake again.* "Is that my phone?" Bellamy furrowed her brow, searching for the source of the all-too-familiar annoying beep.

"It sounds like it." Jenna scooped the iPhone up from where Bellamy had tossed it on the counter the night before and flipped it to her.

Holly planted her hands on her hips and stood in the doorway of the kitchenette like a bulldog in fuzzy slippers. "No way! You're seriously going to shut me down on the dirt?"

Bellamy pressed her lips into a tight line. "There's no dirt. I'm dirtless, dirt-free, utterly devoid of dirt of any kind. Clean as a whistle." She tried to keep her face neutral as she flicked her phone to life.

Wait . . . how could there possibly be eleven unread texts and four voice mails on her phone leftover from a

Saturday while she was on vacation? Nobody liked her *that* much.

"Hey, was there some kind of weird crisis last night that I don't know about? I have a ton of . . ." Realization hit Bellamy when she saw the caller history screen, making her heart take a swan dive toward her perfectly pedicured toes. How were *all* of these messages from her boss? She dropped her head into her hands and hoped that nine thirty wasn't too early to drink.

"What?" Jenna asked with a furrowed brow.

"Bosszilla is on the warpath."

Bellamy pressed the phone to her ear. She had a sinking feeling that unless she figured out how to alter the time-space continuum to manage being in two places at once, she was definitely going to have to head home and figure out a way to come back for the Miata on Friday. Her boss was bound to flip into the stratosphere at the idea of Bellamy waiting in the mountains for her car to be fixed.

"Seriously? That witch needs a hobby," Holly said, thankfully letting Bellamy slide in the naughty gossip department.

Jenna gave a humorless smile and nursed her coffee, leaning against the narrow counter dividing the kitchenette from the common room. "I think making Bellamy's life a living hell *is* her hobby."

"Well, she's getting really good at it," Holly quipped.

Bellamy jerked the phone away from her ear, her boss's recorded voice so grating and awful that the harping would be perfectly audible even if she laid the thing on the counter.

"Bellamy, I understand you're away until Tuesday." The words *away until Tuesday* dripped with so much disdain that Bellamy cringed. God forbid she try to have a life on her days off. "But I absolutely need that Anderson contract on my desk first thing when you get back to the office."

Bellamy swallowed. The Anderson contract, a.k.a. the Doorstop, was sitting, half done, on Bellamy's desk at work, and her boss had told her she had at least a week to finish the research. How was she possibly going to pull this off?

The voice mail droned on. "Oh, and another thing. We've moved up the deadline for the research on the project you've been working on with Cooper, and I'm going to need all of those figures no later than midweek."

The message continued until the time limit for voice mail cut off, but far be it for a little thing like that to stop ol' Bosszilla. She'd just called back and left her litany in installments. By the time Bellamy got to Mission Impossible, The Final Chapter, she was exhausted just from listening. Meeting these new deadlines would be difficult even if she was back in the city. There was no *way* she could pull it off while being stranded in the mountains with no car and the paperwork a hundred miles away.

"I don't think I can handle this." She propped her elbows on the counter and dropped her head into her hands. "You know, when I finished my MBA two years ago, this is *so* not what I had in mind."

"Oh, honey. You had no way of knowing you'd get stuck working for such a heinous troll. Can you move within the company? Maybe there's an opening for an analyst on another team," Holly said, giving Bellamy's back a gentle rub.

Man, she must be toeing the line of pretty pathetic to garner the sympathy-pat before breakfast. Bellamy sighed, peeking out from the thick tendrils of hair draped over her fingers. "Yeah, but you know what? That might just be a quick fix for a slow problem."

Jenna drew her brows inward, leaning toward Bellamy from the other side of the counter. "What do you mean? When Bosszilla's not hounding you—which, granted, is half the day—you're great at your job."

Bellamy managed a tiny smile. "Thanks for the vote of confidence."

"I'm not stroking your ego just for the hell of it. That's the truth." Jenna's voice was straightforward as her eyes focused in on Bellamy's over their coffee mugs. "You graduated twelfth in your class at the most prestigious freaking business school in the country. Come on, admit it. You don't exactly suck."

"Just because you're good at something doesn't mean you love it, though. It's just not what I thought it would be, that's all." Bellamy thought of all the hours she spent holed up in her office, meticulously researching contracts and negotiating deals for clients. The overwhelming majority of those hours had been spent wishing she were somewhere else. Somehow, all of her hard work and accomplishments just didn't seem to outweigh the negatives.

Holly's eyes went wide. "Are you saying you want to quit?"

"No!" Was Holly nuts? "I'm just bitching about my job, is all. I can't quit! I busted my ass to get a degree. I just took the boards last year, for God's sake! What else would I do?" Wow. Her job sucked and all, but there was no need to jump on the crazy train. She hadn't fought her way through UPenn to toss it all away when the going got tough.

"What else would you *want* to do?" Jenna's question threw Bellamy off-kilter, and it stopped her halfway between the counter and the cabinet over the mini-fridge, where she'd stashed the homemade muffins from the bakery at Joe's.

"What do you mean, what do I want to do? I want to come up with a pain-free way to get my ass home tomorrow night so I can work on the stupid Anderson contract until daybreak and get Bosszilla off my back. Can I just ride with you guys?" She'd simply have to suck it up and have the Miata towed back to the city once Shane fixed it. Not ideal, but there were no other choices on the table.

"No. I mean, if you could do something you really love, what would you do?" Jenna asked, point-blank.

Bellamy grabbed the bag of muffins and gave one to both Jenna and Holly before shrugging. "I don't know. I guess I could go into marketing." She took a bite of her muffin, savoring it. At least *someone* knew how to get the whole blueberries-to-batter ratio right.

"That's the best you can come up with?" Jenna smirked.

"Hey!" Holly protested around a mouth full of cakey goodness. "I'm in marketing, you know. And oh my *God* are these good. But not as good as yours," she amended, nodding at Bellamy.

"Exactly my point. You're in marketing because you love it." Jenna acknowledged Holly with a nod, then flicked her gaze back to where Bellamy had just parked herself on a bar stool at the counter. "But not everybody loves her job, obviously."

"You're forgetting the fact that I spent years going to school for this. Everyone expects me to have a business-oriented career. Plus, not to pat myself on the back or anything, but I *am* pretty good at it," Bellamy replied, brushing the crumbs from her muffin into a tidy little pile.

"Oh please. Everyone who? Your parents? Sweetie, you're twenty-seven. It's time to cut the strings," Jenna said.

"Not when the strings have owned a very successful realty business together for over twenty years and supported me while I went to grad school full-time. It's no secret that they're expecting me to join their company as soon as I get enough experience. Sure, they love me, but it would be kind of tough to swallow if I waltzed in and said I suddenly hated big business. Plus, what the hell would I do? Sitting around resting on my laurels isn't going to pay the bills."

Jenna cranked out a grin. "Your answer's right in front of you, you know."

Holly frowned and pulled back. "I don't get it."

"You just said it yourself. Who makes the best blueberry muffins you've ever had?" Jenna's eyes lasered in on Bellamy, and her implication hit like a crate full of cannonballs.

"Oh, come on, Jenna. You can't be serious. You think I should sell muffins for a living?"

"No, dumbass. But becoming a chef wouldn't be such a bad idea."

Bellamy barked out an involuntary laugh as shock ricocheted through her veins. "Please! Whipping up a batch of goodies for you guys here and there is one thing; trying to make a living of it when you have no experience and no training whatsoever is *quite* another. Culinary school takes years, and even then I'd only make peanuts for my troubles."

That's why they called it a dream job, right? Because clearly, Bellamy would be dreaming if she thought someone would pay her to cook for a living.

"You know what, B? Your being a chef isn't a half-bad idea." Holly looked at her with a sheepish nod.

Great. Now they were both crazy. Bellamy made a mental note not to bitch about her job quite so loudly anymore. "It's insane. Now if you'll excuse me, I have to figure out this mess before that yoga-pilates fusion class that's supposed to leave me stress-free and give me a butt you can bounce a quarter off of."

Jenna shook her head with a soft chuckle. "Okay. But I'm telling you. You should think about it."

Right, Bellamy thought as she scrolled through her phone to access her e-mail. Like anything more unlikely could happen than her blazing off on a new career path.

It made the whole impulsive evening making out under the stars with Mr. It's-Not-You look rational in comparison.

Shane lay flat on his back, looking up into the belly of the Mach 1 and thinking he'd be a billionaire if he could come up with a cure-all for being a complete jackass.

Oh, that and he wouldn't feel like shit over how his night with Bellamy had ended.

He replayed the whole thing in his mind for the nth time, picturing her green eyes glaring at him up on the Ridge. He hated that he'd been unable to meet those pretty yet pissed-off eyes before she walked away with nothing more than a clipped good night and her head held high. Man, how come doing the right thing felt so crappy?

Maybe because if he'd been smart in the first place, he'd have stayed the hell away from her.

"Shane? You in here?"

Shane's face creased in confusion as he pushed himself out from under the car with a booted heel. "Grady? What're you doing here on a Sunday?" Even from his vantage point on the floor, Shane could see the concern on the old man's face as he walked into the garage.

"Lookin' for you," he said, his gravelly voice going all matter-of-fact.

"You found me. Is everything okay?" Shane sat up, nursing a twinge of concern.

Grady gave a singular, solid nod in the affirmative and looked around the garage. Shane winced as Grady's gaze swept over Bellamy's Miata. It was obvious not only that Shane had pulled out the old tranny to make way for the new one, but that Grady knew Shane had done it without him. The last thing he wanted was to overstep his bounds.

"Been busy, I see."

Shane would've rather heard anger than the recognition that went with Grady's words, as if he'd pegged exactly why Shane had been spending so much time in the garage.

"Yeah, sorry. I was bored. I just figured I'd keep my mind straight by starting on it." He nodded over at Bellamy's car, trying not to let his thoughts slip to its driver.

"Jackson help you muscle the old one outta there?"

Guilt washed over Shane in the silence that followed. He should've waited for Grady, or at least called him to tell him he was going to pull the transmission. Shit.

Grady continued. "You're good, but I got a feeling that tranny was locked up tighter than Fort Knox. It probably gave the two of you a run for your money, yeah?"

Hell if the old man didn't miss a trick. It had taken all the muscle Shane and Jackson had to pull the fried transmission out of that Miata.

"Yup. It was a nightmare. Be glad you missed it." The consolation didn't work for a second, not that Shane really expected it to.

"You want to tell me what's goin' on here? I know you need the cash," Grady rasped. "But all of this workin' feels like somethin' else."

Shane stood up slowly. He knew he owed Grady more

than a bunch of double speak and canned excuses, but his iron-clad defenses wouldn't let the real reason past his lips.

"I've, ah, had a lot on my mind. Working just helps. I didn't mean to step on your toes, though." God knew this was the truth. Nothing else calmed Shane like working on cars, even the grunt work like oil changes and tune-ups, but he wasn't about to disrespect Grady in order to right his head.

Grady measured Shane with a knowing, steel-gray stare. "You can't hide from this forever, you know." It wasn't an accusation, just a simple statement of fact. And one that deep down, Shane knew.

"I'm not hiding. This is who I am."

The words made Grady chuckle. "Oh, no denyin' that. You are who you are. But you got some loose ends to tie up, and they're gettin' pretty tangled while they wait for you."

Damn it. Grady was nothing if not right to the point. "You don't cut any corners, do you?"

"'Fraid not. You work as much as you need to, Shane, if it'll get your head right. Just don't let it get in the way of what matters."

Shane frowned, looking around the garage. "This is what matters."

Grady's laugh was long and loud. "Boy, you got a lot to learn. Good thing you don't have to do it all in one day." His eyes glinted over Shane's in a knowing glance that told Shane not to argue. Still, the look told him that Grady was onto him, which made his stomach ache with unease.

The expression lasted for only a second longer before it busted into a silvery-stubbled grin. "Now pop the hood on this thing and let an old fart see what'cha been doing with all your time, would you?"

Chapter Twelve

"Surpriiiiiiise!"

Jenna and Holly could barely contain their excitement as they held up a cream-colored envelope, both grinning like total lunatics.

"Okay, you're freaking me out. What did you do?" Bellamy eyed her friends from where she sat on her bed with pages of scribbled notes in her lap and her cell phone glued to her hand. She'd spent three hours piecing together what she could from various e-mails, trying to make heads or tails of the impossible task in front of her. Without the contract in-hand, the research was spotty at best. Not even taking a break for that yoga class had calmed her, even though the yogi had been very male and oh-so limber. Of course, no matter how enticing the view of his Downward Facing Dog was, men were still on Bellamy's shit list.

"Well, when you were—" Jenna paused to clear her throat. "*Out* last night, we cozied up to one of the resort managers."

Holly interrupted with a snort. "And by 'cozied up to,' she means 'flirted mercilessly with.'" Bellamy's brows popped, prompting Holly to raise her hands in an I-didn't-do-it gesture. "Her, not me. I don't share."

"Anyway," Jenna interrupted right back. "He told us all about this little event the resort is hosting this evening. It's a very small, very exclusive and very hush-hush thing, but of course . . ."

Holly picked up where Jenna left off. "We, and by 'we' I mean 'she,'" Holly pointed at a devilishly beaming Jenna. "Just *happened* to run into the manager again after breakfast while you were getting your *om* on . . ."

Jenna took the baton and ran. ". . . and he mentioned that he might be able to snag three tickets to this little shindig . . ." Her eyes shone like runway lights, and her grin was a perfect match.

". . . *and* since we knew you were having a really bad day and could use some cheering up, she made out with him so he'd fork the tickets over!" Holly squealed in the gossip-girl's version of a grand finale.

It took Bellamy a full minute to process the verbal tennis match. "Wait a second, let me get this straight. You made out with a random guy to get us tickets for some top-secret exclusive event?" Helluva way to take one for the team.

"First of all, Chase isn't some random shmo. He's Pine Mountain's events coordinator. And he's a very nice guy who's taking me out for drinks later because, as much as I love you, you're not the only reason I kissed him." Jenna held the envelope out. "Here. Open it."

A current of excitement rippled up Bellamy's spine as she took the envelope with the Pine Mountain Resort crest stamped in the corner, and by the time she'd opened the flap, she was laughing right along with Jenna and Holly. She felt like an idiot, but at least she was a getting-happier idiot. A girl could only handle so much drama before going off the deep end.

"Seriously, you guys, what could you possibly . . ." Bellamy's voice trailed off as she read, then re-read, the square of card stock that slid out of the envelope. "Wait." Her heart went from zero to oh-my-freaking-God in about three seconds.

No. Way. Her brain was malfunctioning. *Had* to be.

"This can't be right. This says that . . ."

"Chef Carly di Matisse, direct from New York City, is doing a one-night-only menu tasting for an intimate crowd of people and we're going?" Holly supplied with an ear-to-ear grin.

Holy shit, her brain *was* working properly!

"Do you guys know who Carly di Matisse is? I mean, do you *know* who she is?" Bellamy released the breath she'd only just realized had been pasted to her lungs, the paper starting to flutter in her hands.

Jenna laughed, nudging Holly. "Told you she'd do this. She gets all fan-girl freaky for those cable-channel chefs. And that's not even the Food Network."

"You bet me she'd hyperventilate. You haven't won until she asks for a paper bag," Holly pointed out with a wry smile.

Bellamy ignored their teasing and pressed on. "Carly di Matisse is only the most awe-inspiring human being on the planet, that's all! Her show, *Couples in the Kitchen* is where I got all of the ideas for my parents' anniversary dinner." She stopped to take a breath, but it was a quick one. "There wasn't a peep of publicity about this on her show, although come to think of it, they've been doing a lot of reruns lately. Still, how the hell did I not know she'd be here this weekend?" She sank to the bed, trying to get a handle on the part of her brain that dealt out rational thought.

Nope. The giddiness that was quickly setting in blotted out every levelheaded cell she possessed.

"Nobody knows. Apparently, she just inked a deal to come run the kitchen in the restaurant they're rebuilding on the west side of the resort. It's part of some mission to restore the place to its former glory. I guess the old one was doing as badly as the room service, so the resort is overhauling the restaurant in the lull between ski season and the summer rush. Did you know a lot of people come for the spa and the lake when it's nice out?" Jenna motioned for Bellamy to move over so she could sit down next to her, and Bellamy relegated her pile of notes to the nightstand as she shook her head.

Jenna continued. "Anyhow. This little soiree is like an added bonus, sort of a kickoff party for her to introduce the new menu she's planning to incorporate. But she wanted to keep her move on the down-low for some reason, so they didn't really publicize things. Apparently, her husband . . . uh . . . what's-his-name . . ."

"Travis," Bellamy supplied. "They do the cable show together. He's really good-looking."

"Yeah! Well, he's running the restaurant in New York and she's coming here, so maybe that has to do with why it's hush-hush. Except for those of us who know event coordinators." Jenna winked with a sly grin. "Everyone else just thinks it's some private party, like a wedding."

Bellamy shook her head in shock, convinced she'd taken up residence in some alternate universe where the world included things like tasting Carly di Matisse's minestrone soup. Not just her recipe, mind you. But food the chef had prepared with her own two hands.

No *way*.

"Oh my God, do you realize that right now it's quite possible I am breathing the same air as Carly-fricking-di Matisse?" Bellamy couldn't help it. The maniacal laugh she'd been trying to suppress flew out as she channeled some serious twelve-year-old-girl vibes from the depths of her adult psyche. Considering the shit factor of her week, it was about time karma showed her a little love.

Holly laughed and climbed onto the bed, sandwiching Bellamy in. "Well, we figured it was going to be the only way we'd get a decent meal around here. Plus, if anybody deserves a break from the crap parade, it's you."

"Are you kidding? If anything will make me forget the kiss-and-diss, it's *definitely* these." She went to hold up the tickets in a jubilant wave, only to see both of her friends staring at her with enough wide-eyed *oh really* to sink a ship.

Well, crap.

"Looks like the boss from hell isn't the only thing putting your panties in a kink," Jenna noted, waiting. The irony of her words caught in Bellamy's chest. Forget a kink, her panties had been downright double-knotted. In the best possible way.

Right up until Shane lame-excused her all the way home.

"It's really nothing," she started, and both friends opened their mouths to throw the bullshit flag at the same time. "Okay!" Bellamy held up her hands. She knew when she'd been beat. "It's really nothing major," she amended.

"Look, sweetie, I know you've had a rough week, so if you don't want to talk about it, that's okay."

Damn it. This really *was* a dream. "Are you serious?"

Bellamy asked, looking at Holly as if she'd sprouted wings or something else equally ludicrous.

"Nah. Spill it before I lose my marbles!"

Bellamy sighed. As much as she didn't want to admit it, she hadn't been able to keep her thoughts from Shane since she'd walked away from him in a huff last night. A well-deserved huff, but still. Maybe if she talked about it, she'd be able to let it go and really enjoy her evening.

Twenty minutes and a giant bag of chocolate chip cookies later, she'd gotten the whole story out, and the only thing she felt was her jeans size going up.

"Wow. He really said that to you?" Holly shook her head in a wordless paraphrase of *what a dumbass*.

Bellamy's nod sent a wisp of hair from the loose knot on top of her head. "Yup. Not that it really matters in the grander scheme of things." Except that she was twelve hours removed from the whole thing and it still burned. Worse than when Derek had said it, which was just plain weird.

"Oh my God, you like him."

Jenna's weird sixth sense for this kind of thing reared its perceptive little head, and Bellamy gave herself a mental kick in the ass for opening her yap in the first place.

"I don't *like* him."

Liar, liar, pants on fire.

She continued, ignoring the little whisper in her head. "And the feeling is mutual, obviously. So now that we're all up to speed on my abysmal love life, or lack thereof, can we drop the whole thing? In fact, it would really make my day if I could just pretend that Shane Griffin didn't exist."

As Bellamy brushed the cookie crumbs from her hands and marched her no-nonsense self to the bathroom to start getting ready for her evening, she came to the realization that just because you liked to lay it all out on the table didn't mean you couldn't bend the truth while you were doing it.

Shane had been awake and ignoring Monday morning for twenty minutes before his alarm clock went off, and he brushed his palm over it to silence the beeping. He thought about going for a good, long run to boil off some of the frustration that had been mounting for days now, but the one he'd taken last night did nothing but move his blood through his body, and given the state of things, he wasn't sure that was the best plan.

God, he'd wanted to do more than kiss Bellamy. A lot more. And didn't that just make lying in bed all by his lonesome nice and uncomfortable. He needed to get up and get in the shower before he admitted that what he *really* needed was to get laid.

Maybe that run wasn't such a bad idea, after all.

His boxers and T-shirt offered little protection from the January cold lingering inside the walls of the log cabin he'd rented since moving to Pine Mountain. The place was small, just the one bedroom and what Shane guessed qualified as mostly a kitchen, although it was really more like a stove, an ancient fridge and a sink crammed in one corner. He crossed the threshold of his bedroom door and made it to the coffeepot in less than five strides, scooping enough grinds to jump-start a rhino into the filter before filling the pot to brew.

There was no room for a couch in the cramped living space, but he had the well-worn recliner and a TV, which suited him just fine. With all the time Shane spent at the garage or running on the trails around the cabin, everything else was basically an afterthought, anyway. Except for the afterthought that had set up residence in his frontal lobe and refused to budge, leaving sultry memories of a velvet laugh and a pair of oh so provocative lips on his . . .

Strike the run. What Shane needed was a nice, cold shower. One that lasted until Bellamy Blake had her keys in her hand and her body behind the wheel of her runs-like-a-dream sports car. Because both times he'd kissed her, it had proven that his gut instinct was spot-on. A girl like her was bad for him, period.

No matter how good a kisser she was.

Shane compromised with his libido and took a luke-warm shower, but promised himself to keep the image of Bellamy out of his head, especially when he wasn't dressed. He didn't seem to have much control over his parts when it came to the thought of her, and he knew if even one tiny flicker snuck its way into the shower with him, his resolve to not call her or see her would resemble burnt toast.

After getting dressed, he rummaged through the pitiful contents of the lone cupboard over the sink. A couple of apples went into a bag, and he grabbed a pre-made turkey sub, courtesy of the deli at Joe's, from the fridge. It wasn't much, but it'd do for him and Grady. Shane turned the collar of his jacket up, but he was greeted with a blast of icy air that shot right through him as if he were wearing nothing but swim trunks and a smile.

"Damn," he muttered. The temperature must have dropped about ten degrees from yesterday, and the unfor-giving wind was back with a vengeance. The F150 protested the trip, warming up just in time for Shane to pull into the side lot of the garage. He'd been there for all of five minutes when a familiar voice snapped him out of his morning routine.

"Hey, I was driving by on my way to work and saw your truck. I'm surprised you're here." Jackson rubbed his hands together, stomping the cold from his boots as he entered the garage.

"Why wouldn't I be here? It's Monday. I've got a little more work to do on that Miata, plus I've gotta make sure the order for the parts is on its way." Shane creased his brow. Why did Jackson look so shocked?

"Dude, do you live under a rock, or what? That massive snowstorm that was supposed to stall out in the Ohio Valley changed course and picked up a ton of steam. We're going to get dumped on, starting any minute now."

Well, that explained the look on Jackson's face. Shit. "I've got to call Grady and make sure he's tight."

"I saw him last night at Joe's, along with everybody else in town," Jackson said. "Looked like he had enough to tide him over."

Shane exhaled. Grady was no stranger to Blue Ridge winters, but still. Shane didn't want him stuck with empty cupboards. "You're heading out, then?"

Jackson cracked a grin. "Hell, yes, although this one's going to be a bitch. Mix of ice and snow, and the wind is supposed to get downright nasty." He paused to shudder. "Still, working for a plowing company this time of year, it's like nickels and dimes falling from the sky, baby. Bring on the snow, I say."

"Yeah, I'd better get some salt out. Bet we'll get a couple of people who need hauling out from ditches." This was standard winter fare in the mountains. Shane walked over to the bags of salt and sand they kept stored on the far wall of the garage.

"I've got a little time before I have to check in, if you want help," Jackson offered, tossing his cell phone and his wallet on the workbench and rolling up his sleeves.

"Thanks, man. I appreciate it. Let me call Grady and tell him to stay put. It looks like we're going to be in for a long haul."

Bellamy burrowed deeply under the luxurious down comforter on her bed, cocooning herself in blissful warmth as she woke up slowly with a big, fat grin on her face. She, Holly, and Jenna spent hours stuffing themselves silly with bite after bite of Carly di Matisse's pure culinary magic. To top it all off, Chase had come through in flying colors, arranging a little meet-and-greet at the end of the night that had Bellamy halfway to the breathing-into-a-paper-bag route. Carly had been so nice, and even graciously listened to Bellamy babble on about how she'd made the "couples special" cedar-plank salmon for her parents' special anniversary dinner, complete with the haricots verts and garlic-roasted fingerling potatoes.

No doubt about it, Bellamy'd had the night of her life and things were getting back to good. Or they would be, if only she could find the source of whatever was giving up that incessant beeping noise and make it go far, far away. She fumbled for the alarm clock, wondering what had possessed her to set it in the first place.

Oh, wait. It was her cell phone that was chiming away like a church choir, and it wasn't even nine in the morning yet. She yanked it under the pillow to meet her ear, trying her best not to mumble. "Hello?"

"Bellamy, we've had a change of plans. I'm going to need the Anderson contract this afternoon."

Well good morning to you, too, O Mighty Ruler of the Underworld. "I'm, um, not in until tomorrow," Bellamy replied, trying to get her bearings and wipe the sleep from her eyes.

Bosszilla's voice made nails on a chalkboard sound like a symphony, and the dreamy memory of Bellamy's night shrank into the recesses of her mind.

"Well the world doesn't stop just because you've decided to skip town. The client wants to move forward, and I'm not inclined to say no."

Bellamy dragged a deep breath into her lungs, cursing herself for looking at the yogi's ass yesterday rather than paying attention to what he'd said about finding her inner Zen. "There was no rush on this when you gave it to me last week, and a lot of the legwork is already done, but—"

"Well, the deadline is close of business today. You're not giving me a whole lot of choice here." The icy implication hung between them.

Bellamy's brain finally kicked into gear. "Why didn't you just tell me you needed it sooner? I'd have prepared it before I left if I'd known you were going to need it so fast." She pushed the covers from her legs, swinging her feet to the carpet.

"What are you implying?" Bosszilla's tone hit arctic levels.

"I'm not implying anything." Bellamy reached for a deep breath, anger welling in her chest to cancel out any last remnants of euphoria from the night before. "I'm just saying—"

Her boss cut her off again. "What you're doing is wasting time, and frankly, I'm sick of these little games. I'm telling you I need that presentation on my desk, complete, by close of business today. Unless you're interested in coming back to clean out your desk."

Something thick and hot snapped from the anger in Bellamy's chest, pushing the words out of her mouth before she could rope them back in. "If you needed that contract reviewed so quickly, you should've said so in the first place, rather than dropping the ball and pinning your ineptitude on me." Momentum coursed through her, double-dog-daring her to speak her mind, and the feeling that swirled like an ominous wind in her gut spilled out with the words. "You want that thing by COB today? Then roll up your sleeves and do it yourself, because I *quit*," she ground out, pitching her phone onto the bed with a satisfying *whump*.

Her gratification lasted for all of six seconds, and then she realized what she'd done. Oh, God. Oh God oh God oh God.

She'd quit her job.

"Bellamy? Are you okay? We heard you from the hallway." Holly stopped short as she rushed into the room, clad in her pajamas and a very worried expression that only got deeper when she saw Bellamy's face.

"I, uh. I don't think so. I just quit my job." She sank to the carpet, dread washing over every inch of her. What had she *done*?

"Are you kidding me?" Jenna breathed, standing wide-eyed in the doorway behind Holly.

Bellamy shook her head weakly. "No." Her mind reeled, so many thoughts flying around that not one of them had a prayer of sticking. She took a deep breath and blurted out a recap before she could lose her nerve, but the retelling only instilled more panic.

"Okay, honey. This is going to be okay." Holly went into

red-alert crisis mode, sitting down on the carpet next to Bellamy and taking her hand.

Her stomach lurched. "How is this going to be okay? I quit my *job*, Holly. What am I going to do now?" Bellamy's brain went right back to the spin-cycle, refusing to let her string together any more thoughts than that.

"You're going to find another job, that's what." Jenna's blunt words made a chink in Bellamy's spiraling dread, and she blinked up at her friend.

"Bellamy, listen to me. This is not the end of the world, okay?" Jenna knelt down to look Bellamy in the eye. "Look, we'll go home tonight, and you can think it through. If you feel like you made a mistake, you can go from there, maybe file a complaint with the VP. It's not like Bosszilla's behavior didn't warrant some kind of reaction from you. She all but strong-armed you into it, for Chrissake. Plus, your track record speaks for itself, and it'll go a long way toward giving you options." Her calm, controlled voice brought Bellamy's sheer terror down a notch, but just barely.

"Is one of my options to throw up?"

"I guess if you need to. Just watch my slippers, would you?"

She loved Jenna more than words right now.

Tears sprang to Bellamy's eyes, and she swallowed hard as she did her best to blink them away. Jenna was right. This wasn't the end of the world. It *couldn't* be.

Oh, God, how was she going to get another job with the words *hissy fit* stamped across the top of her résumé?

All three women jumped at the unmistakable sound of Bellamy's phone ringing from where it lay half buried on the duvet. Bellamy dropped her face to her hands, unable to think clearly yet.

"I can't talk to her right now, honestly. Please, just turn the damn thing off."

Holly sprang into action, plucking the phone from the bed. "I've got you covered," she said, scooping up the phone to take it away.

"Bellamy, I mean it. You're a tough cookie. This is going to be okay." Jenna sat down next to the spot where Bellamy slumped against the bed frame with her elbows propped on her knees.

She gave up a tiny nod that looked more like the tremble of her chin than anything else. "I know, it's just . . ." Bellamy's words died out as she caught sight of Holly's expression, both puzzled and reticent. "What?" Jeez. Bosszilla couldn't have cleaned out Bellamy's desk *that* quickly, could she? An image of all her stuff scattered across the city block where the bank's offices stood flashed across her mind, and she felt a wave of panic swoop in for the kill.

"No. Uh, it wasn't your boss." Holly exchanged a glance with Jenna so quickly that Bellamy might have missed it. Except she knew that look from a mile away. It was a warning look that things were about to get worse.

How could life *possibly* get worse?

"It was Grady's Garage. And whoever called left a message."

Chapter Thirteen

"Hi, you've reached the voice mailbox of Bellamy Blake. I'm not available right now . . ."

Jesus. Even prerecorded, she sounded hot as hell.

Shane shifted uncomfortably in the archaic desk chair in the office, watching the steady snowfall on the other side of the frost-edged windowpanes. As Bellamy's voice mail let out a soft beep, he straightened in his seat as if she could see him.

"Hey, Bellamy, it's, ah, Shane, from the garage." *Right. Because she knows so many Shanes. Idiot.* "I'm afraid I have some bad news about your transmission." His eyes flicked over the information he'd gotten from the distributor's website, and he frowned. "I know I promised you I'd be done by Friday, but I've run into a bit of a problem. So just call me when you get this. I'll be at the garage." Shane left the number, then pressed the button on the cordless to end the call. He knew she was already pretty irritated, and this wasn't going to do anything to make him more endearing, but it's not like he had any say in the matter.

Shane had already given the fast-talking manager at the distributing warehouse his best shot, trying to nice-guy him into putting a rush on the order. But Bellamy's new transmission was stuck in the same snowstorm that was currently doing its damnedest to sideline a good chunk of the East Coast. Far be it for Shane to mess with Mother Nature. That tranny would just have to wait, and irritated or not, Bellamy would have to wait right along with it.

Making sure the ringer on the phone was turned up high, Shane flipped the radio on. Bach's Cello Suite No. 1 drifted from the speakers, loosening the morning's grip on his muscles. He looked at the Mustang, its lines stark in the overcast shadows thrown through the windows, and something tightened in his chest. Running his palm down the driver's side quarter panel, he walked alongside the car with reverence, taking his time to look at it from every angle.

He knew the money he'd get from working on Bellamy's car was a temporary fix, a delay of the inevitable. The Mustang would have to go, and even then, it wouldn't be nearly enough. When he'd come to Pine Mountain, there were no grand illusions, no intentions of anything permanent. No plans for it to become what Shane had known, deep down, he'd been made for from the beginning.

Funny thing about life. Sometimes it did its own thing and you were just at its mercy, hoping you came out okay once the dust cleared. Of course, there was one way Shane could make the whole thing disappear, erase the problem as if it had never existed and right the debt he'd struggled to repay.

No. The option was a non-option. He'd sell the car; hell, he'd sell everything he owned including the shirt off his back before he sold the one thing that meant the most to him.

After all, his soul was the only thing Shane had that he couldn't buy back.

Shane popped the hood and started tinkering with the car, just grateful to have it under his hands. It was harder than usual to slip into a calming groove, but after a while, his mind let go and he gave in to the feel of the sleek steel and intricate details, as if he could memorize them by touch.

A dual slice of halogen high beams cut through the front windows of the garage, snapping his head up in surprise. He squinted through the glass, trying to make out the vehicle in the lot.

"Jackson. Gotta be," Shane muttered, pushing off from the car.

Jackson had called about an hour ago to say he'd left his wallet behind when he'd tossed it on the workbench to help Shane spread salt. He was probably coming by in the plow to grab it. The snow was really coming down now, so whoever it was had to be driving one hell of a truck, or better yet, a tank. The mountain roads were merciless in bad weather, even for the locals. Without four wheel drive, you didn't have much beyond a prayer.

The side door banged open on a gust of wind, and Shane's brows nearly lifted off the top of his head at the sight before him. Bellamy Blake stood as tall as her five-foot-six frame would let her, with her hands on her hips and her slush-coated boots planted firmly over the concrete floor. Big, fluffy snowflakes lay scattered throughout her blond curls, and her face was flushed through with what looked like an even mix of anger and cold.

"What do you *mean* you've run into a problem?" she demanded, pressing her lips into a thin line.

Shane opened his mouth, but his vocal cords were

noncompliant. Had she seriously driven here in the middle of a snowstorm to pick a fight with him over her car?

And was he seriously turned on beyond measure at the sight of her?

"The parts are in Ohio," Shane managed, and she narrowed her eyes on him.

"But you said they'd be shipped today," she said, her voice shaking ever so slightly.

Shane rebounded, gesturing toward the windows. "Well, yeah, before Armageddon out there changed course. The trucks are all snowed in, Bellamy. They can't leave until the storm stops. Getting here—getting *anywhere*— on mountain roads in weather like this is next to impossible." He served her with a disbelieving stare. "Did you actually come out here in the middle of a snowstorm to argue with me about your car?"

Bellamy didn't flinch. "Yes. Is that . . . Beethoven?" Her face crinkled in confusion, and she turned to stare at the old radio as if she'd never seen one before in her life.

"Bach. How the hell did you get here?" Shane took a few steps toward her to look out the window at the side lot.

"Jenna's BMW."

God, she was certifiable. She could've been killed a dozen ways in this weather in a car like that. "Do you have any idea how dangerous that is?"

"I already have a mother, thanks. So what do I have to do to get the transmission here?" The stubborn look returned to her face with a vengeance.

Shane laughed without humor. "You have to wait, that's what."

"But you said Friday!"

"Jesus, Bellamy! I'm good, but I can't control the goddamn weather!"

The tears that filled her eyes took him by complete surprise.

"One thing," she murmured in a voice so quiet that Shane barely heard her. "All I wanted was *one thing* out of this whole disastrous week to go right. I can't even get stranded in the mountains without it blowing up in my face." She closed her eyes and took a deep, trembling breath. "I'm sorry I came out here to yell at you. I just . . . I just . . ." Tears started to flow from beneath Bellamy's closed eyelids, and her breath made her chest hiccup under the cream-colored sweater she wore. "I'll be at the resort. Just call me when you have an update."

"Bellamy, wait." Shane took a couple more steps toward her, until he was within arm's reach. "You can't drive back to the resort in weather like this. You'll never make it." The wind howled, rattling the windowpanes for good measure.

"Don't be ridiculous. I made it here just fine," she said, but there was no fire in her voice. She turned her face from his, presumably to hide her tears.

He stepped right in front of her. "You don't look just fine."

All the heat he'd felt when he'd seen her standing in the doorway coalesced into something a lot softer but just as strong, and Shane's hands moved before he could register the thought that he'd commanded them to.

"I'm sorry about your car." Without thinking, he lifted a hand and brushed a tear from her cheek with the pad of his thumb.

Her eyes jerked open and flew to his, and he froze. "I, uh. I didn't mean to, well. You know."

Ah, hell. He shouldn't have touched her.

But then she leaned against his shoulder, fighting the

sobs even as they escaped from her chest, and Shane was powerless not to put his arms around her and gather her in.

I am a simpering idiot.

The thought crossed Bellamy's mind, somewhere in the way back, but it was drowned out by the moronic bawling she just couldn't stop. Shane put his arms around her, steady and unyielding, which only egged the waterworks on.

"I could handle the stupid Derek thing, you know? That would've been fine. It *is* fine," she rambled into Shane's chest. "And my boss, I don't know, ex-boss, I guess. If I hadn't lost my cool, that would've been okay, I could've sucked it up." More shaky breathing, during which Shane patted her hair. Oh, God, here came more tears. "But I really do hate my career, even if I couldn't admit it until now, so where does that leave me? And now, with the car, I just heard your message and snapped. I have no control over anything, and it's just . . . it's . . ."

Nope. She was no good. The tears took over, and Bellamy couldn't do anything but let them have their way as she blubbered into Shane's chest.

"Okay. Hey, it's okay," he whispered into her hair, squeezing his arms around her shoulders and enveloping her with that intoxicating, woodsy scent.

Bellamy's throat knotted around another sob. "It is *so* not okay! I have no job, I hate my chosen field, and my ex-boyfriend is a consummate ass. I'm stuck in the mountains, which probably wouldn't be too bad, except that I'm standing here like a total basket case, bawling over something I can't control." Surely, the ground was late for its cue to open up and swallow her whole. Bellamy gave a loud, ungraceful sniffle, followed by a groan. "And I'm getting snot on your shirt!"

Shane's chest rumbled beneath her cheek, and her head sprang up in shock.

"Are you laughing at me?"

Shane pulled his head back and blanked his expression, but his twinkling eyes gave him away. "No! Not at all."

But it *was* kind of funny. In a pathetic meltdown kind of way.

"You totally are," she accused without anger, a tiny smile dancing on her mouth.

Shane's cough was completely contrived as he tried to cover up a laugh. "Okay, but only about the snot thing, I swear."

Oh, crap! She yanked her arms out from around him and covered her face with both hands, realizing that now she had no recourse but to wipe her disgusting nose with either her fingers or her sleeve. Could she get any more downright gross? Now he probably thought she was off her rocker *and* had terrible hygiene.

He laughed again, this time out loud. "Come on. There's a bathroom in the office."

Bellamy shook her head, trying to surreptitiously give her nose a delicate swipe with her fingers. "I'm really sorry. I'm such a jerk." She followed him through the garage, and he stepped back to usher her into the small office.

"Tell you what. Let's call it a draw, since I was a jerk the other night. What do you say? Truce?"

She nodded and sniffled. "Truce."

"You won't be offended if I wait until after you've washed your hands to shake on it, will you?" The corners of his mouth kicked up into a smirk.

"You're funny." Bellamy tried her damnedest to glower, but she was chuckling too hard.

Shane's laughter eased into a smile. "Take your time, okay?"

After doing a decent enough salvage job on her appearance, she washed her hands twice for good measure and walked back out into the garage.

"I made a pot of coffee, if you want some." Shane jutted his five o'clock shadow at the coffeepot sitting on the workbench. The aroma wafting from it was pure heaven.

"That sounds great." She leaned against the bench with one hip while he poured. "So are you really not going to let me drive Jenna's car back to the resort?"

He sent out a look that suggested she was nuts. "Have you seen the drop-off over the guardrails on the main road?"

Bellamy swallowed hard at the memory of the steep slopes. Okay, so it might be a teensy bit dangerous now that the snow was really coming down. But still, it wasn't as if she could walk back to the resort. "Well, how am I supposed to get back, then?"

"I can take you in the truck. I'm going to head out of here pretty soon anyway. I can't do anything without those car parts, and it looks like it's only getting worse out there." As if on cue, the wind battered the side of the garage, gusting snow against the wall in an angry scatter.

Bellamy shivered and threaded her fingers around the coffee mug Shane had offered her. "Does it snow like this a lot up here?"

"Yeah, but it's not usually the national crisis that everyone in the city makes it out to be."

"Considering that snowplows in Philly are a dime a

dozen, you'd think getting dumped on there wouldn't be such a big deal," she agreed. "Although this storm looks kind of nasty."

"Yeah, we had one just before Christmas that was about this bad." He paused, his dark eyes resting on her. "You'll probably be stuck here for another day or so, regardless of the transmission thing. That Beamer won't make it anywhere until the roads are cleared."

She sighed. At this point, the only thing she had to look forward to was filing for unemployment. And telling her parents she'd impulsively quit her job. Ugh. On second thought, let it snow. "Jenna and Holly will need to get back, and now they're my only way home. I'll have to find a way to come back and get it when you're done, I guess." Her eyes swept the space around them, settling on the car he'd been working on both times she'd arrived at the garage. "It won't be taking up space you need, will it?"

Shane shrugged and gave a smile, only it seemed forced. "I think you'll be fine." He looked at the car again, his eyes lingering, and hers followed.

The metal was the uneven dark gray of primer, and although it was clearly a sports car, it was nothing like her zippy little Miata. No, this car had a rough, masculine edge to it, more leather-jacket tough than two-seater flashy.

"So, the quitting your job thing is recent, then?" Shane asked, pulling her back to earth. He hooked his thumb through a belt loop, leaning against the rough wooden workbench.

Her lips popped open in surprise, but she didn't shy away from the question. Better to start facing the music. "Well, that depends. Is this morning recent enough for you?"

His eyes widened with momentary shock. "I'd say so."

He waited another beat before asking the dreaded question. "Do you want to talk about it?"

Bellamy meant to open her mouth to offer a heartfelt thanks but no thanks. It was really nice of him to offer to listen to her crap, but there were probably forty-two things he'd rather be doing than listening to a relative stranger do the woe-is-me song and dance.

But then she caught Shane's eyes, open and unpretentious and smolderingly sexy, and the words that crossed her lips were definitely not *thanks but no thanks*.

"Wait, wait. Let me get this straight. Your boss called you in the middle of a dentist's appointment and was pissed you didn't answer while you were getting your teeth cleaned?" Shane's forehead creased as disbelief took over his features.

Bellamy nodded and leaned back in the lone chair Shane had dragged out of the office for her to sit on. She flipped her hand up to signal scout's honor. "Yeah. Her rationale was that my ears still worked just fine. I'm sure she thought it was a bonus that I couldn't exactly protest, either." She shrugged, propping her empty coffee cup on one knee.

From where he sat, perched on the workbench with his boots dangling over the edge, Shane shook his head. "Okay, truth?" he asked, still giving her a look as though she might be pulling his leg.

She wished. Bosszilla had given her such a hard time about that stupid call, too. "You haven't learned the answer to this question yet?"

"Right, of course." He nodded, sending his black hair

over his eyes before he flipped it back with a nonchalant toss. "It sounds like you're way better off without that job."

Her insides gave a little quake, but it was less scary than the full-on fear tremors she'd had earlier. "Yeah, remind me of that when the bills come rolling in. I mean, I have some money saved, but the reality is, I wasn't really happy there even before my terrible boss came onto the scene."

Shane opened his mouth to answer her, but was cut off by the shrill electronic ring of the office phone.

"Ah, that's probably Grady, calling to see if I've left yet," he said, giving her a guilty look before swinging his legs down from the workbench to grab the phone.

"God, I'm sorry. It's been really good of you to put up with my psychoses and all, but we really should get on the road."

Shane looked at her over his shoulder. "I'm not worried about the truck handling the snow. Just let me grab this and then I'll get you back to the resort."

Bellamy stood up and stretched her legs, walking over to look out the window at the snow. Thick, fat flakes were still dumping from the sky, and they swirled in brisk drifts over the gravel drive and the road beyond. She squinted through the glass in confusion. The tire tracks she'd left on her way in had been swallowed whole, and as she looked more closely, Bellamy realized she had no idea where the drive ended and the road began.

And there were easily five inches of snow on both.

"Uh, Bellamy?"

She knew without turning around that she wasn't going to like the look on Shane's face. He leaned in the door frame, phone still in his hand, and met her eyes with an oh-shit expression that made her stomach bottom out somewhere around her hips.

"What? What's the matter?"

"That was my buddy Jackson, who drives a snowplow for the county. They just closed all of the roads going to and from the mountain due to whiteout conditions."

Her eyes went round and wide as he shook his head and met them with his own.

"It looks like you and I are kind of stuck here."

Chapter Fourteen

Bellamy's eyes were as round as pretty, green dinner plates, and she stared at him, wary. "Define *kind of stuck here*."

Shane tried not to wince. "Well, they closed the roads to everyone but snowplows about fifteen minutes ago. Jackson said visibility is pretty much nil, so the cops set up roadblocks until the snow eases up." He didn't add that two cars had skidded right into the guardrails, and that Jackson had almost gone off the road himself a time or two.

"Are you serious?"

Shane shifted in the door frame, trying to look at anything other than the doe-eyed expression on her face. Keeping himself in check when she got all hot-girl-feisty was hard enough. The sweet, vulnerable thing? Shit, an army of him wouldn't stand a chance against that.

"Unfortunately, yeah. Listen, I'm sorry. I should have just taken you back earlier." He probably would've gotten stuck at the resort that way, but at least it would have been better than being stranded here at the garage. Just the two of them. Alone.

Right. Because the garage is so romantic. Get a grip.

Bellamy shook her head. "No, this is all my fault. If I hadn't come down here like a total lunatic, we wouldn't be stuck here like this. God, my screw-ups know no bounds."

The look on her face sent a hard kick of remorse to his gut. "If you hadn't come down, I'd be stuck here alone. So look at it this way. It was kind of like doing me a giant favor." He pushed out of the door frame to reenter the garage, phone in hand.

Bellamy lifted a golden brow at him, a look of stubborn doubt belying the delicate features of her face. "You are so full of shit."

Her blunt words made him do a little stutter step, stopping him short with a laugh. "Okay, fine. I won't humor you. You're stuck with me until it stops snowing. Why don't you call your friends to let them know you're okay, and I'll see what we've got by way of food. According to the weather report Jackson heard, the snow won't start tapering off until later tonight."

"Thanks for trying to make me feel better. And I really am sorry." Bellamy twisted the sleeve of her sweater in a tight spiral with her thumb.

On legs that didn't quite belong to his free will, he stepped in close to meet her eye to eye. "No apologies."

Sure. Except for the big, fat *sorry, you may not kiss the rich girl* that his neurons were trying to send to the impulsive part of his brain.

"Okay." Bellamy took the phone and dialed, pacing the floor in a loop. She brushed her free hand through her hair until her forefinger snagged on a lone curl. Moving her wrist through a gentle roll, she wound the curl around her finger as she assured Jenna that she was safe but definitely stuck until the storm passed through.

The graceful way she carried herself was so unexpectedly beautiful that it captivated him, and even though he knew he was supposed to be doing something, he'd be damned if he could remember what it was. His stomach growled, sending up the hungry-man's version of a slap upside the head. Right! Food.

"So, what've we got?" Bellamy finished her lap around the garage, returning to where Shane stood with nothing to show for his efforts but a smile made up of pure bravado and a prayer that she hadn't caught him staring.

"Well, we always keep bottled water around, and there's half a case of it in the office." Thank God he knew that without looking, having snagged some the day before. "I've got a turkey sub and two apples in the mini-fridge, but there's not much else. Oh, except for the jelly beans." They were such a staple around the garage that Shane had almost forgotten about them.

"Jelly beans?" Bellamy looked at him, surprised.

He nodded. "Grady keeps a stash of them in a jar in the office. He swears they're how he quit smoking," Shane replied, going into the office to retrieve the jar. The thing was half full, and while they might get one hell of a sugar high for their trouble, at least it looked like he and Bellamy wouldn't starve.

"That's kind of an unorthodox way to go." She looked at the jar with curious eyes.

Shane thought of the old man and grinned. "Yeah, he has a helluva sweet tooth. Those damned things work, though. It's been sixteen years since he had a cigarette."

He put the jar down on the workbench with a plunk and shuffled through the contents on the shelf over the coffeepot. "We have plenty of coffee, too. That and the blanket from my truck should keep us from getting too cold."

A look of panic seeped into her glance. "What?"

Shane was quick to diffuse her worry. "Relax, as long as we have power, there's heat. It's just that it's drafty in here with all the windows, and we're not exactly well insulated, like a house. So you might want to keep your coat handy after it gets dark and the temperature drops, that's all."

"Oh. Okay." A hopeful look flickered over her face. "You know what? I think I saw a safety kit in Jenna's trunk when she took her suitcase out the other day. It might have something useful in it."

Shane laughed. "Like maybe a snowmobile?"

Bellamy crossed her arms over her chest, but the laugh she was trying to press between her lips was obvious. "Well, there might be an extra smartass in there. Just in case I need a matched set."

Okay, he had to give her credit. That was pretty good. "All right. I have to venture out there to get the blanket from the truck anyway. Give me the keys and I'll check the trunk."

The indignant look he got in return was just as much of a turn-on as the banter that followed. "I think I'm capable of making it to the side lot to check the trunk for a safety kit, Shane."

The way her lips kicked up over his name sent a blast of heat right through him. He shouldn't flirt with her. He should. Not. Flirt with her.

Oh, fuck *that*.

He took his coat from the hook by the door and pulled his ski cap low over his brows. The wind could get bitter enough to curl a polar bear's toes in a storm like this, but far be it for him to stand in her way.

"By all means. Ladies first." His stare offered no quarter, mostly because he wanted to make her squirm, but a tiny part of him just couldn't look away from the sexy fire in her emerald gaze.

She didn't flinch, but the longer he held the eye contact between them, the more her glance softened, as if she were surprised he'd conceded. "Okay, then." Bellamy sauntered to the side door and slid into the coat she'd abandoned there earlier. She set her cute little knit gloves in place and palmed the key fob to the BMW, squaring her shoulders before opening the side door. The gasp that flew out of her turned into a squeal as soon as she was met by the wall of wind and snow four steps past the threshold.

"Oh my *God*! That is so unfair!" She cursed in Shane's direction, hugging her arms around her body to ward off the blast of cold air as she took a few more steps through the relentless snow.

Shane bit back a shudder. Damn, it really was bone-chilling, and he was used to the weather up here. "What's the matter? I thought you were all over this," he joked. Guilt didn't let him stand there for very long, though. She stopped, and he stepped in close to block her from the stinging wind, letting it force the snow against his back instead.

"I was. I mean, I am," she said, but her cheeks were already flushed from the biting wind.

Reaching down to catch her gloved hand in his, he slipped the keys from her fingers. "You proved your point, tough stuff. I can get the safety kit."

Bellamy lifted her eyes up, unwavering. "I'm not going back." She shivered, but her determination was crystal clear.

He curled the keys back into her palm, returning her gaze with his own surety. "Suit yourself."

Neither one of them moved, and Shane knew right then

and there that he wouldn't be able to keep his hands off of her this time.

Bellamy couldn't tell if it was the frigid temperature around her or the blazing heat coursing through her, but either way, if she stayed where she was, it was going to land her in deep shit.

"I'll just take a quick look in the trunk, then." She ducked her head and stepped away from Shane's guard, regretting it the second the wind slapped her in the face for her trouble. A furtive glance told her he'd turned to trudge toward his truck in the side lot, so she made quick work of slogging through the shin-high snow to the spot in front of the garage bays where she'd parked Jenna's BMW. She dusted off the lock on the trunk to spring the latch, silently kicking herself.

How could she have been so stupid? she thought as she rummaged past a handful of reusable grocery bags. Her fiery attitude had gotten her stranded out in the middle of nowhere with a sizzling hot car mechanic whose sharp tongue wasn't limited to his snappy wit.

Good Lord, maybe a quick stint in the arctic wind was a good idea after all. How the hell else was she going to cool off?

"Find anything?" Shane called from over her shoulder, blanket in hand.

Bellamy brushed off her overactive imagination to zero in on the plastic crate in the trunk. She yanked it from the car, balancing it on her hip as she replaced the trunk lid. "I'm not sure what's in it, but I'm not going to stand out here to find out." She hustled back to the side door of the garage, noticing the thick layer of snowflakes clinging to

Shane's dark ski cap. It had only taken five minutes, and they were both covered in a glittering crust of ice and cold.

"Here," Shane said, gesturing as he removed his coat to shake the snow from it. "You're pretty much soaked. We can put this stuff over by the heat vents to dry." He reached for her coat and gloves as she took them off, throwing them over his arm with his own.

Bellamy scooped up the blanket and the crate, bringing both over to the workbench. She placed the crate in front of her and started rifling through the contents. "Oh, thank God. There are a couple of those heat packet thingies in here. You know, the ones you use to warm your hands. Brilliant." After rummaging past two bottles of water and a set of flares, Bellamy struck gold. "Granola bars never looked so good." And the fact that there was a whole box of them made her feel like she'd won the oatmeal raisin lotto.

"Excellent." Shane nudged a fresh cup of coffee into her hands before looking over her shoulder from behind. He was barely a step away, and she let out an involuntary shiver.

"You're freezing," he said, so close she could smell the warm, woodsy scent of his skin.

Bellamy was far, far from cold.

"I, uh . . . well, it's kind of snowing." Great. Because that little mouthful of obvious didn't make her sound ridiculous at all.

Bellamy squeezed her eyes shut. Come on. They were both grown-ups, here. She could handle close quarters with a member of the opposite sex without it becoming . . .

Shane stepped in to reach over her head for the box of sugar packets on the shelf, inadvertently brushing against her. They both froze for a second, his chest a tight fit against her back, and every rational thought Bellamy had been fighting for was lost in a sea of *oh, so good*.

"You're trembling." There was the barest hint of hesitation before he swept her hair over one shoulder, the rough calluses around his fingers a sharp contrast to the heated skin of her neck.

"I'm sorry," she blurted.

He chuckled, a low rumble that Bellamy felt vibrating under her skin, and his warm breath fanned out over her neck. "No apologies, remember?"

Bellamy answered in a rushing sigh as he wrapped a lean arm around her rib cage, muscles flexing against her with hot suggestion. "Okay. I'm not sorry." Leave it to her to botch being seduced. Oh, God, the heat of him, so unyielding against her, was distracting as hell. She felt him smile into the spot where her neck sloped into the soft knit of her sweater, his lips parting over the skin there in the barest of kisses.

"You are very beautiful when you're flustered. Did you know that?" Shane held her fast, sliding his mouth over her neck in a silken trail that threatened to knock her knees out from under her.

"I'm not flustered," she protested in a voice so velvety, she wasn't convinced it belonged to her.

"Mmm." The kisses teased behind her ear before returning back down her neck, each one shattering her resolve further. "Do you want to be?"

With that, Bellamy loosened her grip on the workbench in front of her and kicked any illusions of holding back to the curb. She swung around, and Shane met the hollow of her throat with a groan.

"Bellamy," he whispered into her skin before lifting his face to hers. She wrapped her arms around his taut shoulders as he parted her lips with a deep kiss that marked every inch of her. Just when she thought she would explode from the intensity of it, Shane pulled back, creating just enough space between them to be excruciating.

"This is still a bad idea," he murmured with a wicked grin, tracing her neck with two fingers all the way down to the top of her chest before stopping to trace a lazy circle over her heart.

Oh, two could play at that game. Her mouth curved into a flirty smile. "Hideous," she agreed, running the tip of her tongue in a delicate swirl over his earlobe. Bellamy wasn't about to be one-upped, no matter how hot he made her.

And he made her hot enough to know that the standing O she was bound to experience if he kept it up had nothing to do with the theater.

She worked her way from his ear across the line of his jaw, trailing little, feathery kisses back to his mouth. The friction of his stubbled chin against her lips was almost enough to blow her dwindling composure.

Bellamy gasped, low in her throat, as Shane answered by cradling his hands around her low back to guard against the rough wood of the workbench behind her, brushing his hips against her belly. He nudged her knees apart with his own, leaving no guesswork to his intentions, and she pushed forward to meet his body heat with her own.

Her hands skimmed the lean muscles of his chest, feeling the tight pull beneath his thermal shirt as his palms rounded the curve of her hips to fist the edge of her sweater. With the muted, gray light from outside creating shadows and nuances on the chiseled lines of his face, the look he met her with sent an unparalleled ache between her thighs.

"You're killing me, you know," he groaned, slipping a

hand over her skin. Lifting slowly, he brushed the backs of his fingers against her lacy bra, and the mere hint of sensation over her nipples sent a shock wave clear through to her spine.

Oh, *God,* was the feeling mutual. She arched into his hand, kissing him hard enough to make her lips sing as her tongue swept against his.

"Do you have any idea how badly I want you?" Shane's hands were at exquisite odds with her body as his fingers dove beneath the lace and lingered.

"Yes. *Yes.*" Bellamy was powerless to stop the keening sigh from spilling over her lips when his words made it past the thick heat of her body and into her brain.

"Shane . . ." Her heart skittered in her chest as she realized all at once exactly where they were headed and exactly why they couldn't go there.

"Bellamy," he replied with a smile so heady that she almost forgot her name, let alone what she was going to say.

She shifted her hands on either side of his face, drawing his shuttered gaze upward so she could meet it. "I, um. I'm going to go out on a limb and assume that Jenna didn't throw any condoms in her safety kit." If it had been happening to *anyone* else, the irony would've been fucking priceless.

A flicker passed over his dark eyes, but then Shane's grin turned even more mischievous. "That's okay. We'll just have to be a little imaginative." His tongue darted and danced around hers in an intoxicating rhythm, proving that his creative side was raring to go.

Gotta love a man who could think outside the box.

Without warning, Shane scooped her toward him, gripping her hips with strong hands and lifting her up to settle her on the workbench.

"Oh!" Bellamy kicked her hips up with a giggle as she rolled her weight off of whatever was caught beneath her left leg. She lifted her knee to retrieve what turned out to be Shane's wallet.

"You should be more careful with this," she teased, handing it over.

Shane drew her hips to the edge of the bench and ran his tongue along her collarbone before he answered. "It's Jackson's." He tossed the wallet to the side with a *thunk,* and it popped open to reveal twenty bucks and two tell-tale foil packets peeking out from the top.

Yes, Virginia, there really *is* a Santa Claus.

Bellamy gave a catlike smile. "So does your offer still apply now? Or am I just out of luck with your imagination?"

Shane looked up from where he stood, hands still wrapped around her hips. "Well, that depends. You sure you want to do this?" He ran his fingers around the top edge of her jeans. Bellamy had a sassy retort preloaded and ready to roll off her tongue, but then she caught the se-riousness on Shane's face. It wasn't seductive banter or sexy flirting. He was really asking.

She didn't even blink. "Yes."

In a motion so swift it made her breath freeze, Shane had his arms around her hips to lift her off the workbench, fitting her into his body and holding her fast. She curled her legs around him, which sent a groan from his chest, but he didn't stop moving until they were next to the car.

Putting her down in one gentle motion, Shane popped the door open and slid the front seat forward without pause to reveal the bench seat behind it. He jerked his head toward the backseat, mouth caught up in a full-on smirk. "You comin'?"

Oh, *hell* yes.

As soon as she settled into the narrow space of the backseat to face Shane, he was on her like wildfire, hands lifting her sweater over her head while hers returned the favor. She clutched the edge of his shirt when his kisses followed the trail of his hands, nails digging into her palms through the thick cotton as his chest brushed against hers.

"Oh." The single syllable came out like the moan it was meant to be, and Bellamy's nipples tightened and peaked through the white lace. She leaned back against the small side window of the backseat, and Shane hooked a thumb beneath the strap on her shoulder, following it around to her back to spring the hook with a nimble twist. Heat shot straight through her and settled between her hips, merciless as his touch became soft and teasing.

"So beautiful." The curve of her spine deepened at Shane's words, his honeyed voice driving her in a way that felt both forbidden and brand-new. He slid over her, and the friction against her jeans was almost unbearable. She arched up, fumbling to both lie down and meet his body at the same time.

"I don't think your backseat was designed for this," Bellamy murmured, trying to shift under Shane's hips, but it didn't deter his ministrations.

"I respectfully disagree." The cool whisper of his breath tightened her nipples even further, and she braced a hand on the front seat to fit herself under his hips. Her composure disappeared like it had never existed as he cupped her breasts with both palms, and when he dipped his mouth reverently from one to the other, Bellamy was certain that she would die from the intensity shooting through her blood.

Out of instinct and pure need, she lifted her hips in search of his touch. The urgency coursing through her was like nothing she'd ever felt, and it wasn't happy about deferring to the restrictions of the car's backseat. Shane lifted his chin to look up at her, his expression hungry and purely male. Keeping his eyes locked on hers, he returned to her mouth, his kiss surprisingly tender.

With boldness that knocked the breath from her, Bellamy pushed against him until he was upright in the middle of the seat. Opening her knees, she settled on his arousal, holding him fast to the backrest.

"Can't say I was . . . expecting that," he ground out against her shoulder, and she pulled away to rest her back on the front seat, which only thrust her sex against his harder.

"You said to get creative. I'm just following your lead."

Shane's eyes glittered with want as they dropped to watch the space where her jeans met his. "By all means," he groaned, sliding his hips under hers in a perfect fit. "Lead on."

Instead of making her blush, the words emboldened Bellamy, and she shifted back to slip a hand into the tight space between his lap and her own.

"Like this?" She stroked his cock over his button fly, following with a push of her hips to trap her hand between them as she continued with another undaunted caress.

"Oh, yeah." The words rode out of Shane on a hiss, and he arced into her hand, hard. She repeated the motion, finding a rhythm as she rocked into him against her own hand. His bare chest was lean and hard on her soft skin, and the contact sent even more sweet pressure to the juncture between her thighs. He released his grip on her hip with one hand, fitting it next to hers to curl his fingers over the seam of her jeans.

"*Shane.*" The pressure building in her sex was no match for the feel of him, his fingers hard and steady over the soft yield of her body, and she thrust against him again and again, unable to stop.

"You are so beautiful like this," he whispered into her ear, pressing into her, sweet and merciless. The combination of the words and the movement between them sent her pitching over the edge, the delicious release of her orgasm rocking through her on a cry. As the wave subsided, her eyes fluttered open to reveal his unwavering gaze on her.

Shane watched with sultry eyes as she freed the top button of his jeans, then the next, sliding back from his body to work her way down. His hungry stare kindled a fresh wave of heat that worked its way through her from the inside out.

Unhooking her leg from over his hips, Bellamy moved next to him in an effort to shuck her jeans and boots as quickly as possible in the tight space, noticing only briefly that he did the same. When she was bare except for her panties, the realization hit her that she was about to have sex with a guy she'd known for all of four days in the backseat of a car while stranded in a snowstorm.

She'd never felt so right about anything in her life.

Bellamy swung back over Shane's hips, nothing between them but a thin layer of satin, and a groan escaped from both of them simultaneously when the fabric brushed his erection.

"You're sure," he whispered, capturing her face in his hands. All of the dark, sexy edge was gone from Shane's voice as his eyes met hers in the shadows of the car. She nodded, sending her curls over her shoulders and her heartbeat into a frenzy.

"Positive."

In a flash, her panties were gone. Shane made quick work of putting on a condom, and Bellamy's breath scattered through her like the howling wind outside. She settled herself against him, flattening her palms on his chest, and he brushed his lips over hers in a slow kiss.

She parted his lips with her own, seeking his heat as the kiss grew deeper. With her hips poised over his, she lowered herself into his lap, his length slowly filling her.

"Bellamy." He bit out her name like a cross between a prayer and a curse as she drew up slightly, only to lower back down with a tremble. Shane's hands found her hips, fingers hot on her skin, and he guided her into a rhythm that made her want to scream. The tension that had broken over her moments before was back tenfold, cresting and demanding all at once as he held her hips to his own. Shane thrust into the heat of her folds, over and over, and all of her muscles squeezed tight before breaking free.

"Oh, *God*." Bellamy dug her fingers into the taut muscles of his shoulders as she came again, even harder than the first time. Shane didn't slow the relentless rhythm on her hips, holding steady as she shuddered on top of him, arching up into her until the grip of his hands tightened with a groan. Fueled by the sound of his voice, Bellamy pressed into him until there was no space left between their bodies, entranced by the sound of her name on his lips as he came.

She leaned her head on his shoulder, her curls a soft curtain between their bodies, and Shane reached up to brush a hand through them. For a moment, Bellamy hung in the balance of time, swinging with the uncertainty that welled up in her chest.

But then Shane slid two fingers under her chin, lifting her face to kiss her softly again, and the worry disappeared like smoke.

Chapter Fifteen

Shane watched a stream of fresh coffee burble into the pot on the workbench. The dark liquid inched up the sides of the carafe and sent out a warm, earthy aroma that did its best to cancel out the snow piling up outside. A glance through the window told him that the wind had only become stronger, forcing the snow into sharp drifts against the north side of the garage. Although the image registered, it didn't linger for more than a second or two.

Shane stood there, eyes wide open, without seeing a thing. He'd just had the most mind-altering sex of his entire twenty-nine years with a woman he barely knew but was so attracted to that it felt sinful just to be near her, and they were stranded together until Mother Nature was good and ready to let them go.

Very bad idea wouldn't touch this with a ten-foot pole.

"Hey." Bellamy stood in the door frame to the office, the sleeves of her sweater pulled low over her hands and a glow on her face that could light up half the Eastern Seaboard. The creamy skin on her cheeks was tinged with a sexy flush of color, although Shane couldn't tell if it was the fantastic sex or the two days' worth of stubble on his face that put it there.

"Hey. I made some fresh coffee." Shane scrubbed a hand down his chin and furtively watched her make her way over to the workbench. He'd done his fair share of sleeping with women, but this was in another league entirely. One minute, they'd been standing there like normal people. The next, he'd been so consumed by lust that he'd seduced her in the backseat of his car. Granted, she'd seduced him right back, but still. He was pretty sure there was no standard protocol for what was supposed to happen after a thing like that.

"It smells good." The cadence of Bellamy's voice so close to him made him want to start from square one, just so he could have her all over again. Shit, he needed to get it together.

"Are you hungry? I mean, you probably are." He turned to crouch down and open the mini-fridge, but she stepped into his line of sight, catching his forearm with a gentle hand. Man, she looked pretty with her hair all ruffled around her face.

"Shane, at this point, I think we can probably skip the small talk."

Okay, wasn't expecting *that*. Shane opened his mouth twice before finally replying, "I, ah. Okay."

She looked at him, just as calm as you please, but her eyes flickered when he met them, giving away the slightest hint of uncertainty. "I'm going to go out on a limb and assume you don't charm every girl you know into the backseat of your car."

Shane's gut tightened. He might not know exactly what was going on between them, but he sure as shit knew what wasn't.

"No, I don't." His look was as unwavering as the truth behind it.

Bellamy nodded once. "All right, then. Seeing as how we're better acquainted now—" She paused to let a tiny grin settle on the curve of her lips. "And it looks like we're both on the same page since I don't make it a habit of being charmed by every mechanic I get snowed in with, maybe we could agree to forgo the weird pretenses. For the sake of being stranded and all."

Huh. Who knew the no-bullshit thing could be so hot?

Shane cocked his head at her, unable to resist. "I charmed you?"

She arched an eyebrow and reached for the coffeepot, so close to him he could smell the clean, intoxicating scent of her hair. "I think that's a pretty good assessment. You're rather charming when you want to be." She poured two cups of coffee, then stood on her tiptoes to examine the shelf over the pot.

"Thanks," he said, reaching over her head to pluck two packets of sugar from the container at the back of the shelf.

Bellamy blinked as he folded them into her hand. "You're welcome. How did you know how I like my coffee?"

"Because you're not the only one who's smart around here, that's how," Shane said, savoring the look on her face.

Oh, they were in for a verrrrrrry long night together.

Shane leaned back against the workbench, watching her stir the two sugars into her coffee just as she'd done the night he took her to the Ridge. If she wanted no pretenses, he could deliver. "So what's a smart girl going to do when she goes back to the city? You think your boss will be calmed down by then?"

Bellamy's shoulders rounded slightly before she pulled

them back to stand tall. "The only way that woman will calm down is with pharmaceutical assistance. I've made my bed, now I've got to lie in it, I suppose. As soon as I get back to the resort, I'll call the VP to officially resign." She sighed, leaning against the workbench. "As crazy as it sounds, working at the bank as an analyst isn't for me." She knelt down next to the mini-fridge and pulled it open, unearthing the bag containing the food.

"Why is that crazy?" Shane fell into a rhythm next to her, unfolding a couple of paper napkins and popping open the box of granola bars.

She tilted her head, concentrating on the food in front of her with that serious yet dreamy look on her face. "Because it's what I went to school to do, and my parents paid my way from day one. They've never said it out loud, but they run a lucrative real estate company. I'm sure they won't be thrilled I'm changing my mind so impulsively. Plus, I don't exactly have a contingency plan for hating a career I spent a ton of time and money to prepare for."

Warning bells went off in Shane's mind, loud and foreboding, but he ignored them. "You can't spend your life doing something you weren't made to do. You'll be miserable."

She took the granola bar he handed her, exchanging it for an apple and a surprised glance. "Easy for you to say. You love what you do. For me, it's not so cut-and-dried."

Shane took a bite of his apple, half out of hunger and half so he didn't have to answer her right away. "How are you so sure that I love what I do?"

Her laugh pinged around in his belly along with his food. "It's obvious. I could see it on your face that very first day you looked at my car." She paused. "Can I ask you a kind of personal question?"

The smartass part of him was tempted to remind her that, as she'd pointed out earlier, they were probably past pleasantries. "Shoot."

"Well, the mechanics in the city make an absolute ton of money. If you love it so much, why stay here, where there's less opportunity to advance?"

Shane's blood seized in his veins, and he put his best effort into a nonchalant shrug that felt anything but. "I belong here. Plus, as much as neither one of us wants to admit it, Grady needs the help. It took me and Jackson everything we could work up to yank your transmission out, and Jackson's a house with legs."

Bellamy laughed again, and his words kept pouring out. "You know who Cesar Millan is, right?"

"The dog whisperer guy?"

He lifted his chin in a single nod. "Yeah. Well, without getting too hokey on you, Grady's like that with cars. He's unbelievable. I mean, half the time he doesn't even need to look at what's in front of him. He can listen to a car, or go by feel of an engine, and bam! He knows what it needs or when it's right."

"That doesn't sound hokey," she said, honesty threading the words together. "It sounds like he's just meant to work on cars."

Something percolated in Shane's chest, and the words continued to flow. "He had a heart attack last year, and now the physical stuff is hard on him." He paused when Bellamy's eyes crinkled around the edges in concern, but she didn't interrupt, just let him keep talking. "Thought he'd have to retire when it happened, but it didn't seem right to close up shop when all he needed was a little help." Shane's mind drifted around the words, spinning back to that first day in the shop, and how he knew by lunchtime that he'd never leave.

What the hell was he *doing*?

Shane cleared his throat in a rough growl and took another bite of his apple before finishing abruptly. "So it might not be glamorous, or pay a buck twenty an hour, but I don't want to be anywhere else. The city and I don't mix." What had made him open his mouth like that, anyway?

Bellamy gave him a beguiling smile, and his edginess fell a notch. She scooped up the other apple to cradle it in the heart of her palm. "Mmm. Well, it seems you've got it all figured out. I wish I was so lucky."

He pulled back to look at her down-to-earth expression, so honest and clean as she took a huge bite. A stream of juice trickled down her chin, eliciting a self-conscious smile from her lips. She rolled her eyes and wiped her chin with the back of her hand before taking another bite.

A warm, unexpected feeling spread out in Shane's chest like it wanted to settle in for a nice, long stay, and he rubbed the spot over his sternum. How could half an apple give you instant indigestion?

He tipped his head at her and shrugged. Time to go vague. "Luck is what you make it."

Bellamy's smile became wistful. "I'm envious."

"Of what? Me?" That just seemed ass-backwards.

"You sound so surprised," she said, gesturing at him with the apple in her hand.

"I just find it hard to believe that someone like you is envious of her mechanic, that's all." He leaned into the workbench to unwrap the sub, sliding the larger half toward her on the napkin.

"What do you mean, someone like me?" The slight

bristle to her words was offset by the curiosity on her face, as if she wasn't sure which one she wanted to go with.

The edges of Shane's lips inched upward at her feistiness. "You just seem to have it all together. I mean, getting your MBA is no joke."

She switched the halves of the sandwich and slid the bigger one back toward him before answering. "Getting my MBA was a lot of work, but I was lucky. It came naturally to me, so I never struggled with it the way some other people did. My parents never outwardly pressured me to go to grad school, but they've owned their own business since I was a kid. It all just made sense at the time." Bellamy picked at the lettuce on her sandwich, putting it on the napkin in front of her.

"But now you'd rather do something else."

"Maybe. I don't know. It's not like I really have the experience to switch careers. I have to do what I'm good at."

A flicker crossed her face, barely a whisper of suggestion, but Shane recognized it. He tipped his chin at her. "If none of that mattered, what would you do?"

"It does matter," she pointed out, finally taking a bite of her sandwich.

Her toughness knew no bounds. Shane cracked a half smile to try and loosen her up. "Don't take this the wrong way, but you kind of suck at the hypothetical game."

Okay, that got her laughing. "Fine. If none of it mattered, I'd probably go to culinary school and be a chef."

"So why don't you?"

"It requires a lot of time and money, one of which I now have, but the other . . ." She held up her empty palms in a soft shrug.

Nope. She might be nine kinds of cute over there, but

he wasn't going down that path. "Yeah, I see your point. Still. Maybe there are ways around it."

"Maybe. But there's something else." Bellamy spread her fingers over the napkin, smoothing out nonexistent creases.

After a full minute during which Shane's curiosity hit an all-time high, he lifted his brows in question. "Okay, I'll bite. What else is there?"

"Well—" She broke off and took a deep breath. "I spent all this time and money to go into business, and now I don't like it. What if cooking for a living made it not-fun anymore? It'd be a hell of a way to find out, and I'm not really sure I want to risk it."

He chewed on that for a second before answering her. "Sure, it's a risk. But what if it turns out that being a chef is something you love even more when you get to do it all the time? I mean, yeah, pulling the tranny out of your car was a pain, but if I'm being honest, I wouldn't want to be doing anything else, even on the hard days."

Bellamy's head sprang up, curls bouncing. "I never really thought of it that way," she breathed.

"Plus, cooking won't ever be not-fun for you."

Her inquisitive stare sent a jolt through his chest, as if she could see every last shred of him with those green stunners. He resisted the urge to look away.

"And you're sure how?" she asked.

"The same way you're sure I love what I do. Your face just looks different when you're around food." *Great.* That sounded totally corny. She probably thought he was an idiot.

"It does?" Bellamy blinked with surprise.

Shane chuckled. How could she not know that? "You get all excited about the grocery store, Bellamy. And I've never met anyone who thought making pasta from scratch was a fun way to blow a Sunday afternoon."

Her cheeks flushed, which didn't make Shane want to let up, so he didn't. "I bet you've de-boned a chicken before, haven't you?" He nudged a soft laugh out of her, loving every second of the deepening rosy glow on her face.

"Well, yeah, but . . ."

Shane continued, not giving her any room to argue. "And you make all your pie crusts from scratch, too, right?"

Bellamy crossed her arms over her chest and looked like she wanted with all her might to say no. But she couldn't. "They taste better that way."

His face got triumphant, and she let out a begrudging smile as he pressed on. "And I'll bet beyond the shadow of a doubt that you know *exactly* what wine is the perfect accompaniment to the thirty-two-ounce porterhouse at Butcher and Singer downtown." It was one of the swankiest steak houses Philly had to offer. She'd probably eaten there a billion times.

"You've been to Butcher and Singer?" Her smile was gone, replaced by total surprise. "I thought you said you and the city didn't mix."

Fuck.

"I live in the mountains, not under a rock," Shane joked, trying to keep his own smile in place. He felt it slipping, despite the effort. "Everyone around here has heard of Butcher and Singer. Plus, I told you, we mechanics do eat from time to time."

What *was* it about her that made him open his mouth without thinking? He cursed silently and took a huge bite of his sandwich as if to prove his point.

"Wow. Guess you don't go halfway, then." She took a bite

of her own before finishing her thought. "And I prefer a nice pinot noir with steak. It enhances the flavors really well."

They ate the rest of their lunch without saying much, the quiet around them punctuated only by the snapping wind outside. When there was nothing left but crumbs and apple cores, Bellamy gathered the trash and tossed it into the wastebasket.

"Thanks for lunch. I guess I owe you one."

Shane shifted where he stood, still wearing a thin layer of unease. "Don't worry about it."

She rocked back on her heels, looking at him with a wide-open, easy expression. "So, what do we do now?"

"There's not much by way of entertainment around here," he apologized, following her gaze around the garage.

"You were working on your car when I got here, right? Is there something wrong with it that you need to fix?" Bellamy peered at the Mustang. Wait, was that a flicker of interest on her face?

Weird.

"No. Think of it like being in front of a pantry full of your favorite foods. I just tinker, kind of play around with it, that sort of thing."

A spark lit her features. "Really?"

Shane's gut stirred. "Sure. There's always something I can fine-tune; plus, it chills me out to work on it, you know? It's just relaxing."

Her laugh sent a straight shot of sexy and sweet right down his spine. "Like making pie crust," she said. "You want to show me?"

What. The. Hell. No girl in the history of the XX chromosome had ever even had so much as a passing interest in his absolute love for cars. "Are you serious?" Shane blinked a couple of times to make sure he was awake and not stuck in some odd dream.

Bellamy chewed her lip and fastened him with a hesitant look. "You don't have to, if it'll be a pain. I mean, I don't know a thing about cars."

A grin spread over his face, slow and sure as a sunrise, as he walked her over to the Mustang and popped the hood. "Well, you're in luck. I happen to know a thing or two, and I'm all about sharing the joy."

Chapter Sixteen

"Truth?" Bellamy cranked her brow at the sight of the shiny, intricate metal guts under the hood of Shane's car.

Shane stood so close she could feel the heat of his body next to hers, which did nothing to help her concentrate. "Of course."

"I have no idea what I'm looking at."

The smile that broke over his face swirled around in her belly like she'd swallowed it. "It's a 1969 Mustang Mach 1." His eyes followed the lines of the car.

It didn't take a math wizard to know that those numbers didn't exactly add up to what sat before them. "But these parts look really new," Bellamy said, peering at the inner workings of the car.

Shane chuckled as if he was thinking of an inside joke. "They are. The engine is a 428 Cobra Jet. I put it in almost three years ago." He pointed to the pristine engine. It looked like it had just come off the factory line.

Bellamy frowned. "Why go through the trouble of replacing something as big-deal as the engine? When the engine on Holly's Jetta blew up last year, the mechanic told her to cut her losses and get a new car."

"I didn't replace the old one because it didn't work. I replaced it because this one is faster." The edges of his lips turned up into a half smile that Bellamy would bet good money he couldn't control.

Oh, the testosterone of it all. "How fast are we talking, exactly?"

The half smile became a full-blown stunner, and the sexy, badass grin on Shane's face kicked her pulse into oh-yeah mode. "The car's got over five hundred horsepower."

"English, please," she said, tilting her head over her shoulder to look at him.

He stepped in close, wrapping an arm around her waist and gently pressing her against the car with his body from behind. "It'll go zero to sixty in the time it takes you to say your name and phone number. How's that?"

Good. That's so freaking good.

"Better," she breathed.

Shane leaned into her, his palm firm on her hip, and gestured into the car with his free hand. "So, when you change out the engine like that, you have to make other adjustments, too. To make sure you get the kind of performance you're after." He pointed out where the transmission was, and gave her a very basic idea of how everything worked. The intricacies were definitely lost on her, but by the time he was done, she had a pretty simple understanding of where everything was and how it all went together. More importantly, Bellamy had picked up on something about Shane that was ironclad.

He might be hot for her, but he was in *love* with the car.

"So, how does a guy come across a 1969 Mustang Mach 1, anyway? It's not like you can just pick one up at the dealership." She looked at the gleaming components under the hood, trying to familiarize herself with the way each one went with the others.

"Well, from the time I hit puberty, I knew I wanted one, so it was just a matter of time. I drove by her on the side of the road six years ago, with a big FOR SALE sign in the window. It was the fastest damn U-turn I've ever made." Shane shook his head, chuckling, and Bellamy shifted the angle of her body so they were face-to-face. Something about his expression was so clean and real that she couldn't make herself look anywhere else.

He continued, clearly caught up in the memory. "I called the number on the sign and told the guy I'd wait right there for him to show up. Nothing like looking desperate right off the bat, right?" His soft laughter twined together with hers before he kept on. "The guy was hard-up to sell it, but not as hard-up as I was to have it. He gave me a good price because it needed a ton of work, but that was half the reason I wanted it. It wasn't about having the car; it was about *building* the car."

The look on his face had Bellamy utterly magnetized, his stubbly jaw set in certainty. She smiled. "So you've always known how to work on cars, then?"

"I've always loved them, yeah." He nodded. "I taught myself some stuff along the way, but everything I really know about cars I learned from Grady. I never would've been able to do any of this without him, although he'll tell you different." The respect Shane felt for the man was obvious as he spoke.

"He sounds like a great guy."

Shane's dark eyes flared with sudden disquiet, but it didn't carry over into his voice, gone as fast as it had appeared. "He is a great guy." He took a step back to close the hood and the conversation, his expression inscrutable.

Bellamy shivered, not from the cold so much as the absence of him close to her body. The look that had been on his face while he talked about the car lingered in her mind, and it sent prickles of something hot and familiar through her.

She was turned on beyond repair, and she wanted to make love to him. Again.

"Hey, you're cold. Let me grab your coat. It gets pretty drafty in here." He started to turn away, and in that moment, Bellamy made a choice that felt like a turning point.

It was impulsive, yet she didn't hesitate.

She reached out, catching his forearm in the grasp of her fingers, not letting go. "I don't want my coat." Her voice was soft, at odds with the piercing stare between them as she moved in, placing herself so close to him that she could see the lean muscles in his jaw go tight with understanding.

"You don't," he said, his eyes dipping to her lips, then back to meet her gaze. It wasn't a question.

Shane's eyes hardened over her as she shook her head, her mouth pulling up into a slow smile. It might not make much sense, but there was something about the way he looked at her that made her positively hungry for him.

"No. I want you."

He didn't hesitate, either.

They didn't so much kiss as collide, their bodies and mouths coming together with an unnamed force Bellamy was powerless to resist. Their tongues rounded against one another, both seeking and finding. Delicious, promising heat pushed its way through Bellamy's body to reach even the smallest places, instant arousal thrumming through her veins.

Shane slipped his hands around her face, his roughly

calloused fingers tracing a gentle sweep into her hair as his touch became slow and deliberate. "I want you, too." His voice was a sexy rumble, low in his throat, as he drew his fingers down her neck to her chest, letting them rest on the soft cashmere between her breasts. "But this time I want you slow."

She almost came right then and there, just from the promise on his lips.

"Oh, God." Bellamy stood on her toes to press into him, folding his hand between their bodies with the force of the upward lift. After a searing kiss, she turned to fumble for the door handle on the car.

"No." He pulled back and captured her hand with a look of controlled hunger, so smoldering that it was palpable. "I have something else in mind this time." Stroking the neckline of her sweater, he followed the deep V to the heartbeat hammering in her chest. "Is that okay with you?"

The memory of being filled to the hilt in his lap took her senses by storm, building the twinge between her legs to a demanding ache. "I'm kind of partial to the backseat of your car." Her voice came out with a seductive edge, and Shane stiffened under her hands at the inflection.

Turnabout and fair play had never felt so sinful or so good.

"This will be even better." The timbre of his words dared her as his hands moved in twin strokes down her rib cage to the edge of her sweater. Her nipples tingled, tight with the anticipation of his touch. "Trust me."

Shane turned and walked to the workbench, grabbing the blanket he'd retrieved from his truck. Instead of returning to where Bellamy stood, he went toward the office, stopping just short of the door frame at a panel of light switches on the wall. With a flick of his wrist, the overhead light disappeared, leaving them bathed in the low shadows of the swirling wind outside. The faint glow of the building's exterior lights strained to shine in through the snowfall, casting a muted gold among the shadows.

It only took a handful of paces before Shane was next to her again, the scent of fresh cedar and pines filling her with recognition and need. He shook out the blanket to spread it on the ground next to the car, then returned his attention to Bellamy by slipping his arms around her where she stood. His touch was electric, even over the fabric between them, and she couldn't help the sigh that spilled from her.

"You feel so good," she murmured, shocked to find it had been out loud. Her cheeks flushed and she squeezed her eyes shut, embarrassed as hell that the words had flown right out. Thinking about how hot he made her was one thing. Telling him, right out loud, was quite another.

Shane drew back to catch her expression in the shadows. He brought his lips to her ear, kissing the soft spot behind it before leaving a whisper in its place. "You shouldn't hold back." His hands slid under her sweater, teasing the skin there. "You're so beautiful when you let go."

Heat pooled low in Bellamy's hips, every inch of her hypnotized by the throaty cadence of Shane's voice. He lowered his mouth to hers in a tender sweep, his lips brushing against hers just enough to create soft friction. Shane parted from her only to kneel over the blanket. As she followed, he wrapped his arms around her to settle her body right in the center before flipping the outer edge to cocoon them both.

His mouth was slow and sweet on hers, each kiss driving straight through her as he settled his weight gently over her body. His fingers skimmed the column of her neck, the skin over her collarbone, making her desperate to have him. Bellamy reached between them to raise her sweater over her head, then slipped her hands low against his body for the edge of his shirt.

Shane caught her fingers, murmuring into her neck. "That's not slow."

God, she was going to die if she didn't feel him on her, skin on skin, heat on heat. "I . . . I . . ."

"Tell me what you want, Bellamy."

Desire shot right to her core at the sound of his words, and she arched toward him, searching. Detailed images of all the steamy, provocative things she wanted him to do flashed through her mind, hitching her breath in her lungs and her words in her throat. She could call it like she saw it all day long, but this took speaking her mind to a totally uncharted level. She couldn't possibly say *those* things, could she?

"Tell me what you want." Shane's hands moved down her bare shoulders, stopping on the thin straps of her bra, both his movements and his words prompting her with the promise of their heat. She buried her hands in his hair as his kisses followed the path of his hands, resting over the top of one breast, then the other, with a feather-soft touch of his lips. "Trust me."

"I want to feel you," she blurted, her cheeks tingling at the words. "I want to feel your skin on mine."

A wicked stare glittered through his eyes as he looked up at her with a dark, seductive smile. Without a word, he shifted from her body to strip off his shirt, revealing the lean, corded muscles in his chest. Bellamy reached up to gather him in as he lowered himself back to her, and the sheer electricity of his skin on hers made her bite back a moan.

"I meant it when I said you shouldn't hold back." Shane's hands brushed over the very tips of her breasts, his palms finding their weight with a gentle caress.

"Don't stop," she rasped, rising into his hands and fitting herself against the hard length between his hips. In one smooth motion, he pushed the straps from her shoulders, freeing her from the lace. With an excruciating tenderness, his fingers turned slow circles around her nipples, and she lifted even farther into the touch. When he followed with his tongue, Bellamy didn't hold back the groan it brought forth.

If she was going to get what she wanted, then so was he, pretenses be damned.

"Touch me. *Please*." She gave in to the words swirling through her head, letting them tumble out unbidden.

Shane's hand traveled over her belly to the seam of her body, his fingers cupping her sex in a lazy stroke that made her draw her bottom lip between her teeth.

"I want to touch you all night, just like this."

Oh, God, Bellamy wasn't going to last ten seconds with his hands on her, let alone all night. She writhed under the slow lift of his fingers, and he coaxed another groan from her with a deliberate touch.

"More. Take them off." The whisper came up from her throat, heady and thrilling as she spoke it. Shane's eyes flew to hers, shining with want and raw sexual heat. He had the button on her jeans undone before she could fully register his movement, drawing the zipper down to bare the swell of her hips and her satin panties underneath. Shane undressed her with care, then took off his jeans and settled over her, brushing her hair from her shoulders.

"Bellamy." He breathed her name into her skin as he kissed her again and again, his sex hardening even more over her satin-covered folds. She reached down between them, riding his cock with her hand, and he hissed out a breath against her. "*Bellamy*."

Something about his voice murmuring her name pushed her harder, and she returned the favor of the lazy strokes that had sent her so close to the edge. His hand wrapped around hers with a groan, joining it in the motion for just a moment before guiding her away.

"What's wrong?" Bellamy's pulse ricocheted through her veins before it froze.

Shane shook his head and kissed her. "Nothing. You're a little too right, that's all." He arched a mischievous brow.

Bellamy flushed, but the implication turned her on just as much as his touch. "Really?" She teased a hand around the waistband of his boxers, hooking her thumb under the elastic.

He gave her a dark look and a smile so slow and provocative, she had to suck in a breath. "Mmm." His fingers delved between her legs to her inner thigh, stroking the edge of her panties. "So right."

Bellamy's knees listed open, screaming for his touch, and he didn't disappoint. He slipped a finger inside her heat, drawing tight circles against her with his thumb.

"Yes. Oh God, *yes*." She had no idea who was in control of the totally wanton voice that came out of her, but as her muscles squeezed around a sweet crest of release, she didn't care. Shane's finger was joined by another, and the steady, slow rhythm sent sparks through her brain. Words tried to form and fight their way from her, but the only thing that made it past her lips was the heavy cry of the orgasm that crashed into her.

"You are perfect when you come undone."

Bellamy's eyes fluttered open to reveal Shane's unwavering gaze upon her face. Never before had anyone actually watched her come, and while a tiny, faraway piece of her consciousness told her she should be embarrassed, she wasn't.

She trusted him.

"Shane." She ran her palms over the scattering of dark hair on his chest, enjoying the shudder it brought from him as she skimmed over his nipples. When her hands reached his shoulders, she guided him over her and lifted her lips to his ear. "I want you inside me." She arched her core to meet his erection, the cotton of his boxers giving just enough resistance against her to tempt her to scream, but she held steady. With one swift yank, the fabric between them was history.

Shane quickly put on a condom and returned to hover over her, trailing kisses from her ear to her open, waiting lips. He nudged her knees wide, fitting into the tightness of her sex with gorgeous strength.

"Like that. Oh, just like that." Bellamy's breath stole from her as they made love with slow intensity; cresting, falling, and cresting again. When Shane gripped her hips to rock into her, fast and hard, her eyes flew open to focus on his face. His expression was an exact mirror of his lovemaking, both fierce and exquisite, and as she watched the look on his face while he shuddered into her body in release, it sent her over the edge right alongside him.

They lay in the shadows of nightfall, wrapped around each other in a tangle of heated skin and sated breath, and talked until their growling stomachs lured them out from beneath the blanket. Over a couple of granola bars, Bellamy told Shane about the disastrous time she tried to take a breakfast shortcut by hard-boiling eggs in the microwave, her first true cooking debacle. The peals of laughter continued through Shane's recounting of the day he discovered—the hard way—that the gas gauge in the Mustang was faulty and he and Jackson had to be rescued by the local Girl Scout troop passing by. They traded stories back and forth with seamless ease, and Bellamy couldn't remember the last time she'd felt so genuinely good.

Only when she shivered from the true chill in the garage did Bellamy realize that night had fallen, and fallen hard. She and Shane snuggled right back beneath the blanket, whispering and laughing about everything and nothing in the dark of the garage, until they were both so tired that they fell asleep in each other's arms.

Chapter Seventeen

The grating scrape of metal on asphalt jolted Shane from a dead sleep, and he lifted his head from his lumpy excuse for a pillow, a.k.a. a balled-up sweatshirt. Sun streamed in through the windows, so brilliant that his eyes had no hope of adjusting, and he went to rake a hand through his hair in an effort to jump-start his brain.

His arm refused to budge. And what was with that *noise*?

"Ugh, shhh," Bellamy murmured drowsily, and she burrowed farther beneath the blanket, rubbing her back against the cradle of his hips before sighing back to sleep. His arms were wrapped around her from behind, the one that lay by her head completely asleep, the other resting right in between her cashmere-covered breasts.

The memory of the night before filtered back into his brain like a series of sweetly wicked dreams, and although Shane was sore as hell from sleeping on the concrete floor, the warmth of Bellamy's body against his kept him happily rooted to the offending spot. He shifted even closer, acutely aware of the rise and fall of her chest under his hand. Man, she smelled so good, even after spending the night on the floor of a garage. How many girls could pull *that* off? Shane closed his eyes, drifting back into the feel of her fuzzy sweater, of the incredible skin that lay beneath it . . .

The side door to the garage banged open with a rude thud, scaring the ever-loving crap out of him.

"Shane? You in here?" Even though he recognized the voice right away, Shane still froze to his spot under the blanket.

Shit. Shitshitshit! Bellamy did the shift-and-snuggle, her slow breaths suggesting she was still very much asleep and about to get the shock of her life. Shane leaned forward to put a gentle whisper in her ear in order to soften the blow, but it was too late. Jackson rounded the passenger side of the Mustang, coming into view.

"Jeez, buddy, I had no idea you'd still be . . . whoa!" Jackson skidded to a halt as soon as he saw the two of them lying on the floor, wrapped up together just as easy as you please. Bellamy chose that exact moment to wake up with a start, looking disoriented as hell. She sucked in a breath at the sound of Jackson's voice, then promptly gave a startled, full-body jerk that landed her butt squarely on Shane's raging morning hard-on.

Right. Because the whole morning-after thing wasn't awkward enough.

"Morning, Jackson," Shane said, trying to come up with a graceful way out of the situation while getting his dick to cooperate and keeping Bellamy's honor as intact as possible. It was a tall order on both counts, seeing as how her body pressed into him from head to toe.

"This is Bellamy Blake." Shane gestured in front of him with his chin before sliding her hips from his in a careful move, despite the nasty dual protest from his brain and his southern bits. "Bellamy, Jackson Carter."

Jackson's eyes could've doubled for a pair of sky-blue Frisbees as they darted from Bellamy to Shane to the door and back again. "I, uh. Wow. I'm really sorry. I didn't mean to . . . wow. Yeah."

Bellamy singlehandedly diffused Jackson's awkwardness and Shane's dilemma with one smooth move. She popped up from beneath the blanket, folding it back behind her to give Shane some breathing room before she stood up and padded, sock-footed, over to the spot where Jackson stood gaping.

"Hi, Jackson. Nice to meet you." Bellamy extended her hand. Her no-nonsense smile made it look like she'd just waltzed into a job interview, not off the concrete floor of a garage where she'd been tangled around the guy's best friend.

Under any other circumstances, Shane would've had a good, long laugh at the look on Jackson's face. As it was, Shane was still working on talking Mr. Happy down from the good-morning-to-*you* ledge, so he shut up and stayed put in his spot on the floor.

"Nice to . . . meet you, too," Jackson said, but it came out like a question. He shook her hand, then turned his attention to Shane. "Sorry to intrude. I finished my shift and was headed home, but I saw your truck. I wanted to make sure you were okay in here. I didn't know . . . well . . . you didn't mention that you had, uh, company . . ."

Bellamy's cheeks flushed, but she didn't look away. "I came by yesterday to check on my car, and we got snowed in when the blizzard warning closed the roads." She squinted toward the windows, wincing at the unforgiving sunlight pouring in.

"Oh. Well, the main roads are pretty passable now. You, ah, want me to plow the lot so you can get out?"

Shane got up off the floor, the ache in his shoulder and neck making him instantly sorry. "Yeah, man. That would be great." He looked out into the lot to the road beyond with unease. "Hey, she's in that Beamer, and she needs to go back up the mountain to the resort." Shane jutted his chin toward the front of the building where Bellamy had left her friend's car. He could just see the thing pitching over the guardrail in his mind's eye, even with the roads cleared.

Jackson let out a low whistle and looked at Bellamy. "Well, you'll probably be okay getting back, but you'll have to take it really slow."

"Oh, I'll be fine." She waved a *no problem* hand through the air, but it lost its *oomph* as both men gave her wary looks in response. "Don't you think?" she tacked on.

"Tell you what." Jackson's eyes shifted to Shane's for a fraction of a second before settling back on Bellamy. "I've got to head that way to get home anyhow. Why don't you follow right behind me? Main roads could probably use another plowing anyhow, what with the drifting."

Note to self. Buy Jackson a round at the Double Shot. Maybe two. The resort was nowhere near Jackson's route home.

Her face crinkled in confusion. "Wait . . . you took the snowplow home with you?"

Jackson's good-natured laugh rang through the space of the garage, and any remaining strains of awkwardness disappeared. "You could look at it that way. I have a plow blade that attaches to the front of my truck for side jobs. I'd guess not a lot of people in the city do that, huh?"

Bellamy shook her head, framing her sheepish smile

with a couple of wisps of hair that tumbled free around her face. "No."

"Well, it's not as big-deal as the heavy-duty trucks, but it'll clear the road for you okay," Jackson offered with a smile of his own.

She wavered. "If you're sure it wouldn't put you out, maybe it would be a little safer that way, since I'm not really used to driving in much snow."

"Not a problem at all."

Shane exhaled a silent breath, and he sent an equally wordless look of gratitude in Jackson's direction. At least now he wouldn't have to worry about her plunging off the side of the mountain. Worrying about why he was so worried was another story, and one he'd have to deal with later.

"Okay. So I'll just go freshen up and call Jenna and Holly to let them know I'm on my way." Bellamy moved like a delayed reaction, letting her words settle into silence before taking a step. Shane busied himself by grabbing the blanket to shake it out, trying like hell to avoid the inquisitive stare of his friend. The last thing he wanted was to have to answer a bunch of questions about whether or not he'd slept with Bellamy. He snapped the blanket for good measure.

Her bra fell to the floor at his feet, the delicate white lace so at odds with the boot-scuffed gray of the floor that even a blind man could see it.

Well, didn't *that* just dispel the mystery.

"Um." Shane took a step back from it as if it were a rattlesnake, coiled and ready to strike, while Jackson poorly fought the urge to laugh his fool head off, fake-coughing into the crook of his elbow to hide his ear-to-ear grin.

"Everything okay?" Bellamy stopped halfway to the office, turning on her heel to look at him.

Shane shifted his weight uncomfortably. "You, ah, dropped something," he mumbled, eyeballing the swath of lace and satin like it might self-destruct. Should he pick it up? Oh hell, it wasn't like the whole scene didn't scream *we did it!* anyhow. Shane scooped the delicate fabric up off the floor and folded it gently into his palm while Jackson grabbed his wallet from the workbench and hightailed it out the side door, stammering something about warming up his truck in between errant cough-laughs. As soon as Bellamy saw the offending object, she skidded to a stop and jerked her arms around her body as if she'd forgotten she hadn't been wearing the thing, but it only pushed her cleavage higher into view down the deep V of her sweater.

"Oh shit," she cursed softly, turning just pink enough to make her freaking adorable. She took a deep breath, and Shane couldn't help but zero in on the curve of her braless chest beneath the cream-colored sweater, his brain trying to convince his nether region that he couldn't see the faint outline of her nipples through the fabric.

Welcome back, hard-on.

Shane tugged his shirt lower over his jeans as he passed the bra over. "Jackson might not have seen it," he suggested in an effort to help her save face.

She didn't even buy it for a second. "Really? Is he clinically blind?" An uncharacteristic giggle escaped from her lips, followed up by a full-on laugh.

"Well . . . okay. But he's cool," Shane said, starting to laugh with her.

She settled her face into a smile. "Now that I've flashed my undergarments at your friend, I guess I should replace them and make that call. Holly and Jenna are probably flipping by now." Bellamy's eyes skimmed the office door, but she didn't move.

"Yeah, okay. I'm going to go help Jackson. I can warm the BMW up for you if you want." He scratched his head and looked at her, simultaneously loving and hating that damned sweater and the suggestion of what lay beneath it.

"That would be great. I'll be out in a second to help." She fished the keys out of her coat pocket and passed them over to him, her fingers touching his for a brief, electric second.

He was never going to get rid of this stupid hard-on.

"Sure. Take your time."

He watched her walk the entire way to the office before turning to go outside.

Jackson went all cat-that-ate-the-canary the second Shane stepped out the door, unrolling the driver's side window down to the door frame in spite of the frigid temperature to fix him with raised eyebrows and a huge grin. The sunlight was bright enough to be borderline obnoxious, and Shane had to squint his eyes down to slits just to see through the glare.

"Hey, hop in." Jackson tipped his head toward the passenger door. "I can have you cleared in a couple of minutes."

Shane yanked the passenger door open and knocked the snow off his boots before getting into Jackson's pickup. There had to be at least a foot of snow on the ground, but it was hard to tell with all the drifting.

"How much snow fell?" he asked, but Jackson shook his head and laughed.

"Oh, no you don't. I'm not talking snowfall totals with you, you dog! How the hell did you end up on the floor with Miss She's-Not-My-Type in the middle of a goddamn blizzard? And sorry I barged in on you," he added, putting the truck in gear.

Shane dismissed the apology with a wave. "Don't worry about it. We were just sleeping." He avoided the other question like it was every strain of the plague.

"Uh-huh. Right. I'm sure that's exactly how her bra made it to the floor. Are you gonna tell me that you made water balloons with the condoms missing from my wallet, too? 'Cause really, I could call bullshit on you all day."

Shit. Time to concede. "Okay, okay. She came out yesterday morning to talk to me about her car and got stuck here in the snow. You think I was going to let her drive that BMW with the roads like they were?" Shane shrugged. "So, you know. You called to say the roads were closed, and then we were stranded together." He trailed off, letting Jackson fill in the blanks.

Jackson shook his head. "Leave it to you to get stranded with a pretty girl. If it had been me, I'd have been stuck with Mrs. Teasdale or something." He arched a brow at Shane, maneuvering the truck to keep clearing the snow. "You know, when I told you I thought you should get laid, I didn't think you'd actually do anything about it."

Something he couldn't quite name needled its way into Shane's system, snapping his head up. "It didn't happen like that." The words came out on a warning, low and with more of an edge than Shane intended.

"Whoa, take it easy. I didn't mean anything by it. It's just that she's the first girl you've been with since you moved here last year. I'm a little surprised, is all." The scrape and rumble of the snowplow was the only sound between them for a long pause.

"Sorry. I'm a little surprised, myself." Shane looked out the window at the snowdrifts. "Thanks for making sure she gets back okay. I know it's out of your way." Jackson really had been stretching the hell out of the truth when he'd said going by the resort was on his way home.

He chuckled. "Look, if you're going to get juiced about a girl, she must be something special. Figure it's not a bad plan to make sure she gets back intact. Plus, I'm just that kind of guy."

Unable to help it, Shane cracked a grin. "Yeah, you're a regular saint." He paused to snicker before continuing. "And I'm not juiced about her. I mean, don't get me wrong. I like her and all, but she's an uptown girl through and through." He thought of Bellamy's fancy background. When she'd finally admitted last night that she'd earned her MBA from Penn, he wasn't sure whether to be impressed or a little sick. It wasn't just one of the best MBA programs in the United States; it was ranked in the top five in the world.

And Shane lived in a five-hundred-square-foot cabin in the mountains and wanted nothing more than to be a grease monkey for the rest of his natural born life. Talk about incompatibility.

Except she'd been so down to earth when she'd told him how she'd made half a dozen eggs explode like a bad science experiment in her parents' microwave, then risked life and limb to scale a nine-foot ladder to clean the ceiling so they wouldn't find out. And her laugh was the perfect combination of provocative and sweet, just enough to make him feel torn between wanting to laugh along with her and kiss her until he ran out of air.

He didn't even want to get started on how good it felt to do more than kiss her. He'd just gotten rid of that hard-on, thank you very much.

"Helllllooo, earth to Shane?" Jackson waved a hand across Shane's field of vision, making him jump.

"Sorry, what?" He really needed to snap out of it. Spacing out like that definitely wasn't his bag, no matter how enticing the vision might be.

"I said, just because she's a city girl doesn't mean it won't work out. Who knows? Maybe she'll surprise you."

Shane shook his head, trying unsuccessfully to blot the thought of Bellamy's laugh from his mind. The sound was there to stay, even if the rest of her was headed back down the mountain in less than a week.

"Maybe." He shrugged, focusing out the window again.

But the word tasted as cold as the snow they were shoveling.

Chapter Eighteen

"Oh my *God,* are you okay and if you tell me there's no dirt this time I will positively die! Twenty-four hours of being snowbound with Mr. Goodwrench *had* to have yielded a little play! And, really, are you okay?"

On the Richter Scale According to Holly, Bellamy's adventure in snowland turned out to rank a lot higher than she'd anticipated.

"Wow. Hello just isn't in your repertoire, is it?" Bellamy asked on a lopsided grin. "And to answer your question, yes. I'm fine." She hugged her friends before heading into the kitchenette with both of them hot on her heels.

Jenna fastened her with a wry smile. "Glad you're back in one piece. There's got to be at least a foot of snow on the ground out there." She clucked her tongue and aimed her glance at the pretty-as-a-picture view from the main room of the suite.

"Fifteen inches, but that's the unofficial total." At least, that's what Jackson had said just before they'd left the garage, with Bellamy following him at an embarrassing fifteen miles an hour. The roads were still pretty slick, but the longer trip back gave her plenty of time to think about all that had happened in the last couple of days.

Some of the images were a lot more appealing than others.

Bellamy pressed her glorious post-sex smile between her lips in an effort to conceal it. "Do we have any food left? I'm starving." Her stomach chose that exact moment to chime in with a gurgle that would've made Sigourney Weaver's Alien look like a wallflower, and for the first time in twenty-four hours, she realized how hungry she really was.

"Oh, God, honey. Of course you should eat." Holly rushed forward to yank on random cupboard doors. "And if you should feel some burning urge to, I don't know, tell us every gory detail of being stuck in a blizzard with the white-hot mechanic guy in between bites, we wouldn't shush you. Pretzels?" She shook a half-empty bag at Bellamy, eyebrows lifted.

"That'll work." At this stage of the game, Bellamy wasn't above instant gratification to keep her stomach from imploding, although what she really needed was an actual meal. "But I'd give my left arm for a good omelet."

Jenna snorted and slid onto a stool at the breakfast bar. "Then don't order one from room service."

"Right. I've got to get back to Joe's. I think I can finagle flatbread pizzas out of that toaster oven if I play my cards right." Bellamy canted her head at the oven where she'd successfully melted the Brie over thick slices of French bread a couple days earlier. The pretzels were kind of a disappointment after the thought of pizza, but she was too hungry to be picky. She started to crunch her way through the bag, much to the delight of her gastric system.

"Why would you go grocery shopping when we'll be

back in the city by nightfall? Ooooh, we can hit up Pietro's for dinner if you want a pizza," Holly said, leaning against the counter opposite Jenna, who chimed in with bright eyes.

"Oh, hell yes. Pietro's might make the fact that I have to get up at oh-dark-thirty for work tomorrow at least a *little* more bearable. We're already a day behind getting back, what with Mother Nature's arctic tantrum. Hey, speaking of which, did you get the thing with your car ironed out? I can run you back up here on Saturday if you want. For a nominal bribe, of course." Jenna winked at her over the rim of her coffee mug before making a face at its contents.

Bellamy pressed her lips together for an altogether different reason than she had a moment before and shifted her weight back and forth in the door frame of the kitchen.

"Yeah. About that." She hedged for just a second before realizing that it was better to just say what had tumbled around in her mind the whole way back from the garage. "I'm not going home with you guys today."

"You're whaaaaa?" Holly was nothing if not eloquent. She pushed off from the counter to goggle at Bellamy.

But somewhere between mile marker 46 and the front gates of the resort, her mind had been made up, and backing down wasn't part of the deal. "I'm not going home with you guys today. I'm going to stay here for the rest of the week until my car is done." Despite the fact that they scared the crap out of her, Bellamy's words felt deliciously good as they rolled off her tongue. Well, maybe deliciously good spiced with just a teensy hint of bat shit crazy, but still. At eighty-twenty, she'd take it.

Jenna's eyebrows lifted so high, they were in danger of merging with her hairline. "Are you serious?"

She nodded with certainty. "Yeah. I have a lot to iron out in terms of my career. I need to figure out what I'm going to do, and making another error in judgment isn't something I can afford, literally or figuratively." Bellamy winced, but continued. "Look, I know me. If I go back to the city to think it through, it's bound to cloud my judgment. I'll get maybe two floors up on my way to clean out my desk before the guilt kills me. Then I'll just end up in HR, groveling for my job back in less time than you can say *pretty please with sugar on top*."

She held up a hand for emphasis. "I'm not saying it's out of the question for me to stay at the bank on another team, or to go somewhere else as an analyst. But I have a lot of options, and they're overwhelming as hell. I need to think about my next step in an impartial setting, that's all." Bellamy felt the tension that had been triple-knotting her shoulders every time she thought about her job stand up and take note.

Good, because she was serving her stress its walking papers, come hell or high water. Or a life of eating Ramen noodles. Or moving into her parents' basement.

Bellamy shook her head. Nope. It wasn't going to come to that. She had a plan.

Please, God, let it work. Ramen noodles would send her over the edge.

"But we already checked out," Holly said, pausing to chew her lip.

"I know, and I know you both need to go home." The fact that they both had jobs to get back to wasn't lost on Bellamy, even if it did sting a little. "Don't worry, I'll be fine. It's four days, maybe five, depending on how long my transmission takes." Bellamy wondered how long it would take before the word *transmission* didn't cause her neurons to automatically fire off the eye-roll signal to her optic nerve.

Of course, her car trouble *had* landed her in Shane's lap. Quite literally. On second thought . . .

"This decision wouldn't happen to have anything to do with a certain tall, dark, and handsome car mechanic, would it?" Jenna's smirk threatened to consume her face, and Bellamy blanked her brain waves as if Jenna had somehow honed in on them.

"Nope. Not at all." She picked some imaginary lint off of her sweater and went across the room to dial down the thermostat. Spending twenty-four hours in that drafty garage must have thrown her system out of whack. The suite was hotter than hell.

"Not even a tiny bit?" Jenna waggled her dark blond brows.

Bellamy pursed her lips over a smile. "Not even a tiny bit."

"Not one molecule of your being is staying in the hopes that you'll see Shane again?" Jenna crossed her arms over her chest, firm with teasing disbelief.

"I'm not staying here to be with him on a molecular level or any other level, no." Her mind flitted back to the lurchy backflip thing her stomach did when he wrapped his arms around her and breathed good night into her hair. Okay, so maybe her molecules had had a weak moment. But it was just the one. And she sure as hell wasn't *staying* just so she could see him again. She had bigger fish to fry.

Even though the bigger fish didn't feel all warm and strong and downright damn perfect against her skin like Shane did.

Holly gave a pouty moue, breaking into Bellamy's thoughts. "That's it? Not one speck of dirt—not one *iota* of dishy goodness? Can you at least tell me if he's still a good kisser?"

Bellamy's mouth curved into a catlike grin. "I said I wasn't staying *because* of him. I didn't say I wasn't going to see him again." She thought of Shane's promise to call her later and it sent her grin into overdrive.

"You tricky bitch!" Holly accused through a giggle, sliding down from her bar stool to wave a finger at Bellamy, who held up her hands in defeat.

"Yeah, yeah, so sue me. He's still a good kisser."

"How good?" Holly pressed. Even Jenna gave a subtle lean in Bellamy's direction to hear the answer.

Bellamy's overdrive went into overdrive. "Good. Really, really good." The breathy, sigh-y thing wasn't normally her gig, but her voice box and her chest were bound and determined to conspire against her in an epic coup against good sense.

Oh, screw it. Good sense went out the window days ago.

"I knew it! I knew you hooked up with him again!" Holly crowed, coming into the main room to plop down on the couch, motioning for Bellamy to do the same.

"Of course she hooked up with him again. You can't manufacture that look on her face." Jenna abandoned her coffee cup on the counter to curl up in a chair across from Holly.

"There's no look on my face," Bellamy said, losing the battle of wills with her smile.

"Hah! Give us a little credit, please. Your face is practically broadcasting *I just had a morning romp in the snow*!"

"It was last night, not this morning," Bellamy said tartly, hand firm on her hip. Take that!

Jenna laughed. "You're so easy to corner, it's not even fair."

Damn it. *Damn* it! Bellamy opened her mouth to flip some glib comment at her, but she couldn't. She was flat-out busted. "Shut up," she replied, letting her smile have its way with her.

"Look, it's not my fault that fabulous sex shows on your face. That's on you and Mr. Goodwrench, okay? What I want to know is exactly how you two got funky in a garage. I mean, the place is logistically challenged, to say the least." Jenna sealed her fishing expedition with a good-natured grin.

Bellamy sat on the couch and drew her knees to her chest with a laugh. "It's not *that* challenged. We just had to get a little creative, that's all. And no, I'm not drawing you a diagram. Use your imagination if you must."

"How can you possibly get creative in a garage?" Jenna's face bent in concentration, but Holly beat her to the *a-ha!* punch.

"Oh, stop it! You did it in your car? I'm never riding shotgun in that thing again."

"Your days of riding in the Miata are safe, sweetie. We didn't do it in my car." Bellamy fielded their twin looks of disappointment with satisfaction.

Not so easy to corner after all, huh.

"Wait, you did sleep with him, didn't you?" Jenna measured Bellamy with careful regard, and Bellamy had to cave in. She'd toyed with them enough; plus, she was dying to say it.

"Of course I slept with him. We did it in *his* car."

All three women burst into a chorus of giggles, and Bellamy doled out enough details to satisfy her friends yet still keep her dignity intact.

"So I assume you're going to see him again, since you're staying here all week?" Holly inquired in the gossip-girl's version of the full court press.

Bellamy nodded. "He's going to call me later, yeah. And

I'll obviously have to see him at least one more time to get my car." She skirted the issue out loud just as well as she did in her head. There really were more important things to consider, like finding a decent meal, making sure she had a place to stay for the rest of the week and trying to pick up the pieces of her career. In that order.

Jenna's eyes flicked over hers, and Bellamy was grateful when she didn't push it. "I wish we could stay here with you, although now I'm not quite as worried that you'll be all by your lonesome. Are you sure you'll be okay up here for the rest of the week?"

Bellamy nodded, squinching her toes into the couch cushions through her socks. "Yeah. It'll be good for me."

"Well, call us if it's not. I'm not going to have you stuck here if you want to be at home."

But what Bellamy wanted was about as far from the city as a girl could get.

She'd intentionally left out the weird backflip maneuver in her gut and the fact that she and Shane had fallen asleep in each other's arms. There was no need for her friends to go jumping the gun and getting all mushy on her, and definitely no need for them—or anybody—to think she was doing something insane like falling for the guy.

Okay, fine, so she'd slept with him, which was a big deal, but it wasn't really her fault. Shane had surprised the hell out of her by being all tender and sweet about the stupid crying thing, and it threw her for a loop. Her defenses had been tongue-tied and twisted the minute he brushed the tears from her face, and they only got more turned around when he laid that kiss on her at the workbench, like some kind of sexual knock-out punch that would've brought a convent full of nuns to their knees.

She'd never been particularly quick about sleeping with

anybody, but that kiss had been her undoing, like a loose strand of yarn on a sweater begging to be pulled. Bellamy hadn't planned on letting him unwind her until she was nothing more than a pile of soft thread on the ground, but that's exactly what had happened. And now she had to face facts.

The acrobatics going on between her chest and her hips every time she thought of Shane's deep, rumbling laugh or every time she caught a whiff of his scent from her sweater were just a by-product of his sweet sympathy for her crying jag and the multiple orgasms he'd given her. It didn't mean she was going to go all ga-ga for him or anything. Period. End of story.

No matter how gut-fluttery the thought of him made her.

In the three hours since he'd gotten home, Shane's phone had morphed into something roughly the size of a moose, and it did everything but dance and sing and scream *pick me up and dial, buddy*! every time he so much as glanced at it.

He'd stuck around the garage for more than half the day, fielding a handful of phone calls from people who'd been in fender benders or needed to be dragged out of ditches. Grady's wasn't set up to do body work, which was a damned shame considering that was the extent of what the fender bender people needed. Still, Shane was happy to keep his body and brain occupied so they wouldn't gang up on him and drift back to the rush of Bellamy's skin on his, and how what he really wanted to do was call her even though he had nothing to say.

Eh. Scratch that. He had plenty to say, it's just that he was pretty sure "I dig you way more than I should and I can't for the life of me forget the incredible way you smell and would you *please* shut me up by saying you'll let me take you out to dinner" would make him look like the biggest idiot on two legs.

But something had clicked inside him the minute his lips found hers at that workbench, something seamless and daring and good. He hadn't been able to put his finger on it all day, even though he'd eventually given in and let himself linger on his thoughts of Bellamy in an effort to get it out of his system. It finally hit him on his way back to the cabin, and he hadn't been able to shake the idea since it had popped into his mind.

She felt right.

"That's just fucking ridiculous," Shane said to the moose-phone, giving it a petulant glare. "I've known the woman for all of five days. Yes, she's pretty . . ."

She's downright stunning, the moose-phone interrupted knowingly.

"And yes, she's nice . . ."

Screw nice. You like *her, and you know it.*

"But let's be realistic. Bellamy lives in the city. She has an Ivy League degree and leads an Ivy League life. And I'm not that guy." Shane's voice went cold over his closing words.

But you slept with her, and she's expecting you to call. You're not that *guy, either.*

Well, shit. The moose-phone knew what the hell it was talking about. Shane had never had a one-night stand in his life, but even if he had, he knew enough about women and sex to know that what had happened between him and Bellamy was definitely not that.

Plus, the stupid moose-phone was right. As much as he didn't want to say it out loud, Shane really couldn't deny the fact that he did like Bellamy. In exactly the way his inner voice implied.

"Fine," he grumbled, swiping the receiver from its base. "But I have the feeling I'm going to regret this."

Or maybe you're terrified that you won't, you big baby. Now shut up and dial.

Chapter Nineteen

"Hello?"

All it took were two tiny syllables for Shane to realize that his inner voice had his number, big-time. Man, the sound of Bellamy's voice was like honey, velvety sweet and so damned good.

"Hey. It's me. I mean, it's Shane." He swung the phone away from his mouth to clear his throat in his sleeve.

Her laugh could've melted butter. "Hey, me. What have you been up to on this fine evening?"

"Truth?" He sank into the Barcalounger, cradling the phone between his ear and shoulder while he kicked up his feet into the long shadows cast off by the fresh sunset.

"Of course."

"I'm sitting at home in the dark in a nasty old chair, talking on the phone with you. What're you doing?"

"Taking a bath." Bellamy's voice was so smooth that Shane questioned his hearing.

"Sorry, what?" Nah. He had to have misunderstood. Surely, there was no way she was naked on the other end of the phone.

"I'm taking a bath. You know, the big, oblong thing in the bathroom, usually full of hot water and bubbles. Well, probably not bubbles in your case, but still. You get the idea, right?"

Oh, he got the idea loud and clear and in Technicolor. Shit, he needed to *not* be lying here in the dark, listening to the purr of her voice and thinking about her hot, naked body in a bathtub. "Do you like burgers?" he blurted, trying like hell to think of his battle-ax of a third-grade teacher, the sludge that came out of an engine when it was way overdue for an oil change, anything other than Bellamy's perfect breasts playing hide and seek with a bunch of bubbles.

"Ohhhkay. A little random, but still a good question. Sure." She paused to laugh again, and Shane could swear he heard the soft trickling of water in the background.

He tried to focus, but his mind—and a couple of other parts of his anatomy—were still stuck on the idea of the bubbles. It wasn't his fault that she had such fantastic breasts, really. Who could blame a guy?

Bellamy cleared her throat at the exact moment a voice from deep in Shane's mind screamed *burgers, dumbass!* but he faked flawless composure as he replied.

"Well, your trip to Pine Mountain wouldn't really be complete if you didn't have one of Lou's burgers. They're a culinary masterpiece."

That got her attention. "Reeeeeally?"

Shane could all but hear her grin over the word. "Scout's honor."

"Shane Griffin, are you asking me out on a date?" Although Bellamy's voice teased its way over the phone line, it tightened his gut with its implication.

Oh, fuck it. The moose-phone was never wrong.

"I believe I am. What do you say, Bellamy Blake?"

"I say how fast can you come and get me? I'm starving."

When she'd asked Shane how fast he could come and get her, it had kind of been metaphorically speaking, although she wasn't kidding about being beyond hungry. When he told her he could be at the resort to pick her up in half an hour, she'd had to eat her words and scramble her butt out of the bathtub, but not before she gave herself a good scrubdown with her favorite yummy-smelling shower gel and shaved her legs with careful (albeit quick) precision.

A review of what was left of her clean clothes told her she'd better figure out a way to hit a Laundromat, because all she had left was a pair of black yoga pants and a matching turtleneck. Thank God her mother had drilled it into her to bring extra underwear on a trip, "just in case," although the unmentionables in question were the one dreaded thong that Bellamy owned. Sometimes necessity, or in this case, yoga pants, dictated the use of such torture devices, and in order to banish weird bum lines, she'd just have to take one for the team. *Not* that anyone would be looking at her butt, per se. It was really just a general rule.

Dear God, if you're up there and you're listening, could you please let Shane Griffin want to look at my butt? I'd really appreciate it.

She made her way down to the lobby exactly thirty minutes after she'd gotten off the phone with Shane and was surprised to see him in the archway of the main entrance. The scattering of stubble that had graced his jaw earlier was now gone, and the rhythm of his body as he walked over to her suggested casual purpose. It was probably a bad sign to start the evening so hot and bothered, but unless a cold front came whipping through the lobby right then and there, Bellamy would have to chill out on her own.

"Hey! Wow, you weren't kidding about the thirty minutes, huh?" She clasped her hands together in front of her, not quite sure what to do with them.

"I don't kid when it comes to women who say they're starving. You look great." Shane leaned in to kiss her on the cheek, just as easy as could be, and the simple gesture sent her nerves packing. This wasn't some awkward date with forced conversation or false pretenses. It was just her and Shane, going out for burgers.

And it felt good.

"Thanks. This is my burger-getting outfit. Glad you like it." Bellamy gave a little twirl before putting on her coat.

Shane laughed. "Well, I hope your friends don't mind too much that I'm stealing you away for the evening. I promise to have you back by midnight."

They walked out to the main entrance of the resort, and Bellamy steeled herself as they got to the front door and Shane pushed it open for her.

"Oh, they left to go back to the city about four hours ago." She jumped when the cold air slammed into her like a brick wall, wrapping her arms around her body in an instinctive maneuver. "God, do you ever get used to that?"

"In a weird way, yeah. Your friends left?" Shane put his arm around her shoulder and they walked in sync through the parking lot, his hip in her side and her imagination going full throttle.

"Oh, ah, yeah. They both had to get back to work. I decided to stay and wait for my car."

"Hmm. That might be just as well, because I didn't

really have any intention of getting you back early." Shane nudged her with his hip.

She bumped him right back. "At least you're honest about your bad intentions."

He fixed her with a look that arrowed right into her chest in a white-hot streak of *oh my God* before responding. "They might be good intentions, depending on how you look at it."

They arrived at his truck all too soon, in Bellamy's opinion, and he let her go to open her door so she could climb in. She was met by the faded scent of cedar and pine, and it made her wonder if everything he touched was left smelling all wonderful and Shane-like.

He popped the driver's side door open and started the truck, which warmed up quickly since he'd just been in it. "So you're staying at the resort by yourself?"

"Yup. I don't have a job, so staying in that suite was out of the question if I couldn't split it with Jenna and Holly. But I talked to Jenna's friend, Chase, who's the events coordinator, and he got me an extended stay rate since I'll be here for more than a week. Plus, the weekday rates go down pretty significantly anyhow, so I decided to stay rather than go home and come back."

Shane winced as he pulled away from the front gate of the resort. "I feel really bad about your transmission being stuck in Ohio. I put in a call to the distributor after you left today and told them I needed it ASAP. The guy said if we're really lucky, it'll get here Thursday, but I wouldn't bet on that." He kept his eyes on the road, but his remorse was clear even in the orange glow of the dashboard lights.

"It's not your fault it snowed, Shane. In fact, it might be a good thing. Sticking around gives me some time to figure out what I'm going to do and explore all of my options. If I job search in the city, I'm afraid I'll be guilted into something because it's in front of me rather than picking it because I want it, you know?"

Shane creased his brow, but kept his gaze on the windshield. "Do you always have a plan?"

Bellamy let out a *doesn't-everybody* laugh. "Well, yeah. I started by ruling out the definite no's, namely staying unemployed and going back to work for Attila the Boss. I bit the bullet and called the head of HR at the bank after I got back today, but it turned out okay. Apparently, my ex-boss has quite the track record." She paused to give her eyebrows a provocative raise.

"Well, that's not really shocking. What, did she get caught eating her young in the break room or something?"

Bellamy was in danger of working her laugh right into the embarrassing snort that popped out only for the really good stuff. "No, but let's just say I'm not the first employee to have issues with her 'questionable management skills.'" She put air quotes around the words and sighed. "In the end, it wasn't just her that made me miserable there, so I politely declined HR's offer to move to another team. At least I know my résumé isn't trashed over the whole thing, though." Having the reassurance of a good reference despite her showdown with Bosszilla really did go a long way toward easing her mind.

"Okay, so what's next then, if you're not going to stay there?" Shane's eyes flicked over her for a second before returning to the road.

Bellamy ran her teeth over her bottom lip in thought. "I'm not sure. My strengths are definitely on the management end, but the idea of sitting in another cubicle with a stack of papers equivalent to nine miles of rain forest makes my skin crawl. I guess I could do something more hands-on, or even go work for my parents, but I'd have to see what's out there to get a better idea of what I'm qualified for."

Shane pulled into a familiar parking lot and scratched his head. "Jeez, this place is packed." He scanned the snow-packed gravel. "I don't see a parking spot anywhere."

"Not to ask a stupid question, but why are we at the Double Shot?" She squinted at the spotlit side of the building, where faded paint boasted the name of the bar just as it had four nights ago when she'd last seen it.

"Oh, sorry. I didn't tell you? Lou works the grill out here. The burgers are incredible." He muttered an indiscriminant curse under his breath as they circled the lot again, coming up on a group of people rushing toward the building.

"Excuse me," Shane called, rolling down his window and catching the attention of someone so bundled up, Bellamy couldn't tell if it was a man or a woman. "Do you know what's with the crowd?"

A high-pitched giggle left no doubt as to the gender of the outerwear mummy. "Yeah. The Screaming Taste Museum got snowed out of the city last night and they needed a place to do their show. It was this or nothing." She giggled again, giving Shane a long look like she wanted to eat him. "See you inside, sweetheart," she finished before skipping off to join her friends.

Bellamy stifled a laugh of her own while Shane shot her a wry glance. "Do I even want to know what the hell a Screaming Taste Museum is?"

She grinned. "I doubt it, but if you figure it out, I don't think I need to know."

He released a slow exhale. "I'm really sorry. It seems I promised you something I can't deliver."

"Well, that leaves you in a jam, my friend, because I am still starving," she said gravely.

God, that whole serious-face thing he did back at her was really endearing. And sexy. Did she mention wildly sexy? He looked borderline worried, and guilt kicked her mouth into gear.

"Shane, I'm kidding. Well, not about being hungry. But this is no big deal. We can always pick something up and go back to the resort if you want."

He shook his head and laughed, pulling to the exit. "Bellamy, this isn't Philly. You can't just hit up Pietro's for a couple of calzones on your way home. Unless you like McDonald's, your options for eating out around here are slim and none, and slim is having a weird rock concert in its dining area right now."

Bellamy pulled away to look at him, and despite the niggling voice in the back of her mind that told her not to, she let her question off the tip of her tongue. "Did you go to school in the city or something?"

It would explain how he knew about Butcher and Singer the other day, and the reference to Pietro's. God, everybody who had ever lived in Philly had horked down a pie or two at Pietro's. The pizza was legendary.

Shane's body went rigid in the driver's seat. "Why do you ask?"

Well, she'd taken a step and landed smack in the middle of what looked like Shane's biggest sore spot. She decided to tread carefully, but tread nonetheless. "Not too many people know about Pietro's unless they've been there. I just thought . . ."

"No, I didn't go to school in the city," he said, cutting her off.

"But you've been there." Her gut told her it hadn't been on the occasional weekend jaunt down the mountain, either.

"It's been a while." His voice made the weather outside look downright balmy.

"Do you want to talk about why you hate it so much?"

"No." Silence stretched around them like a blanket of thorns.

When he didn't elaborate, Bellamy nodded. "Okay." After a minute that felt more like an hour and a half, she decided to go with her gut. "Shane, I'm not really sure what I said to make you uncomfortable, but whatever it was, I'm sorry."

He snapped his gaze to hers, his eyes looking almost black in the diffused streetlight from the parking lot. "Jesus, Bellamy. I'm the one who should be apologizing. It's not you, I just—"

Before he could finish, she snatched up his hand and squeezed it hard enough to cut him off. "Let's make a deal, you and I. I won't say anything about the city until you feel like talking about it if you don't ever, ever utter those three words to me again. Fair?"

Shane blinked, shadowy lashes playing against his skin. "I feel like an ass. It's just not something I like to talk about. With anybody." His fingers tightened around hers, and he lifted their hands up so hers rested just under his lips. While the serious look he'd given her when she teased him earlier had been open and sexy, the expression he had on now told her not to pry. So he wasn't a concrete jungle kind of guy. Big deal.

She could live with it if he could.

"A wise old man once shared his sage wisdom with me, and I believe it applies here. What was it that he said . . . oh, right. No apologies." The corners of Bellamy's mouth hinted upward in the slightest of smiles.

"I'm only twenty-nine, you know."

Shane's bemused expression made her want to chuck any plans for dinner so she could have him instead, but she held her ground.

"And wise beyond your years," she teased, enjoying the glower that was doing a poor excuse of covering his lop-sided grin. She lifted her brow at him, smiling. "Now do my stomach a favor and head back up the main road toward Joe's Grocery, would you?" She didn't let go of his hand as he lowered it to the armrest between them, keeping her fingers twined around his.

God, they felt good there.

"Let me get this right. You want to go grocery shopping at seven o'clock on a Tuesday night?"

Bellamy's lips curved into a devilish smile. "If we can't go to dinner, then dinner is going to come to us instead."

"Cart or basket?" Shane asked, surveying the front of Joe's Grocery.

Bellamy chewed her lip before caving in. "We'd better go with a cart. I need some stuff for my room back at the resort, too. You're the car guy, so you can drive."

He pulled a cart from the row where they were lined up by the entrance. "So what'd you have in mind for dinner?"

"I'm not sure yet. I want to let the food talk to me."

"You want to *what*?" Shane laughed.

Bellamy's face flushed, and she walked over to the first

row of produce, lined up in baskets by the front window. "I want to get a feel for what's good, what I'm in the mood for. Sometimes I don't know until I see it. Like the other day when I was in here, the Brie and figs looked so good, I just couldn't say no." She scanned the pears and navel oranges carefully, but gave them a reverent pass-by.

"So the food talks to you?" Shane creased his brow, trying not to crash the cart into anything as he watched her moving along. Damned if she wasn't just as captivating as the first time he'd seen her here.

"Well, not literally. I'm not crazy." She stopped to give him a healthy nudge, then reached past him. A flicker of interest passed over her face, like a light on a dimmer being turned up to a soft glow. "But look. These are just so pretty."

Bellamy's fingers brushed over a handful of deep red fruit, the look on her face shifting from honesty to pure, pared down beauty and back again. She scooped one up, cradling its weight in her palm. "See? The color is perfect. And here," she murmured, reaching down to place the ruby-colored globe in his hand. "It just feels right. So no, this pomegranate isn't sprouting lips and starting casual conversation with me right here in the produce aisle, but it's speaking to me all the same."

Shane knew, in a far-off, disembodied kind of way, that he should be saying something to Bellamy, making some kind of witty remark or flirty banter. At this point, even a grunt or nod would do the trick. But he couldn't.

He was too busy wondering how the hell he'd met a woman who looked at food—hell, at *anything*—the exact same way he thought about cars, and trying with all his might not to fall in love with her on the spot.

"Sorry. I'm sure that just sounds crazy to you." She slid

the pomegranate from his hand and gently put it in the cart, then turned toward the apples with a sheepish look that bordered on embarrassed.

"It doesn't sound crazy to me at all." Oh, thank God. He had a voice box after all.

Her laugh stirred around in his chest. "Really? It sounds a little crazy to me, and I'm the one who said it. But it's really how I look at the whole thing, so . . ." She trailed off to fill a bag halfway with apples, placing them in the cart.

"That's how I knew I was meant to work on cars." The words slipped out of him quietly, but they stopped Bellamy in her tracks.

"It is?" she asked, her eyes on him like emerald velvet over steel, both soft and unyielding.

The logical part of his brain, the one that had ruled everything about him until the minute he'd laid eyes on her four days ago, told him without hesitation to close his mouth. He shouldn't dive into any of this with her, because it was going to open up a can of don't-go-there that he'd jammed the lid over, one he swore would never get opened again.

But the words came out anyway.

"Just because I always knew I loved cars doesn't mean I always knew I'd be a mechanic. For a while, I wasn't. But I was never happy, not like I am now, because nothing else ever spoke to me the way cars do. They feel right under my hands, and the complexities that turn a lot of people around when they look under the hood just make sense to me."

Shane registered her lips parting in surprise, but kept on regardless. "So while there are plenty of things I could do with my life, a bunch of things I'm good at, I had to pick the one that spoke to me. The one I just knew was a part of me. So no. That doesn't sound crazy to me at all. In fact, it makes perfect sense."

They stood there in front of the baskets of apples for a long minute, just looking at each other. Bellamy's eyes never wavered from his, and even though his mind screamed with vulnerability, the only thing that passed between them was understanding. Finally, she gave a tiny nod and spoke.

"It does, doesn't it?"

And in that moment, Shane knew he was in over his head with Bellamy Blake.

Chapter Twenty

"Whoa. You really weren't kidding when you said all you had was ketchup and a frying pan." Bellamy took a step back and put her hands on her hips, surveying Shane's kitchen with a sinking heart. This wasn't going to be easy.

He gave her an apologetic grin. "Yes, but there's wine." He bent down and rummaged through the bags at their feet until one hand shot up, victorious.

Bellamy lifted a brow. "Very nice, Sherlock. You got a corkscrew for that?"

"Oh, shit."

Her laughter was automatic and felt so good it ached. "You mind if I help myself to the kitchen here? The sooner I get started, the sooner we can eat." She gestured to the tiny space. The stove had to be circa 1960, but it was a sturdy son of a bitch, and all four burners looked functional. Come to think of it, she'd cooked on worse.

"I take it you want the frying pan and not the ketchup, but be my guest to either." Shane reached into his back pocket to reveal a Swiss army knife, and started to open the bottle of sauvignon blanc that Bellamy had been thrilled to find at Joe's.

"Thanks." She washed her hands at the sink, looking over her shoulder at Shane. "Your cabin is nice." Her eyes swept over stacked log walls the color of honey and the woodstove in the far corner across from the kitchen. True to what he'd said earlier, a recliner that looked to be conservatively four hundred years old stood sentry in the middle of the room, with an end table and a small TV stand rounding out the view. It might not be the biggest or grandest thing going, but it was cozy as hell; perfect for its surroundings and definitely perfect for Shane.

"Bellamy, your room at the resort is nice. This bottle of wine"—he paused to free the cork from the bottle with a flick of his wrist, the muted pop serving as a soft punctuation mark to emphasize his point—"is nice. I don't think I'd put my cabin in the same category. But it keeps me dry and warm, so really, I can't complain." His eyes gleamed over a half smile as he reached up to open one of the three cupboards in the kitchen.

"You really are a skip-the-pleasantries kind of guy, huh?" she said, rooting through a drawer for a knife.

"What gave it away?" Shane poured the wine into two juice glasses and handed one to her. "Sorry about the glasses. It's this or nothing."

She held hers up and clinked it against his. "This is great, thanks. You want to make yourself useful? I could use a hand." Bellamy was in her element, the ingredients already spinning around in her head, whispering about how they should be put together. She eyed the sweet potatoes and apples, mentally trying to work in how she wanted them to go with the pork chops still nestled in the bag. Thank God she'd grabbed fresh rosemary and some olive oil in case Shane hadn't been kidding about having the barest kitchen in town. Yeah, this would work out just fine.

She looked up at Shane, realizing he hadn't answered her question, or even moved since she'd started scrubbing the potatoes at the sink. "What?" she asked. He had the funniest look on his face, and hell if she could place it. "Do you hate sweet potatoes or something?" Oh, shit. He'd seen her put them in the cart, but still. Maybe he just wanted to be polite or something. She should've asked.

"No, they're my favorite."

"Oh. You just had a look on your face, that's all. Are you sure they're okay? I don't have to put them in." Eh, that was only sort of true. The dish would be kind of weird without them, but she could figure something out.

"Are you always this comfortable when you cook?" Shane's expression shifted but didn't change all the way, fluctuating into something sensual as he hooked his thumb through the belt loop of his jeans and leaned into the counter, facing her.

Heat shot through Bellamy's body and pooled between her hips, reaching down into her core with fiery twinges she had no hope of ignoring. "I, um . . ." *Focus. Focus. Focusfocusfocusfocus on the food.* "Yes."

Shane kept his eyes on hers as he moved so close she could feel the warmth rolling off of his body. He snaked an arm around her waist, and she drew in a sharp breath at his touch.

"You don't have any idea, do you?"

If she'd had any damned willpower to speak of, she'd have reminded him that she was supposed to be making dinner. But he was sliding her turtleneck away from her ear with fiery suggestion, sipping on the skin of her neck with such sweet little nibbles that her knees threatened to go on strike. Never mind what the rest of her wanted to do.

"Have any . . . oh, God, that feels really good," Bellamy

sighed, tilting her head to give him better access to her now-bare neck. Would it be bad form to just whip her shirt off in the kitchen? "Have any idea of what?"

"How happy you look around food, even in my shoe box of a kitchen." He traced his tongue around the outer curve of her ear, following with the edge of his teeth.

"We're never going to eat," she murmured in the world's weakest protest. Those pork chops had looked good, too.

"Oh yes we are," Shane said, pulling back to give her a suggestive grin.

She couldn't help it. She broke out laughing. "Shane!"

"Okay, okay." He held his hands up, laughing with her. "But you do, you know." He took a step back from her, and she felt a pang of disappointment mixed in with the rush of anticipation of what she was in for later as he washed his hands and reached for the knife and the sweet potatoes.

"What, look happy around food?" She got to work taking the pork chops out so she could season them.

Shane nodded. "Everything about you changes a little when you look at it. How do you want me to cut these?" he asked, motioning to the counter.

"Chopped would be perfect. They're kind of a pain, so be careful." Bellamy tilted her head at the pork chops and got to work.

He chuckled. "You say chopped like it means something other than 'cut in half.' You want to be more specific for those of us who are culinarily challenged?"

The edges of Bellamy's lips curved into a smile. "Sorry. Pieces about this big, give or take." She held up her fingers about two inches apart.

"Now we're talkin'." He started to wash the sweet potatoes, laid back as ever next to her in the kitchen. "So, can I ask you a personal question?"

Bellamy thought of what they'd just been doing and fought off the urge to giggle. If Shane wanted to get personal, she was all for it. "Sure."

"Why are you really afraid to go to culinary school?"

Her head snapped up. "I'm not."

He slipped a dubious glance at her, but didn't argue. "I'm just asking because it's obvious, even to a gearhead like me, that you'd be great at it. It doesn't make any sense to skip out on what you're really made for unless you've got a damned good reason. Especially when it's right in front of you."

Bellamy hedged, starting to chop the apples with the knife he passed her way. "I was thinking maybe I could go into management for a catering company or a restaurant or something," she admitted. She'd done a casual Internet search after she'd gotten off the phone with the head of HR at the bank and found that she was pretty well qualified to do both of those things, although she'd need to really do her homework about the industry to make it work.

"Yeah, but that's only half the brass ring. Are you really going to be able to watch chefs do their job while you do yours in a power suit on the sidelines?"

"Ouch," she said, frowning at him. "I'm not sure I like the whole skip-the-pleasantries thing when it comes to stuff like this."

"Look, all I'm saying is that you've got this crossroads in front of you. What would it hurt to try culinary school?"

She opened her mouth to protest, but Shane cut her off with a smoldering quirk of his lips, putting a hand on her arm that sent a little thrill of contact all the way up to her shoulder. "And I'm not buying that line about how it might wreck it for you. You're not going to hate it, darlin'. That much is crystal clear."

Bellamy wanted nothing more in that moment than to tell him that he'd known her for only four days, thank you very much. He couldn't possibly give her sound advice on something as big or impulsive as a sudden career change.

Except that, goddamn him and his sexy little smile, he saw right through her. And he was right.

"There's a little more to it than that." She kept working on dinner, and the fact that she was in Shane's kitchen, making a casual meal just like she would at home, went a long way toward chilling her out. "I know it sounds stupid, because I'm twenty-seven, but what my parents think is kind of a big deal to me, and I don't think they'd approve."

Shane's movements jerked to a halt, freezing him to the spot where he stood next to her. Well, who could blame him for thinking it was weird? Most adults didn't really worry about what their parents thought about their career, unless they were doing something deranged or illegal.

Bellamy bit her lip, then figured she'd opened the bag, so she might as well let the cat prance right on out. "My parents have owned their own realty business since I was a little girl. They started it from the ground up, just the two of them." She prepared the food while she spoke, and Shane stepped out of her way, just giving her space to move and talk.

"So when other girls were dressing their Barbies in ball gowns, mine was bossing Ken around in board meetings. I always thought I'd be this powerful executive, because running a business looked so exciting and cool, and for my parents, it was. I don't mean that there weren't difficult times, because they both worked their fingers to the bone for what they built. But they love every second of it. And I know it'll disappoint them that I don't, so this is hard for me."

A muscle ticked in Shane's jaw as he stood, stock still,

next to her at the counter. Wow, she knew it wasn't light conversation, but he looked like someone just ran over his dog. She should've just kept her trap shut.

"In the end, you're the only one who can decide what's right for you. I just thought you should know how it looks from the outside, that's all," he said, his voice tight.

Confusion tumbled in Bellamy's brain before finally, something clicked into place. His expression wasn't about her at all. "You feel like talking about it?"

Shane's eyes widened for a fraction of a second before narrowing to the food in front of them. "There isn't really anything to talk about." He shrugged and took a sip of his wine. The tension that had masked his face just moments earlier was gone as if it had never existed, leaving Bellamy to wonder if she was projecting her anxiety out into the world and poor Shane had just gotten caught in her web of weird neuroses.

"Oh. Well, sorry for laying all of this on you. Like I said, I know it's kind of weird." She reached deep into the bottom cupboard for a sheet pan that looked like it had doubled as a snow sled. More than once. Bent and wavy was better than nothing, she supposed.

"It's not weird." Shane's glance took in the cookie sheet. "Hey, I have one of those?" His nod was akin to a big, fat *who knew*?

Bellamy laughed, the strain of a couple of minutes ago swept under the rug that was her issues. "You think you're surprised now, wait'll you see what you can actually do with one of these babies," she cracked, spinning it around.

His laughter joined hers, and the sound of it warmed her, not just with its sexual heat, but with something else, something even more provocative.

She felt right, like she wanted to be here with him, just like this, indefinitely.

Ooookay, just because she was playing Suzie Home-maker in the guy's kitchen was no reason to go thinking she was falling for him or anything. They'd known each other for less than a full week, and while the chemistry between them would put most science experiments to shame, it would be silly to believe that raw attraction was the same thing as, well, a straight shot to the L-word.

"So, tell me about Pine Mountain," she said, in an effort to move her mind from the land of the utterly ridiculous.

Shane's dark brows popped, as if it was the last thing he'd expected her to say.

Which made two of them.

"What do you want to know?" he asked with a tilt of his head.

Bellamy shrugged, focusing on the food in front of her. "I don't know. Surprise me."

And that was how they spent the evening, with her as happy as a clam in his kitchen and him telling her about all of the intricacies of Pine Mountain. She got a little giggly over the wine, which turned out just fine, because Shane came dangerously close to gushing about the food, to the point that she actually blushed at the praise. Who would have thought that pork chops with a pomegranate reduction sauce could bring a tough guy like Shane to his knees?

A tough guy who, at that very moment, was looking at her with some seriously seductive eyes, like he wanted to have her for dessert.

"It gets kind of chilly in here at night. Why don't I make a fire?"

Too late, Bellamy thought, trying like hell to ignore the tingle that was vibrating through her like the waves of a sexed-up tuning fork. "That sounds great," she said, trying to convince herself that it was the wine making her want to sit down.

Sit down, tackle Shane to the ground and have her way with him . . . what was the difference, really?

Bellamy tucked her legs beneath her as she perched on the recliner, since it was the only place in the room to sit other than the tiny breakfast table where they'd just eaten. Wow, despite its age, the chair was really comfortable.

"So, um, do you want to watch TV or something?" Bellamy's eyes flitted over the darkened screen before settling on Shane. He stacked a handful of logs in the stove and lit the fire as if he'd done it a thousand times before.

"I only get a couple of channels, and the reception's not the best." Shane's eyes were back on her, sending that *whoa, Nelly* feeling right into her gut again. He had something on his mind, all right, and it wasn't the Tuesday night lineup on ABC.

"Oh, right." She peeked up at him. He was kneeling down, next to the fireplace, but his eyes were fully on hers. Want mingled with need and moved through her, replacing her blood and breath.

"What are you thinking about?" Shane asked, his voice a perfect balance of genuine curiosity and suggestive huskiness.

"Me?" Bellamy felt her cheeks flush as soon as the word was out. *No. The other babbling blonde in the room, you dumbass.*

Shane's laugh was a low, sexy rumble. "Yeah, you. You've got a look on your face."

"What kind of look?" Maybe if she stalled, she could come up with something non-embarrassing to say.

He raised a delicious brow. "You looked like you wanted to come over here."

Holy hell. Now he was a mind reader, too. She'd better get it together, otherwise she was going to be reduced to a great, big puddle of wine and hormones, right there in his only chair.

"Okay." All it took was three steps before she was next to him, sitting cross-legged in front of the woodstove. The fire crackled, filling the room with intimate warmth. "This is nice." Bellamy gestured to the stove. "Although if I'd known, I'd have bought marshmallows."

"Do you always think about food?" Shane picked up her hand and curved it over his, pausing to kiss the top of each of her fingers. Ohhh, mixing sweet with sinful like that was downright criminal.

"No." She hesitated when he lifted his eyes to meet hers, the doubt on his face clear.

"Not *always*. But a lot," she admitted.

His lips parted in a smile that she felt in every inch of her body. "Then we can do the marshmallows next time." He grazed his fingers up her arm, toward her shoulder, and she felt powerless to resist how electrifying the simple touch felt, even through her shirt.

"Oh, that's good," she murmured, letting her eyes fall closed.

Shane leaned in nearer, his lips so close to her ear that she had to fight back a sigh. "You must really like marshmallows."

She squeezed her eyes even tighter, torn between a laugh and the sigh that was still fighting for escape. "No, I meant . . ."

Shane feathered his lips over her neck, and the sigh won out.

"I meant you." Her eyes fluttered open just in time to see him tense before her, and for a second she thought she'd said something wrong. But then Shane pulled back so she could see his face, his eyes black and round with desire, and her breath caught in her throat. Everything about him, from the woodsy, masculine way he smelled to the feel of his rough hands on the softest parts of her filled her up and tangled in her mind, mingling inextricably with all that had been there before in a way that she was certain could never be undone.

And she wanted it that way.

"Do you know what you're doing to me?" His voice sent tiny quakes through her insides that only intensified as he hovered over her ear again. Bellamy shook her head, unable to find the words to answer, and Shane's breath heated her skin as he continued. "How every time I see you, I can't think of anything other than how good you taste?" Shane dipped his mouth to her neck again, and she felt a soft moan slip from her lips. Bellamy wrapped her arms around him, pulling him in. If she didn't have him right *now*, she was going to explode, plain and simple.

But he resisted. "Uh-uh. No more floors, no more backseats of cars." He sent a look over her that positively sizzled on her skin. "I want to make love to you in bed, like you deserve."

Something hot and wicked snapped in Bellamy's veins, and it screamed with raw satisfaction as she curled her fingers around his shirt to push him onto his back.

"I like the floor," she breathed, swinging a leg over him to settle in his lap. The feel of his arousal, hard and ready and oh so snug against her, derailed any chance she had at rational thought. She bent down, greedy for his kiss, but when he arched up into her hips, she stopped over his lips to bite back a groan. The split second was all the leverage he needed to make her insides go liquid. Again.

"Nice try. But you're not getting what you want. Not this time," Shane amended, reaching his arms under hers to scoop them back to sitting. In one swift move, his legs were beneath him, carrying them both to his room. Bellamy was getting *exactly* what she wanted.

And she wanted it forever.

Chapter Twenty-One

Shane couldn't breathe or think or see. The only thing he knew as he carried Bellamy to his bedroom was that he wanted to have her until the sun rose. He wanted to watch her eyes fly open, glittering bright green like summer grass under sunrise, as she unraveled beneath him. He wanted to bring her to the sweet edge between aching need and lusty release so many times that she forgot her name. He wanted to follow her there with reckless abandon, lose himself in the smell of her hair and the salt of her skin.

He wanted her to stay.

Bellamy squeezed her legs around his waist, and the wicked friction of her hips over his jeans almost made him walk into the doorjamb. Holy *shit*, every time she came out with one of those breathy little sighs, it damn near killed him. She buried her face in his shoulder, lining his neck with kisses hot enough to make him question his sanity.

"Bellamy," he ground out, loving the exquisite feel of her name in his mouth. There was something so passionate about her, so unguarded and real, that he didn't even want to let her go to lay her down. They tumbled onto his halfway-made bed, and Shane relished the tight fit of her body under his in the midst of the rumpled comforter.

Bellamy unlaced her legs from around his waist to let her knees fall open, reaching down between them for the edge of his shirt. The heat of her sex against his cock was just a tantalizing sliver of what he knew would follow, and it made him harder still as he fit himself tightly against her hips.

She teased tiny circles around his tongue with hers before letting him in more deeply, and when she gave in, he didn't wait. He'd never been with a woman who could drive him out of his mind just by kissing him, but the push and pull of her was goddamn flawless.

"You are so beautiful." He parted from her only long enough to utter the words, and the thrum of noise it brought from her in response made it worth it. He slipped a palm under her shirt, the hot silk of her skin enticing him to take it off.

Bellamy beat him to the punch, though, winding her fingers into fists and pulling his shirt over his head. She was the perfect combination of give and take as she moved under him, rocking up into his hips with irresistible heat.

Desperate for the delicious slide of his skin over hers, Shane drew back to lift her shirt over her belly, circling it with his palm before pressing back into the cradle of her hips. It was going to take every ounce of control he had not to rip those cute little pants off of her, but he was going to do his damnedest to take his time and savor every nuance, from the honeyed taste of her skin to the unfettered look on her face when she came.

"Do you want me to take this off?" Shane shifted his hand upward, toward the breasts he ached to touch, and lifted her shirt to reveal what lay beneath.

"Yes. God, *yes*." Bellamy writhed under him, knocking his concentration down a peg. Man, he'd wanted to do this slowly, to feel every second of being with her, but if she kept it up, he wasn't going to make it.

They'd just have to do it again. Maybe twice.

Shane pulled her shirt over her head to expose her creamy skin, bound softly by a black satin bra that made him cut out a groan. Bellamy arced up, eager for his touch, but he grazed over her with gentle caresses, savoring her taut nipples beneath the glide of the fabric. His fingers turned lazy circles over one, then the other, driven by the feel of the hard peaks under lush satin. Aching to taste her, he dipped down to circle his tongue over one perfect pink nipple, still sheathed in the thin fabric of her bra.

"*Oh*, don't stop doing that," she keened on little more than a whisper, so provocative that he couldn't deny her. Heating both the satin and her body with his mouth, he laved her, meeting her want with his own. Bellamy reached down on a gasp, cupping his face with her slender fingers. Her hands moved from his face to the curve of her rib cage as she slid them beneath her breasts.

Ohhhkay, he definitely wasn't going to make it, because that was hot as hell.

Shane lifted his eyes to Bellamy's just in time to watch the recognition flash over her face. The corners of her lips kicked upward into the sexiest smirk he'd ever seen, and she braced her elbows under her body, fingers still lightly cupping the underside of her breasts.

"It's in the front," she said on a husky breath. She fingered the two edges where the inky satin came together to hug her curves, but didn't make a move to unclasp it. Shane could just make out her eyes, wide in the dark of his room, through the moonlight spilling in from the window.

They were unwavering on his, striking a flawless balance between tenderness and desire.

He wrapped his fingers around hers, holding the weight of her breasts and her hands in his. Bellamy's chest hitched under them as she sucked in a breath, pushing hot need through his body.

"You do it," he said on a hoarse whisper, watching her eyes gleam in response in the silvery moonlight.

"I . . . um . . ."

Shane sensed the hesitation mingling in with her hunger, and he kept his eyes on hers. "Do you trust me?"

Bellamy answered without pause. "Yes."

"Then let me show you. Let me show you how beautiful you are."

Shane slipped his fingers over hers, curling them into the warm V between her breasts. Slowly, he guided her hands around the clasp until it popped open. Twining his hand around hers so their fingers were side by side, he brushed over her, barely grazing the tips of her nipples first with her fingers, then his own. Bellamy dug into the pad of his hand with her thumb, and it stayed his focus on her body. The second pass came with bolder strokes, evened out by light caresses as he guided both of their hands from one breast to the other, using her fingers to build the sweet tension between them.

"Oh," she murmured, her hair splayed across his pillow in a riot of golden curls. Shane shifted his body over hers to nuzzle the hot fold where her neck met her shoulder, inhaling the clean scent of her. Working her hand in quicker sweeps, he felt his breath catch in his lungs as she tightened and lifted beneath his body.

"Don't . . . oh my God, *please* don't stop," she begged, her voice ragged with the plea. The words snapped through him, daring him closer, and he went without looking back. God, she was beyond compare when she danced right on the edge, and he knew he'd give anything to watch her eyes spring wide with pleasure.

"Open your eyes, Bellamy." Shane bent down to take her nipple into his mouth at the same time she fluttered her lids to look at him. He felt the heat of her stare as his tongue slid over her, bringing her closer. "Can you see how breathtaking you are?"

She canted her hips to meet his just once before pulling back to drop a hand between them, firmly cupping his cock over his jeans. Every thought in Shane's mind was completely canceled out by the feel of her, replaced by raw want.

"What about you?" Moving her hand in a steady stroke, Bellamy tucked her bottom lip between her teeth as she gave him the most seductive, teasing look he'd ever seen in his life. "Can you see how breathtaking *you* are?"

The friction between her hand, the layer of clothing that separated them and his skin was excruciating in the best possible way, to the point where Shane was sure he wasn't going to make it out of his jeans. He had to turn the tables on her, do something, *anything*, otherwise this night wasn't going to end with the kind of bang she was surely expecting. Bellamy's lips curved into a wicked smile, her bottom lip still caught in her teeth.

Without thinking, he reached up to release her lip from her teeth, his fingertips barely touching her soft skin. Gasping, she stilled her hands halfway down his button fly, parting her lips to taste the rough edges of his fingers. The look on her face was pure passion, and as she looked up at him, green eyes sparkling in the shadows and moonlight, Shane felt something in his chest rise up and break loose.

"I don't want to wait, Shane. Please don't make me stop."

He didn't stop her as she unbuttoned his jeans, but when he went to slide her pants down her hips, she caught his hands with hers.

"My purse," she said, catching him completely off guard.

"Your what?"

Bellamy turned to her side, bringing him with her. "There are condoms in my purse." She buried her face in his shoulder and started kissing her way across his chest. If ever there was a way of making him not want to stop, she was hot on the trail to finding it.

Thank God they wouldn't need to go rummaging for wherever she'd left her purse. Shane turned to his back, reaching out blindly for his tiny bedside table. He'd covered every hopeful *maybe* earlier that day, not wanting to leave anything to chance.

"Got it." He barely got the drawer open in between groans at her ministrations as she kissed her way across his chest, and when she drifted lower across his belly, he hissed out a breath.

"We're not going to get to use this if you don't stop," he ground out, and she looked up at him with a surprisingly naughty grin.

"I thought you liked creative," she said with an arch of her brow.

Shit. She was killing him, she really was.

"I do like creative," he replied with every last ounce of willpower he possessed. "And you're about to find out how much."

The only thing better than the feel of Bellamy's hands on him was the feel of her body under him.

Taking care not to hurt her, but not giving her an inch

to protest, Shane swept an arm under her to swing her firmly onto her back. He rolled the waistband of her pants over his thumbs, stroking her hips with his fingers while he served her with an exact replica of the wicked grin she'd just given him. Trailing his tongue down the column of her neck, he made his way to the sinuous curve of her belly, freeing her pants from her hips to reveal a triangle of lace and satin that made his heartbeat jackhammer in his veins.

"God, these are hot," he rumbled, breathing into the skin just above the fabric.

"I hate them," Bellamy blurted out, and he had no choice but to chuckle.

"Then let's take them off." Shane guided the thin strings down over her hips, fixing her with his gaze. He slipped the panties from her, then worked his way back toward her center with slow, deliberate strokes of his fingers and mouth. She tasted just like heaven, and even though he wanted to be inside her so badly that he could have screamed with need, he held back, pleasuring her with his mouth and his hands instead.

"Shane. *Shane.*" Bellamy's hands fisted the comforter, and she arched her back off the bed. He slid his palms between the small of her back and the gorgeous curve of her ass, holding her fast as she shuddered under him.

Watching her come was the most striking thing he'd ever seen in his entire life, the intensity and pure sweetness of it so matchless that Shane wanted to have it forever.

"Shane," Bellamy whispered, slipping her hands around his face. Her breath carried the word right through his chest. "Come here."

He kissed his way gently past her still-trembling thighs, up the tenuous rise and fall of her chest until he reached her face. A sated smile played on her lips, and he outlined it with the pad of his finger.

She caught his hand with hers and laced their fingers together. "I want to make love to you."

Honesty rang through her words, which made him want her all the more. Bellamy ran her hands reverently from his face down his neck, gliding across his chest to land around his waist. His fumbling for the bedside table hit the mark on the second try, and he found the condom he'd left there and put it on. Returning to the warmth of Bellamy's body, he snaked an arm around her ribs to cradle her shoulder with his palm. She gave an ever so slight shake of her head and hooked a leg over his hip.

"No. I want to make love to *you*." Using the arm he had braced beneath her and the momentum of her weight against his, she swung him over so that the weight of her lithe body was poised right over his. Before Shane could even register being on his back, Bellamy had curled her fingers into his shoulders, the intoxicating heat of her core so close to his cock that he couldn't think about anything else.

"Bellamy." Her name felt perfect coming out of him, as if he was made to say it, and she responded wordlessly by lowering herself over him. She balanced over his body until their hips joined together, skin on skin, heat on heat, and Shane knew that if a million girls came along after her, he would still never be the same.

Bellamy moved over him with slow fierceness, both intense and beautiful. The rhythm of her body on his felt so good, and he guided his hands to her hips to steady her while she made love to him. When her movements quickened, he held her even tighter, watching with awe as she shuddered over his body in a wave of release. Only then did Shane let go, grasping her so close that there was no space between them and calling her name as he came.

She leaned forward, breath still spilling out in ragged bursts, to cover him with her bare chest. Shane folded his arms around her to gather her in, tucking her into his body like she belonged there and nowhere else. Without thinking, the words in his mind found breath and tumbled out.

"Stay. Please stay."

Bellamy nuzzled his neck, releasing one of those soft sighs that made him forget everything that stood between them.

"I don't want to go back to the resort tonight," she admitted, settling against him.

Shane shook his head. "No. I mean don't go back to the resort at all. Stay with me for the rest of the week."

Her head lifted from his shoulder, blond curls brushing the space between their bodies. Goddamn it, he knew he shouldn't have opened his mouth, or his heart, or whatever it was that had made him ask her to stay. He knew he couldn't be with her in the long run, but the way she made him feel every time she looked into his eyes or said his name had pushed the stupid, reckless words right out of him.

"You want me to stay here with you," she said, like she was making sure she'd heard him correctly. Shane could feel her stare, honest and unfeigned, and he met it even though it scared the hell out of him.

"Do you want to?" He couldn't quite bring himself to say that yes, he wanted her to stay more than he wanted to fucking breathe, but Bellamy seemed to get the idea just fine without words, which was one of the reasons he wanted her to stay so badly to begin with.

She got it. Despite how different they were, she got *him*. And even though Shane couldn't have her in the long run, he wanted her for every second until she had to go back where she belonged.

"I do want to. As long as *you* want me to." Bellamy paused to give him one last glance in the shadows, searching for an answer.

Shane nodded, pulling her close. He didn't want to waste a single second of the time he had with her worrying about the fact that, eventually, he had to let her go. For the next couple of days and nights, he had her.

And he was going to make the best of it before she went back to her life, in the only place he couldn't follow her.

Chapter Twenty-Two

Bellamy rolled over and slid her arms beneath her pillow, cradling it under her cheek as she inhaled the fresh cedar scent she was fast becoming addicted to. She didn't open her eyes, just breathed in deep and memorized the feel of the flannel sheets, soft against her body, and the comfortable quiet of the cabin.

She'd told him she would stay.

In the grander scheme of things, staying with Shane made sense. It wasn't exactly a secret that she liked him, and the feeling seemed pretty darned mutual, especially after last night. They had some time before she had to leave to go back to the city, and he wanted to spend it with her. It wasn't as if they were getting married or anything, for Pete's sake. It was four days. Ninety-six hours. Nothing major.

Then why did she feel it would make or break her?

"Hey, you awake?"

Bellamy fluttered her lids open just in time to catch Shane putting a steaming mug on the bedside table. He leaned in, his hand brushing her curls, but didn't sit down on the bed.

"Coffee's fresh."

Her insides tightened. Shane was already dressed in his trademark jeans and thermal top, lean muscles of his forearms showing just enough from the pushed-up sleeves to make Bellamy's pulse hopscotch through her veins.

"Mmm, thanks." She sat up, rubbing her eyes for a full ten seconds before she realized she was naked as the day she was born. Modesty made her scoop the covers to her chest, trying to hold them in place with her palms. Shane's eyes flared darkly from where he stood next to the bed, but then he looked down, probably to give her at least a little dignity as she tried to figure out where her unmentionables had gotten to. Bellamy patted awkwardly through the bed with one hand, using the other to try to cover her nakedness.

Oh, screw it. It wasn't like Shane hadn't seen her sans apparel. He was the one who'd taken the damned things off in the first place. She twisted her hair up in a knot and launched a full-on rummage for her bra while he examined the floorboards. Her cheeks burned as she found it tucked in the folds by her feet and put it on, following quickly with her shirt. Looking around for her clothes like this should feel awkward, right? Things could be so different by the light of day, after all, and . . .

Was that bacon?

"I have to go to work in a little while, but I made breakfast if you're hungry. It's nothing fancy," Shane added. His eyes were back on her, and they'd lost none of the intensity of the moment before. "But I kind of figure you can't go wrong with bacon and eggs."

Bellamy's stomach rumbled, letting her know it was more than interested. "That sounds really good."

He nodded. "Okay. I'll just let you get dressed then."

She waited until Shane had his back turned before sliding out of bed to scoop her pants and panties off the floor, grimacing slightly at the thought of putting the torturous G-string back on. Measuring her options, she decided to forgo undergarments in favor of good old-fashioned commando. After all, she was only headed back to the resort.

Or was she? Her heart played a healthy game of pinball in her rib cage as she remembered Shane's request. Maybe he hadn't been serious when he'd asked her to check out of the resort and stay with him for the rest of the week. Worse yet, maybe he'd said it in the heat of passion and was now totally regretting having asked her. It wouldn't be the worst thing in the universe, right? I mean, sure, it would be a blow to her healing ego, but still. The sex they'd had would've made her babble like a topographical map full of brooks . . . if she'd been able to speak at the time. So he'd let it slip in the thick of things. People said all kinds of crazy things in bed.

Please let him have meant it.

"Bellamy?" Shane's dark gaze rested on her face. He'd stopped in the door frame, eyes crinkling in what looked like concern.

She pasted on a too-bright smile and scrambled for her wits. "Sorry, I'm slow to wake up sometimes. You were saying?" She brushed an errant curl from her face and tucked it behind her ear, fully dressed except for the tiny slip of lace and string surreptitiously balled up in her fist. Shane's eyes swept over her hand, and his jaw ticked under tight muscles. Good Lord, this was embarrassing.

"I just said to help yourself to whatever you need in the bathroom." He gestured to the narrow door right outside the bedroom, but didn't move otherwise.

Bellamy's bare feet whispered over the floorboards as she rushed to escape. "Right. I won't be long, and then we can head out."

"Stop."

Okay, the Jedi mind trick thing was *so* unfair. Her feet defied the *go* message from her brain, bringing her body to an abrupt halt at the foot of the bed. Bellamy steeled herself as she peeked up at him.

"This is about what I said last night, isn't it." There wasn't even a hint of a question in his voice, and his black-coffee eyes were on her, steady and unnervingly hot.

Here we go. "Look, it's really no big deal for me to stay at the resort. If you think I should. If you want me to, I mean." Ugh! She really needed to work on quality control with her common sense. What the hell was *wrong* with her?

Shane lifted a sable brow. "Truth?"

No. "Of course." Bellamy fought back the waver in the words.

"I want you to stay."

Her lips parted in surprise. "You do?"

He nodded, stepping in. Oh, the smell of his skin so close to hers was just plain cheating!

"Look, I'm not going to lie to you, but I don't think you'd want me to." Shane paused to let a wry little smirk lift one corner of his mouth. "We have four days before I'll be done with your transmission. I don't know what'll happen after that, but I do know that, until then, I don't want you to go."

His honesty startled her. "I don't want to go," she admitted, the words spilling out of her.

"So stay. Stay the four days with me, and we'll figure the rest out when your car is done." Shane's eyes sparkled under the sooty frame of his lashes. He dipped his head to place a kiss on her neck, the softness of his lips canceled out by the brush of stubble on his chin. "Just . . . don't go."

Not speaking your mind had never made sense to Bellamy. But what if the thing you needed to say scared the hell out of you? Then what?

Guess she'd just have to be scared, that's what. Bellamy steadied her hands and slipped them under Shane's chin, lifting it to look him straight in the eye.

"Okay. I won't go."

"Okeydokey . . . darks over here, whites over . . . here." Bellamy rooted through the suitcase she'd propped open on top of an oversized wash basin. "And slutty underwear over here," she snickered, reaching into her purse for the scrap of lace and string that she might consider wearing again, just for the look it brought to Shane's face.

She'd been eternally grateful to find a small Laundro-mat in the basement of the resort, and although she had a sneaking suspicion it was reserved for staff, her need for clean undergarments outweighed the fear of getting busted using their facilities. Even in spite of the fact that she was checking out in a matter of hours.

To stay with a guy she'd known for all of five days, but felt like she'd known for six lifetimes.

Time to focus on the laundry.

Bellamy filled two of the four washing machines in the tiny basement room, feeding them with the requisite amount of quarters and laundry detergent she'd gotten at the resort's drugstore. Once her clothes were doing the swishy-samba with the water and bubbles, she plunked herself into the only chair in the cramped space.

"No time like the present," she said quietly, and popped

open her laptop. Before her conscience or common sense could stop her, she pecked *culinary school, Philadelphia* into the search engine and hit Enter.

"Two hundred forty-six *thousand* hits? Are you kidding me?" Her breath left her lungs in a burst of no-freaking-way as she scanned the list.

Well, at least she had options.

Forty-five minutes and two spin cycles later, she'd scribbled a page and a half's worth of meticulous notes on a legal pad. Culling through the list was proving easier than she'd thought, and yielded a couple of very viable options.

Sure. Provided she had the balls to follow through on applying.

A loud crash just outside the open door frame brought her to full attention. Bellamy scrambled into the narrow service hallway, where she found a well-muscled, platinum-blond brick wall of a man, wearing chef's whites and cursing up a blue streak at the plates and serving tray littering the floor.

"Are you okay?" she asked, bending down to help collect the dishes. "Wow, it looks like you got lucky. I don't think any of them broke." Bellamy glanced at the scattering of kitchenware on the thin layer of carpet lining the hallway.

The stormy hazel glare she got in return for her trouble made her regret opening her mouth. The guy flipped the tray over and filled it with startling efficiency, looking more at her than at the clean dishes he was stacking.

"Am I okay? Well, let's see. I've been waiting for a produce shipment for over twenty-four hours, my boss, bless her dark little heart, expects the impossible from me, and don't even get me *started* on the sorry excuse for wanna-be line cooks cowering in the kitchen. Apparently, it's too much to expect that even one of them might be able to break down a chicken without destroying the damned thing. Even the easy stuff is out of the question. Hell, at this point, I doubt that half of them can even wash dishes with much success."

By the time his tirade was halfway to rant status, he'd righted the tray under his massive hands and stood up to rake his cold, hard gaze over her. "I don't suppose you're any good at washing dishes and have a couple hours to kill, hmm? It would make you the bright spot of my shit morning."

Bellamy narrowed her eyes at him. She didn't care that she didn't know this guy from Adam. No way was she going to let some hard-edged kitchen jockey bully her around.

"Of course I can wash dishes," she shot back, thinking for only a split second before putting a hand on her hip and matching him tone for tone. "But I'm better at breaking down a chicken."

Brick Wall's dark eyebrows kicked up in the direction of his bottle-platinum hair, and Bellamy noticed that one of them had a stainless steel barbell pierced through it. Shit. She just had to get mouthy with a guy who looked like he belonged in a motorcycle gang, didn't she?

"*You* can de-bone a chicken without rendering it useless?" Brick Wall's expression clearly suggested he thought she was full of crap. He frowned for added emphasis.

Bellamy stood as tall as possible without rising onto her tiptoes even though her heart had taken up permanent residence in her throat. "Yup."

He gave her a long up-and-down look as if she *was* a chicken, and her muscles grabbed tight around her bones. *Bad idea! Getting flip with the big man was a bad idea!*

She took a quiet half step backward. Maybe she could get back to her laundry and her Google search unscathed if she just shut her mouth and went now. Never mind that she really *could* break down a chicken, and make twenty different things with it, to boot.

"Well what're you waiting for, Sunshine? Believe me when I tell you I don't have all day." He jerked his head down the hallway marked STAFF ONLY, and Bellamy creased her brow in response.

"But I'm not . . . I don't work here," Bellamy stammered, willing her bravado back to the mother ship. She fastened him with an uneasy look. She couldn't just go marching around in the resort's kitchen, could she?

Brick Wall cracked an evil smile. "Technically, I don't either. Not yet, anyway. Look, I'm weeded up to my armpits, so really. If you wanna put your mayo where your mouth is, now's the time. Otherwise, I'm a ghost."

Bellamy squeezed her eyes shut on the fastest prayer she could muster and slung her laptop bag over her shoulder, running to catch up. She did her best to block out the chorus of *what the hell are you doing*? coming from the back of her mind.

"I'm Bellamy Blake," she said, following the guy's brisk strides to the end of the dingy back hallway.

"Adrian Holt," Brick Wall replied with a nod, bumping the door in front of them open with an elbow before barging through like he owned the place.

Bellamy's heart skittered in her chest as the name sank in and did the recognition dance in her brain. "As in, Carly di Matisse's sous chef, Adrian Holt?"

His evil grin reappeared. "One and the same, Sunshine. Now go grab some whites from the back room and let's see what you're made of, shall we?"

* * *

After the third time Shane checked the same engine valves in Lucky Gunderson's Cadillac, Grady arched his brow and followed it with a knowing grin.

"You wanna tell me what's on your mind, or are you gonna keep daydreamin' and tell me it's nothing?"

Shane did his best to hide his smile in his flannel sleeve as he pushed his hair back from his face. It was pretty much a no-go.

"Sorry," he said, bracing himself with both palms against the Caddy. Lucky wasn't exactly living up to his name as far as the Coupe de Ville was concerned, but that was okay with Shane. It gave him something to do other than watch the clock.

"Nothin' to be sorry about when you're wearing a smile like that." Grady's laugh echoed through the garage on a rumble. "So what's her name?"

Damn, Grady's sixth sense was just unnatural. "Who said I'm smiling over a woman?" Shane's attempt to blank his expression fell woefully short, and he ended up grinning like a fool at the Caddy's engine.

"I might be old, but I ain't stupid, son." Grady chuckled as he examined the contents under the Cadillac's hood, running his hands from the engine to the oil filter. "Only one thing brings out a smile like that on a man's face, and that is a pretty girl."

Shane shook his head. He knew when he'd been beaten. "Her name's Bellamy. She's here for the week. As a matter of fact"—he paused to jut his chin at the Miata—"the two-seater is hers. She's waiting for us to fix it before she can go home."

"And where would home be?" Grady kept his eyes on the car, but Shane felt his skin prickle at the question.

"She lives in Philly." He kept his tone purposely neutral, but Grady didn't follow suit.

"Huh. You do like a hornet's nest, don't you?"

Shane exhaled, long and slow. "I know, all right?"

"Do you, now?" There was no accusation in Grady's tone, and the honesty of the question made Shane realize that he had no good answer for it.

"It all happened kind of fast. I didn't exactly plan on . . . you know. Any of it. But it's no big deal," Shane tacked on. The lie might as well have left scorch marks on its way out, considering how bad it tasted and how hard it burned. Still, big deal or not, Bellamy was headed home before the weekend was out, and there was nothing he could do about it.

"Does she know?" Grady looked up from the Coupe de Ville to pin Shane with a questioning stare before lowering the hood.

Shane folded his arms over his chest. "No."

"Mmm." Grady turned his eyes back to the car and got behind the wheel to start it up, but Shane couldn't tell whether he was just listening to the engine or waiting for a response.

God*dammit*, the last thing Shane needed was guilt over this. Knowing she was leaving was hard enough. Baring his innermost secrets to her would only take things from bad to worse.

"It's pointless to tell her, Grady. She's going back to the city. It's where she belongs."

The old man scrubbed a hand down the silvered stubble on his chin and killed the Cadillac's engine. "Places are places, Shane. You come and you go, but in the end, it ain't the places that matter. It's the people you had with you that counts."

"The places matter to me," Shane said, his voice cold with finality.

Grady shook his head, and the faintest trail of a smile crossed his jaw, like he was thinking of something familiar. "You'll learn. Now hand me that wrench, would you? The valves on this lifter are shot, and if we don't pull it for a new one, it ain't ever gonna run right."

Chapter Twenty-Three

"I gotta admit, Sunshine. When I first saw you, I didn't think for a second that you could hold your own." The fact that Adrian's face only held slight disdain was a weird little comfort to Bellamy as she stood, exhausted and elated, at a food-splattered kitchen station deep in the bowels of the resort.

"What do you think now?"

"I think you'd better clean up your workstation before Chef di Matisse catches you. You're a fucking mess."

Bellamy wrinkled her nose at him, but only to cover up the grin that wanted to work its way over her face. She still wanted to pinch herself at the fact that she'd spent over an hour working on a list of techniques and test dishes in a professional kitchen. It blew the tiny yet functional kitchen in her condo out of the water, and she was still kind of in shock that Adrian had let her come down here to play even after she'd told him she was just an armchair cook with no professional experience. It didn't seem to matter, as nobody questioned her presence while they worked side by side on the same test dishes. Bellamy remembered that they were overhauling the restaurant. How freaking cool was it that she was getting to reap the benefits of menu-testing firsthand?

"You'd better hope your cooking's better than your kitchen management, girl. I'm not kidding about the mess." Adrian tapped his foot impatiently, but Bellamy could see traces of a smile under the few days' worth of dark stubble on his face.

"You're a real sweetheart, Chef Holt. Really. I'm swooning over here," she muttered, starting to tackle the mess in front of her with fastidious hands. He couldn't be serious about Carly catching her. Chef di Matisse would probably be pissed if she knew Adrian had let her come into the kitchen just to mess around, but she didn't want to leave any signs that she'd been there, just in case.

"If you want to have a prayer in the kitchen, you'd better be able to handle it. Nobody pats you on the head in this business, that's for damn sure." Adrian flicked a glance over the cavernous kitchen, bustling with movement and smells and sounds. He tipped his platinum head at her before turning to walk down the row of stainless steel counter space, each with stations that looked like different variations of the one Bellamy was currently cleaning.

"By the way, I gave one of your test dishes to Carly. She'll be back from her break in five."

Bellamy was ninety-nine percent sure that the not being able to breathe thing would subside eventually.

"You never said . . . I mean, you didn't . . . she's not supposed to *taste* any of it!" She scrambled for wits that seemed to have no intention of surfacing. Adrian's impromptu invitation to come show her stuff in the kitchen was supposed to be a fun-and-games kind of thing. She didn't even have formal training, for Chrissake!

Adrian crossed his arms over his retaining wall of a

chest and eyed her. "This is a kitchen, not a playground. What do you think all of these people are doing here?"

"Um, working?" Reality started to sink in, hard and fast.

"Competing for jobs, sweetheart. This isn't a swanky cooking class just for fun. This is the nitty-gritty, right here." He creased his forehead, knitting his brows into a dark slash over his eyes. "Clean up your station. Anything for dishwashing goes on the tray under your table. You can take it back there." Adrian thrust a meaty finger toward the back of the kitchen.

And he was gone.

"Don't feel bad. At least Chef di Matisse saw yours. Some people's test dishes didn't even pass plating earlier. Chef Holt pitched one based on smell alone."

Bellamy swung around to see a tall brunette in splattered chef's whites meticulously scrubbing down the workstation next to her.

"Are you serious?" Bellamy reached out to brace herself with both hands, the coolness of the table seeping into her palms. Oh God. Oh God oh God oh God.

The girl nodded, but didn't even break stride with the bowls in front of her. "And he's not even the hard-ass of the pair. Chef di Matisse sent two people home before lunch without even tasting their stuff. You don't get where she is without being tough as nails."

Bellamy broke out of her panic long enough to furrow her brow. "But when I met her the other night, she was so nice," she said, confused. They *were* talking about the same woman who had patiently listened to Bellamy prattle on about plank salmon, right? Oh, this was going to be really, really bad.

One brown eyebrow arched up from behind the adjacent

workstation. "Let me guess. You weren't working for her then, were you?"

"I'm not working for her now," Bellamy said, trying to swallow the knot of fear that had taken over most of her throat.

"Oh yes you are, or at least you're trying to. Look out."

The girl had no sooner given the set of swinging doors at the head of the room a pointed look than they flew open in one heart-sickening swoosh.

"Adrian! *Please* tell me that we have fresh produce. That stuck-in-a-snowstorm excuse is wearing thin. I can't make something out of nothing over here!" Chef di Matisse glided through the kitchen with graceful, latent strength, her dark eyes scanning the entire kitchen in less than ten seconds. "I'm not having messy workstations, people. Sloppy stations equal sloppy food. Neither one of those is happening in here."

She continued moving through the kitchen, stopping to shake her head, her chestnut-colored French braid swishing down her back as she peered into a bowl at someone's workstation. "No, that's not going to cut it. I can't put re-moulade that looks like that on anything, I don't care how good it is. People eat with their eyes first, and if it looks like Elmer's paste, that's what they'll taste. The recipe's right in front of you. Do it again."

Adrian leaned in to murmur something in Carly's ear, and both sets of eyes lasered in on Bellamy's workstation, which was still dotted with dirty mixing bowls and utensils. She scrabbled to collect them and then wipe down her station with blinding speed, then bent low to snatch the tray from under the counter. Maybe she could hide under there if it got really bad.

"You made chicken piccata."

Bellamy jumped and banged her head on the lip of the table. How the hell had Carly made it down the row so fast on those short little legs? It just wasn't natural!

"I, ah. Yes," she admitted, straightening and clutching the tray. Damn, the woman was intimidating for such a tiny thing. Bellamy had a good four inches on her, and yet she felt as if Carly was ten feet tall and bulletproof. A flicker of recognition appeared in Carly's dark glance as she looked at Bellamy closely.

"Where did you learn how to cook like that?"

"In my kitchen," Bellamy squeaked. Where else would she have learned how to cook?

Adrian chuckled over Carly's shoulder, but a head-turn, eyebrow-lift maneuver from Carly cut him off pretty fast.

"When we met the other night, you didn't tell me that you'd gone to culinary school, Miss . . . ?"

Bellamy's heart made a beeline for her shoes. "Bellamy. I mean, Blake. Bellamy Blake," she corrected herself, cheeks flushing. "I'm sorry. I didn't tell you that because I don't have any formal training." She was tempted to add that she'd *told* Adrian that when he'd set her up at this work-station to begin with, but she knew it wouldn't matter. God, this had been a crushing mistake. As boring as it was, she belonged in an office with the suit and briefcase set.

"Mmm. Chef Holt?" Carly perched her chin on her shoulder to fasten Adrian with a stare. "Can you please escort Miss Blake to my office?" Her eyes skimmed over Bellamy's, and even though she wanted desperately to look down, Bellamy stood her ground.

"I'd like to have a word with her in private."

* * *

"Jesus, Bellamy," Shane said, his gut twisting at the serious look on her face in the low light of the cabin. The thought of some huge sous chef and his iron-fisted boss giving Bellamy a hard time made his insides churn. Maybe he'd just have to go over there to let them know that toying with people's dreams wasn't very good manners. He pondered Bellamy's description of the guy for a second. Maybe he'd take Jackson, just in case.

"I know. It was all I had not to throw up right then and there." Her cheeks had a rosy glow in the firelight from the wood-burning stove, and she recrossed her jeans-clad legs as she sat across from him on the floor. Man, she was beautiful.

"So what'd she say?" Shane tried to keep the tension from his voice, but he was pretty sure he was doing a bad job of it.

Bellamy's face curved with a wicked smile. "She said my chicken was the only decent representation of her recipe that she'd tasted all day, and that while my workstation was unacceptable"—Bellamy paused to wince, but then continued—"she wanted to see me do a few things herself. After about twenty excruciating minutes, a little bit of slice and dice, and some aioli later, Chef di Matisse put my name on the list of people she and Chef Holt are considering for their new staff. They're going to choose their line cooks next week, once they've seen enough candidates."

Shane's brows felt permanently lifted in shock, and Bellamy tossed her head back and laughed.

"Wait, so she didn't . . . oh, you little cheat!" he said, starting to laugh. *Damn* was Bellamy's poker face good.

And the face she had on now was downright stunning. Shane was on her in a second, bracing an arm around her back as he softly tackled her to the floor. She gave an uncharacteristic squeal and a set of giggles that made his insides turn soft and his outsides turn decidedly *un*soft.

"Fooling me like that isn't fair, you know." He kissed the supple skin where her neck met her ear.

Bellamy threaded her fingers in his hair, which didn't make him want to stop kissing her. "I know. But you should have seen your face," she sighed, arching into him. "Plus, having my name on the list just means that now I have an ice chip's chance in hell rather than no chance at all. I hardly think it's worth getting my hopes up for."

"You're such a pessimist," he said, nipping at her earlobe.

She rewarded him with a laugh that he felt all the way to his fingertips. "I'm really not kidding when I tell you that the list of hopefuls is as long as my leg. And they're all talented, probably with impressive résumés. Comparatively, I'm a nobody."

"I wouldn't recommend this level of confidence once you get back in the kitchen. You're going to have to do better than that." Shane pulled back to kiss the cute little crease in her forehead.

"I'm just trying to be realistic. It's really cutthroat, and I doubt I'll make it."

Shane turned her so they could lie side by side in front of the woodstove. "You're a cutthroat kind of girl. And I mean that as a compliment," he added when she parted her lips to protest. "Come on. You whipped up tonight's dinner with a handful of things we grabbed on the way back here, and it was amazing. You're great in the kitchen."

Bellamy rolled her eyes even though she wore a sheepish smile. "It was lasagna, Shane, with sauce that came from a jar. I could've made it in my sleep."

"Uh-huh. Right. The sauce tasted homemade by the time you were done doctoring it," he joked. That lasagna she was trying to pass off as nothing special had been the best Italian food he'd had since . . . well, ever.

Her eyes lit with remembering before he could argue with her any further, and she smiled. "Oh! That reminds me. There's a ton left over, so I wrapped up a bunch in one of those plastic tray thingies we snagged at Joe's. That way you can bring some to Grady."

Shane's heart lurched in his chest, and he pulled back to look at her. "What?"

Her green eyes grew wide. "Well, you said that you sometimes get extra groceries for him, so I thought maybe he'd like it." Bellamy looked at him, tiny lines of confusion etched on her face.

He'd mentioned the extra groceries thing in passing when he'd grabbed a bag of jelly beans for the stash at the garage, never thinking anything of it. Sure, Bellamy's gesture was small—she'd just packed up some leftovers—but it felt important, special somehow.

She felt important. Important enough to open up to.

"Shane? Is something wrong?" The confusion on her face crossed the boundary into concern, and she propped herself up on an elbow to look at him more closely. Her green eyes were flecked with gold in the firelight as her stare wrapped around him, and he knew she was seeing more than he meant to show.

Bellamy's voice came out on a whisper. "Do you want to talk about whatever this is yet?"

In that split second, Shane wanted to say yes. He wanted to open his mouth and tell her all the secrets that swirled around in his head, including how right and pure and good he felt lying here next to her.

But he couldn't. In four days, she was leaving, going back to the city where she belonged. All the talking in the world wasn't going to change that.

"There's nothing to talk about." Shane leaned in to kiss her, drowning out the secrets with the feel of her lips on his. "Unless it's me thanking you for dessert."

Bellamy sighed softly under his lips. "You mean dinner. We didn't have dessert."

Shane slipped her lithe body beneath his, entranced by the instant heat of her, and his face broke into a devilish smile. "Not yet, sweetheart. But I'm workin' on it."

Bellamy chewed her lip and looked out the passenger window of Shane's pickup. The midmorning sunshine made it impossible to get more than two steps from the cabin without sunglasses, and even then it sparkled over the snowcapped pines in a brilliant display of shimmering white on evergreen. She balanced the tray of lasagna in her lap, fiddling with the lid as she stared through the glass.

After they'd made love in front of the waning firelight, she and Shane had stayed up until the darkest hours of night gave in to the velvet of predawn. He listened as she finally confessed how badly she wanted the job on Carly's staff, taking in every word before assuaging her doubt with quiet confidence. His dark stare made it clear to her that he meant what he said; that despite knowing her for all of a week, he believed in her even when she wasn't sure she believed in herself.

When he took her to bed and made love to her again with the gentle fierceness that seemed to define him, she knew that going home wouldn't be as easy as a scenic ninety-minute drive. She'd come to the mountains to get away from it all, at least temporarily, so she could get back on track. Now there *was* no track, and the out-of-control feeling that pulsed through her every time Shane so much as looked in her direction left her both breathless and scared stiff.

She knew she had to go home. But oh God, she didn't want to go alone.

"That is some deep thought you've got going on over there," Shane said, smiling over the words and breaking her from her reverie. "Care to share?"

"Truth?" Bellamy stalled, casting a sidelong glance at him.

"Of course," Shane quipped, just as she knew he would. *Shit.*

She pulled in a deep breath and let it rush out with her thoughts before she could change her mind. "I was thinking I'd really like it if you'd come see me after this week."

Shane didn't move for what felt like an eternity. "You want me to come see you in the city." His tone was quiet yet inscrutable. Why was her heart pounding so hard?

"Yeah. I do." She used the cover of her sunglasses to sneak a sidelong glimpse at him, but it didn't yield much more than a peek at *his* sunglasses. Damn it.

"Bellamy," he started, but didn't continue. God, opening her mouth—and, okay, maybe her heart—like this had been a mistake. This had *it's not you* written all over it, and she should've known that her zero-tolerance policy for all things subtle would bring it out.

She cut him off with a preemptive strike in an effort to save her battered ego. "Look, you don't have to say anything, really. I know you're not exactly Philly's biggest fan." That much was clear with the dodge-and-deflect he pulled every time she so much as breathed the words *bright lights, big city.* Had she really thought he might come to a place he clearly couldn't stand just to see her again?

And what was with the tears suddenly rimming her eyes? Oh thank God for sunglasses, because really? This was too much embarrassment for any girl to take.

"So, you know, never mind. We said we'd spend the week together, and we are. Let's just forget I brought it up," she said, the words so rushed and nervous that they all kind of blended together.

"Okay."

Her heart sank as though it had been shrink-wrapped in lead. "Okay," she whispered, tamping down the urge to let the hot tears cross the threshold of her eyelids. God, she was an idiot! They had a couple of days left together, and there she was, getting all mushy on him. As much as she wanted to stay, maybe she should just save herself the heartache and go home. If she called as soon as they got to the garage, she'd probably be able to convince Jenna to come pick her up before nightfall. Then at least she could have her cry in private, with a little dignity and a whole lot of chocolate.

"When?" Shane asked, his voice hoarse.

Bellamy's heart sped up while time slowed way down. "When what?"

"If you want me to come and see you, I should probably know when to show up." He pulled the truck onto a narrow-as-hell shoulder, the pop and crunch of the gravel under the tires doing a number on her already shredded nerves.

"But I thought . . . I mean, you said okay, like, okay we should just forget it . . ."

Shane took off his sunglasses, revealing dark eyes thick

with emotion. "I meant okay, I'll come see you. I don't want to forget it."

He gave her a tentative smile, so different from the sexy smirks and cocky come-ons that she was used to him dishing out. As they sat in his truck, staring at each other rather than the gorgeous view over the guardrail, Bellamy was struck by the irony of being on the edge of something so stunning and yet so terrifying at the same time.

"Oh. Well, in that case, how does next weekend sound?"

Chapter Twenty-Four

The unease that had parked itself squarely on Shane's chest the minute he lied to Bellamy didn't even budge when they pulled into the side lot of the garage.

I didn't lie on purpose, he countered to his sneering conscience. *And I meant it when I said I don't want to forget it.*

But the glaring truth didn't have to do anything other than exist for him to know he never should have told her he'd come to the city. It wasn't just as easy as sucking it up and getting on the highway for a few hours. He'd sworn he'd never go back, and he'd damn well meant it. He had good *reasons* for his vow, damn it.

Not that he could tell her that.

"Shane?"

Man, those big green eyes were going to be the end of him, they really were. "Sorry, I must have been zoning out." Shane scooped her hand up and planted a quick kiss on her gloved knuckles.

"About what?" Tiny lines of worry ghosted over her brow, but her lips twitched with the naughty suggestion of a smile.

He snatched it up and ran. "If I tell you, it'll just ruin the surprise later, you know." Shane arched a suggestive eyebrow at her. The image of her face, unguarded in the throes of climax, slipped from his memory to his mind for an extended stay. Shane felt all hope of getting anything productive done melt away as his imagination had its way with her.

"You're terrible," she giggled.

"You like me that way." He pulled her closer until the irresistible taste of her was on his lips and under his tongue.

"You're going to be late for work," Bellamy warned with no tenacity whatsoever, parting her mouth to kiss him back. Her teeth took a gentle slide over his bottom lip, barely scraping him, and he groaned.

"I'm already late for work." Shane threaded his hand through her hair to cup the back of her neck. Her skin felt like magic under the roughness of his hands.

Bellamy smiled into him, and when she pulled away, his brain didn't waste any time hollering at him to bring her back. "Let's go, before we *don't* go."

Oh, he was screwed. And not in the good way.

"Okay." They crunched over the snow-packed gravel of the lot and through the side door, and Shane stuffed down the unease bubbling in his chest.

Just spend time with her for the next couple of days, like you told her you would. You can figure out how to get out of going to the city later. For now, you've gotta take what you have.

It was all too easy to let his inner voice take the ball and run like mad.

Shane hadn't been late for work once in the entire fourteen months he'd worked at Grady's, but that didn't stop the guilt from flooding through him at the twenty minutes that had dropped off the clock in his absence.

"Morning, Grady. Sorry I'm late." Shane didn't volunteer an excuse, mainly because Grady was no dummy. Whatever lame explanation Shane offered up would be canceled out by the fact that the *real* reason was standing right next to him, looking cute as hell with that blue hat framing her curls.

Grady looked up from Lucky Gunderson's Cadillac, a grin splitting his silvery stubble. "No apologies. 'Specially not when you've got a pretty girl with you."

Shane chuckled and shook his head. It figured that Grady would pull out the old-man charm for Bellamy. She was the first girl Shane had ever brought around the garage. Guess he had this coming. "Grady, this is Bellamy Blake."

"Nice to meet you." Bellamy balanced the lasagna tray in one hand and extended the other, wearing a smile that could make a dead man sing.

"Good to see you, darlin'." He wiped his hands carefully on a rag before taking hers in a firm handshake.

Bellamy drew her brows down in a slight pull, as if she was trying to place Grady's accent. Shane suppressed a chuckle. Grady was a product of the Blue Ridge, through and through, but he doubted she'd peg the cadence of his words without having grown up here.

"I, ah, brought you some lasagna that I made. In case you get hungry later." She offered the tray with a tentative smile and a quick blush. Shane chuckled. Man, she had nothing to be nervous about. That lasagna was freaking amazing.

"Well, that's right nice of you. Thank you." Grady took the tray and put it in the fridge. "So, that's your sports car we've got over there?" Grady jerked his head toward the Miata, which sat in the bay next to Shane's Mustang.

Bellamy nodded. "I'm really grateful you're able to fix it for me."

"Ah. Piece of cake, those trannies. Don't you worry your head over it. We'll get you fixed up just right. Soon as those parts get here, anyhow." Grady's eyes flicked over Shane for just a second, but then settled back on Bellamy with a wink.

Shane straightened and he turned toward the office. *Speaking of which.* "Hey, let me call the distributor. Your transmission might actually get here today," he suggested, but Grady cut him off.

"Don't go holdin' your breath. Bet it'll be tomorrow before you see that tranny. In the meantime, why don't you get out of here? It's not good manners to leave a pretty girl all by her lonesome."

Shane pulled back, staring at Grady in surprise. "But we need to finish replacing the lifter on this Cadillac."

Grady shook his head, his gravelly chuckle filling the garage. "If I can't manage a new lifter after all these years of owning a garage, then shame on me. Go on. Get out of here. I'm not askin'." He aimed a steel-gray stare at the door, but still wore his trademark easy smile.

"Oh, I wouldn't feel right keeping Shane from work," Bellamy said. "Really, I was just going to go back to the cabin and do some research online. I'll be fine on my own for the day."

"Ain't much work to keep him from until those parts get here. No more excuses. Scat, both of you, so I can get to it with this Caddy."

Shane didn't like the tired shadows under the old man's

eyes, but he knew all the arguing in the world wouldn't change Grady's mind. Plus, the idea of spending unexpected time with Bellamy *was* kind of tantalizing. He hedged.

"If that tranny comes in, you call me," Shane said, giving Grady his best and-I-mean-it look.

Grady's belly laugh rumbled while he ignored Shane in favor of his much prettier companion. "Nice to meet you, sweetheart. Take good care of him, now. He ain't seen a day off in over a year, so he might not know what to do with himself."

Bellamy's eyebrows shot up. "Over a year? Seriously?"

Shane shifted uncomfortably and hooked his thumbs through his belt loops with a shrug. It wasn't his fault there had been stuff to do all that time. Jeez.

Grady's eyes twinkled. "Ah, I'm tellin' his secrets, now. Go on. Have fun. And thanks again for dinner." He jutted his salt-and-pepper chin toward the fridge.

"You're welcome. Next time I can add some dessert if you want," Bellamy volunteered, eyes sparkling as she studied him in the wash of bright sunlight pouring in through the windows.

Grady grinned. "Now you're talkin'."

Shane chuckled and walked Bellamy to the side door. Figured Grady would be all over the sweets. Maybe Bellamy could come up with a jelly bean pie or something. That'd be right up Grady's alley.

"Okay, well, call me if you need anything," Shane said, meeting the old man's eyes over his shoulder.

"Bye now." Grady shooed them toward the door with the arch of an eyebrow. Something sparked in his eyes, and Shane paused for half a step. It hit him quick, like a sucker punch.

Approval, he thought. *He likes her.*

Guess that made two of them.

Bellamy stood with her hands on her hips and her bottom lip between her teeth, thoroughly dissatisfied.

"They're still not quite right," she said, shaking her head at the ancient belly of the oven. Two pairs of disbelieving eyes met her worry head-on, both clearly intending to show it the door.

"Are you kidding? These are the best chocolate chip cookies I've ever had," Jackson mumbled through a mouth full of crumbs as he reached for his glass of milk.

Shane nodded in agreement, putting his elbows on the tiny kitchen table. "Gotta go with the big man on this one. These cookies are out of bounds." He reached down to grab another one from the plate between him and his friend, polishing it off in a single bite.

Bellamy exhaled. She really wanted to get these cookies just right. Shane had said they were Grady's favorite, and although she couldn't quite put her finger on anything concrete, there was something about the man that was just so endearing. Familiar, almost.

Not being able to pinpoint it had been bugging her all day.

She tipped her head, putting the thought aside for now. "You wouldn't say these cookies are good just to humor me, would you?"

"Yes, I would," Shane replied, rendering Bellamy speechless. Jackson gave a low *are you stupid?* whistle, and Bellamy's hand went right to her hip. "But," Shane scrambled to continue before she could protest or hit him or take his cookies away, "I wouldn't eat a dozen of them just to humor you. They really are good, babe."

Bellamy's cheeks flushed. Shane *had* eaten at least ten cookies. "Okay, fine. I still think they need more brown sugar," she said, calculating the ratios in her head.

"Perfectionist," Shane teased.

He had to be kidding, right? "Pot. Kettle. Helllloooo?"

Well, that shut him up.

Jackson laughed. "Well, y'all, I'm going to roll out of here. And I do mean that literally." He rubbed a hand over his midsection, and Bellamy fought back the urge to snicker. There wasn't an ounce of fat anywhere on him, but whatever floated his boat. Leave it to a man to cram down over a dozen cookies with no fat repercussions.

"Thanks again for letting me come over and test out the cookies," Jackson said, tipping his blond crew cut in her direction. "They really are awesome."

"Thanks for being my guinea pig." She stood on her tip-toes to hug him good-bye, and after a hiccup of surprise, he enveloped her in a bear hug right back.

"Anytime. And I really do mean that, especially if you get some urge to go the oatmeal raisin route."

When Shane had said Jackson was cool, he'd known what the hell he was talking about. They'd only spent a couple of hours hanging out in Shane's cabin, but Bellamy had felt instant affection for the guy. It wasn't every day you met a man whose pro-wrestler-esque veneer covered up genuine down home charm.

"You're on." She grinned, waving as Jackson slid into his jacket.

"See ya, dude," he said to Shane, jerking his head in parting as he headed out the door.

"Jackson's sweet," Bellamy said, nibbling the edge of a cookie. Okay, they *were* pretty good, brown sugar notwithstanding. She took another bite.

Shane laughed, pushing back from the table. "Yeah, he's just sweet enough to get away with not doing any dishes," he pointed out, gesturing to the kitchen.

It hadn't been easy to make those cookies on one warped cookie sheet, and the aftermath clearly showed in the tiny space. Bellamy had managed to get flour and sugar all over the narrow counter, not to mention using every kitchen utensil Shane owned. All three of them. Thank God she'd snapped up some plastic measuring cups at Joe's, but still. They added to the mess.

"Yeah, that's my fault." Bellamy chewed her lip and turned toward the sink, but Shane's playful smirk stopped her in her tracks.

"Where I come from, if you cook, you don't clean." He edged past her to snap up a dish towel, starting to swipe it over the flour-scattered countertop.

"And where I come from, we clean up our messes. Draw?"

His smirk lingered, weaving its way through her with sexy heat. "Draw."

Bellamy ran a sink full of hot, soapy water and started to scrub the sheet pan, and he whistled softly as he scrubbed the counter clean. It felt all too good to be standing there in the kitchen with Shane, even doing something as simple as everyday chores.

God, she didn't want to leave.

"Thanks for showing me around Pine Mountain today. It's really beautiful up here."

"I'm glad you finally got to have one of Lou's burgers,"

Shane said, stacking the dirty dishes he'd collected next to the sink.

Bellamy's stomach groaned in pleasure at the memory. "The man knows his way around the grill, I'll tell you that." Even the fries had been perfect—not too thick or greasy, just perfect for dipping. She rinsed the cookie sheet, brain still stuck on her fantastic lunch.

"Yeah, well it's a good thing we took that hike afterward, otherwise I'd have been in a food coma all damned day." Shane laughed. "The loop behind the cabin is nicer than the cleared trails by the resort, but with all the snow still on the ground, we'd never have made it." He took the cookie sheet Bellamy passed his way and began to dry it.

She smiled into the sink, continuing to wash the dishes while Shane dried. "The Ridge was still my favorite part, though." They'd both been surprised to see that the path to Carrington Ridge had been cleared, probably by some locals wanting to see the sunrise over the snowy mountains. Wrapped in blankets and passing a Thermos of coffee back and forth, Bellamy and Shane had sat in the bed of the truck and enjoyed the gorgeous view, talking and laughing until their fingers were numb. Every minute had felt seamless and perfect, and it just hammered home Bellamy's completely unrealistic desire to stay right where she was.

"Yeah, me too. Not a whole lot of people get to see the mountain the way you did today." Shane slid open the lone kitchen drawer, its occupants giving a metallic clank as he tossed in one of their freshly cleaned friends.

"I just hope I can return the favor next weekend. You've probably seen all the touristy stuff in Philly, though," she replied, thinking out loud. Shane didn't really seem like the Liberty Bell kind of guy anyhow.

He stiffened, then shifted his weight as if he didn't want her to notice. "Yeah."

Bellamy's heartbeat stuttered in her chest. The air around her felt thicker somehow, but she hauled in a breath of it anyway. "Shane, what's going on?" Damn it, she really needed to get a handle on her lack of brain-to-mouth filter, but something just wasn't right here and she didn't think she could ignore it anymore.

"You're woefully behind on your dishwashing, that's what." He cocked his dark head and gave her a smile that would seduce the panties off a schoolmarm.

Something twisted deep in her rib cage, telling her not to bite, but the heat between her thighs begged her to shut up. So he had some mysterious aversion to the city. It's not like that was a shocker—he'd told her about it days ago. Plus, he'd said he would come see her regardless, and Shane wouldn't lie to her. Pushing him to talk about it would only sour their evening, and it was one of the last ones they had left together, for now anyway.

"I guess I am," she finally agreed, letting her hands slip into the water.

Shane moved behind her, the combination of his heat and his touch making her forget about the sink full of kitchenware in need of washing.

Bellamy sighed and leaned into him, her back against his lean, strong chest. "Dishes," she said weakly, but Shane just chuckled in her ear.

"Leave 'em." He slid his hands over the front of her hips from behind, fingers biting into her as he curled them over the denim. A moan shuddered from her as he pressed his arousal to her body, pinning her without force against the sink.

"If you insist," she murmured in a throaty whisper,

thrusting the cradle of her hips back into his erection. With one swift move, Shane swung her around so they were face-to-face. Bellamy arched forward to close the slight space between them, but the reverent look on Shane's face stopped her before they could touch.

"God, every part of you is just exquisite," he breathed, his eyes prickling her skin as they moved over her, as palpable as a touch. He leaned in just enough to dance his tongue over the shell of her ear with hot suggestion, and she shook her head against his ministrations.

"But you are," Shane whispered, sliding his fingers through her hair. "Your hair looks perfect when it's lying over your pillow in the early sunlight." He traced his way down her neck with both hands, letting his mouth follow their lead, and Bellamy couldn't resist the raw urge to curve up under his touch and let his words fill her as he spoke them.

"Your skin tastes like honey, right here." He paused to kiss her, lightly scraping his lips over hers with excruciating heat, then dipped his tongue to the spot where her shoulder met her collarbone. "And here, you're even sweeter."

Shane lowered the flat of his hands to her hips, sliding them under her thin sweater. Bellamy had no choice but to suck in a breath at the contact of his skin on hers, heat sparking right to the center of her hips before burning a path to her core.

"Shane, please." Her thoughts were so disjointed from wanting him that her plea short-circuited with the desire that created it, but Shane heard her all the same.

"Oh, I've barely just begun," he assured her, stroking the sides of her body with sure, even touches as he lifted her sweater over her head. Her nipples pebbled and strained against the lace of her bra, screaming to be touched. When he parted his hands over her breasts to balance their weight in his palms, an unfettered groan worked its way from Bellamy's chest to her lips.

"Don't you see how beautiful you are?" He cupped her breasts over the fabric, making her clamp down on her lip to hold back a whimper. "Here," he whispered, rolling her nipple between his thumb and forefinger. "And here," Shane continued, and Bellamy's bones threatened to melt right inside the heat of her body. Never in her life had she wanted anyone or anything with so much white-hot intensity, so much pure, uncut desire, and she couldn't wait another second to have it.

"Shane, *please*," she begged, her voice thready with want. "Please take me to bed. I want you so much." She drank in every nuance of him as he stood before her in the low light of the kitchen, the contrast of his skin against the richness of the amber walls of the cabin making them seem to glow.

"But I haven't even gotten to the best part," he protested in a drawl that rippled up her spine. "The sweetest thing about you is right here." He paused over her slamming heart, pressing his palm over it with care. "And here." His hands moved to cradle her face as if she were a treasure. "Because your openness is so unbridled. Your honesty makes you beautiful." He paused again, this time to let his eyes give her a message that even his words couldn't.

He meant every word, not just as pillow talk, but as the simple truth. He meant it.

Bellamy couldn't do anything other than look into the emotion banked in Shane's dark eyes. The truth on his face made tears prick her eyes, unbidden and hot.

"Please," she whispered, afraid to utter anything other

than the one word, lest the tears start pouring out and the words racing through her mind follow.

As he led her to his bedroom, over the threshold and over the edge of want and need and reason, Shane made love to her like she was the only woman on earth, and Bellamy knew. Just like she knew she needed air to breathe and food to eat and somewhere to sleep at night, she needed Shane Griffin. It was as simple as the rightness in his words and the look in his eyes when he saw her, and somehow, even though they lived in separate worlds, being with Shane made perfect sense.

Because she was in love with him.

Shane smoothed his hand along one of Bellamy's curls, catching its softness between the pads of his fingers and the pillowcase. Christ, she was gorgeous with that glow on her face, almost angelic under the sliver of moonlight passing through the curtains.

"Get some sleep, sweetheart." He placed a kiss on her forehead, inhaling the crisp scent of her for just a moment before pulling back. Her big green eyes focused in on him, unwavering, as they lay side by side in the shadows.

"I'm not really that tired." She didn't say anything else, just captured his eyes with hers and held on tight.

She gets you. And she deserves to know the truth.

The explanation rattled around in Shane's head, stark and serious, and although none of the words sounded right, he'd held them in for far too long to keep them buried now. Not when there was a chance Bellamy would understand.

"Shane?"

The way her whisper shaped his name perked through his blood, and he brought his eyes back to hers. "Hey." The word arrived on a slight tremble, and he opened his mouth to just let the rest out; to tell her that as much as he didn't want to be away from her, he couldn't possibly come to the city to see her; to ask her to come back to Pine Mountain instead . . .

The shrill ring of the phone on his bedside table made him jump out of his skin.

"What the hell?" he blurted, the curse edged in anger. He propped himself up on an elbow to squint at the clock. It was barely ten P.M., but still. "No one ever freaking calls me," he said, fumbling for the phone in the near-dark. Whoever it was had pretty crappy timing, and was about to get an earful for it.

"Maybe Jackson left something." Bellamy sat up while the phone let out another ring that grated his nerves like sandpaper on silk.

Finally, Shane connected with the damned thing and snatched it from the cradle to press it to his ear.

"Hello?" If this was a wrong number, so help him . . .

"Shane? Jesus, Shane! Get your ass to the garage right fucking now." Jackson's words were as garbled as they were panicked.

Shane sat up in bed, fear bolting through every inch of him. "Jax? What the hell, buddy?" He barely registered Bellamy's hand on his back, sudden, cold fear coming off her in waves.

"The garage! Hurry up. I think they just got here!"

Shane could hear voices, indistinct but clipped and serious, muffled in the background. "Who? What the fuck is going on, Jackson?" Dread gripped Shane all the way to his bones, and he jammed his legs through his jeans without feeling a thing.

"Paramedics. Grady had another heart attack, and you need to get down here *now*."

Chapter Twenty-Five

Shane never took the main road any faster than was necessary, mainly because the forty-foot drop-off made it just plain stupid. Plus, the ride between his cabin and the garage took less than ten minutes to cover.

Under the muted moonlight, with his old F150 protesting like mad, Shane made it there in five, barely stopping to throw the thing into Park before flinging himself out the driver's side door. From the corner of his eye, he caught sight of Bellamy through the windshield, presumably grabbing the keys from the still-running truck, but he didn't stop. He ran toward the garage, dizzy from the eerie red glow of the ambulance lights that pulsed over the building and the sickening *whoosh* of his own blood in his ears.

Shane barged through the side door and tried to focus, but there were so many things in the garage that didn't belong there, he couldn't process any of them, much less make himself speak. Bellamy's Miata was up on the lift, transmission parts littering the floor like scattered toys. The cordless phone lay, sunny-side up, in the midst of them, and the display glowed green as if it was still on. Jackson stood stock-still in the doorway of the office, his face grave and his cell phone locked in his grip. People Shane had never seen before raced around in front of him, crouching down and shouting things that made no sense.

"Pulse is thready! BP is one-oh-six over seventy."

"Sir, can you hear me?"

A grunted response from the floor shattered the disconnect between Shane's brain and everything around him, and all at once, everything crashed from slow-motion to real-time in an unforgiving snap.

"Grady!" Shane lunged toward the office, where two paramedics huddled over Grady's limp form, their movements sharp and efficient.

This wasn't happening. It wasn't happening.

Jackson jerked to attention. "Damn, that was fast!" He cut the distance between himself and Shane in only a few brisk strides.

Shane met his friend's eyes for less than a second before trying to elbow his way past in an effort to reach Grady, but Jackson reached around him and held firm.

"Dude, you gotta let them do their jobs. They're trying to help him."

"I'm all that man's got," Shane growled at Jackson. "And I'll be goddamned if he doesn't know I'm here when he needs me." He struggled against Jackson's unyielding torso. Why wasn't Grady answering, damn it? "Grady!"

"Shane?" A tall redheaded paramedic he'd also seen tending bar at the Double Shot from time to time looked over her shoulder, but Shane was so worked up that it barely registered. "*Shane!*" she barked again, and the word sank in enough for Shane to realize it had been directed at him. Jackson's hold weakened, and Shane took full advantage, pushing past him to answer the woman.

"Yeah?"

"Teagan O'Malley, Pine Mountain Fire and Rescue. When was the last time you saw him?" Her hands moved in a flurry of sure activity over Grady's body, and she leaned in to murmur something to him before glancing back at Shane. Grady looked so pale and fragile that Shane's heart thudded around in his chest.

"This morning. He was . . ." Tired. Grady had been tired, and Shane had known it. "He was fine." Shane forced himself to look at Grady's face. *Please wake up. Please.* "Hey, Grady. We're gonna get you fixed up, okay. Just hang in there."

The old man's gray eyes flashed open at the sound of Shane's voice, showing a mixture of fear and pain that made Shane's blood turn to ice in his veins.

"Call . . . him . . . you have to call . . . make it right . . ."

Shane reached in to grab the old man's hand, giving it a squeeze. "Okay. Okay."

Grady closed his eyes again, and Teagan cut in roughly. "It's better if he doesn't talk unless he has to. Know any medical history?"

Shane nodded, but couldn't speak.

"Any drug allergies that you know about? Past history of heart attack? He had one last year, right?" More movement, and the other paramedic made purposeful strides with a wheeled stretcher. Oh, shit, this was bad. No, no, no, no.

Shane forced the answers from his mouth. "Uh, no allergies. But yeah, he had a mild heart attack fourteen months ago. His meds are in the cabinet in the office." Both hemispheres of Shane's brain were bound by a fog that made it difficult for him to think, and he felt as if his entire universe was crashing down over his head.

"I'm going to need those. Now would be good."

Shane's legs refused to move. He couldn't leave Grady's side, not even for the two seconds it would take to grab the medication bottles from the shelf in the office. "You can't let him die." He'd meant the words to come out firm, forceful, but instead, they were a vulnerable plea.

"I'm going to do everything I possibly can to make sure that doesn't happen, okay? But you've got to let us do our job here."

Shane caught a flash of movement, blond hair and plaid flannel, and someone handed the fistful of orange bottles to Teagan.

"Ah. Thanks." She scanned them quickly and rattled off a bunch of syllables to her partner that sounded odd together, like some sort of code. Bits and pieces, fragments of things, crossed Shane's field of vision, but nothing made any sense. Why was Bellamy's car on the lift? And what the hell had Jackson been doing here?

"He's stable enough for now, but we need to get to Riverside Hospital. They have an advanced cardiac unit, so they'll be better able to diagnose and treat him than Pine Mountain's medical facility. Is Grady his first name or last?"

"First." This couldn't be happening. Why hadn't Shane been there? Guilt pushed through him, relentless and fast.

He should've been there.

"You work with him. Do you know his last name? We're going to need to find his family, if he's got any." The male paramedic began strapping Grady to the stretcher with care, and Teagan aimed an expectant look at Shane.

His heart wrenched in his chest, his voice utterly cold as the words formed in his brain and forced their way from his mouth. "His last name's Griffin, just like mine. The only other family he's got besides me is his son, Charles Griffin, Esquire. My father."

Bellamy blinked at Shane and took an involuntary step backward as she reeled in an equal mix of shock and confusion.

Shane was Grady's grandson? But why hadn't he said anything to her?

Recognition shot through her as she stood, dumbfounded, next to Jackson. No wonder Grady had seemed so familiar to her when she'd met him that morning. Shane's mannerisms were an exact mirror of Grady's, right down to the inflection in his voice when Shane had called her "darlin'" the other day. Even if the physical resemblance was only slight, they were definitely cut from the same cloth. How had she not seen it before?

"Jesus," Jackson said, his chiseled jaw falling open. "Grady's his grandfather?"

"You didn't know either?" Shock rebounded through her chest.

"No. He never said anything," Jackson replied in a low voice, shaking his head. "After Grady had that heart attack last year, Shane just showed up. I always thought it was a stroke of luck for the old man, you know, that some drifter came along to save the day. But Shane never told me where he came *from*."

Bellamy nodded, her thoughts racing on fast-forward. Shane's devotion was a little clearer, but still. Jackson was right. He had to have come from somewhere, left something behind, in order to help Grady out.

Wait a second . . . Charles Griffin, *Esquire*? Bellamy's stomach dropped like a rock.

Oh, *God*. He couldn't possibly be Charles Griffin, Philadelphia's most prominent attorney, could he? Bellamy had heard the name in certain circles at the bank, and while his offices didn't specialize in real estate, per se, everyone who was anyone in the world of business had at least heard of the law firm. His name was in the papers on a regular basis, in both local news and on the social page.

But of course she hadn't connected the dots. Why the hell would she?

Shane's voice, loud and argumentative, yanked her focus back to the garage. "I'm going with you," he insisted, following the paramedics and the stretcher to the door.

"Standard operating procedure, Mr. Griffin. No passengers." The female paramedic's words were curt and suggested zero wiggle room.

Shane didn't seem to care. "Like hell. I'm going."

Bellamy sprang into action, shoving her fist into the pocket of her jeans where she'd stashed Shane's truck keys, and they all moved toward the door in a bustle of movement and sound.

The paramedic stared him down. "What you're doing is wasting precious seconds of my time. I get that you're worried, but if you want me to save his life, you have to get out of my way and let me *do it*."

Shane stopped short at her order, helplessly watching in defeat as she and her partner loaded the stretcher into the back of the ambulance. Bellamy passed the keys to Jackson, who wordlessly went to start Shane's truck. Out of sheer instinct, she put her hand on Shane's shoulder, realizing only after the fact that he might not want her to.

He clutched her hand for a second before slumping into

her, and she barely got her arm around him in time to hold him up.

"Okay," she whispered into him, biting back tears with every breath. "Okay. Jackson's waiting, Shane. We're going to follow them the whole way there. Come on."

The redhead jumped out the back of the ambulance, slamming the doors to the rig with finality before turning toward the driver's side.

"I'm sorry," she said over her shoulder. "I really am. But I promise we'll do all we can to keep him safe."

Shane's eyes surged with raw emotion as he looked at her. "I'm holding you to that."

With a nod, the woman climbed into the ambulance and pulled out into the dead of night.

Shane fought the urge to vomit as Jackson navigated the turns on the main road down the mountain. His head reeled with unanswered questions and impending dread, only one of which he could do anything about.

"How . . . how did you know about Grady?" he asked Jackson, whose stony blue gaze didn't move from the road as he answered.

"After I left your place, I stopped by the Double Shot to see what was going on. It was pretty dead, so I decided to take off, and I saw the ambulance pulling in as I passed by on my way home. Teagan said Grady called nine-one-one, complaining of chest pain. That's when I called you."

Shane reached behind the seat for Bellamy's hand. She'd managed to squeeze herself across the narrow bench in the back of the truck, which couldn't be comfortable, but she hadn't even hesitated to get in.

"He was working on that tranny, doing the job by

himself," Shane realized out loud. From the looks of things, Grady had gotten a good deal of the work done, too, so he had to have pulled a ten-hour day, maybe even twelve, considering Lucky Gunderson's Cadillac. That kind of day would've turned even the healthiest guy into a zombie.

Shane swallowed past the Sahara desert in his throat. What would it end up doing to Grady?

"He said he would call me. He was supposed to call me when that stupid tranny came in." Shane let out a low curse under his breath, and Bellamy's hand froze in his.

"This isn't your fault, Shane."

"This is *absolutely* my fault," he snapped, his gut triple-knotting. "He's my responsibility, and I should've been there."

"Okay, take it easy. Getting upset sure won't fix anything," Jackson said with care. "Let's just get to the hospital. Do you want to try my cell to call your, uh, father?"

Oh, *fuck*. This was going to go from bad to worse. Shane pinched the bridge of his nose. "No." No way was he having that conversation with the two of them in the car to overhear it. It was going to be bad enough as it was. God *damn* it, he hadn't had a chance to tell Bellamy the truth.

But he couldn't worry about that now.

"My father hasn't wanted to see Grady for twenty years. A few more hours should suit him just fine."

As soon as his father showed up, every secret Shane had ever kept would be out in the open, and there would be no hiding from any of it.

With that, he let Bellamy's fingers slip from his, letting her go before she could beat him to it.

* * *

Bellamy stared into the Styrofoam cup of cold coffee in her hands, catching her distorted reflection in the dark liquid. The clock on the wall showed half past midnight, and although she was weary down to her bones, sleep was the furthest thing from her mind. She rubbed her forehead as if the motion would jump-start her brain into making sense of the last few hours.

Shane had bolted inside the hospital doors the minute Jackson pulled up to the glass and brick façade of Riverside Hospital two hours ago, and they'd met him in the waiting room of the ER. All of their questions had been met with the polite yet firm assurance that the doctor would come out and speak with them shortly. As soon as it had become clear that *shortly* was a rough translation for *a dog's age* in hospital-speak, Shane disappeared for about ten minutes, presumably to call his father.

His father, who Shane had gone out of his way to avoid mentioning. He had to have something to do with why Shane hated the city so much—Charles Griffin was a paragon of Philadelphia high society. Even his money had money, for God's sake. Bellamy's family was well-off, sure, but they didn't hold a candle to *that*. Her head pounded between her temples, and disquiet squeezed her chest into tightness.

He'd lied to her.

Shane prowled the ten by ten path of linoleum in the waiting room on a restless loop, his work boots echoing a hollow thud into the squares with each step. Jackson had given up on trying to sardine his large frame into the hard plastic chairs in the waiting room, opting instead to lean back across the entire row for a better fit. A year-old *Car and Driver* magazine sat in his lap, untouched, as he stared at the walls, and Shane did yet another abrupt about-face in the corner of the waiting room. The steady *clomp-clomp* of his steel-toed Red Wings alternating with the deafening silence set Bellamy's teeth on edge, but she said nothing. Finally, the doors leading to the ER hissed open on automatic breath.

"Shane Griffin?" A tired-looking man in pale green scrubs stared at the trio with kind yet serious eyes.

"That's me," Shane said, nearly hurdling the row of chairs between him and the doctor. Bellamy's heart beat so wildly against her rib cage that she half expected it to break free.

"I'm Dr. Russell. I'm taking care of your grandfather." He extended his hand for the obligatory one-pump man-shake, then flipped an electronic chart from under his arm. "As I'm sure you suspect, your grandfather suffered a myocardial infarction, which is the medical term for a heart attack. We've ruled out the need for angioplasty, but we have him hooked up to the ECG to monitor his heart rhythms. He's also getting oxygen, so his body won't have to work so hard at breathing."

Oh, sweet Jesus. Just breathing on his own was too hard? Bellamy slammed her eyes shut over the pool of tears forming there. She would *not* cry.

"We're also giving him some beta-blockers, which help to lessen the strain on the heart, and some pretty heavy-duty painkillers to ease his discomfort. I want to get him in for an MRI so we can see what we're dealing with here, and he'll probably spend some time in the ICU, just to be on the safe side." The doctor paused, probably to let everything sink in for a minute, but Shane didn't waste a single second.

"I want to stay with him."

Dr. Russell shook his head. "Visiting hours are strict in the ICU, and nearly one A.M. doesn't qualify. I'm sorry. Plus, what he needs above all else right now is rest. The first twenty-four hours after a heart attack are the most precarious. We've got the best cardiac unit in the area, so he's in great hands. But he's not out of the woods yet. After he's stable, we'll see what the MRI says and go from there."

Shane nodded in defeat. "Thank you, Dr. Russell. Come get me if he needs anything. I'll be right here."

"Do yourself a favor, Mr. Griffin. Go home and get some rest. He'll be here with us for a while, so you're going to need it. We'll be sure to call you if anything comes up." The doctor shook Shane's hand one more time before disappearing behind the double doors.

Bellamy stood, unmoving, on the green and gray flecked linoleum, torn between wanting to ask a billion questions and throw her arms around Shane. His usually warm brown eyes fell on her with dull sadness, and she felt a distance stretch out between them as it slipped under her skin to invade every part of her.

"Why don't we go back to the cabin to lie down for a bit? Then we can come here in a few hours to see him," Bellamy said. She fully expected Shane to protest, and had already made up her mind that she wouldn't push it if he did. Those chairs in the waiting room weren't too bad, and anyway, she'd do anything to ease the pain on his face.

"Okay, yeah."

Jackson jumped to action. "I'll pull the truck around, buddy. Just hang tight." He hustled his gigantic frame out the lobby doors and into the frigid night.

Bellamy wrapped the sleeves of her shirt over her hands, curling the edges over her fingers and into loose fists. They'd been in such a hurry that she'd snapped Shane's flannel from the floor of his room, and she just now noticed that she'd missed a button in her haste to get dressed.

"I'm really sorry, Shane." Maybe it was lame, but the apology was what she'd been thinking, and apparently her speak-your-mind habit didn't have a crisis mode. Plus, she had no idea what else to say.

"For what?" Shane asked, but he didn't look up. His face had aged fifteen years in the last few hours.

"I wish this hadn't happened to Grady. To you. Why didn't you tell me he's your grandfather?"

The question felt so utterly benign as it left Bellamy's lips that she was unprepared for the reaction it brought.

"Because it's none of your business. It doesn't have anything to do with you."

Bellamy recoiled as if she'd been slapped, the words reverberating in her skull so hard she'd swear they'd leave a mark.

"But I . . ."

"Forget it." He cut her off. "I just want to go home."

"O-okay." Bellamy wrapped her arms around herself to suppress the shudder working through her. Shane was stressed beyond measure, and she knew she should cut him some slack. But now she didn't know if that meant staying close or leaving him alone, and the confusion rattled her brain. She turned toward the lobby doors, trying to hide the sting of his words. "I'll just see if Jackson's here yet."

"Bellamy, wait."

She hovered a few steps between Shane and the doors, not moving toward either. Her disloyal legs refused to move her one way or the other, even though she commanded them to just head for the damned door.

"It's fine," she managed to croak. "Let's just get you home."

Shane exhaled a shaky breath. "Listen, I . . ."

"Shane."

The word came from behind them, a deep baritone that sang of seriousness and quiet power. Bellamy turned toward Shane, who didn't move except to close his eyes. The man stood in the mouth of the hallway leading from the main hospital, his stance still and imposing. His face was a perfectly sculpted older version of Shane's, with the exception of the steel-gray eyes coldly fixed on Shane's back. Bellamy blinked in surprise, too shocked to speak.

Shane squared his shoulders and opened his eyes to give her one last, fleeting look before he turned on his heel toward the man.

"Dad."

Chapter Twenty-Six

All of the breath and blood in Shane's body felt as if it had been replaced with permafrost the minute he heard the familiar timbre of his father's voice behind him. Leave it to Charles Griffin to come up behind Shane and catch him off guard. Even in a crisis, he was all about strategy.

Shane turned to meet his father head-on. Charles Griffin stood with his back to the hallway, looking as polished as if he'd walked out the door for a business lunch at Del Frisco's. The perfectly knotted silk tie seemed so out of place under the circumstances that Shane had to fight the urge to cough up a bitter laugh.

"I'm surprised you're here," Shane said, measuring his father's stance with careful eyes.

"Is that because of my relationship with him or you?" his father returned coolly.

God damn, he should've figured it would go this way right out of the gate.

"I'm not the one who's sick," Shane volleyed, hoping his father would bite. He didn't want to talk about himself, but hell if he was going to back down, either.

His father nodded, a smooth stroke of his elegantly graying dark head. "Have they told you anything?"

Relief swirled in Shane's chest at the successful diversion, though he knew it wouldn't last. "Grady's headed up to the ICU. They won't really know the extent of the damage until he's had an MRI. For now, the doc wants him to rest while they monitor him." Shane knew his father would double-check every detail with the doctor anyway, but he wished there was more to tell. At least that way, they'd be talking about Grady and not him. Not that it probably mattered.

"He's a tough old man," his father said, and for a minute Shane wondered if it was meant to be reassuring rather than just a statement of fact.

But his father was a statement-of-fact kind of guy, the cold bastard, and Shane felt the resentment well up within him.

"How would you know? You've seen him what? Four times in twenty years? Last time this happened, you were all set to just let him rehab with strangers and watch the business he loved fall to pieces," he bit out, each word laced with accusation.

His father was unruffled. "You're upset."

Damn, the man was such a manipulator! Anything he didn't want to discuss got conveniently swept under the rug without a second thought. Well screw that. Shane had plenty to say.

"And you're not upset enough," he hissed, floodgates he'd locked bursting open as he took an angry step closer. "That's your father up there, and you could give a rat's ass. Just like last time."

His father's gray eyes flared, his mouth pulling into a thin slash. "Don't think for a second that I don't remember where I came from and who raised me. As a matter of fact, you might do well to remember that on your end, son. You and I have unfinished business, don't we?"

Shit. *Shit.*

"My business with you is done," Shane said flatly, knowing the blanket statement wouldn't hold.

His father sneered. "Your business with me never really got started, did it? You're into me for a lot of money, Shane."

"What are you talking about?"

"I'm talking about the law school loans you're two months behind on paying. You see, I had a nice, long conversation with the senior loan officer when she called the firm looking for you the other day. It seems you had *two* work numbers listed on your account, and she was covering all the bases to try and get you to pay up."

"I talked to a loan officer last week," Shane ground out, on the defensive as his father moved toward him. "My debt is to them, not you. Plus, I'm paying it."

The older man lifted a cold brow. "Not fast enough, according to them, but don't worry about being in the hole. I paid your loan off four days ago. You owe *me* that money now, and I want it the right way."

Panic clutched at Shane's gut with iron fingers, and he heard a small gasp behind him, but it sounded very far away. "You paid off my loan?"

His father's smile was more of a grimace. "I didn't want to have to do it like this, but you gave me little choice. You went through three years of law school at Princeton, passed the goddamn bar, and for what? To piss it away."

"I tried," Shane argued, although his voice didn't want to cooperate fully. "I put in time at the firm."

"And those two years were just enough time for everyone

to expect great things from you before you disappeared."
His father paced around Shane slowly, his unforgiving
stare forcing its way under his skin. "I'm done watching
you fool around out here in God's country, son. Playtime's
over. You need to get your ass back to Philadelphia to start
putting your credentials to work."

Shane cranked his hands into fists so hard that he knew
they should hurt, but he didn't feel a thing other than the
sudden, blinding rage that kicked his mouth into gear. "It
must piss you off beyond measure that with all your money
and power, you can't buy me," he said, calm despite his
shredded nerves and the adrenaline pinging over them.

His father narrowed his eyes at Shane, but whether
it was in defense or anger, Shane couldn't tell. He forced
out a contemptuous smile of his own and continued, undaunted.

"The irony is priceless, really. Your only son was born
and bred to take over your prestigious law firm, only he'd
rather be a shop jockey like your old man, working on cars
instead of court cases." Momentum coursed through Shane
so hard that he felt almost dizzy with it, but he refused to
stand down.

"You need to come back to the city, son," his father said
without moving. "And do what's right."

All that was left of Shane's restraint unraveled like a
hot, angry thread. "I *am* doing what's right. If it takes me
the rest of my goddamn life, I'll pay back your fucking
money, but I'll do it as a mechanic, not an attorney,
because that's who I am. And speaking of who I am, don't
call me 'son.' I'm not coming back to the city—*not ever*—
so don't go holding your breath for that one."

The silence between them felt like fog, cold and thick,

and it stretched around them in a haze of tension until Shane's father broke it.

"Do you feel better? Now that you got that out of your system?"

No, Shane wanted to scream, but instead he stood silent, anchored to his spot on the ugly floor tiles. His pride wouldn't let him drop his father's gaze, although the emotions banked in the man's gray eyes made Shane want to look away.

His father's expression was as blank as his stare. "I don't either. Go get some sleep. I'll see you in the morning, son."

Bellamy lost count of how many times she'd been emotionally sucker punched in the last twenty-four hours. Jackson, having sensed something wrong when Shane and Bellamy failed to appear outside the ER to go home, had come inside just in time to hear the entire exchange between Shane and his father. The ride back up the mountain had been full of stiff, uncomfortable silence that crashed against Bellamy's ears, clotting her already muddled thoughts as they dropped off Jackson and Shane pulled up to the cabin and wordlessly got out of the truck.

Twelve hours ago, she'd have been more likely to believe that Shane was the man in the moon than the son of Philadelphia's most high-powered attorney, with his name all but stamped on the letterhead right next to dear old dad's. He was a mechanic with a simple life—hell, he was the one encouraging *her* to be true to herself.

Just went to show how gullible *she* was. Right about now, Shane might as well be the man in the moon for all she knew him.

"You should get some rest," Bellamy said, her voice stilted, as she raked a hand through the snarl of curls around her face. Holding out for much longer wasn't going to be an option for her, and she'd be goddamned if her pride would let Shane see her cry.

"I wanted to tell you," Shane said, although his hollow tone suggested otherwise. "But it's complicated. Obviously."

Bellamy's eyes fell on the sink full of dirty dishes, the now-cold, murky water a stark contrast to what had happened in front of it just a handful of hours before. She felt her composure snap and start to unravel, and she pinned him with an angry stare.

"How do you figure lying to be any less complicated?" she asked, cursing the honesty as it rolled off her tongue.

He flinched, but still didn't look at her. "I didn't mean for it to happen this way."

"Did you mean any of it, period?"

Shane's eyes flashed to hers, wide and roiling with emotion. "Yes," he protested, but she barreled on, realization thick in her chest.

"God, it all makes perfect sense now! No wonder you hated me at first. I'm a city girl, head to toe, from my freaking Ivy League degree to my cute little sports car you keep turning your nose up at. I'm like the ultimate reminder of everything you can't stand. And here I was, buying into all of your crap about being true to myself, taking these huge risks and letting you encourage me to change when you just didn't want to see your past every time you turned around. Jesus!"

"None of that is crap, Bellamy! It's why I'm *here*. I left my father's law firm because I *hated* it. You left your job because you hated it. I'm with you even though you come from the city. You can't be any more true to yourself than that!" he exploded, bracing himself against the short stretch of kitchen counter.

If Shane thought she was going to go the shrinking violet route at a little yelling, he had the wrong girl. Bellamy's pulse hammered through her, ushering out her anger. "Yeah, you were so true to yourself that you lied through your teeth to me about who you were! I don't even know you, Shane. I don't know anything about you!"

He winced. "Okay, fine. So I let you believe some things about me that weren't necessarily true, and yes, I kept some things from you. But you know exactly who I am. I never flat-out lied to you."

Bellamy's heart bottomed out as her next words tumbled from her lips.

"But you never told me the truth, either. You were never going to come see me in the city, were you?"

Please, God. Please let him say yes. Please . . .

Shane exhaled as if she'd punched him in the stomach, and the tears that had been threatening her with their presence rimmed her eyes, ready to fall.

"No. I wasn't."

A traitorous sob worked its way up from her chest, and Bellamy used every ounce of her willpower to swallow it whole. Shane had intended to let her walk out the door with her head full of delusions. She'd believed him, thought she was in *love* with him, for God's sake, and the whole thing had been a total farce, based on a man who didn't exist.

And didn't that just make her the biggest jerk on the face of the planet.

"I see. Well, then, I think it's time for us to end this little charade, don't you?"

"God damn it, Bellamy, you don't understand—"

Everything that was left of her resolve crashed down around her. "Really?" she snapped, her nerves beyond frayed. "Then explain it to me, Shane. Explain how you lying to me every step of the way should make me trust you."

"It's . . . it's complicated . . ." he stammered, pulling his arms over his chest in a tight fold.

"Yeah, you said that." Her chest fluttered with adrenaline and sadness and something else that she couldn't quite pin with a name. The silence between them was covered in nails, and Bellamy stood, stock-still on the scuffed floorboards, torn between hating Shane for playing her for a fool and wanting him to grab her and hold her and tell her the whole thing was a big misunderstanding.

Or was it more like a big mistake?

A muscle ticked beneath the stubble on Shane's jaw. "I just . . . I need to get out of here. I feel like I can't even think."

All the breath in Bellamy's body left her in a soundless rush, sucked out into the cold air with finality. "Don't let me stop you."

"I'm sorry," Shane whispered as he made his way to the door. "I really am. It's not you."

Bellamy cursed his name until the sound of his truck faded into the deep folds of night. Only then did she sit down on the floor and start to cry.

Shane autopiloted his way to the garage, thoughts pressing against the sides of his skull like a nasty hangover. Getting elbow-deep in a car was his only hope of getting his head semi-straight, and he was suddenly grateful for the pain-in-the-ass job of replacing a tranny. He stood in the frame of the side door for a minute, the cold wind and dark night conspiring against him at his back. His heart twisted in his chest as he flicked the fluorescent lights on, and all of the night's events threatened to flash back over him in vivid detail, making his stomach churn with bitterness and bile.

The cordless phone, still flashing a dull green in a pile of socket wrenches on the floor, snapped Shane's glazed-over stare back into focus. Grady must have dropped it there after he'd called 911. He should put it back on the hook, in case anyone tried to call the garage. Yeah. It wouldn't do to leave it off the hook like that.

Having that one small purpose steeled Shane's nerves, forcing his boots to move over the buffed concrete floor toward the lift. Okay. He could do this. He could figure out a way to deal with his father, to help Grady get better, to fix everything. After all, fixing things was what he did.

Who the hell was he fooling?

"Shane?" The sound of Jackson's voice rattled through Shane's thoughts, and he swung around, blinking.

"Jackson? What are you doing here?"

His friend's sheepish smile looked faded and tired. "Too jacked up to sleep. I thought a drive might clear my head; plus I figured someone should come out here and make sure everything was locked up." Jackson shut the side door behind him and stuffed his hands in his pockets.

"Thanks." Shane picked up a socket wrench from the cold concrete. "I'm going to stick around, finish up with this tranny."

"You're gonna need some decent muscle to mate that thing to the bell housing, you know," Jackson said, pulling his coat off to toss it on the workbench.

"Yeah. It's not for the faint of heart."

"Lucky for you I know just the guy to help you out. Hand me that input shaft, would you?"

Shane stopped, overwhelmed again by everything flying around in his mind. "Thanks, man."

Jackson lowered his arms from the Miata's undercarriage. "You want to talk about it?"

He meant to say no. He meant to just work on the car, get his mind good and straight, and come up with all the answers. But instead, when Shane opened his mouth, the whole story came bubbling up.

"When I was a kid, my parents would host these fancy parties in the city for Philadelphia's up-and-coming socialites. They were no place for me and my sister, so we'd come up here to spend long weekends with Grady and my grandmother, Ella. We thought it was the coolest thing in the world to come play in the garage bays, eat homemade chocolate chip cookies and stay up past our bedtime to look at the stars. I used to peek under the hood of every car that came into this place, and Grady helped me memorize the makes and models while Ella played with my sister in the fields out back."

Jackson's brow twitched in thought. "I don't remember Grady ever being married."

Shane exhaled on a small, sad smile. "You moved here when you were eleven, right?"

Jackson nodded, and Shane went on. "She died the summer I was nine, and my sister and I never came back. By the time I was old enough to realize it wasn't Grady's grief so much as my father's strained relationship with the old man that kept us away from Pine Mountain, I was in middle school." Shane shook his head at the fogged-over memory of it. "For a couple of years, Grady came up to the city to visit at Christmastime, but my dad was always conveniently in court on those days. After a while, the visits just stopped. I didn't see Grady at all when I was a teenager." The guilt that threaded around the words hung in the air like a heavy aftertaste.

"So then you just went to college and law school? How'd you end up back here from there?" Jackson asked.

The smile that crossed Shane's lips grew a little bigger, and he tipped his head toward the Mustang. "On an impulse, I bought the car the summer after I graduated from college. It pissed my father off something fierce, which was half the reason I did it. But in the end, I'd earned the money for it by grunting it out at the firm, so there was nothing he could do about it."

Recognition flickered in Jackson's eyes, and Shane could see him starting to fit the pieces together as he finished.

"So I kept the car at a hole in the wall garage outside of Princeton, fixing it up whenever I could, but I didn't know my ass from my elbow and I got in way over my head. I called Grady up, just for a pointer or two, and you know what he did? He showed up in Princeton three hours later."

Jackson chuckled. "That sounds like something Grady would do."

Shane shifted his weight, squinting through the harsh fluorescent glare of the garage. "We never talked about the ten years we spent apart, not that weekend or any of the others when he came to Princeton to help me with the car, but it always ate at me that I wasn't there for him when I should've been. Even when I graduated and passed the bar, I still stayed close with him, even though my father never knew it."

"And that's why you came last year."

He nodded, a single dip of his rough chin. "Yup. It was

a no-brainer. I couldn't let Grady lose his business, not when he loved it so much. My father scoffed at the idea, even though he begrudgingly agreed to let me have the time off. We both thought it would be temporary, but as soon as I spent one day back here, I knew I wouldn't ever go back to the city."

Jackson cleared his throat and looked at his boots. "So, uh, will you now?"

Shane's heart sped up in his chest. "No. Nothing's changed. I meant what I said in that hospital. This is who I am. I belong here."

"And what about Bellamy?"

The sound of her name jolted through Shane, and he instinctively reached up for the bell housing on her transmission, itching to keep his hands busy so his brain would slow down. "I don't know."

Seeming to sense that Shane was nearing the end of his rope, Jackson backed off. "Right. Let me grab a rubber mallet. We're going to have to pound the hell out of this input shaft to get it back in there right."

Shane rubbed his palm over the ache in his chest, flattening it for just a second to hold the thought of Bellamy there, close to him. She'd been right about his keeping the truth from her, but goddamn it, it wasn't like he could just come out with all of it in casual conversation. *Yeah, by the way, I'm the son of one of Philadelphia's most powerful men, but we're not speaking because I decided to give up a prestigious career for a simple life in the middle of nowhere.* She'd probably have thought he was insane.

Christ, she probably hated him right now.

Yeah, well, she's not the only one, he thought, rolling up his sleeves to finish what he'd started.

Chapter Twenty-Seven

"Sorry for calling you in the middle of the night."
Bellamy stared out the window at the purplish light of
predawn, seeing nothing as the scenery whipped by on
Rural Route Four.

Jenna shrugged, her sloppy, honey-colored ponytail
doing a haphazard dance behind her. "What're friends
for?" She paused for a minute. "So do you want to talk
about it?"

"No." Saying out loud that she'd fallen in love with
Shane, only to have him play her for the world's biggest
sap sure wasn't going to make the truth sting any less.
Hadn't her past taught her pride it was a bad idea to lie
down on the job?

It was better to just forget what had happened. God, she
needed to put her stupid, trusting heart on lockdown. Look
at what an idiot following the damned thing had made her.

"You're pretty upset," Jenna ventured again, gently
pressing.

Words percolated up from Bellamy's chest, followed by
an ache and what was sure to be an avalanche of tears.
How could she say any of this without it knocking her

down even further? What her ex, Derek, had done paled in comparison to this, and admitting that she'd been played for a fool and then a *super*-fool all in time span of a week might just be enough to send her over the edge.

Oh, no you don't, her pride roared, forcing different words from her lips.

"I'll get over it. I just want to go back to the city. I want to go home."

Bellamy stuffed down the urge to talk about Shane—to even think about his dark, brooding eyes or the ultra-masculine, oh-so-good smell of him—with all her exhausted might.

She wasn't letting him get the best of her ever again.

"It's complicated . . . complicated . . . it's not you . . ."
Bellamy covered her ears to force the words away, but they echoed, loud and sure, in her head. The smell of cedar and pine surrounded her, invading her senses, making her heart ache.

"Shane," she murmured, reaching out.
But he wasn't there.

Bellamy's head popped off the cool glass, jarring her awake with a gasp.

"What the hell?" She squinted against the sunlight filtering into the car.

"Effing potholes. Sorry," Jenna said, making a face. "And it's rush hour, so you know. We're going to eat the bumper of this moron's Corolla for a while. No-driving bonehead," she muttered with a shake of her ponytail. "Anyway, it's good that you got some sleep."

Bellamy blinked, her brain railing against the command to catch up. "Oh, right." Had she honestly been dreaming

about the way Shane smelled? Hello, lame. She tucked her
chin to her chest, surprised to feel the brush of flannel on
her face. Damn it. She'd never taken off Shane's shirt,
the one she'd snatched up off the floor on her way to the
garage. Bellamy considered taking it off, right there in
Jenna's car, but she was only wearing a thin tank top underneath it. Probably better not to flash morning traffic on 295
just to spite her ex . . . whatever Shane was. Boyfriend?
Lover? Guy who stomped on her ridiculously trusting
heart?

It was going to take forever to forget him.

"I should probably give you a heads-up. Holly's waiting, and she's at Defcon Oh-my-God. I told her you didn't
want to talk about it, but you know how she gets." Jenna
hissed a curse at the box truck in front of them and
swerved to avoid another pothole.

"You *told* her?" Bellamy felt what little energy she had
seep out of her. Fan-freaking-tastic. *Hi, welcome home.
Have some rehashing to go with that heartbreak. Little
helping of feel-like-a-gullible-jackass to go on top? Don't
mind if I do.* Bellamy sighed.

"Of course I told her. We're your best friends, dummy.
She's making you breakfast."

Bellamy groaned. "You let her into your kitchen?"

A wicked smile crossed Jenna's face. "Nope. I let her
into yours." She took a quick exit and headed toward
Bellamy's building. "But don't worry. Last time I checked,
her breakfast-making skills were totally limited to order-
ing Starbucks and pouring cereal."

"Great," Bellamy mumbled. At least her kitchen was
probably safe. Her cereal, not so much. "I'm telling you, I
really don't want to talk about it."

"Okay. Just breakfast it is, then."

Bellamy wrapped her arms around herself and slumped back into the passenger seat. She stared at the traffic, vowing to take the stupid flannel shirt off and stuff it in the Goodwill box the minute she walked in the door.

She was going to erase Shane Griffin from her memory if it was the last thing she ever did.

Shane worked on Bellamy's transmission until his fingers were numb, letting the movements and the feel of her car under his hands calm him into rational thought. Finally, somewhere between replacing the bearings and seating the bell housing, the answers started falling into place, and by the time the sun came up, bright and unyielding over the mountain, Shane knew what he had to do. He thanked Jackson for all his help and sent him on his weary way before flipping the cordless into one hand, cradling it in his palm as he dialed.

"Riverside Hospital," the woman's pleasant voice purred into the phone.

"I need to check on a patient in the ICU, please."

"Just a moment."

After a brief conversation with one of the ICU nurses, Shane learned that Dr. Russell was scheduled to make rounds before his shift ended at nine. Shit, that wouldn't give him enough time to get back to the cabin to talk to Bellamy if he wanted to make it out there before the good doctor left. Measuring his options and liking neither, he coaxed the cordless to life one more time.

"Come on, baby. I know you're pissed. Just pick up the phone . . ."

When he was greeted by his own prerecorded voice, he

wasn't exactly shocked. He was one hell of a candidate for the old silent treatment.

"Hey, Bellamy, I know you're there. Just hear me out." Not that she had much choice. The cabin was so small, you could hear the machine from its four corners with sound to spare. "Listen, I know I screwed up. I should've told you the truth from the beginning. You have every right to be really mad." He paused, hoping maybe she'd pick up the phone. "Anyway. I'm going to go to the hospital to check on Grady before Dr. Russell leaves. I'll be back soon and we can talk. I mean, I'd really like it if we could talk." Man, he was no good at this. No wonder she wouldn't pick up. "Right. So I'll be back soon. I . . ." Shane stopped short, squeezing his eyes shut.

"I'll see you. Bye."

"All in all, you're incredibly lucky, Mr. Griffin. Even though your episode last year was rather mild, people who suffer more than one heart attack usually have more tissue damage." Dr. Russell flipped through the results of Grady's MRI, explaining the details. "You'll have to stay with us for a little while as you recover, but I don't think you'll need the ICU after today. We'll continue to monitor you, and you'll have to stay on your meds after you leave, of course. But for now, what I really want you to do is keep resting."

"Got plenty of time to rest when I'm dead," Grady rasped. His slate-gray eyes didn't miss a trick, even if he did look like he could use the rest and then some.

Dr. Russell chuckled. "Well, lucky for you, that day won't be today. Now if you'll excuse me, I'm going to go fill Dr. Edwards in on your status before I head out. I'll see you tomorrow." He paused to look at Shane, who finally let himself sigh a breath of relief from the visitor's chair crammed in the corner. "Press the call button if you need anything, Mr. Griffin."

"Thanks, Doc." Shane got up to walk him into the hallway. Once he was positive they were out of Grady's earshot, Shane cleared his throat. "How long a recovery do you think we're talking about here?"

Dr. Russell weighed Shane carefully with his eyes. "It's difficult to say. It depends on how well he responds to the medication, but I'm not going to lie to you. For a man his age, it's not an easy road. I assume he's retired?"

Shane snorted. "Are you kidding? He was changing out a transmission last night before this happened."

Dr. Russell's eyebrows skipped up. "Well, those days are done. Don't get me wrong," he added in a rush, no doubt responding to Shane's look of panic. "I'm not suggesting he sit in a rocker all day. But at this point, he's going to have to dial back in order to stay healthy, that's all."

Shane nodded mutely. Oh, this had bad things written all over it. Grady was stubborn in his sleep, for Chrissake.

"Look, let's not put the cart before the horse. As he gets better over the next few days, we'll work on a plan to keep him that way. For the next six weeks, he's looking at a lot of rest and not much else, but he's a lucky man. Not everyone has family members so close by who can help out. Speaking of which—" Dr. Russell stopped to eyeball Shane's rumpled clothes with a pointed look. "Go home and get some sleep. I meant it when I said you won't be able to help him if you're dead on your feet."

"Thanks, Dr. Russell." Shane watched the man disappear down the hall before heading back into Grady's room.

"Done talking about me, are you?" One corner of Grady's mouth lifted slightly in a halfhearted smile.

"For now." While there wasn't much sense in lying about it, Shane wasn't about to wax poetic on the subject, either. "The doctor says you need to rest, so rest is what you're gonna do. You want me to see what's on TV?" Shane started to rummage for the remote to the TV anchored on the wall across from Grady's bed.

"I owe you an apology."

The words took Shane by complete surprise. "For what?"

"I told you I'd call you when that tranny came in, and I didn't. Guess I lied to ya a bit so you could spend time with your girl. I'm sorry." Grady was breathless just from the handful of words.

"I'm not worried about the tranny, Grady." The last thing Shane wanted to do was open up the can of worms that involved Grady's work habits. That conversation would have to wait for another time. "The only thing that matters is you're okay."

Grady managed a throaty chuckle. "Boy, you don't even know what you don't know. Someone offers you an apology, you got two choices. You either accept it, or you don't. It's called making amends." More raspy breathing.

Damn it, this wasn't resting! "Okay, okay. I accept your apology. Jeez, Grady. You need to take it easy."

"And you need to pay attention, son."

"Huh?"

Grady gave him a knowing smile, and recognition flooded through Shane as his gut did that foreboding end-around thing it did whenever he was about to get into a fight.

"I take it he came to see you, then." Shane's voice was

full of tension. It was just like his father to beat him to the punch.

"Ayuh. Left just before you got here." Grady nodded, unwavering steel eyes on Shane's dark ones. He could read the message in the old man's eyes from a mile away.

"I'm not making amends with him, Grady. It's too late for that." Shane crossed his arms over his already-tight chest. Hell, no. He'd rather be skinned alive than kiss and make up with his father, no matter what Grady said.

"Funny, he said the same thing. Crossed his arms just like that too. Hardheaded, both of ya. Too stubborn to see past what you want to know what you really need."

Shane set his mouth in a mulish line. "Really? And what is it that I need?"

Grady laughed in a short little burst. "Swift kick in the ass, same as your father." His face sobered as Shane scowled. "Listen, Shane. Life's too short to argue like this. He might blow a lot of smoke over it, but he's finally figurin' out that deep down your passion is for somethin' other than the law. You really gonna blame the man for wanting you to love what he loves? You're his son."

Well, fuck. Of course the old man had to go and make sense.

"It's not that easy," Shane argued. "He paid off my loan to blackmail me. Wanting me to love the law is one thing. Not giving me a choice in the matter is another." He thought of his father's ultimatum. Fact of the matter was, his father had wedged him between one hell of a rock and a hard place. Shane had no idea how he was going to pay off his law school debt working at the garage.

Grady arched a graying eyebrow. "Ah, you've always got choices. You may not like 'em, but you still got 'em."

"Grady, I don't know how I'm going to pay him back.

Selling the car won't even turn up a third of what I owe him, even if I get what it's worth." Dread pinballed through Shane's chest at the thought of selling the Mustang. He wasn't even sure it would be worth it.

"I'm retiring, Shane."

All of Shane's thoughts slammed to a halt in his head. "You're closing the garage?" No way. No *way*.

Grady shook his head. "No. I'm giving it to you."

Shane's mouth fell open. "What?"

"I'm gettin' too old for this, son. You practically run the place, anyway. It's about time we just made things official."

Shane gave his head a vehement shake. "I don't want the garage."

Grady chuckled, a small, gruff sound. "Even so, it's done. I told your father."

That must've been a hell of a conversation. "What did he say?"

"That's for the two of you to discuss." He dismissed the subject with a wave. "Where's your lady friend?"

"Don't change the subject," Shane warned.

"Don't avoid the subject," Grady returned, eyebrows raised. "You look like hell, and I ain't vain enough to think all that worry's for me."

Shane exhaled and gave in. "Bellamy's back at the cabin."

"And what does she think of all this?"

He scrubbed a hand down his face. "I kept all of it from her, so she's pissed. She's, uh, a little headstrong."

Grady's eyes twinkled in the sunlight slanting through the window. "Oh, she's perfect for you, no doubt. And from the looks of things, I ain't the only one who thinks so."

The words in Shane's mind lodged in his throat before he forced them out. "Yeah, well, I screwed up royally. I don't know if she's going to forgive me, to be honest." Oh, hell. That hurt to say.

"Go, then. Make amends with your girl and let an old man rest, would ya?" Grady shifted beneath the covers and closed his eyes so Shane had no choice. They'd have to have it out about the garage another time.

"The thing is . . . I'm not really sure what to say." None of the words in his head felt like they'd be enough to make her understand.

"I've found tellin' the truth to be the best way to make amends. But do it quick, you hear? You don't want a girl like that to get away."

Shane swallowed hard and nodded. Letting her get away was the last thing Shane wanted.

Bellamy jammed the last of her clothes into the tiny washing machine in her condo and closed the lid, filling the dispenser with as much detergent as it would allow before starting the wash cycle.

"Damn, girl. You must want those clothes uber-clean," Jenna said, arching an eyebrow over the lid of her Starbucks cup from the end of the hall.

Bellamy closed the laundry closet door, making her way toward Jenna and the kitchen with the cuffs of her beat-up pj's swishing around her ankles. "Yup."

Take that, super-Shane-smell. If only a healthy dose of Tide would erase the rest of him, too.

"If you're looking for cream cheese, there's some on the top shelf," Bellamy offered as she breezed into the kitchen, gesturing to the stainless steel fridge with a lift of her chin.

Holly snorted and reached into one of the distressed

pine cabinets for a plate before unloading the contents of the brown paper bakery bag across the counter.

"Are you kidding? A crisis like this overrides bagels in a heartbeat. We're in pastry territory, sweetheart." Holly pulled two cranberry streusel muffins roughly the size of softballs out of the bag, following them with a couple of pumpkin scones and a chocolate éclair. "Breakfast is served," she chimed, passing Bellamy the éclair.

"I don't need an éclair for breakfast. I'm not that bad off." Bellamy frowned, picking at the satiny exterior. How pathetic could she get? And oh my God, was that ganache beautiful.

"Ooooh, goody. Pass it this way then," Jenna said with an expectant wave as she plopped herself down at the farmhouse table in the middle of the dining area.

Bellamy clutched the gooey chocolate shell hard enough to sink fingerprints in it. "I didn't say I didn't want it. I said I didn't *need* it," she clarified, taking a bite. She parked herself next to Jenna before breaking off the other end of the pastry and passing it to her friend. "I'm honestly fine."

Holly pursed her lips, a network of worried creases outlining her forehead. She plunked the plate of muffins down on the table, sliding into a chair with her latte. "Sweetie, denial like this isn't healthy." She held up her hand to halt Bellamy's protest. "And I'm not just saying that to get the scoop from you. I'm saying it as your friend. Something made you call Jenna at two o'clock in the morning to come get you, and no way am I buying that it was a run of the mill argument."

Well, crap. There was that.

Holly continued. "So if you really don't want to talk

about it, then we'll just have breakfast. But really? You might feel better if you got it off your chest."

Bellamy sighed, her eyes starting to sting despite her pride screaming like a banshee for them to knock it off. "He lied to me," she finally managed on little more than a whisper.

Holly's eyes widened with concern. "Oh, sweetie. After Derek? What a jerk."

"Believe me. What Derek did is nothing compared to this."

"God, B." Jenna lowered her half of the éclair, uneaten, to grab Bellamy's hand. "What did Shane lie to you about?"

Bellamy's voice quavered despite her very best efforts to kick it in the ass.

"Everything."

Shane pulled up to the cabin, watching the midmorning sunlight stream around the trees as he pondered his words for the billionth time in the last twelve hours. He palmed his keys and made his way to the front door, pulse pounding with every step he took toward the tiny porch. Bellamy was just beyond the scuffed wooden threshold, maybe waiting to give him the cold shoulder, or worse, throw something at him. Not that he didn't deserve it. Still, Shane was long overdue to tell her the truth; the words banged around his head in an effort to escape.

Please, God, let them make sense.

"Bellamy?" Shane squinted into the cabin, eyes adjusting too slowly to the dark interior. The quiet that Shane normally craved pinged off the amber log walls, making the hairs on the back of his neck stand at attention. "Bellamy?"

he tried again, and the silence grew more eerie and twice as loud. Shane bolted through the stillness of the main room, past the wide-open bathroom door and into the empty bedroom. His bed was made, his cabin utterly still, and any sign that Bellamy had ever been there had vanished into thin air.

Shane's brain railed in a silent yell. Maybe she'd tried the trails behind the cabin to try to chill out. But then where was her stuff? The suitcase that had taken over what little room existed next to Shane's dresser just last night was now gone, and the empty space where her things had been only hours before wrenched a hole in his chest.

In a daze, Shane stumbled back into the main room. The sink sat, empty and clean, just like the rest of his small kitchen. Hadn't there been dishes? The memory of Bellamy, so sultry and unassumingly beautiful as she stood in front of the sink full of bubbles assaulted his mind, and he sank into the recliner from weak knees. The answering machine blinked a knowing bright red, and Shane pressed the button as he repeated a silent, one-word prayer in his head.

Please, please, please . . .

"You have . . . one . . . new message . . ."

The sound of Shane's own voice, weary and soft, met his ears, and his heart dropped into the pit of his stomach. It was the message he'd left Bellamy earlier—God, how long ago had that even been? But she'd never heard it.

She was gone.

"Okay, think. Where the hell could she be?" He stalked over the floorboards, his mind tumbling with possibilities. Each one turned out to be more absurd than the last, and finally, he snatched up the phone, gripping it in frustration. He'd just call her cell phone until she picked up. Sure, it was a total twelve-year-old move, but what choice did he have? He was that fucking desperate. Shane settled into the Barcalounger, resolve hardening, when the phone rang in his hand, startling him clear out of his mind.

"Jesus!" he barked, flipping it over to check the caller ID. *Midtown Mazda*. A chill rippled up his spine, leaving a bitter taste in his mouth on its exit path.

"Hello?"

"Oh, uh, sorry, is this . . ." There was a pause and the sound of some papers rustling on the other end. "Grady's Garage on Pine Mountain?"

Shane frowned until he remembered forwarding the garage phone to the cabin. "Sorry, yeah. This is Shane. Can I help you?"

"I've got an order here to pick up a 2009 Miata from you, kind of a weird request. Owner said you're replacing the tranny, and she wants us to tow it back here when you're done. Ring any bells?"

Shane's entire universe pitched at an odd tilt, and he had to close his eyes just to keep his balance even though he was sitting down. "Yeah," he said, trying to keep his voice steady. "I know the car. You said you have an order to pick it up?"

"Yeah, a, uh, hold on . . . Bellamy Blake called it in a little while ago. Just between me and you, the tow is going to cost her a ridiculous amount of cash, but she was pretty clear she couldn't leave the city to go get it and wanted it towed when you're done. Anyhow, you got a time frame on it so I can get this on my books?"

If Bellamy was making arrangements to have her car brought to the city, it was a good bet she wasn't just blowing off steam locally. Somehow, she'd gotten the hell out of Dodge without hearing his side of the story. For a second, Shane was tempted to tell the guy that there had been a huge mix-up and that he should forget coming to get her car. If Shane drove the frickin' thing to the city himself, then Bellamy would have to see him.

But he couldn't break his vow, especially not when his father had the upper hand. There was too much at stake for him to go back to Philadelphia now, and he couldn't leave Pine Mountain. He couldn't leave Grady.

If he crossed those city limits, everything would change.

The guy on the other end of the phone cleared his throat, jolting Shane back to the reality of the cabin and the finality of his next words.

"I'll be done with it by Monday. We're open from nine to five. Just call me when you're on your way."

"I've got an order here to pick up a 2003 Miata from you, kind of a weird request," Shane said. "You're replacing the tie rods, and she wants us to tow it back here when you're done. Ring any bells?"

Shane's chin involuntarily pitched at an odd tilt and he had to close his eyes just to keep his balance even though he was sitting down. "Yeah," he said, trying to keep his voice steady. "I know the car. You said you have an order to pick it up?"

"Yeah, ah, I did on—Bellamy Blake called it in a little while ago. Just between me and you, the tow is going to cost her a ridiculous amount of cash, but she was pretty firm she couldn't leave the city to get it and wanted it towed when you're done. Anyhow, you got an hour, maybe on it so I can get this on my books."

If Bellamy was making arrangements to have her car brought to the city, it was a good her she wasn't just blowing off steam locally. Somehow, she'd gotten the bed out of Dodge without hearing his side, the story. For

Chapter Twenty-Eight

"What do you think? Not enough oregano, right?" Bellamy set her teeth over her bottom lip in determination and eyeballed the stockpot of sauce on the stove. Yeah, definitely more oregano.

"Are you kidding me with this? You need to sell this stuff and make a fortune. It's amazing," Holly said, swiping a hunk of crusty bread into the bubbling pot.

"Hrmph." Bellamy frowned. She measured some oregano into her hand, crushing the dried herbs against her palm with a spoon before tossing them into the pot. "Meatballs should be done soon."

"Don't take this the wrong way, but can you please kiss and make up with Shane? You haven't stopped cooking all afternoon, and I think I've already gained five pounds over your breakup," Jenna said, giving Holly a gentle nudge to the ribs. "Quit hogging the pot, would you?"

Bellamy put on a nonchalant expression, giving the new version of the sauce a taste before bending down to the storage cabinet in her kitchen island. "First of all, you can't break up with someone you were never with in the first place. And secondly, I'm not even going to see him again, much less make up with him." Where the hell was that pasta attachment for her stand mixer? She knew she'd stashed it around here somewhere.

"So you're just going to let the dealership in the city go get your car and then what? You'll mail Shane a check and that's that?" Holly's look broadcast her doubt, but Bellamy refused to budge.

"That about sums it up, yeah. A-ha! I knew this thing was in here." She gave the pasta attachment a nimble yank to unearth it from beneath her waffle iron. Bellamy stood up just in time to catch the tail end of the eyebrow-lift Holly and Jenna had exchanged over her head.

"Don't," she warned without elaborating. She should've known better than to spill her guts to them. How was she supposed to forget about Shane if Holly and Jenna kept bringing him up?

"Don't what?" they chorused.

"Don't *start*." Bellamy dragged the stand mixer from its perch on the granite countertop and started putting on the pasta attachment with a series of precise tugs for emphasis. "Everything out of Shane's mouth is a lie, so talking to him would be a waste of time." She felt her chest tighten up with sure, steady fingers of pressure around her ribs, and took a steadying breath to diffuse the sensation. No way was she going to start crying again. The huge handful of Kleenex she'd gone through as she told Jenna and Holly everything the first time had been embarrassing enough. No, she was done. Done with crying, and done with Shane Griffin.

Her chest hitched. Fucking traitor.

"You have every right to be mad at him." Jenna punctuated her words with the bob of her blond head. Well, good. Her friends were on her side after all.

"But are you sure he's not worth hearing out?"

Bellamy's lips popped open in surprise, which didn't waste much time morphing into anger. "Yes, I'm sure! Why would I want to do something as stupid as that?"

"Because I think you're in love with him, and I'd hate to see you lose a chance to be with the guy if he loves you, too."

"Whoa," Holly whispered, giving Bellamy a chance to recover from the bolt of shock arrowing through her.

Nope. Not happening.

"Clearly, he doesn't love me, since he couldn't even be bothered to tell me the truth about who he really is." Bellamy's voice was more wooden than she'd have liked, but at least she was able to force the words from her mouth. Of course Shane didn't love her. After all, he was the one who had said they should just spend the week together. *She* was the one who'd jumped the gun, following her foolish heart instead of facing facts.

"Come on, B. He spent all that time with you, and he even asked you to stay with him. Don't you think that counts for something?" Holly asked with a sheepish glance.

"I don't think any of it matters now. And it's not like he's trying to call me to explain things, anyway." This little truth had picked its way into Bellamy's brain somewhere between stewing the tomatoes and making the meatballs, and it lodged itself in good and tight.

Shane didn't want to talk to her.

Fine and dandy, her pride snapped. *That makes two of us.*

"Sweetie, I think Jenna's right. Maybe you should give him another chance."

The ridiculous tremor in Bellamy's chest started up again, as if to agree. Oh, for the love of all things holy, she couldn't be yanked in two different directions forever. It was time to end this, once and for all.

"Another chance at what? Lying to me some more? Look, the reality is this. No matter how I feel about it, what Shane and I had is over. All the maybes in the world aren't going to change that."

As if on cue, Bellamy's cell phone began to ring.

"You look like hell." Shane's father stood in the entryway to the tiny hospital waiting room, his perfectly pressed dress pants and cashmere sweater making him look only casually imposing instead of all-out intimidating.

Shane glanced down at his own attire, pushing aside the hollow thud in his chest. Funny, he'd heard that once already today, and that was *before* he'd taken a shower and changed into clean jeans.

"Thanks." Shane's tone suggested how little he meant it. The last thing he was in the mood for after being jilted by a girl who hated his guts enough to leave without saying good-bye was another tangle with his father.

"Is Grady settled in his new room?" His father tipped his dark head toward the hallway, and Shane noticed he was more gray at the temples than he had been last year.

He shrugged. "Yeah. They took him for another ECG, and the doctor's in with him now. Figured I'd give them some privacy." Shane crossed his arms over his chest, adrenaline perking through him like an antsy pre-argument wake-up call.

"I see." His father sat down across from him, leaning his forearms on his thighs. "You and I are long overdue for a conversation, don't you think?" The older man's gray stare pierced Shane's dark one, and for a moment, neither of them moved.

"If your version of a conversation involves telling me what to do with my own life, I'm not really interested. You'll get your money soon enough. I never planned to skip out on my debt. But I'm not coming back to the city."

His father's mouth was drawn into a humorless smile, a network of worry lines creasing around his eyes. "You really think I care about the money?"

Shane pulled up in shock. "Yeah." Wasn't that kind of the point of his father trying to drag him back to Philadelphia in the first place? He'd gone so far as to pay off Shane's loan just to back him into a corner, for God's sake.

"You don't even know what you don't know," his father muttered with a shake of his head.

"What did you just say?" Shock prickled through Shane, and he stared, wide-eyed, at his father. *Boy, you don't even know what you don't know.* Grady's gravelly voice rumbled through Shane's mind.

His father frowned, and he brushed off the question. "I don't care about the money, Shane. I paid the loan off because I knew you were struggling. I thought . . ." He broke off for a breath, steepling his fingers together over his knees. "I thought it would be a wake-up call for you to come home. Clearly, you don't want to leave." A flicker crossed his features, one that his father was quick to erase, but Shane caught it nonetheless.

It looked like remorse.

"No, I don't. This is where I belong." He'd meant to deliver the words with a sting in his voice, but they didn't come out that way.

"I suppose it might help you to know why this is difficult for me." His father drew in a breath while Shane did a terrible job of keeping the shock from his face.

"People who are raised in small towns either love them or can't wait to leave them. There's really no middle ground. Your grandfather's a lifer." A small, wry smile crossed his father's lips, but it didn't last. "But I never was. The old man never quite understood why I wanted to leave Pine Mountain for the city. He's a man of a simpler life, but I wanted more. At the time, and for a long time, I thought what I wanted was a better life. So the minute after I graduated, I left. My mother recognized that I just wasn't cut out to stay here, but your grandfather could never quite come to grips with the whole thing.

"So when she died, I felt there was nothing left here for me. My father disapproved of my choices, and I wasn't interested in defending myself. I was an adult, with a career I'd worked hard for and loved, but to him, it never made sense. So I stayed angry, and stayed away. But I was foolish."

His last words snapped Shane's head up, just in time to see that odd smile cross his father's lips again.

"You were what?"

"I was foolish," his father repeated. "All that time, I saw disapproval. But really, it was disappointment that my passion was for something else. Only I was too stubborn to recognize it, and he was too stubborn to point it out. Until today."

His father's words scattered around him, all the pieces falling into place with startling clarity, and Shane kept listening, too mired in shock to speak.

"In hindsight, I think I always knew you didn't have a love for the law like I do; I just didn't want to admit it. Don't get me wrong. You were good at it, no doubt. But you never got that light in your eyes for it like you did when you talked about that car. And when Grady had his first heart attack, you were so quick to come out here, and even quicker to stay. I was too proud to admit that your passion might be for something else, for that simple thing that I left here. Let's face it, working at the firm isn't exactly low-pressure. I thought you were taking an easy out. But last night you showed me that's not the case."

"Why didn't you just tell me all of this when I left?" Shane asked, his mind buzzing.

This time his father's smile was more genuine. "Because I was mad. We Griffins tend to be a bit hotheaded and stubborn, in case you hadn't noticed. I thought your grandfather would get back on his feet, you'd get being a mechanic out of your system, and things would go back to normal. But then you didn't come back, and I said I'd be damned if I was coming out here to get you."

His father exhaled a long breath. "When the bank called my office last week and I found out how you'd been struggling to repay your loan all this time, I'll admit that I initially paid it off so you'd owe me. I really thought . . ." He paused, letting out a gruff sigh. "I thought it was just the thing to make you come to your senses and snap out of it. But I can see now what you're made for. It's not disapproval on my face when I look at you, son. It's disappointment that I didn't pass on my love for the law."

"I don't know what to say," Shane managed to breathe.

"You can start by thanking the old man. He's the one who pointed it out to me, even though I didn't want to hear it. He said he couldn't live with himself if another twenty years went by and two more Griffins didn't make amends."

Make it right . . . make it right . . . Jesus. Was *this* what Grady had meant last night? And all that talk about making amends?

Suddenly, it made all the sense in the world. Shane hadn't realized it, but he'd spent the last fourteen months, hell, the last seven years, covering up who he really was. It was time for the out loud truth, no matter what the consequences.

"I owe you an apology," Shane said, and although he expected the words to stick to his throat, they flowed easily. "I should've been honest with you from the beginning, but I didn't think you'd understand."

His father arched a dark brow. "Before now, I doubt I would've."

"I *will* pay the loan back," Shane insisted.

His father chuckled, and in that moment, Shane could see something familiar cross the man's features. There was no rasp in his father's laugh, but it was a reflection of Grady's nonetheless.

"I know you will."

"Grady told you. About the garage."

His father nodded once. "He did. All things considered, it makes sense for you to run the place. After all, it's a family business."

"And you're okay with that?" Shane's eyebrows puckered, his face laced with doubt.

"I'm not going to lie to you. It'll take a bit of time for me to be truly okay with it. But it's the right thing, for you and for Grady."

"I'm just not cut out for the city, Dad. I'm sorry, but I'm never coming back."

"Don't apologize for who you are." His father's voice broke slightly over his words, startling Shane. "You belong here. That's just something I'll have to learn to live with."

As he met his father's eyes with respect and conviction, Shane realized that while he belonged on the mountain, there was still an empty part of him that had gone to the city.

And he was going to get it back.

* * *

Bellamy rang the bell of the elegant, three-story brownstone and waited, fidgeting like mad on the brick threshold. It was cold enough for her to see her breath on every nervous exhale, and she drummed her gloved fingers together to a tuneless beat.

"Bellamy! Oh, sweetheart, why do you ring the bell like that when it's freezing outside? Come in, before you catch your death." Her mother pulled the door wide, ushering her inside with a warm embrace.

"Hi, Mom. Sorry to barge in on you and Daddy like this." Bellamy's heart raced against her rib cage, and she hoped her mother couldn't feel it as she returned her hug.

"Nonsense. You grew up in this house. You can barge in any time you want. Have you eaten dinner yet? Maybe we can talk your dad into pad Thai." Her mom grinned, moving through the living room toward the kitchen.

Bellamy followed, resisting the urge to start fidgeting again. "Oh, uh, I'm not hungry." She thought of the tons of food she'd had her hands on in the last eight hours, none of which she'd been hungry for. "I actually came because I need to talk to you guys." In all of the strategizing she'd done over the last few hours, cutting right to the chase seemed to make the most sense. After all, not even her trampled pride could make her a beat-around-the-bush kind of girl.

Her mother stopped short, a few paces away from the kitchen, and turned to stare at Bellamy with round, worried eyes. "What's the matter?"

"Relax, Mom. I'm fine." Eh. Mostly fine, but she wasn't about to get into her ruined love life with her mom.

"You don't look fine," her mother protested, drawing

her brow in tightly. "Bob!" she called, but Bellamy's father was already in the kitchen doorway.

"She looks beautiful to me. Hi, baby!" He greeted her with his standard hug-and-kiss combo that could still take the sting out of any bad day. A little bit, anyway. Bellamy let him squeeze her a little extra, just for good measure.

"Hi, Daddy." She blew out a sigh. Holy shit was this going to be hard.

"She has something to tell us," her mother warned, her green eyes clouding over with concern as she motioned for Bellamy to sit next to her on the living room couch.

"Oh?" Her father's glance darkened a shade, his worry matching her mother's. He came in to sit in a chair next to her mother. "What's going on, Bellamy? Are you all right?"

"I'm fine," she insisted, tugging at her gloves and sitting down.

Now or never, girlfriend.

"I, uh. I quit my job."

Silence flooded through the room, and Bellamy counted a handful of deafening heartbeats before her mother finally responded.

"Are you switching banks?"

"No." Her nice, deep breath barely made it a fraction of the way to her lungs. "I've decided to switch careers."

"You're leaving real estate?" Her father drew back in his chair, eyes wide.

"I'm leaving business." Bellamy sucked in all the air she could muster, opting for the blurt-it-out method so she wouldn't lose her nerve. "I know that you guys have always wanted me to go into business like you, and I tried, I really did. I just . . . I don't love it. I don't even think I like it, to be honest. Working at the bank drove me crazy, in a quiet, boring kind of way. No offense," she scrambled to add, trying not to trip on her words, "but I was miserable there, so I decided to quit."

Her mother's lips parted in shock. "But what will you do?"

The butterflies that had taken up residence in Bellamy's stomach a few hours ago reminded her again of their presence. "I'm going to train to be a chef."

"A chef," her father repeated, sounding certain he'd misunderstood.

Bellamy nodded. "Do you know who Carly di Matisse is?"

"The little Italian gal on that cable show with her husband?" her father asked, blinking.

"Yes. She's the new head chef at the restaurant in Pine Mountain Resort, and she called today to offer me a chance to work for her as a line cook."

"Is that why you went to the mountains? To get a job?" Her father creased his brow.

Bellamy gave her head a quick shake. "No, not at all. It just kind of happened really fast." She proceeded to give them a condensed version of her unorthodox kitchen audition with Adrian and the meeting with Carly that had ensued.

"But you haven't even gone to culinary school," her mother said, confused. "Doesn't that put you at a disadvantage?"

"Yup. It sure does. And I know I'll probably have to go at some point in order to really move up in the ranks." Truth rang in Bellamy's voice, and it steadied her. "Chef di Matisse made it clear when she offered me the job today that she was taking a flyer on me and if I couldn't hack it, she'd fire me without a second thought. I'm going to have to do a tremendous amount of work on my own time just to keep up, and the reality is that no matter what I do, I still might get canned. But I want this, in a way that I've never wanted anything else. So even if I screw it up, I have to be true to myself."

A wave of relief washed over Bellamy at the words, but it mingled with the uncertainty on both of her parents' faces, leaving her uneasy.

"And you're sure this is what you want?" her mother finally said, eyes firm on Bellamy's.

Bellamy didn't even think twice. "Yes."

Her father scrubbed a hand down his clean-shaven jaw. "It's a hell of a risk, sweetheart. But if I'm being honest, you've loved to cook since you were a kid. I always thought it was a hobby, but if you want to make a go of it, then I think you should."

"*We* think you should," her mother corrected, nodding.

"Wait, you . . . you do?" Bellamy sputtered around the shock in her chest.

"Of course we do. Did you think we wouldn't support you?" her father asked, starting to smile.

She gave a tiny nod. "Well, kind of. Yeah. It's a little crazy."

"About as crazy as the day the two of us stood in your grandmother and grandfather's house and told them we were going to start our own business on nothing more than a shoestring and our own determination. But it was what we wanted, and it's obvious that this is what you want," he answered.

Tears pricked Bellamy's eyes, quickly spilling onto her cheeks. "I really do," she nodded, letting her mother gather her up for a tight hug.

"You have to be true to your heart, honey. You get that part down, and everything else has a way of falling into place."

As she stood in the embrace of both her parents with tears streaming down her face, it was all Bellamy could do to convince herself that the only thing following her heart would get her was that job.

Chapter Twenty-Nine

Bellamy could hear the shrill electronic ring of the phone in her condo before she'd even slipped the key all the way into the lock.

"Coming, coming, hang on!" she mumbled between her teeth, fumbling to get her key out of the lock and shut the door safely behind her before rushing toward the kitchen.

"Hi, you've reached Bellamy Blake. I can't take your call right now . . ."

She let out a curse under her breath and flipped the phone to her ear. "Hello?" But she was met with the steady hum of the dial tone.

"Oh well. Couldn't have been that important, I guess," she muttered, checking the caller ID. *Out of Area.*

Right. Didn't telemarketers have anything better to do on their Friday nights?

Bellamy surveyed the contents of her fridge and settled for a bottle of water. What she really wanted was to crack open that bottle of pinot grigio, but she was pretty sure it was upper-level pathetic to drink a bottle of wine all by your lonesome not even a whole day after being jilted by a guy you thought you knew. A guy you thought you might even love.

On second thought, where was that corkscrew?

Bellamy poured herself a healthy glass of wine and trudged down the hall to her bathroom to draw a bubble bath. As soon as she started the water, the sound of the phone interrupted her again, only this time she was prepared. She lifted the phone from her bedside table, glancing at the caller ID.

"Hello?"

"Hey, how did it go?" Jenna asked.

Bellamy let out a little smile and ran a hand through her hair. "Pretty well, all things considered. Aside from the normal parental concern over the whole taking-a-big-step thing, they were kind of excited, actually. Thanks for letting me borrow your car to go see them."

"No problem. Is it cool with you if I come grab the keys in about half an hour? My roommate's going to be out your way, and she said she could drop me off so you don't have to make a trip tomorrow."

Bellamy eyed the bathroom door, thinking. "I was going to get in the tub. Why don't you use your spare key to get in, and I'll leave them on the kitchen counter for you." God, did that bone-weary voice really belong to her?

"That sounds good. You sure you're okay? I can stay, if you want company. We can do the chick-flick, ugly slippers, drink too much wine thing. Talking about it totally optional."

Bellamy paused for a fraction too long before answering. "No, thanks. I'll be fine. I'm just tired, that's all. I think I'll feel better once I get some sleep."

Jenna paused equally long, but finally conceded. "Okay. Have a good soak. I'll talk to you tomorrow, but if you need me before then, just call."

"Thanks." Bellamy replaced the phone on the cradle and returned to the bathroom. Peeling her clothes off and tossing them into a heap, she slipped into the steaming tub. Her skin tingled, deliciously painful under the borderline-too-hot water, and she let herself sink in against the slope of the porcelain. The tangled ends of her hair fanned around her neck and chest in the water like an intricate blond spiderweb, and Bellamy spiraled her fingers through them with an absent stroke.

Your hair looks perfect when it's lying over your pillow in the early sunlight . . .

Hot tears filled Bellamy's eyes, and she squeezed them shut in an effort to forbid them to fall. She would *not* let Shane Griffin get the best of her.

Your skin tastes like honey, right here . . .

"Please stop. Please. I just want to forget him," Bellamy whispered, her voice wavering to give away the lie.

But the sweetest thing about you is your honesty . . . because it makes you beautiful . . .

Bellamy dropped her chin into the bubbles and let herself have a good, long cry.

Shane parked his truck in the visitor's lot, letting his eyes sweep the busy suburban neighborhood just outside of Philly, proper. The outline of the city buildings, visible from the highway, didn't stir Shane's gut like he'd expected them to. They simply stood, sleek and glittering, against the night skyline, just as they had when he'd left, a testament to a place he'd thought he hated. But it wasn't the place he hated so much as the things that had gone on in it.

Hell if Grady hadn't been right. Shane really did have a lot to learn.

He got out of the truck and eyeballed the neat brick buildings until he found the one he was looking for. With his determination brewing, Shane headed toward the well-lit courtyard dotted with a handful of doors set in colonial brick.

"Okay . . . 101, 102, . . . ah, here we go. 103. Bingo."

Okay, Romeo. Now what?

Shane stood outside the glossy black door, hand over the tiny brass doorknocker, and took a deep breath. He'd driven all the way down from Pine Mountain knowing full well that the girl of his dreams was going to curse him six ways to Sunday and send him packing, but it didn't matter. Hopefully she'd hear him out first, and he'd get a chance to say what he should've told her from the beginning.

The truth.

"Here goes nothing," Shane said to himself, but before he could lift the doorknocker, a familiar voice froze him, mid-movement.

"She doesn't know you're here, does she?"

Shane spun around, his heart whacking around in his rib cage like a loose hockey puck. Bellamy's friend, Jenna, stood at the mouth of the courtyard, a bemused expression on her face.

"No. She has no idea."

"I'm guessing she didn't exactly leave you her card in her rush to leave this morning. Can I ask how you found her?" Jenna's brow pulled in, as if she was trying to figure out a puzzle.

Shane shrugged. "There were three B. Blakes listed in the online phone book for this area. Bonnie Blake assured me she'd never heard of a Bellamy sharing their last name. The second B. Blake was a man. Bernard, I think. He'd never heard of her, either. But the third one was her machine, and since the address was listed right along with the phone number . . . here I am."

Jenna cocked her head at him, clearly thinking. "I'll give you points for being clever and consistent, but you still did a number on her. I doubt she'll want to see you."

His gut plummeted toward his boots, but he stood firm. "I know. But she's got it all wrong. I might've kept some things from her, but she knows exactly who I am. I didn't lie to her about what matters."

"I figured."

Shane's brows popped. "You did?"

Jenna nodded. "Any idiot can see you're crazy about her, even if you have a weird way of showing it." She sighed. "You're not going to break her heart, right?"

"No. God, no. I just want her to hear me out."

"Well today's your lucky day." Jenna held up a set of keys, and they jingled softly against her palm. "Here's what we're going to do."

As soon as her tears slowed to a dull trickle, Bellamy wiped her face with the back of her hand and sank into the water, letting the bubbles cover everything but her face. It swished over her ears, distorting the sounds around her into a series of creaks and thumps and groans. One big one in particular caught her attention, and she jerked out of the water to listen.

"Bellamy? You still in the tub?" Jenna's voice floated through Bellamy's bedroom and past the cracked-open bathroom door.

She sighed with relief. At least she didn't have to go all bathtub Ninja and figure out how to get to the can of

Mace in her bedside table. "Yeah. The keys are on the counter. Thanks again."

"No problem. Listen, I'm leaving something here for you. But don't let it sit for too long, 'kay?"

Bellamy's face creased in confusion. "What?"

"You'll understand when you see it. I'll call you tomorrow, sweetie. Bye!" The front door thunked shut before Bellamy could respond.

Huh. That was weird. Maybe Jenna had stopped at Mr. Wong's Szechuan Gourmet for Chinese takeout. Jenna knew that hot and sour soup was Bellamy's favorite comfort food, and it did get kind of nasty when it was cold. Her stomach growled, sending up a rude reminder that it had been a while since Bellamy had thrown anything down the hatch other than a few sips of wine.

"Okay, okay, I get it," she grumbled, starting to salivate over the possibility of the soup. She popped the drain on the tub and dried off, throwing on a pair of ratty pajama pants and a three-sizes-too-big Philadelphia Phillies T-shirt. No need for pretenses like a bra for hot and sour soup, thank God. Bellamy jammed her feet into her purple fuzzy slippers and twisted her wet hair into a thick knot. She cradled her glass of wine in her palm, letting the stem dangle between her fingers as she padded out of her bedroom and down the hall.

"If you tossed in spring rolls, I'm really going to owe you big, Jenna," she said under her breath, peering into the semidarkened main room from the mouth of the hallway.

"Hey."

"Oh, God!" Bellamy yelped, clapping her free hand over her heart and sloshing wine all over the other. She blinked, hard and fast, at the source of the voice coming from the living room couch, and her pulse sped up even faster. "What the hell are you doing here?"

Shane stood up, but didn't move toward her. Wow, he looked like hell. Bellamy's heartstrings did a little dance before she could stop them.

He looked at her, seeming to measure his words with care. "I came to talk to you, and I, ah, ran into Jenna outside. I'm sorry if I startled you, but she . . . well, neither one of us thought you'd let me in any other way."

Bellamy closed her eyes and drew in a deep breath, then another to steady the adrenaline squeezing through her veins. "You're probably right about that," she said, slapping her resolve into place and blanking her tone. "How's Grady?"

Shane's eyes flickered. "He's okay. Recovering. They moved him out of the ICU today, and he got to eat some normal food. He said it's definitely not your lasagna, but it would do."

Even though Bellamy tried to resist the urge, a faint smile flitted across her lips. "I'm glad he's okay. I've been thinking about him." She clutched the stem of her glass, wine turning slightly sticky in her palm.

"Me, too. I've been thinking about a lot of things, actually."

There's nothing he can say that will make things different, her pride whispered.

Shane straightened, taking a small step toward her. "I owe you an apology, Bellamy. I never should have kept anything from you."

Except maybe that.

"But you did," she whispered.

"I did, and I wish I could change it. I was . . . foolish." He paused. "I was scared you wouldn't understand. Hell, I didn't even understand it. And it turns out the whole thing was pretty stupid, anyway. I was afraid of coming back to a place that I thought would define me, but really, everything that defines me has been here all along." Shane brushed a hand over his chest and took another step toward her. "You taught me that."

Her head sprang up, sloshing another trickle of wine over the rim of the glass. "I did?"

He gave her a half smile. "Yeah, you did. You kind of snuck up on me, with all that honesty. It threw me for a loop at first, but then it made me realize what an idiot I've been. I just didn't know it until it was too late."

Bellamy felt a tremble work its way from the center of her body and start to radiate outward. "So you came all the way out here to tell me that? Why didn't you just call me?"

The half smile became a familiar chuckle. "Because you'd have hung up on me, which I'd have deserved. And because I wanted to come here, to the city. To you. I don't want to be without you, even if that means being here. I don't want to leave Pine Mountain, I really don't, but I don't want to be without you more. So whatever I have to do to make that happen, I'm going to do, even if it means being here."

Shane met her eyes, unwavering and strong. "You want to know who I am—who I really am? I'm the guy who's in love with you, Bellamy. I'll do whatever it takes. Just trust that you really do know me and give me a chance."

Bellamy stood, speechless and shaking, in the middle of the floor, measuring the words in her head very carefully.

"Truth?" she asked, not letting go of his dark gaze.

Shane exhaled a shaky breath, but locked his eyes on hers. "Of course."

"I do know you, and I trust you. Pride be damned. I love you, Shane Griffin, and the last twenty-four hours have been hell on earth. So if you could please come here, I would really like for you to hold me and not let go for a really long time."

His eyes went wide, and she cracked a grin as he processed her words.

"You . . . hold on . . . you . . ."

"Yes. I'm waiting." She laughed, and Shane closed the space between them in two long strides. He threw his arms around her, and she buried her face in the gorgeous angle of his shoulder, inhaling the scent of him down to her toes.

"God, I love you. And I really mean it. I'll come here on the weekends, we'll figure something out. I can't be without you," Shane said, bending down to kiss the damp crown of her hair.

Bellamy laughed again, pulling back to peer up at him. "Oh, you don't have to. As a matter of fact, you might be able to help me out. See, just today I was offered this great new job in Pine Mountain, working in the kitchen with Carly di Matisse. Maybe you've heard of her?" she said with a wink. "Anyway, I have to start next week, but I don't have a place to stay. Can you recommend anything?"

"Oh, I think I can help you out. Whenever you want to go, my door is always open." Shane dipped his mouth to hers, brushing her lips with a soft caress.

"Mmm, good. But let's not hit the road just yet. I'm pretty sure I spilled an entire glass of wine down the back of your jacket, so you may want to take it off and stay a while."

"Tell you what," he said, his eyes going dark with a look Bellamy knew all too well. "How about I take off more than my jacket, and stay with you—wherever that may be—forever?"

Bellamy smiled, and eased her hands around his face to look him right in the eye.

"I say forever sounds great."

Recipes

Bellamy Blake's Late-Night Guacamole

Perfect after a late night out with girlfriends!

<u>Ingredients</u>:

- 4 ripe avocados (Haas preferred)
- Freshly squeezed juice of one large lime
- ½ teaspoon kosher salt
- ½ teaspoon cumin
- Tabasco to taste
- Roughly ½ of a medium red onion, small dice (adjust amount to taste)
- One medium tomato, seeded and diced (in a pinch, you can also use about ¾ cup of jarred salsa, but fresh is much better)
- One large clove of garlic, minced fine
- About a tablespoon of chopped, fresh cilantro (also to taste)

Cut avocados in half and remove the seeds (one good whack with a sharp knife should help it pop right out, but be careful!). Scoop the pulp from each avocado into a large bowl (I like to use my hands for this, but a spoon works too). Discard skins. Add lime juice, salt, cumin and Tabasco. With a potato masher, work mixture to desired consistency. Note: texture is important in good guacamole. Over-mash, and you end up with baby food (eek!), but not enough, and it won't "dip" without destroying your chips. You want the chunky feel of salsa.

Add onion, tomato, garlic and cilantro. Stir gently to combine well. Let sit (for flavors to really pop) for about an hour in the fridge with light cover. Serve with tortilla chips, preferably to your friends after a late night out. Licking the bowl is optional, but encouraged.

Sharing food doesn't have to be an intimate thing between lovers—it can be what ties us together with anyone we love or care about, such as our family and friends. One of the big mantras in my house is that "food is love," and Bellamy's guacamole in *Turn Up The Heat* is a prime example. As an aspiring (and closet) chef, Bellamy cooks from her heart, and in turn that makes everything she prepares into a feast for the emotions. Even late-night guacamole! Bellamy's desire to feed her friends shows how much she cares for them, and following the path of your heart is a big theme in *Turn Up The Heat*. Give this recipe a try, and share it with some friends (over margaritas!) to embody "food is love" in your house, too.

Grady's Favorite Chocolate Chip Cookies

*Make sure to leave lots of space between these cookies
on the sheet pan, as they like to have lots of room
to spread out as they bake. Also, make sure
you've got a big glass of milk for dunking!*

Ingredients:

    2¼ cups all-purpose flour
    1 teaspoon salt
    1 teaspoon baking soda
    1 teaspoon ground cinnamon
    1 cup (2 sticks) unsalted butter, softened
    1 cup granulated sugar
    1 cup light brown sugar
    2 eggs
    1 teaspoon vanilla extract
    1 bag high-quality semi-sweet chocolate chips

Preheat oven to 375 degrees. In a medium bowl, sift together flour, salt, baking soda and cinnamon, and set aside.
In a mixer fitted with the paddle attachment, mix butter at
medium speed for one minute until pale and fluffy. Add
sugars, and blend well, scraping down the sides of the bowl
as necessary. Add eggs and vanilla. Mix until combined.

Slowly add flour mixture at medium speed, blending until
just incorporated, but not over-mixing. Stir in chocolate
chips by hand. Drop by rounded teaspoons (try not to go
bigger, as these cookies really like to grow as they bake,
and they will "melt" together if they're too big) onto a
parchment or Silpat-lined baking sheet. Bake for 9–10
minutes, until cookies are just brown and your kitchen

smells unbelievable. Cool for 10 minutes on cookie sheet before moving to a wire rack. Cool completely.

Makes 3–4 dozen, depending on how ambitious your rounded teaspoons are. The author recommends eating them warm. The author also *highly* recommends eating them warm in bed, while snuggled up with the one you love!

Pomegranate Pork Chops for Two

*Every night should be date night
when these are on the table!
Recipe can easily be doubled to feed more.*

<u>Ingredients</u>:

  1 shallot, diced fine
  1 tablespoon olive oil
  ½ cup white wine (I used a Chardonnay because it was
      open, but really, it's to taste!)
  ¾ cup pomegranate juice
  1 teaspoon sugar
  2 teaspoons balsamic vinegar
  ½ cup pomegranate-flavored dried cranberries
  2 boneless pork chops
  Salt and pepper for seasoning
  2 tablespoons all-purpose flour
  1 tablespoon fresh chopped rosemary (no stems)
  Olive oil for skillet

In a medium saucepan, warm 1 tablespoon olive oil over
medium heat. Add shallot and cook 4–5 minutes or until
soft and translucent. Add wine, scraping the bottom of
the pan to deglaze, then add pomegranate juice, sugar,
balsamic vinegar and cranberries. Bring to a simmer, lowering heat if necessary, but keep the mixture at an active
simmer. Stirring often, let mixture reduce (20–30 minutes)
and cranberries "pop" (expand and soften).

While mixture reduces, season pork chops with salt and
pepper, both sides, to taste. Combine flour and rosemary
in a shallow dish and dredge both pork chops through

mixture, coating well and shaking off excess. Warm olive oil in a skillet over medium-high heat, and cook pork chops for about 5 minutes on each side, until golden and cooked through. Remove to plate and cover with foil to keep warm if your pork beats your reduction sauce to the punch.

When the sauce is thick enough to coat a wooden spoon, divide evenly and pour over pork chops. Serve with your favorite sides (ours are rice and green beans!) and enjoy with the one you love!

If you loved Kimberly Kincaid's
sweet and sexy
take on modern romance,
come back to Pine Mountain
this June for

Gimme Some Sugar.

Out of the frying pan . . . and into the fire!

Desperate to escape the spotlight of her failed marriage
to a fellow celebrity chef, Carly di Matisse left New York
City for a tiny town in the Blue Ridge Mountains. The
restaurant she's running these days may not be chic, but
in Pine Mountain she can pretend to be the tough cookie
everybody knows and loves. Until she finds herself
spending too much time with a way-too-hot contractor
whose rugged good looks melt her like butter . . .

Jackson Carter wasn't looking for love. But he's not
the kind of man to walk away from a worksite—or from
a fiery beauty whose passionate nature provides some
irresistible on-the-job benefits . . .

It's the perfect temporary arrangement for two ravenous
commitment-phobes—except that Jackson and Carly keep
coming back for seconds . . . and thirds . . . and fourths . . .

Thrilling Suspense from
Beverly Barton

Books by Bestselling Author
Fern Michaels

___**The Jury**	0-8217-7878-1	$6.99US/$9.99CAN
___**Sweet Revenge**	0-8217-7879-X	$6.99US/$9.99CAN
___**Lethal Justice**	0-8217-7880-3	$6.99US/$9.99CAN
___**Free Fall**	0-8217-7881-1	$6.99US/$9.99CAN
___**Fool Me Once**	0-8217-8071-9	$7.99US/$10.99CAN
___**Vegas Rich**	0-8217-8112-X	$7.99US/$10.99CAN
___**Hide and Seek**	1-4201-0184-6	$6.99US/$9.99CAN
___**Hokus Pokus**	1-4201-0185-4	$6.99US/$9.99CAN
___**Fast Track**	1-4201-0186-2	$6.99US/$9.99CAN
___**Collateral Damage**	1-4201-0187-0	$6.99US/$9.99CAN
___**Final Justice**	1-4201-0188-9	$6.99US/$9.99CAN
___**Up Close and Personal**	0-8217-7956-7	$7.99US/$9.99CAN
___**Under the Radar**	1-4201-0683-X	$6.99US/$9.99CAN
___**Razor Sharp**	1-4201-0684-8	$7.99US/$10.99CAN
___**Yesterday**	1-4201-1494-8	$5.99US/$6.99CAN
___**Vanishing Act**	1-4201-0685-6	$7.99US/$10.99CAN
___**Sara's Song**	1-4201-1493-X	$5.99US/$6.99CAN
___**Deadly Deals**	1-4201-0686-4	$7.99US/$10.99CAN
___**Game Over**	1-4201-0687-2	$7.99US/$10.99CAN
___**Sins of Omission**	1-4201-1153-1	$7.99US/$10.99CAN
___**Sins of the Flesh**	1-4201-1154-X	$7.99US/$10.99CAN
___**Cross Roads**	1-4201-1192-2	$7.99US/$10.99CAN

Available Wherever Books Are Sold!
Check out our website at **www.kensingtonbooks.com**

More by Bestselling Author
Hannah Howell

__Highland Angel	978-1-4201-0864-4	$6.99US/$8.99CAN
__If He's Sinful	978-1-4201-0461-5	$6.99US/$8.99CAN
__Wild Conquest	978-1-4201-0464-6	$6.99US/$8.99CAN
__If He's Wicked	978-1-4201-0460-8	$6.99US/$8.49CAN
__My Lady Captor	978-0-8217-7430-4	$6.99US/$8.49CAN
__Highland Sinner	978-0-8217-8001-5	$6.99US/$8.49CAN
__Highland Captive	978-0-8217-8003-9	$6.99US/$8.49CAN
__Nature of the Beast	978-1-4201-0435-6	$6.99US/$8.49CAN
__Highland Fire	978-0-8217-7429-8	$6.99US/$8.49CAN
__Silver Flame	978-1-4201-0107-2	$6.99US/$8.49CAN
__Highland Wolf	978-0-8217-8000-8	$6.99US/$9.99CAN
__Highland Wedding	978-0-8217-8002-2	$4.99US/$6.99CAN
__Highland Destiny	978-1-4201-0259-8	$4.99US/$6.99CAN
__Only for You	978-0-8217-8151-7	$6.99US/$8.99CAN
__Highland Promise	978-1-4201-0261-1	$4.99US/$6.99CAN
__Highland Vow	978-1-4201-0260-4	$4.99US/$6.99CAN
__Highland Savage	978-0-8217-7999-6	$6.99US/$9.99CAN
__Beauty and the Beast	978-0-8217-8004-6	$4.99US/$6.99CAN
__Unconquered	978-0-8217-8088-6	$4.99US/$6.99CAN
__Highland Barbarian	978-0-8217-7998-9	$6.99US/$9.99CAN
__Highland Conqueror	978-0-8217-8148-7	$6.99US/$9.99CAN
__Conqueror's Kiss	978-0-8217-8005-3	$4.99US/$6.99CAN
__A Stockingful of Joy	978-1-4201-0018-1	$4.99US/$6.99CAN
__Highland Bride	978-0-8217-7995-8	$4.99US/$6.99CAN
__Highland Lover	978-0-8217-7759-6	$6.99US/$9.99CAN

Available Wherever Books Are Sold!

Check out our website at
http://www.kensingtonbooks.com